What Dreams Remember

This is a work of fiction. Names, characters, places, and incidents either are the product of the author's imagination or are used fictitiously. Any resemblance to actual persons, living or dead, events, or locales is entirely coincidental.

Cover art by Benjamin Ezra Cremer

ISBN 978-0-615-24885-1

This one's for me and my girls...

It is said that from Sarasvati; the Hindu goddess of the arts, beauty and knowledge in all its forms, flows inspiration, benevolence and nourishment for body and soul and that only through the acquisition of knowledge, which flows into her followers, can there be liberation from reincarnation.

Part 1
The Present

1

Miss Windell

Thud…her heart jumped into her throat and lodged there, slowing to a dull thud in her ears, which began to drown even the noises of the aggravated longhouse, causing everything to fall into a sort of muted haze. She was left then with an all-consuming awareness that somehow didn't require thought for the processing of what she suddenly knew or how she knew it, she simply did. Some there might have called her fey, might have dismissed with a descriptive which has been integrated into our daily vocabulary but isn't truly understood; calling it 'déjà vu', but it was more. The retreating sounds of the longhouse, now losing themselves in the rush of blood to her ears, were more real than anything her senses could currently assimilate, the chain around her ankle more familiar than could be explained and yet it too was from the dream, her link to him.

Thud…sound was still there, the dull now distant thud that remained in her ears and yet not, more of a feeling that told her mind that her heart still beat somewhere below her temples and warmth, there was warmth too. The warmth that came from the fire at her back, which put unreasoning fear in her bones but that she always kept blazing, not for her but for him. The one thing she could do for him on so short a length of chain. That was the thing she knew, somehow, deep down, she needed to focus on: this chain, link after iron link, colder than it should be so close to her fire. Not the hound beside her, snoring contented, paw over bone, not the duel- edged axe gleaming beside the mound of furs that passed for a bed, but the metal tether that had changed everything, that bound them and yet came between, that she cherished and loathed simultaneously.

Thud…he hadn't done more than glance at her since attaching the shackle to the wall. It had been a sad replacement of the gold and silver trinkets and bells that had graced her ankles before him, but those eyes, they remained with her. They held more heat than any flaming hulk of wood she'd ever brought herself to push back into the depths of the blaze she had taken as her charge. Those eyes, like his fingers, where they had met her skin for mere seconds when checking that shackle, crackled with a life more vibrant than anything she had ever encountered that she could remember, and she remembered a lot.

She remembered this dream, the dream that was more than a dream.

Thud…she knew, knew it would be him, that it was him even now, coming toward the bearskin drape that served as a door to the little chamber that had been her only home for weeks now. The warmth at her back took on a new depth and life all its own and began to race through her, up her spine to play in the short hairs at the base of her skull before finding her ears and cheeks to settle in. This warmth, this heat ran down the back of her thighs quickly, all the way to the shackle and back again, to settle somewhere in her abdomen and flutter, it reminded her of the butterflies for a very long moment as the room faded even further into obscurity.

Thud…again, the sound that wasn't sound pounded in her over-heated ears as she stood still as death, shackled before a hearth in a room that was no more now than wood smoke and living shadow, in the corner of a long forgotten longhouse with a master only she remembered. Her own heartbeat acted the soundtrack to this dream, its centerpieces a cold iron shackle, a bearskin drape, and a memory that wasn't a memory, in a dream that wasn't a dream.

Thud…the bearskin flapped softly as her vision tunneled to crystal clarity, for the briefest of moments taking in the large blond head and those eyes that saw right into her, finding her instantly every time he was near. It seemed

3

for a heart stopping second he might see, truly see, like she could, as his eyes quickly cut through the smoke and shadow seeking her form out immediately. The way they focused, so keenly and quickly, she feared and hoped in the same breath that he might even see the dream for what it was.

Breathe...

She shot straight up from her pillow, gasping for the breath she had subconsciously told herself to take, and fighting to slow her heart as it seemed to thump so desperately in her chest that it would burst free at any moment. The cool darkness of her room seemed heavy and oppressive in comparison to the warmth of the room her subconscious had just been ripped from. A part of her wanted to cry for the loss of it. The rest was simply thankful to have remembered to breathe, yet again.

She had a desperate fear that someday she wouldn't be so lucky.

"This has got to stop," she cried softly, trembling.

Glancing over quickly and self-consciously to be sure her sudden movements hadn't woken the man beside her, she remembered just as quickly that he was no longer there. He hadn't been there for two months, two weeks, two days and some random number of hours that wouldn't seem random enough when she figured it out later quite by accident while trying to convince herself it didn't matter.

She lay back slowly, trying again to control her breathing and wondering absently how it was that a human being could survive such a rapid heartbeat. It reminded her of bunnies for some reason, Thumper in specific. How strange that Thumper should come to mind after such a dream. Wasn't Thumper 'twitter-pated', in love? And she didn't believe in love like that anymore.

She reached over, tugging on the cord of the bedside lamp beside her and quietly withdrew her dream journal from the nightstand's top drawer. Quickly, she wrote down all that she could remember by the meager light that managed to find its way in around the layers of window coverings and out from under her lamp's black shade. Most of her journal was filled with

4

failed attempts at capturing emotions and feelings in words and random bits of landscape descriptions. It made little sense, she knew, but she still tried, as she always had, to capture the essence of her dreams before they completely escaped her.

Then slowly, quietly, she flipped the blanket back, thinking to crawl from beneath its warmth and make her way down the cool dark hallway to the bathroom without waking her dog and having to let him out for the same relief she sought. But she found herself sometime later, staring at her ankle, unable to move.

The red mark that encircled her lower leg, just above the many anklets she had collected over the years, was fading now just like the vivid dream she had just been having and the tight buttery knot it had put in her stomach. She moved those many gold and silver chains, with a slight tinkling of bells and charms, as she lightly rubbed at her skin, erasing any traces of remaining redness.

The bed shook suddenly, jarring her from her stupor and causing her to squeak. It was only Angus, she realized, fighting to steady her heart rate yet again. "You have a bad dream too, buddy?" she asked the nearly four year old Wolfhound beside her; at least that's what she had come to figure his age at.

She wondered even as she labeled it such what it was exactly that had made hers a "bad" dream. And, really, she could find no reasoning to have thought it such other than the fact she'd obviously forgotten to breathe during it and that it had made her heart race as if she'd been running from the very devil all night.

A huge huff of expelled breath, very much like a human sigh of disgust, was the only answer she would get from Angus as he blinked at her a few times then rose and slowly got halfway off the bed. With his front feet now firmly on the floor and his rear straight up in the air, he then proceeded to enjoy a large stretch.

"Don't you fart, you nasty thing," she said, falling back across the bed to reach him and swatting at his haunch just in time to cause him to leap off the bed rather than defile the air of their bedroom.

"Out," she continued, rising again and pointing out the door in one motion. She watched him absently as he made his way slowly around the foot of the bed then followed him as he dutifully sauntered out of the room and through the kitchen to stand patiently before the back door.

"How is it that you always get to go to the bathroom first?" she asked, opening the door and watching him walk idly out into the still mostly dark morning of the back yard without bothering to answer. "Men," she huffed, closing the door and heading back through the kitchen to the bathroom to find her own relief.

As she made her way through the cool dimness of her home she thought for just a moment that she'd caught the scent of a fire but it was gone before she could be positive. The smell itself began to seem more a memory as she wondered who would be burning anything at this hour, in this part of town. She finally convinced herself that no one would and that she had to have been mistaken.

She was just flushing the toilet when an insistent, heavy scratching began again with its slow destruction of the back door. "Hold on," she yelled as she rounded the corner back into the kitchen, flipping on the light this time as she passed it. As she reached for the handle, another heavy scratch shook the door again.

"Jeez, Angus," she grumped, as she threw the door wide and watched his large, scruffy, tarnished silver form saunter right back in and straight for his food dish as though he had done nothing at all uncalled for and deserved to be rewarded with an early breakfast for letting her know he was ready to come back inside.

"The landlord's gonna keep my deposit, ya know," she told the back of his huge, unfazed head as she scooped a healthy helping of dry kibble from the plastic bin beside the microwave cart. Replacing the lid she poured his breakfast into the bowl she'd sunk into an old wooden chair for him to eat out of. She'd had her grandfather cut the hole in it so Angus could eat at a more comfortable level when he'd amazed her, and the people at the pet store, by tripling his size after they had pronounced him a full grown Greyhound, Wire Fox Terrier mix.

She grinned to herself remembering their assurances those were adult teeth in his head and he was a large breed mix when helping her to choose a dog food. Come to find out from his vet, when she found him one a month later, yes, they were his adult teeth, because he was probably about six or seven months old, but those teeth were brand new and he was only getting started when it came to how big he was going get.

If he had been large then he was a true giant now. How what had grown up to look like a purebred Irish Wolfhound had come to be running, skinny and scared, along the side of the highway was anyone's guess and her good fortune. She had taken that route out to her grandparents' house, and had scooped Angus up on an inescapable impulse. It was a mystery to this day why he'd never been reported missing by his owner.

She patted his large head gently, remembering the day she'd forced herself out the door and into her new used SUV to go out to Papa's and ride old Shanks. She'd thought the brief escape back to purer childhood joys was just what she'd needed to help her through the sad transitional days of getting used to the new house and the being alone after she and Jordan had split the first time. Her ex-fiancée had never wanted a dog, he'd couldn't explain why, he just didn't like them or maybe it was more fitting to say he'd never understood the need for them as pets.

Somehow, pulling off the road and coaxing the frightened beast to her side with what was left of her drive-through burrito and finally getting a dog had seemed to make their split acceptable. Angus had done far more to ease her transition from fiancée to alone, than any day of horseback riding out at Papa's place. Angus had pulled her through the deep depression that tried to follow her move to her new home by giving her cause to crawl out of bed every morning, even if only to save herself the need to clean the carpets daily.

When she had gotten back together with Jordan a few months later, he had had little choice but to accept Angus but things had changed during their time apart and only continued to from there. Angus was just the first of many things she would take a small but steady stand on and those stands would later see her here, still in her own place and once again with only Angus for company.

Angus merely crunched his kibble contentedly, oblivious to the two hundred and fifty dollars his impatience would eventually cost her and basking in the fact she eternally found him worth it. He gave her no more response to her rhetorical conversation than he normally did as she gave him one last scratch and went about putting on a pot of coffee despite the fact she really just wanted to crawl back into bed. The coffee had once again won the long standing battle between painting or risking another dream. It was when she turned to cross the kitchen, from the sink to the counter that held her coffee maker, for the second time, with the pot now full of water, that she noticed the blood.

"You're bleeding," she gasped, staring at Angus.

Quickly she dumped the water in the back of the coffee maker without removing her eyes from him and hit the start button reflexively as she turned the rest of the way toward her beloved dog. Angus raised his massive head and looked back to see what the fuss was about as she went to her knees beside him and began running her hands over every square inch of his huge form, checking her hands for blood and looking for any sign from him she might have found a sore spot. Finally, having found no sign of injury on her boy, she stood back up, suddenly assailed by a new fear. She ran into the dining room adjoining the kitchen and tugged on the cord hanging in its center, turning on the light.

Standing before the huge mirror that hung there, she examined herself, turning this way and that. She saw no wounds, nothing hurt; the red mark she'd discovered earlier, on her ankle, was completely gone and definitely hadn't bled. She pulled off her oversized tee-shirt and took another long hard look at herself, twisting her long, dark chestnut hair up around her hand and looking over her shoulder at her back…nothing. She turned again then and moved closer to the mirror, peering intently at her oval face with its high Indian cheekbones and dark brows and lashes, her dark brown eyes focusing first on themselves then her ears. After assuring herself all her earrings were still there and none bled, she finally examined her nose ring and even looked up her nose. No blood.

Angus came up behind her licking his lips and staring at her like she was performing some new trick he'd never seen but found mildly interesting. "This is crazy," she whispered as much to him as to herself as she bent to retrieve her hastily discarded shirt from the floor at her feet. Thinking she needed to calm down and go back to the kitchen to check and be sure it was even blood and not paint she had seen spotting the white linoleum, she tugged the old tee-shirt back over her head with a sigh of disgust at her own panic. As she straightened again though, she caught a glimpse of Angus's gaping maw in the mirror as he panted his vague appreciation of her newest display of insanity.

"You!" she said whirling on him and dropping once more to her knees before her favorite beastie, "you *are* bleeding! What did you do?"

Grasping both sides of his huge muzzle, she pulled his lips back and opened his mouth, noting the blood that had dried on the wiry hair around his snout. Angus patiently sat down and allowed his crazy human to do as she would, licking his lips as frequently as he could manage, trying to keep the blood and taste of it down around her grumbling and prodding ministrations. Unable to find any obvious wounds, cuts or broken teeth, nothing other than just a slow seeping of blood from his gums, she finally gave up trying to figure out what he had done and called his vet.

Lucky for her, hers was the first call the still sleepy tech had gotten that morning and three hours later found a somewhat calmer young woman escorting a very bored and fractionally overweight Angus in to see his doctor moments after the doctor himself arrived. She was calmer now only due to the ten-minute conversation the patient tech had taken the time to have with her about such things as bleeding gums and their serious inability to be immediately life-threading to her beloved companion.

"Well, hello again Angus, Miss Windell," said the now wide-awake and cheery tech, nodding first at the dog then at her, as he came quickly out from behind the counter with their file already in hand.

"Pretty bad, huh?" she said sheepishly, taking note of the tech's obvious recognition and readiness for her arrival, and tucking her hand into her hoodie to fiddle nervously with her cigarette case.

"No, as I said he will be fine…," the tech began, thinking Miss Windell still needed reassurance her beloved pet was going to survive this new trauma.

"No, I mean that I have obviously been here so frequently you know Angus and me by name," she grinned and giggled at herself, "I bet you guys think I suffer from Munchausen's by proxy."

"Nah, you just love your dog," the tech laughed, "and I'm sure the doctor and his suppliers are glad you do." He tussled Angus's ears and patted his head saying, "Besides, who could forget Angus, he's the biggest dog I've ever seen. What'd he finally top out at?" He flipped open the file in his hand and glanced down at it. "Yeah, wow, 40 inches at the shoulder. We got a Dane comes here, made 38, but Angus takes 'em all."

"Him's just a baby!" Miss Windell gushed at her dog.

"A giant baby," the tech laughed. "I'll go tell Doc you're here, it'll be just a second. He just got in and barely poured his coffee. How are Angus's ears now, by the way?" he threw back over his shoulder as he walked toward the door at the rear of the room.

"Better now," she replied, "thank you."

Moments later the tech returned with the veterinarian right behind him and waved them back behind the partition which separated the large room from the exam area. "So what is going on with Angus today?" came the vet's also cheery voice from behind the layered wooden slats standing vertically between them.

"His gums were bleeding this morning," she answered, coming around the edge of the divider, led by Angus who headed straight for the scale on the floor.

The dog stepped immediately up onto it and sat down expectantly, awaiting the praise he was sure would come.

"Good boy," she said, not letting him down.

"Good God!" the vet said just as quickly, staring over her head at the little monitor reading 203.3. "I thought we talked about his weight, no more table scraps," he chided.

"I'm not!" she defended quickly. "We're down to one scoop in the morning, one at lunch and one more at night. He's doing good!"

"He's obese," the tech corrected in good-natured jest. "When you buy a "scoop" in Lawn and Garden it's really called a shovel!"

"He's just fluffy," she said sheepishly, flipping her cigarette case over in her hoodie's pocket again and picking at a spot of dried paint on her sweatpants before patting Angus's furry back and assuring him he was perfect.

"He's a Wolfhound, they're wire-coated and meant to be built more like a Great Dane. They don't come in fluff, just fat," the vet replied, grinning with good-natured sarcasm.

There was no attempt to try to get Angus up on the exam table, it was a well-known fact that he could instantly double his already excessive weight via sheer will power to avoid the process, so after a brief examination was conducted on the floor and a few more jokes were made about his weight, all of which Angus took quite well considering, a diagnosis was pronounced.

"He's probably chewed on something," the vet announced. "Sometimes when they chew on something hard, such as a fallen branch in the yard *or a large bone*," he paused and looked sidelong at her, daring her to deny she gave him bones, "they will irritate their gums enough to cause them to bleed for a bit, much like you would if you brush your teeth too hard for a long period of time. With no other signs, no broken teeth, and no cuts, nothing wrong other than he may need a good cleaning soon to knock some of that tartar off those back molars, I'd say he'll be fine."

The vet patted Angus on the head and thus dismissed the dog and any avowals Miss Windell may have been preparing to make as to the fact she hadn't given him any bones since their last talk. With that permission-slip of a pat, however, the point was moot. Angus, dismissed and thus ready to go, became quite unruly and hard to manage. She paid for the office call while playing tug-o-war with his leash and then followed the dog out the door.

With the better part of her unexpectedly early morning off wasted with worrying over her dog, Miss Windell let Angus and herself back into the small house in the middle of the dead-end street they called theirs, absently thinking to head back to bed for a few more hours of hopefully undisturbed sleep before her shift at the bar. She made her way through the house to the back door, behind Angus, and let him out into the back yard again. Following him out, she found herself wandering the yard with him as he sniffed a bit, then stared at her inquisitively, then sniffed a bit more.

Miss Windell realized after a moment that she was searching for anything he may have chewed that could have been hard enough to cause his gums to bleed, but even as she did so she knew she wouldn't find anything. Her grandfather had just been over to mow the lawn for her the day before and anything that might have been there would have been removed. Not to mention, she knew Angus hadn't been out there long enough that morning to have chewed anything. His insistent scratching, demanding reentry and access to his food dish, had begun even before she had finished her own pee that morning.

She stopped dead, under one of the trees, once again thinking she had caught the scent of something burning. She tested the air, reminding herself of Angus, in a way that might have amused her, had the dog not seemed unaware of anything odd in the air. Once more she was forced to second guess her senses, unable to catch another whiff and determine where it might be coming from and why.

Then suddenly she was questioning all of her senses, not just her nose, everything seemed out of whack, as a freak mist appeared to roll in swiftly, out of nowhere, and shroud the edges of her vision. The tall privacy fence, barely a few yards away, disappeared completely as the smell of burning wood and something more assailed her. She was almost completely sure of the smell this time and tried to locate Angus through the shroud to see if he had caught it. She grew frightened when she couldn't find the dog as the air thickened, stiflingly around her. She was just beginning to think it was not mere mist but smoke itself rolling in around her when she heard someone scream.

Whether it was smoke or mist no longer mattered as she froze, listening for any further sound. She spun in a circle, trying to determine where the scream had come from, who had made it and why, and realized she couldn't see anything but smoke. Miss Windell spun again, choking on what she was positive now was smoke that hung oppressively heavy all around her. She was scared to death. She heard another scream and spun in the direction she thought it had come from, but could see nothing at all. Angus was nowhere in sight.

"Angus!" This time it was she who screamed.

She had no clue how long she'd been lying in the grass in the back yard but her clothes were damp from soaking up the morning dew. Angus lay beside her, alternately licking her ear and nosing it, obviously finding her choice of sleeping arrangements very out of the ordinary.

She sat up, wiping her ear absently on the sleeve of her hoodie and patting Angus's head, wondering where the smoke had gone and what had made it and then suddenly a very scary thought occurred to her: she smelled no smoke now, and there would have to have been something of it left had it been real. She hadn't then, nor did she now, hear any fire trucks, and with the kind of fire it would have taken to create that much smoke there should have been dozens. She had gone to school for this, even if she had never graduated. She recognized the signs. She was quite sure she was losing her mind.

13

The thought scared her deeply. She had studied the human mind because she had always known hers worked just a little different than most and had hoped desperately to figure out why. All her years of "higher education" had taught her was that she was indeed very different. All the schooling in the world had never shown her how to resolve her persistent feelings of déjà vu; her almost precognitive intuitions, or translate her terrifyingly real dreams with any success. So once again, she settled, as she always did these days, for telling herself it was merely the fact that she'd been up late at the bar and early with the dream. The stress of the entire situation with Angus hadn't helped either. She told herself she just needed a real good sleep, one free of disruptive visions she could never figure out but somehow deep down knew she desperately needed to.

"Just go take a nap," she told herself, "in your bed this time."

Sleep had always been a thing she cherished, she couldn't seem to ever get enough of it, and almost always resented the alarm, but lately, especially, a good sleep had been scarce. The dreams had gotten worse, since she and Jordan had their most recent split, or maybe more insistent was a better description. There was nothing, really, about most of them to make them nightmares, per se, but they never left her as rested as the rare dreamless nights by any means. They were like those dreams that everyone in the service industry seems to have had at some point, that they are the only employee in attendance on the busiest of days and they wake up exhausted like they did indeed just work the shift from hell.

Miss Windell had always had vivid dreams, dreams that seemed not so much like dreams but memories. She had asked her grandmother once if she had ever been to Europe with her mother and just not been old enough to remember it clearly, but she had been assured her mother's travels had been mostly centered around India and that the things she'd dreamed, things like a Scots-like seaside view, must have been born of some forgotten movie's scenery. Even then she had wondered how it was that she'd even come to feel deep down that it was a European seaside and not some random coast anywhere in the world.

14

She had known even as a child that there was a difference in the things she dreamed versus other kids her age. What she knew in her dreams and what she had learned up to then from life quite often did not coincide, and she'd put her mother through many an unexpected midnight conversation coming to those realizations. She had wrestled often recently with whether or not she should take them as past life memories and examine them, or just call herself crazy and leave the puzzle be. Such things as the fact she was indeed strange, if not mentally ill, only became more and more clear as she got older and began studying and finding out what other people dreamed and what those dreams were said by "the experts" to mean.

She desperately wished at times that she could just talk to her mother again, ask if there was something she should know about her past that might help her to understand these things her subconscious seemed to hint at, ask if maybe there were things her grandparents didn't know that had led up to her being left with them and her mother's return to India and subsequent death. Some brief adventures through Europe? Those where things she would never be able to ask, those answers and a thousand more had long since gone to heaven with her mother.

As her head hit the pillow, she chided herself reflexively, knowing how her grandmother would tell her there was no such thing as reincarnation, only the Lord and salvation. Her grandmother had spent all that had remained of her teens, when she had gone to live with her, trying to eradicate all her mother had allowed her to study and learn from her beliefs and she still felt the occasional twinge of guilt when she would find herself reflecting on such an unacceptable theology. But sometimes, it was all that she could do, when one had to choose between diagnosing oneself as clinically nutty or simply believe in past lives and the possibility of memories of them, the choice seemed clear...sometimes.

She could smell roses and hear the simpering, overly feminine giggles that were lost in the occasional robust and hearty laugh of one of the men in attendance, as those jovial party-goers, to the annual ball, held in the old manor

15

at the end of the oak-lined lane, got further into the punch. The House of Ruin it was lovingly called by the Ton, the Rune Estates, renowned or mayhap rather infamous for the parties those halls had hosted, and most infamous of all was the annual ball which had never required any further title to lure the jaded masses to its door. The mist had rolled out just enough that the merrymakers could barely be made out through the windows looking out on the well-manicured hedges of the lawn from the ballroom. The mood was high and spirits higher, the tension was palpable as she stood there collecting her courage.

This was to be a special evening, she knew, she remembered, only she was a he and meant to ask her to wed. Her, at the top of the stairs just there, her blond hair trussed up in pure perfection, her angelic form encased in a satin creation that could shame the clearest sky with its genius and hue. Her, whose beauty and innocence was in drastic contrast to the very walls of this place and who's every naive and beatific smile begged she be taken from it and kept forever safe.

It was a long shot, he knew, but he also knew they both felt the bond, the kinship, the love he did. From the moment their eyes had met, a mere three months before, he had known. Each brief conversation, stolen in some mutual acquaintance's parlor or local tea house, each time he'd felt her fingers tremble when he brought them to his lips and pressed them tenderly, told him he was not alone. He was royalty, yes, but Indian royalty from a British-occupied India, it didn't mean much, but he had been among them for a little better than three years now and his wealth was known, love would be enough for them, and money enough for her sire. All that was needed was her consent; just one word from her lips and the rest would be made well with her sire via pure, unadulterated greed.

He straightened his deep blue waistcoat and fingered the ribbon at the nape of his neck which held his shoulder- length unpowdered black hair out of far-away eyes. He took in one last deep breath, focusing on the woman he loved through the widows of the ballroom before him and took another step forward –

tink-tink-tink- only to be halted with all the other partygoers in the shadow of one final oak by the steady tink of silver on crystal.

An announcement: "Your attention please…"

Everything but his heart went deathly quiet, as his vision blurred to a tunnel that ended in her and the masked terror her well-trained features quickly rearranged themselves to hide. She was to be wed, and not to him, the knowledge slowly hammered its way into his head as she went pale before his eyes. Excuses were made quickly, for her sudden inability to remain among the revelers, excuses all expected but none believed. Sheer happiness…doubtful, but purchased by all for the sake of merriment and another round. Frantically his mind worked round and round, as the party resumed and the sounds of it flooded back in and magnified themselves under the microscope of his panicked pain. How to change it?

How to change it? Could his wealth create some fiction by which her sire might retract the engagement? Could he outwit cruel fate and steal her hand?

Suddenly there came a different sound, many different sounds: the screams of horrified women, the shattering crystal of dropped beverages, the rush of richly-shod feet across the polished wooden floor ending just beneath the banister. A horrible misstep? A terrible tragedy? Overcome by her happiness and unable to see through her tears of joy, she had stumbled and fallen over the banister to an untimely death? Doubtful, but purchased by all.

All save him, as she stumbled backwards in his nightmare, bouncing off an old oak tree's unyielding and abrasive trunk and tumbled heartbroken and beaten into the collapsing mist. Defeated and guilt-ridden, suffering the constant beating of a million tormented remembrances and lost opportunities, he sat unwashed, unshaven and uncaring, under some long-fallen archway over a lane no longer there, on a night London had long forgotten. He cradled a memory and a musket; a lone hound bayed far off, calling to him a mournful sound which he felt he truly understood, as he slowly raised the barrel to his head. Another tear rolled down his stubbly cheek.

She woke up crying again, with a terrible headache, and her hands, pressed to her wet cheeks, still tingling from the feel of stubble in her palms. She hated that one! She much preferred the ones from which she woke herself up with her own laughter, even if she could never recall what had been so funny. Not a funny dream this time, by any stretch, and it wasn't the first time she had had that dream. No need to write that one down, though certainly this time had been the most intense. The deep sadness that had taken root inside her while she slept would remain with her for hours, sometimes days; she would find it hard to smile even when she was happy. She wiped at her eyes and reached without looking for the bottle of aspirin and glass of water that would be on her nightstand.

A few deep breaths later she finally turned to glance at the clock and saw it was time to get up anyway, no need worrying about whether or not she could get back to sleep without the dream returning to finish itself; no need to worry if she would wake from it; if she *could* wake from it, after the musket was fired. She needed to get ready for work. Throwing back the covers purposefully, as if throwing the dream away, she woke Angus and he followed her from the room to the back door where she let him out before heading to the bathroom again herself.

She heard him scratching while she lathered her hair but ignored it, knowing he would give up eventually and go lie down somewhere under one of the trees in the back yard and fall back asleep until she went to let him in. Idly it occurred to her, as she raised her second leg to the tub's edge to shave it clean, that was probably why he was putting on so much weight even though she had cut back his food and cut out the table scraps altogether. All he did these days was sleep, hell, all she did these days was sleep!

Sadly she told herself she would get up early enough one of these days to take him for a walk and still get what she needed to get done before work, but even as she did so she knew she wouldn't. She was filled with a sense of sad defeat, such things never went as planned and it wasn't the first time she had told herself to do something that would detract from the amount of sleep she could get and never brought herself to do it.

As she put the cream rinse in her hair, piled it up on top of her head and began brushing her teeth, a small, somewhat detached surge of enjoyment did actually manage to rush through her despite the overall depression she had woken with. Jordan hated her brushing her teeth in the shower. "Yeah, well, what's it to you," she thought, feeling a bit of the strength she would need for the coming evening come into her. She was the one who cleaned it she thought then, sadness quickly stalking back in and taking the thought over, so really, what did it matter?

She stood there a long time, allowing the water to not only rinse the conditioner from her hair but try to wash some of her problems away as well. Once again she was forced to question her senses as she suddenly had the odd sense she was in the open, as if the shower curtain, even the walls of the bathroom, had disappeared. She felt that if she opened her eyes she would be standing under a waterfall, hip deep in a cool pool, out in the middle of a wide glade, but the feeling was gone before she could rinse her eyes and open them to see. She shook her head, trying to physically dislodge whatever it was that had her so screwed up lately. She simply couldn't afford to go crazy right now.

Stepping from the tub, she pulled a towel off the rack over the door and, flipping her head down, wrapped up the long mass of deep chestnut that looked black just now and tucked it atop her head. Shaking her head a little again, trying to loosen the more depressing thoughts more so than check to be sure the towel was firmly attached, she then grabbed another towel and wrapped it around her body and went to let Angus in.

Standing in the back doorway, in only her towel, calling for her dog, again she felt another little surge of enjoyment. The satisfaction of knowing Jordan would disapprove and that it no longer mattered what she could and could not do while maintaining his perfect level of happiness. But her satisfaction was quickly washed away as surely as the sleep had been from her eyes by the tears she had woken up crying. One of these days she would have to tell people the engagement was off, again; eventually someone was going to figure it out like Genie. Her best friend had, the moment she'd

19

walked into the indoor flea market where Genie kept a booth, Angus in tow, suddenly wanting a new collar for her dog, eyes still swollen because some things just wouldn't change no matter how hard she tried.

She patted her dog as he brushed by on his way in, as much to comfort herself as him. For now, though, she still kept the most recent breakup to herself. No one at work knew, not even her grandparents, just Genie. Why? Because there was still that nagging fear that she might somehow, under some unforeseeable circumstance take him back, yet again, and that she would look even more the fool than she already felt, unable to let go of something she never had. It just seemed safer with only Genie knowing, not that she could have avoided that one finding out anyway.

2

Win

The ritual of donning the Armor of Win went on undisturbed for the most part, except for the random memories that floated through her head in regards to her two most recent dreams. At least the unshakable sadness that had settled in her stomach, left by the latter of the two, had finally squashed the butterflies. All thoughts of her sanity, or lack thereof, slowly faded as she dried her hair, put it back up in a ponytail, and put on her makeup, steadily pushing back the hurt and fear she saw staring back at her as she put on the finishing touches to Win's face. Showing such sadness where Win worked would never do! She pursed her lips and made a smile; now she could see why people looked twice, now she actually felt beautiful.

She was mildly amused for the thousandth time by how she separated her true self from the person she became to work that bar and earn her living. Becoming "Win" to intoxicate the masses required she wear nice, sexy, flattering clothes; that she put on makeup and have sassy, vague comebacks for every comment which the customers could take any way that was profitable because the possibilities were endless, based merely upon her smile. It was also necessary that she let rudeness and idiocy slide off her back and force that smile, "gnashing her teeth for the public," to earn the tip that may or may not come.

So she took another look at her butt in her leather pants and adjusted her cleavage in her corset one last time for maximizing effect. Finally, approving herself for departure in the large dining room mirror, she left the worry-wart Miss Windell, who had raced her beloved Angus to the vet on three hours sleep, at home and took Win out to the Gentlemen's Club.

Gentlemen's Club. "Were there such creatures still in existence to even frequent such places?" Win mused to herself, as she pulled into her parking spot, beneath the sign that tried to assure one and all that they did indeed. Win didn't mind really, whether they wanted to be thought of as gentlemen and order a cigar to go with their overpriced scotch or if they were proud deviants, demanding she keep that mug chilled for the next "college boy" and watch them drink their beer from the pitcher with barbarous gusto. She poured the drinks, they poured the money and to Win, that was what mattered. Any further contemplation was mere entertainments for the mind while the hands did their own work.

She opened the door of her SUV and unfolded one long leg, stretching one sure high heeled boot down to the ground. Then peeking one last time in the mirror to be sure Win was perfect, out came the other boot, now just as sure. Win needed to be perfect; not only was she about to be surrounded by some of the most beautiful girls in the city, but it was what would get her through tonight and pay the bills. Intoxicated men rarely questioned and less often insulted perfection; usually they just dropped their jaws and their paycheck. Gone now were the paint-stained sweatpants and oversized hoodie; the sheepish grins and nervous fiddling with her cigarette case when among those she considered friends.

Miss Windell had been left home with Angus; Win was here to work.

"Good evening, Win," greeted the tall blond kid they'd hired a few months back to work the door, "you look great as usual."

"Thank you, Gamble," she replied with little thought and even less attention.

She'd long ago quit paying attention to them; the endless troop of testosterone junkies that came seeking employment as soon as they recovered from the brown bottle flu they contracted on their twenty-first birthdays. The endless parade of naive boys, who still thought being the bouncer at a strip club was a dream job second only to Madonna's bodyguard or porn star, had ceased to do much more than mildly amuse her. They never seemed to realize in time that those iconic girls gracing the stage and giving them the eye had come here just as naive as they were, looking for the same glamour and quick cash. In the end all found the illusions fun while they lasted, entertaining as much as they entertained; endless wood for the rumor mill that left even the most jaded with splinters of some kind.

Of course the cursory warning was always given when someone was hired; no fraternizing between employees, but get real, like lust ever listened to reason, especially when it believed it was love. Still, as long as they were large and imposing, the bouncers were accomplishing their real job. The moments they grabbed the spotlight with a dancer would either prove enlightening or burn them but that part was not Win's problem. She learned their names because it was polite and once in a purple moon she might actually need one to carry something, but otherwise, most other details were needless trivialities Win had no use for. Let the girls play out there in the spotlight with the new eye candy if they wanted, she played behind the bar.

Win walked past him through the door he held politely wide and headed straight for the bar, allowing her eyes to adjust to the darkness inside the building as she went. Taking quiet note of the stares of appreciation she let the loud music permeate her being and the final strap of the Armor of Win was secured. She felt the usual surge of power she felt whenever Win walked in this place- yes, power! She had never understood it but when she was Win people stared; sometimes they complimented, sometimes they got intimidated, but they rarely looked away very fast and most were inexplicably compelled to please her.

Some people immediately thought Win was a bitch, "don't mess with that one, she looks like she'd tear you apart," they'd say to themselves and anyone who'd listen, what other explanation for the things they saw and later learned of her? Others didn't know what to think, but if anyone were to ask, those who felt they knew her would say, that's just Win and to them it seemed a perfectly satisfactory answer for any questions about her. None of it really bothered Win, it told her that her armor was on right and nothing was going to hurt her feelings that night because she hadn't brought them with her.

It would often make her laugh what a little make-up and leather could do for a heartbroken twenty-four year old woman with bruised confidence. She thanked God quite often for Jadin, the long-time friend turned single mother and stripper, both quite accidentally in the same year, who had come home with a carton of ice cream, a pair of leather pants and an invitation to an opportunity to get her life back on track the first time Jordan and she had split.

"I know you'd never strip, you ain't got the balls for it, but you've waited tables before," Jadin had said, handing her a huge bowl of Chocolate, chocolate chip ice cream and the fateful leather pants, before sinking down into the couch beside her a little better than three years ago, "it's the same only better; easier orders for more money. Just pretend you are someone else who actually enjoys the attention from their drunk asses and might give up the digits, smile, and shake your ass in those things when you walk away. You'll have money for a car and a place in no time. Hell, you could even go back and finish school."

She got the money all right, but first she'd knocked the crap out of a guy who had smacked her ass that first night and then proceeded to give him what for all over again, only verbally, in the silence that followed the DJ's accidental and reactionary silencing of the music. It had been a thoughtless reflex, something she would have never had the balls to do had she actually thought about it, but she had never regretted it. She'd suddenly found herself in the very spotlight she would eventually grow to dread; only that time it had served to enlighten. She was suddenly seen as someone she didn't know she could be, a strong woman who demanded respect and got it, plus a healthy tip. Some called that a bitch and if that's what it meant, then so be it, she didn't mind, she had worked hard from that moment forward to perfect it.

She'd managed to save nearly a thousand dollars in the first month and that was with paying her share of the bills at Jadin's place. But that hadn't been enough because then she needed an alarm for the beautiful gas-guzzling SUV she'd set her heart and not her head on, since she was now parking it at the Gentleman's Club every night and then she needed a place of her own to park it after work. With that place came the yard that somehow suddenly needed a dog that she hadn't been able to have before. With the dog came veterinary costs, with the SUV came large expensive tires. With life in general came bills.

The money was easy there, but so were the debts it made you feel you could handle and so the cycle had continued, until three years later what had been a weekend night job to supplant her mind-numbing receptionist gig, answering phones for a psychiatrist she would have hated to have to analyze, had turned into her main means of income. Jordan had called, they had tried to mend things but just ended up fighting every step of the way as she'd gone from part-time cocktail waitress to full-time bartender and gave up on juggling phone calls and a hormonal boss altogether. She never had gone back to school, though she always meant to, she had settled for merely reinventing Win to save her thin skin and continued to rake in the dough and argue with Jordan.

Win had always been inside of her, the strong-willed, aggressively independent core that had been gently tortured into submission by her grandmother's desperate desire to save her soul as she felt she had failed to do with her own daughter. She had just needed some fine tuning and a little coaxing to come out of her corner and fight again for the things she wanted.

"Little Win", she had been, when the original Miss Windell had led them traipsing all over India in a Greenpeace tee-shirt, allowing, no encouraging, her to learn and believe whatever her heart led her towards. Little Win had disappeared for a while, lost along with her first nose ring and her favorite black eyeliner pencil, which her grandmother had thrown away when she had gone to stay with them at the formative age of twelve. But Win had reemerged, years later, with a new nose ring and attitude to match.

Win counted down her drawer, talked briefly with the bartender she was relieving about anything she might need to know for the evening ahead and in general surveyed her domain; making sure all was in order for her shift. The other bartender, who was just getting off and appeared she needed to have done so hours ago, walked up with two shots of Goldschlager in hand, her purse already over her shoulder and raised her glass for the traditional passing of the torch.

"To Money," they said in unison and slammed it down with relish.

Ahhh, she loved being Win! This had been one of the main things she had taken a stand on when she and Jordan had gotten back together that first time, trying to work things out, how could she not? She had refused to give up the ability to care for her own needs again; to see to her own dreams. She'd come from the dorm on foot, to borrowing his car and living in his home. He'd made a huge mistake allowing her to glimpse the true freedom of being self-sufficient. He had been welcome to hang some clothes at her place, she had been content to stay at his occasionally, but she'd swore she would never again be so reliant on another.

It was addictive, she knew, not just the money which came easy in this place but the power of feeling beautiful and wanted; that you could get anything you asked for if you played your cards right. But more so, the biggest thrill was knowing she didn't *need* to; that she needed no one to give her anything, all that she needed, she could and had earned, by using her wits and what the good Lord gave her.

She never played the standard games, of course not, that would be karmically wrong and her mother would haunt her worse than any strange dream ever could were she to cross that line. Even without that knowledge and genuine belief in karma, she had seen first-hand what happened to those who played rough in the glass house rather than simply enjoy the view through the skylights as she did. She wouldn't tread that path, but it was

26

intoxicating to know she could if she wanted to and with an ease few could match.

The night started slowly as usual, a few mixed drinks, a pitcher or two, mostly shots for the girls to help put the finishing touches on their own alter ego's armor. Jadin was no longer among them; this six-foot-plus in high-heels collection of girls that lined her bar in the early part of the evening, less than eagerly awaiting their turns on the stage before the tip rail was lined. Jadin had retired recently for the forth or fifth time, and settled down with a boy she met in a bar, never a good sign if you asked Win. But then Jadin rarely did, unless she wanted the voice of reason to talk her out of something she already knew was a bad idea.

That was the kind of friends they were though, much more like family, in the sense that they might not hear from each other for the better part of the year and then, one night, show up on the other's step, suitcase in hand, heartbroken and in need of a friend. Jadin was the sister she never had, the other half of her. Come those cliffs where Miss Windell screeched to a halt a few yards back and not even the ballsy Win would dare do more than glance down, Jadin would run past, full speed, jump, and scream all the way down about the wind in her hair.

They had met in high school over a knot-tying lesson in the ladies room. Jadin had walked in behind her, yanked on her shirt, un-tucking it, and then turned her around, tying it in a knot around her rib cage. She'd told her, "You really are too damned pretty to go around all stick up the butt." It had been the beginning of a beautiful thing. Come to think of it, Jadin hadn't been heard from in awhile. Tonight was just the usual collection of girls, some Win loved dearly, in her own detached sort of way, and some she barely knew, but none here really knew her. They knew Win, and that was how she liked it.

Someday one of them might think to ask about her boyfriend, fiancée, significant other, or whatever, that they knew existed since she never flirted or went out or played as they did. Win always made excuses, went home, became Miss Windell again and got cozy in the bathtub with a novel

27

while Angus snored on the bathroom rug or got lost in a canvas and her passion for paint. So eventually someone was bound to ask about her man or lack thereof, and at that time she would deal with it but until then she kept it simple. How was school? How were the kids? When are you graduating? Win relied on such mundane questions to keep them doing the majority of the talking and leave her the luxury of non-revealing silence that was simply listening. When she did talk it was usually about Angus or her most recent paintings; entertaining, but again, safe.

First one waitress arrived, a pretty, dark-haired girl with kinky curls falling between her shoulder blades. Her name was Jovan and she'd come from New Orleans after the disaster, with skin a little darker than Win's and an engaging way of displaying her accent, that told the world of her intriguing heritage. Then another arrived, a tiny blond, appropriately named Pixie whom Win liked calling imp instead when she'd done something that brought trouble on herself. It always seemed to lighten the girl's perpetually changing moods. Win had never taken the time to find out what the girl's real name was, which honestly, in this age, could have really been Pixie. Then the evening really began to pick up and the dancers filed away from her bar one by one, finding a regular or some promising new face and wallet to keep them in drinks and dollar bills for the evening.

The second bouncer arrived shortly thereafter, a guy named Jimmy, fresh back from the war; a personal fact which one of the girls had made quite the big deal about when calling first dibs. He was military-thick and fresh-out shorn, he still walked almost too erect, and so Win would have gathered that on her own even had the dancer not gushed it at her bar. He was also late again. He took up post at the back of the stage, between it and the rear exit, accepting the arched brow she gave him that said, You better get a new excuse. Occasionally he was known to catch Win's eye and nod his head in something that resembled a handless salute, thus satisfying himself he had done his duty in checking up on her and any needs she might have, without having ever had to move from his self-appointed position near the stage. He probably wasn't going to last much longer.

Win gradually lost herself in the steady ebb and flow of mixing a drink, pouring a pitcher, mixing another drink or two, then finding time for a drag off of a cigarette. A few times a customer she remembered or liked, in her own detached sort of way, would come toward her and she made the effort to have their preferred drink ready and waiting along with a smile. The tip jar began to fill up and she started politely declining drinks. Three was enough and after the first one the other two had shown fine returns both monetarily and in an elevated mood that would carry her through the rest of the night. She always stopped about then, wanting to be sure she had a full four hours or better to clear her head before the drive home.

Sometime in the course of the night, somewhere close to midnight, the new guy, Gamble, made his way to her bar and asked her if she needed anything. It was sweet, she thought briefly, that he always thought to actually ask, but then Win looked over his shoulder, told him she was fine, and referred him back to his post at the door where another small group of already half-inebriated young men where lining up, IDs in hand, waiting for him to be the first to take their money that night.

Last call was a bit of a haze, as it tended to be, but she managed to get all the tabs added up and handed out to the right cocktail server or patron in time to get them all signed. She leaned against the reach-in cooler behind her and lit a cigarette as she watched the last few patrons file out the door. She watched with some mild interest as she noticed Gamble catch a man who stumbled into him on his way out. Gamble steadied the man by his elbow then reached into his pocket and pulled out his cell phone. He then turned the man and sat him down in the chair behind the door where he'd sat periodically throughout the night and had him wait. She was about to comment that it was time to lock the doors, no patrons could remain, when a cab pulled up and Gamble all but carried the man out to it and shoveled him in.

Interesting, this one just might last a minute, she thought to herself, then turning and snuffing out her cigarette, she began collecting the fees from the girls as they slowly made their way to her to pay their dues and cash in their ones for bigger bills. After all the patrons had left the parking lot and she'd asked each such things as, "You do good tonight?" or "You good to drive?" or "You turned in your schedule for next week, right?" as she took their house fee, she cleared each one to leave. One by one they were escorted to their cars by the doormen and soon the bar was all but empty.

The silence eased over her as she began sliding open the drawers to the cooler she'd been resting against, while everyone else left for home, and began surveying the damage the night had done to her stock. Vaguely she was aware of Jovan, arguing with the vacuum out loud, amusing herself with her own comments on how it wouldn't suck and that made it suck. The girl was spicy, she liked her. She hoped she'd stay around awhile and not end up another good cocktail waitress lost to the call of the ever-alluring stage.

"Leave another note for Gina, so she knows we need it fixed again," she called to Jovan whom she didn't need to look back at to know that the sound she got in response was that waitress smacking the vacuum with one of her already-vacated heels. "But see if it's just another straw holding everything clogged in the hose first, so I don't have to hear how we night girls suck again," Win added as an afterthought.

Win heard nothing more as she finished compiling her mental list of what cases of beer she would need to bring up from the back cooler, so she couldn't help but jump when someone tapped her shoulder unexpectedly.

"Jeeezz," she exclaimed, whirling to find one of the doormen, Gamble, had come up right behind her, "don't sneak up on me like that!"

"I'm sorry," he said, taking a few quick steps back but grinning in a way which appeared not the least bit apologetic, "I said your name three times...."

"Whatever," she said, frustrated he'd caught her off guard and maybe even a little embarrassed he'd made her jump, "what do you want?"

She was also more than a little annoyed by her short-circuiting senses. These brief moments of seeming deafness she had been experiencing lately were nearly as upsetting as the smell and sight of smoke appearing from nowhere or any other number of odd feelings she had been subject to

30

more than usual lately. It was inexplicable to her why all sound would fade, much like it did in her dreams, only there seemed no pointed reason. At least in the dreams it seemed meant to focus her mind on the visuals.

Win shook her head as if to clear it, wondering if maybe it was only the years behind the bar, with the huge speakers on both sides of her, finally taking their toll on her hearing, only to be forced to recall her doctor had assured her there was no good medical reason, which happened to be less than assuring. Coming back to the present she reprimanded herself that here was not the place for thinking about the dreams, she needed to finish her work and get home and out of these boots; she needed to let Angus out.

She didn't look up as Gamble took another step back at her abrupt response and the silence that she let follow it, expanded. She wasn't really trying to be rude, she simply awaited his answer, assuming he'd ask for a shift drink, the free beer the guys had taken to getting after each shift, but again he surprised her.

"Is there something I can help you with?" he asked, still grinning, when she finally glanced at him inquisitively.

What in the world had crawled up this kid's butt, she asked herself, he was entirely too happy after an eight-hour stint on his feet and far too eager to find more to do. But then maybe she was just suffering the added weight of the defeated sadness left her by the dream that afternoon. Again she pushed all thoughts of the dreams aside and tried to focus on his unexpected question as the sounds of Jovan vacuuming came sharply into focus again and made her head suddenly ache. Well, at least the vacuum was working now, she thought distractedly.

"The boss said I was to stay with you and help you while he was gone," he added, looking askance at her when she didn't respond.

What an odd boy, she thought, but finally managed to answer, "Nah, just grab a beer and sit down, this is my job- you're doing yours just being here till I've stocked the bar and counted the money and got it into the safe."

He looked disappointed of all things! She'd let him out of hard labor and he was upset? Win walked down to the other end of the bar and bent down, retrieving her purse from under the cabinet, she began digging through it for her bottle of aspirin. As soon as she found it she went to the coffee machine and poured the last of the pot she'd been drinking on the last half of the night into her thermal mug and swallowed three like they were salvation pills. Gamble sat down heavily in one of the bar chairs behind her, twisting the cap off the beer he had taken at her word. She could feel him staring at her back as she bent to put her purse back under the cabinet.

"Headache again?" Gamble asked her unexpectedly.

"Yeah," she replied without looking back.

The word again echoed in her head as she pretended to assure herself the cabinet had closed well and wondered just how many holes Win's armor had developed and what other personal things the young man might have noted. She stayed crouched with her back to him just a tad too long, she knew, but she was trying to rearrange her features to hide the surprise that she knew had registered unexpectedly on her face. His acute observation made her desperately want to escape his obviously all too discerning gaze.

So hiding inside Win, she left her simple yeah hanging rudely in the air and walked back to the cooler to retrieve the first few cases of beer she required. She was just barely finding her comfort zone again, walking back undisturbed from the cooler for the third time, when he shattered her composure yet again.

"Do you ever have nightmares?" Gamble said suddenly into the quiet just as the vacuum went silent and Jovan yelled for Jimmy to walk her out to her car.

Win dropped the two cases of Bud Light she held stacked in her hands just a bit too heavily on the top of the cooler, shocked and wondering how in the hell he had managed to figure that out. The headaches, okay, he'd probably noted her taking aspirin more than once, that was acceptable, if you were observant, she supposed but... How the hell could he have figured out she had nightmares?

"I had the weirdest dream this afternoon," he continued as though it was normal for her to slam cases of beer down or he simply hadn't noticed.

She breathed a silent sign of relief, chiding herself for being silly and paranoid as he began to ramble on about this dream he'd had and how it had felt so real. At some point when he was talking about how it had been even more disturbing when he had woken with an ache in his ribs right where he had been stabbed she started to actually pay attention. She remembered how she'd awoken with a headache right after her heartbroken man-self had put the muzzle of the old musket to his head. She didn't, however, remember whether she had remained him even as she pulled the trigger or woken up a fraction of a second before hand. She never could figure that out.

"You know how people say if you die in your dream you die in real life?" Gamble continued as though they were old friends and he had been reading her mind like Genie always seemed to.

No telling, really, why she suddenly felt compelled to join the conversation rather than nod and allow it to hang, becoming a rhetorical question which would force him to continue on his own as he was proving to be quite adept at. That was Win's art, what she was good at, the well-timed nod that allowed her not to have to join a conversation but kept the other person talking and comfortable. Maybe it was just that she too wondered about such things and hoped to prod him into shedding more light on the subject. Or maybe that was his art, making someone feel so comfortable they couldn't help but interject their opinion. No telling really.

"Did you actually die?" she asked, stacking the last of the beer in the cooler without looking back at him.

"No," he laughed, "I'm still alive."

"That's not…" Win stammered, then sighed in frustration that she had even walked into this position and now felt she needed to explain herself so as not to feel so foolish. "What I meant was to find out whether or not you had managed to prove the theory wrong by surviving a death in a dream," she fairly snapped.

She had just stammered! What the hell? Win didn't get tongue-tied or not know what to say. Win always had the witty comeback already on the tip of her tongue and always said it just right. Her feet hurt, her head hurt, the Armor of Win was failing fast, she needed to count the money and get home. What was she thinking getting into a real conversation in which personal things could be revealed, rather than getting safely home with her illusions unscathed?

"I know what you meant," Gamble, replied displaying that huge grin for which she couldn't comprehend the origin, "I was just trying to be funny, you always seem so detached, like only half of you is here…"

Now it was his turn to stammer and somehow it made the fact she had just a little bit okay. She knew just how aloof and stand-offish she could sound sometimes, especially when her self-defense mechanism was tripped and she explained herself in the manner she just had, as though the making of the explanation in the first place was an act beneath her and that the person she was making it to was an idiot for requiring it be made at all. It bothered Miss Windell that she had just been so snappy, she knew what it was like to be made to feel stupid, but that was Win, it was how Win was, it had kept her emotional core safe thus far and at this point she wouldn't know the least bit about how to change it.

"I was just trying to lighten things up," Gamble said, after a moment of silence and picking at the label on his beer bottle.

"Well, if you die," she said, putting on her best smile and purposefully making her tone playful, "be sure to let me know."

It was the best Win could do on the spur of the moment with her mind in such disarray, but it seemed to suffice as he burst out laughing and leaned back to slam the rest of his beer. Nothing more was said as she pulled the drawer and he walked to the door behind Jimmy and locked it again behind the last employee besides themselves. Such a situation as this, being left just the two of them, would have freaked Miss Windell out to no end, but that was one of the very many reasons why Win had been re-invented, so she finished counting the money and then locked it in the safe, purposely paying no mind to the large young man lounging in the corner waiting to walk her out and head home himself.

"Everyone has headed over to Jimmy's for a little after-party-birthday-thing for Firefly," he said as she set the alarm and locked the door. Having received no response, he added, "You coming?" as he moved ahead of her and reached for her door handle, opening her car door for her then stepping politely out of the way, the consummate doorman.

"Excuse me?" she asked, realizing he had obviously asked her something which she hadn't caught but that he felt warranted a reply, given the expectant look on his face as she sat down behind the wheel.

He pushed her door closed as she rolled the window down then took a step back as she started the car. Standing a few feet away, as though he feared she might run him down, he finally repeated himself with a raised eyebrow and that big grin of his which was beginning to unnerve her.

"I need to get home and let the dog out," she said with her usual dismissive but thankful smile. "But give Firefly my love and best wishes, please," she added putting her purse in the seat beside her and releasing the brake.

He took the hint and yet another step back as she put the vehicle in reverse and drove away, but even as she widened the distance between herself and the place where Win worked a few things that should have been left there kept digging at her and kept her mind busily looking for answers. So she took the long way home. Why had she felt compelled to add the extra sentence? To send her good wishes via a door guy to someone she had already given a card, a shot and her best excuses to earlier that evening, but even more disturbing, why had she felt compelled to alleviate the feelings of stupidity that Miss Windell related to but Win felt no pity for? Why had Miss Windell even been active then and there to have felt anything? And, for goodness sake, what in the world had compelled her to use Angus as her excuse just then rather than the no longer truly applicable Jordan which had always served so well.

She was tired, her feet hurt, the dreams had been too much today and the Armor of Win had nearly failed; it was the best she could come up with as she put the pedal down a little further and headed toward the house.

She opened her front door with one hand, already pulling one of her boots off with the other. Angus was right there at the door waiting and began backing up around the coffee table while still facing her and panting his happiness to see her. She hopped on the sore balls of one now freed foot and struggled to free the other, proving a lot less adept at avoiding obstacles than Angus as she fell against the T.V. cabinet in the process.

She leaded heavily against the door as if blocking any of the night behind her from following her in and turned the knob, locking it. She smiled at Angus; it always made her giggle how she could hear the beep of a backing garbage truck in her head every time Angus backed out of a room to give her leeway to enter. Both boots in hand now, she moved forward and patted his head then bent to kiss his nose, flipping one of his lips up as an afterthought she looked at his gums before setting him free.

"Free dog!" she said with more enthusiasm than she really felt, strictly for his sake, and the excitement he got from it. Then she ran behind him as quick as she could, given her current, sore state, as he raced through the house to the back door.

As Angus reclaimed his property and checked on his trees she filled his bowl, belatedly realizing this was going to be his fourth meal in less than eighteen hours but there was nothing she could do about that now. Surely he had heard the kibble hit the bowl and would give her no peace, whatsoever, were it not to be there when he came back inside. She meant to paint for just a few hours, just till the birds began to tell tales about the dawn and she was tired enough that she might not dream, and Angus would have her back and forth to the kitchen door the whole time if he didn't find his food there right off. He had this strange notion that it appeared by some magical means only during his absence and was quite adamant at times that she allow him to depart the mystical bowl's presence long enough for it to do its wonderful trick.

She took the time that Angus was busy outside to head back to her room and peel off the remaining Armor of Win, wiping it down with a mink-oil-soaked cloth to remove the evening "train wreck" and its smell from the leather. Restoring it to the closet with the rest of Win's things she pulled on her sweat pants and trusted hoodie, then Miss Windell answered the call of Angus before he scratched the door down.

She smiled as he headed straight for his bowl as usual, and then started herself one last cup of coffee in the single cup maker she'd bought for just these kinds of nights. It was ready before Angus had finished his dinner and she took it and went back into the dining room where her latest love sat awaiting her tender ministrations.

She stared for a moment at the half-filled canvas, walking around it a few times, viewing it from every angle, as it lay amongst the beautiful disarray that was all her paint and brushes and wash pots spread across her dining room table. Jordan would have shit himself to see the mess, but Genie was going to love it (not the mess, Genie wouldn't even see that, but the painting). It was going to be Genie's birthday gift and house warming present all in one, a huge portrait of a fairy, sitting perched atop a daisy, holding her knees to her chest and looking timid but serenely alluring- pure Genie!

Problem was that with the Armor of Win now shed, Miss Windell felt the sadness of the dream creeping back in on her full force and the fairy seemed more heartbroken now than timid, more beautifully damaged than serenely alluring. She really should straighten up, she thought, organize the mess at least a little. She pushed the thought away angrily, it was an old thought, a habit born of years of pleasing another and never bothering to wonder what pleased her.

She took a sip of her coffee, smiling despite herself; fresh coffee at four in the morning pleased her. The mess on the dining room table pleased her, it told her she was alive and well, doing what she loved, creating something beautiful from nothing but herself, her imagination envisioning it, her hand guiding the brush and giving it form, her heart giving it life. Simple, small things pleased her. Angus came in, having finished his dinner, and after doing his little turns a few times laid down with a huff of satisfaction at her feet; that was what pleased her!

She pulled her chair up and sat down, relaxing the angle of the canvas on the table top easel she'd just bought last week and took another long hard look. Then twisting her long hair up and piling it on top of her head she shoved a paint brush through it by the handle and grabbing another, started filling in the details. They came out with a hint of the sadness that remained but a little defiance as well. A few of the blades of grass that surrounded Genie's fairy and its flower chair may have been broken but they were still a healthy gree, a green she spent much time mixing and perfecting- she needed it to speak of life. The deeply blue, overcast evening sky in the background may have been full of clouds, pregnant with pain, but it wasn't raining yet. She was bemused by how much time she spent on those two background shades, how much it seemed to matter that they be just right, they were just background after all, but Genie was worth it!

Two hours later the birds had begun gossiping, and the light beginning to make its way through the blinds and sheers was nearly enough to turn off the man-made lights inside her house. She took one last look at her creation and sighing her satisfaction signed her name to the corner with her smallest brush. She woke Angus by purposely sliding back her chair noisily and then let him out one last time before bed while she went to brush her teeth and relieve herself.

Dumping the remains of her now chilled coffee in the sink, and the ashtray full of cigarettes that had smoked themselves while she painted in the garbage can, she locked the door behind Angus and prayed for a dreamless day as she followed the dog to bed.

3

Genie

"Aizlyn, tell me what's so funny!"

The sound of her name, the name her mother gave her, and the feel of the world shaking, were dim realizations that barely penetrated her sleeping mind as Aizlyn giggled again and continued to dream.

"Aizlyn, tell me what's so funny!"

Aizlyn opened one eye, a part of her slowly losing grip on the dream, the same part that was not even aware enough to focus on the short little ball of fire that was shaking it loose by calling her name and flopping down on the bed beside her. The other part was still greatly amused and still giggling.

"Wha?" she finally managed.

Genie leaned over her, a cup of coffee in hand and said again, "What were you laughing about?"

"He...," Aizlyn trailed off as the smell of the coffee worked its way into her brain and she began to think about the question and the best friend who had asked it of her. "Did I forget something?" she asked suddenly, pushing herself up in bed and focusing on her friend a little better.

She was wracking her muddled brain for why Genie would be waking her and worried she had left her friend hanging on some plan or other she couldn't currently recall. Then she remembered the painting on the dining room table her friend was not to see until Saturday evening, when it was presented properly as a birthday gift, and she was suddenly fully awake.

Aizlyn twitched nervously as she swallowed her first sip of the proffered coffee, wanting desperately to throw off the covers and race to hide the painting she'd just finished a few hours before. She knew, however, that would just draw even more unwanted attention to a piece that might have otherwise gone unnoticed among all the others in the dining room.

"I let myself in when you didn't answer the door or your phone," Genie said, studying her friend's face, "I heard you laughing and I thought if I could catch you at just the right moment you might tell me what you were dreaming. You don't remember now, do you?" Genie said sadly, as she saw the look of confusion come into her friend's eyes.

"I was laughing again?" Aizlyn asked, even though she knew from the giddiness inside her that stood in stark contrast to the hurt of the night before that she had to have had another one of those nights from which she'd have eventually woken herself up laughing.

"Yes," Genie replied sadly, realizing once again they would have no answer to the eternal question- what makes Aizlyn so happy? "You did, however, say 'he' so we at least know it's something to do with a man that makes you so happy," she laughed.

"Doubtful," Aizlyn replied sarcastically, "unless I was laughing *at* one."

"Don't kid yourself, Aizlyn," Genie chided, "the way the joy sticks with you after one of those dreams I doubt you're laughing *at* someone. Someone is making you genuinely happy."

Aizlyn kicked off the covers, smiling at her friend rather than starting up the old argument about love and what it does for you. She was filled with energy and in an impressively good mood considering she had been woken rather than woke on her own, and felt no desire to ruin it with another talk about her disillusionment and her friend's steadfast belief she needed to get over and get on, that the "right one" would change her mind.

Suddenly she paused though, as she stood by the bed yawning happily, coffee held high, and looked around her. Before she could even put her finger on what was out of place Genie answered her unformed question saying, "I let him out already."

Aizlyn smiled at her friend yet again. Genie had to be part mind-reader, she'd almost swear to it. Still stretching big, arms wide, she finally registered the cool air on her bare legs and giggling again she dashed in her tee-shirt and socks to the bathroom, coffee still in hand. As she peed, Aizlyn realized how odd her friendship with Genie was, considering how she was with so many other people she met. It usually took her forever to get to know someone, to let them in on who she really was and be herself around them.

They had met just after Jordan had left that first time. Genie had been selling hand-branded leather collars at the swap-meet when Aizlyn had taken Angus for their first of many walks there. She had been lured to Genie's stand, wanting to buy something special for her new little man, and ended up talking the day away with the delightful little artistic strawberry blond. Genie had branded out her dogs name with a collection of what had appeared to be strange screwdrivers resting in a coal burner on the brown strip of leather and they had barely stopped to breathe as they had chatted.

It had been the oddest thing for Miss Windell, and even odder still, was when it was time for Genie to pack up her stuff and leave; they still had more to say. They had agreed to meet and exchange lessons in various artistic skills and hobbies. When they had exchanged numbers, and laughed that they were just barely exchanging names, Genevieve had instantly become Genie in her mind. And Genie had, just as quickly, taken to calling her by her first name, ignoring the nickname, "Win," which Aizlyn had also offered. With Genie it had always suited. With Genie, she was Aizlyn, not Miss Windell, not Win, but a little bit of both and a whole lot more.

They had been hard to separate from that day forward. It seemed her only competition for Genie's time and adoration from then to now had been her equally adorable six-year-old son, Nathan. Now, years later, Genie had a key to her place, she, a key to Genie's, and the nine-year-old had keys to both and spent his time equally between them, hanging with whomever was home and making the most appealing items for dinner. Genie's husband drove a truck and when he was home, admittedly, Genie was a lot little less her constant side-kick but even then he was soon off again and the same movies were still at the theater when he was gone.

Genie and she both tended to get lost in their artistic endeavors too, so it was nothing for them not to bother to walk the two blocks that separated them, or drive as had been the case until Genie had gotten the new place two months before, for three or four days. Then one or the other would show up with their newest creation in hand, to show off, along with a DVD, and they'd spend an evening together. Even during their few almost-too-busy-for-even-your-best-friend times, they would at least call each other twice a week if for no other reason than to talk each other's ear off while folding their laundry or painting their toenails.

Aizlyn flushed the toilet and washed her hands and face then headed toward the kitchen, where she could hear Genie dumping food in Angus's bowl and letting him in. Aizlyn cringed slightly, realizing the dog was eating yet again far before a meal was truly necessary but there was nothing to be done about it now. Genie already had a pot of coffee made, so she simply refilled her cup and added the cream and sugar as she watched her friend pat Angus's over-fed, happy head.

"One of these days we'll figure that one out," Genie said, turning to refill her coffee cup too and taking in Aizlyn's newest but ever amusing case of perm-a-grin.

Genie knew about the dreams, it had been unavoidable, and had tried more than once to help her sort through and make sense of them. They had even flipped through together and read some of the entries in the worn-out journal which her mother had her start ages ago. But they had never gotten very far with it, as far as answers went. The entries in the old book were, for the most part, jumbled, badly written by half-awake hands that were sometimes obviously shaking, and made little sense as they stood, incomplete except for in her own head.

42

Genie felt, and was quite adamant about it, that they were indeed past-life memories trying to tell her something, often insisting she needed to try to examine them further, ask herself questions and try to remember more while she was in that state where they were accessible to her. Where as Aizlyn was, most of the time, more inclined to think herself half crazy and trying to work out this life's problems in a very disturbing way. Citing the fact, as would make her grandmother and her psychology professor proud, they seemed to come in waves, when she was most stressed, as reasoning for her half-hearted belief. After she'd been left with her grandparents, right before she left home for college and just before her first split with Jordan, the dreams had plagued her those stressful times, just not nearly as bad as they were now.

She was constantly trying to make her dreams fit normal interpretation using color and symbols that rarely fit but made more logical sense than having memories from some other life fighting for your mind at dream time. Of course Genie would then say it was in those stressful times that her memories tried hardest to show her answers through knowledge gleaned in past lives, but that was merely another old discussion they had never come to any solid agreement on.

"I had the one where I was a man again yesterday afternoon," Aizlyn said, between blowing on her coffee and scratching Angus's nosing head. "Have you ever been a man in your dreams?"

"I think you've asked me that before," Genie said, studying her friend's mood as she always did when she managed to catch her right out of a dream and wondering what the real thing bothering her was. "I've always been a woman."

"It was more intense, my heart hurt so bad, it felt like I was losing Jordan for the first time all over again, almost worse really," Aizlyn went on, ignoring her friend's pushing of the past life explanation via her assertion she'd always been a woman.

"Maybe you were. So that was it, Genie thought, Jordan's on her mind. Single-minded she pushed her point again. "Maybe your dreams have gotten stronger because you have lost him *again* and these memories are coming up because it is not the first time. For whatever reason maybe you guys haven't had much luck getting it right and doing the happily ever after. Maybe your dreams are trying to illuminate a way to make it better this time around."

"Yeah," Aizlyn said sarcastically, "like maybe he needs to not be so backward-ass and realize I can't, won't, make his life the way his mother made it for his dad?"

Aizlyn's bitterness clawed up her back far quicker than she expected after over two months and this not being the first time he'd taken his clothes and walked out on her. She'd thought she'd be numb to it by now but she still couldn't help resenting his mother for raising him to expect such nineteenth-century, third-world crap from a woman. His mother might have been content with how she was raised and want the same for her son as she had been happy to give his father but it wasn't for Aizlyn. It sure as hell wasn't for Win and it had barely worked for Miss Windell, in the beginning, before he broke out all the real bullshit and expected her to swallow it.

It seemed as soon as she slid on the engagement ring and moved in with him, quitting college and taking over the home, that he began to change. Gone was the boy she'd met in India, happy to run about town with another half breed such as himself and make mischief equally. Gone was the young man who had looked her up upon his return to the States, come to visit her, stayed to court her, even chose a school that kept him close to her. Here came a man, full on his mother's wisdom as to what a good woman would be and do for him. Aizlyn had slowly and painfully come to realize she didn't fit that description and so, she thought, had he. They just hadn't been able to fully accept it yet and implement the realizations.

She was never going to be content to stay home and clean the house while carrying a kid on her hip and making fresh nan only to paste on a smile and wish him well when he left before dinner for an impromptu night out with the guys but couldn't fathom the thought of her wanting to go anywhere without him. It was hypocritical and he couldn't see it! It was an old, old fight between them, a fight that constantly saw him storming off in anger for longer and longer periods of time. Their fights went far beyond falling asleep angry; they often found her falling asleep alone. Yes she was half Indian but she was raised very American and what was good for the goose was good for the gander. If he wanted considerations when he left early and trust when he arrived late, he needed to learn to give them.

Certainly his penchant for collecting a gaggle of beautiful women to hang on his every word and every note he played was not a big help either or the fact the place he chose to still work and the places his friends liked to hang out seemed to have an endless supply of the giggling creatures. His job had made no end of havoc, he had all the money he could possibly need, his father's business saw to that. Even if he didn't have his father to fall back on, he had a great education, but he still insisted on working where he had throughout college. He didn't want to let his employer down, he'd say. Be damned if him in that environment made her uncomfortable or made her feel that her hours on the phone making appointments for the crazy therapist so he could finish school and get a regular job were wasted, be dammed if she felt let down. Damn a man who could play a piano! And damn piano bars!

"If we knew each other in a past life," Aizlyn quipped, "we were more probably combatants than lovers. I will admit something draws me to him that I have to fight on a daily basis. Every time he crosses my mind, I have to force myself to avoid a phone but I don't think it has ever come to anything good, if we have lived before and crossed paths, and definitely not this time."

Aizlyn stared out the window, suddenly caught up in a memory that was only half formed but that her own words seemed to have brought on. She was simultaneously having yet another argument in her head with her grandmother, another of which she would never have aloud with her. The second she had graduated she had headed off to college and moved into the dorms. She'd gone and bought a new nose ring and a whole slew of black eyeliner pencils too. She was proud of them and never hid that from her grandmother those few occasions she might note them, but she still had never again spoke of or forced such deeper issues as her very varied beliefs and widely controversial theories.

"What?" Genie asked, her cutting into her swirling thoughts.

"Well, damn," Aizlyn sighed, hushing her grandmother's insistent tisking in her head, "you know it almost makes more sense if these are past life memories I am dreaming. I mean, they don't really fit as far as normal dreams go, no matter how much I try to make them. The more you talk to me about it the more I wanna just go with your explanations, and quit going back and forth in my head about it, because otherwise it won't seem to work right." Aizlyn laughed at herself then added, "I have had dreams of being a concubine to an Indian prince. We are both half Indian after all and his precious bar piano, surrounded by adoring women, makes for a great modern-day harem."

"Really?" Genie cocked her head and stared at Aizlyn. "You never mentioned those dreams."

"Well, it was neither here nor there," Aizlyn defended seeing Genie seemed genuinely disappointed. "It's not like it is one of the ones I forget to breathe in that scare me to death that someday I won't remember in time, or one I wake up with a terrible headache just in time not to figure out whether or not you really do die if you die in your sleep. They are certainly not as intriguing as the ones I wake up laughing from and never know why."

"Well," Genie prodded. "What do you feel?"

"Nothing?"

"You must feel something," Genie pushed. "Nearly every time you dream you wake up in a certain mood. Your dreams set the tone for the day. You just have to remember what those ones make you feel." Realizing Aizlyn was not looking as sure as she was, she added, "Think. When was the last time you dreamed one of those ones? What did you feel the rest of the day? Even better, what did you feel when you were dreaming it?"

"I dunno," Aizlyn replied, taking another distracted sip of her coffee as she guided them back to her room to sit on the bed, deftly avoiding the dining room and the painting that hid in plain sight. "I can see what I have written down."

Aizlyn sat on the edge of the bed closest to the nightstand and began to thumb through the old journal that rested there while Genie sat down at the foot of the bed and watched her with much interest. Angus helped himself to the entire rest of the queen-sized mattress, turning in a few bored circles before flopping down in a huff that spoke volumes of his lack of interest in what the two humans were doing. Soon he was snoozing away, running free in some random dream while Aizlyn looked up one in particular.

"Here," Aizlyn said triumphantly, "I had it last, just before we broke up this last time."

"Well," Genie prodded, "read it to me."

"It's not written out here," Aizlyn said, "I just wrote, 'had the concubine dream again' and here," she added, flipping back a handful of pages, "I wrote, 'I will be the thirteenth wife of the prince again.' I've had it a lot, sometimes I just write something like that. I don't always write them out."

"Disappointed?" Genie asked trying to read into what her friend read so nonchalantly, "Disillusioned?"

"Maybe, yeah, a little," Aizlyn continued to thumb through the journal distractedly while she tried to put her finger on her feelings and give them a name. "I think it's more like defeated but used to it. Does that make sense?"

"Too much! Well, find one of them and read it to me already. Maybe more will come back to you," Genie said, exasperated with Aizlyn's apparent lack of excitement at what appeared to her as a breakthrough via obvious similarities between the here and now and a dream. "This is a good thing, Aizlyn! Think about it if you can figure out what the dreams are trying to remind you, you might find peace of mind. You tell me all the time that you couldn't be the woman he wants because he wants a submissive stay at home woman who will do everything like his mother and allow him to do as he pleases. That sounds like a man used to a concubine way of life to me. But I think the hardest part for you was him working at that piano bar with all the women fawning over the good looking "Italian" guy and knowing you would never be as important as the piano itself and the fans it made him and the feeling that gave him, like a thirteenth wife, who doesn't like sharing the man." Genie smiled at her own imagination and wit.

"But," Aizlyn said slipping back once again into logic, "what if I dream those dreams merely because that situation left me feeling less important than I felt I should be and I am simply relating it in my subconscious to the feeling a thirteenth wife might have had ages ago. You know what I mean, I dream I am dancing my heart out for someone and I don't get nearly the recognition I had hoped for it, that sort of thing."

"Dancing?" Genie queried.

"Yeah, I dance," Aizlyn answered, "I dance, I win him…"

"Or," Genie cut in, still dead set that she was right in this matter, even though her mind was spinning, "you dream you were one of many wives because once you were and the feelings then are the same as now, whether you had married him yet or not. Maybe you put off the marriage in the first place because you somehow recognized he has always been this prince you dream of and was once again making you feel that way, at some point, to some extent. You want to change that, to show him that you are equals and you deserve to be treated as such, you're fighting for a better relationship this time around. You want to be loved more than anything, be the most important, not just another love among many."

Aizlyn had paused in her backward thumbing somewhere toward the front of the book and seemed to have gotten lost in the page before her or the thoughts her friends words had provoked. Had it been anyone else besides Genie who'd been so blunt, Miss Windell would have broke down crying or Win would have told them to mind their own karma and get bent. But it was Genie and that meant Aizlyn just took it in, swirled it around and tried to swallow it down to see what nourishment it might provide.

Genie had stirred up enough possibilities in her own mind to cause her to get a little lost too, trying to fit together what she already knew with what she could only guess she was about to hear, so as the silence lengthened it was enough to cause first Genie and then Angus to jump when Aizlyn suddenly began to read:

"The drums were pounding so hard they nearly drowned out the sound of my own heartbeat in my head, certainly they sped it up and made it match their rhythm. My chest was heaving in time, dragging the hanging bells, coins and gems, which dangled beneath my breasts, encircling my ribs, up and down my tense torso and I hadn't even begun to dance. The excitement of what lay before me had already heated my face, making me distinctly aware of the cold, cut emerald my mother had so carefully hung between my brows. It made my toes and my fingertips go numb, oblivious to the hot blood that raced through my entire body, making my whole being feel as though it were humming. I resonated like a bow strung almost too tight that had been plucked by a child and was just waiting for a man of strength to set my true power free. My muscles were leaden, heavy on my bones, but I felt beyond powerful, ready to spring over the heads of all those gathered. In short, I was nervous but sure and wanted the dance done and over with.

"The look on my mother's face had changed, as I glanced at her for the tenth or so time, it told me I could take the floor the first second the beat dragged my feet forward. And that was how it should be, she had always said, the beat should move you; you did not move yourself to a beat. Still I waited, I wasn't quite sure why, the cool expanse of marble leading up the dais where the prize lounged was clear, had been for some time. All those over-eager young women had near trod each others' heels in the parade they made before him but I had not taken my place among them. I had not raced to come between them. I had waited. Now I was all that was left and I still wasn't sure when my feet would move me.

"I could have sworn I had done this all before, that I felt no great desire to do it so eagerly all over again; that if I was to do it at all, I wanted to be different and stand out.

49

"Now I would.

"The drums stopped, the parade was over and I had not gone out onto the floor to try and capture his attention beyond all those gathered. Silence descended, you could have heard a pin drop as all waited to see him point out his choice and for her to come before him once again, that he might place his jewel upon the woman who had captured him. Instead they all heard the bells about my ankles as they clinked hard together following the drop of my heel as it swung down from the pendulum that was the balls of my left foot and my extended hip. Again I moved just the heel, hard left and up then dropped it back into place. A third time.

"Well I wanted to be different!

"A single drum could not resist following me as I moved slowly forward in this manner, one hip at a time, thrusting up and forward along with its respective heel and dropping heavily, creating my own beat. When I had reached the center of the marble floor I raised my arms out to either side and threw my hair forward. I began elevating my chin by minimal degrees in time with that solitary drum, while moving only my shoulders one at a time and still slamming down that one heel with its wonderful bells that had started it all.

"I could barely make him out through the veil of my hair but I continued to stare through it anyway. I knew even without being able to make him out that he would be beyond beautiful, my heart could see him just fine. It was a terrible mockery of greeting, directed toward the dais, as another drum and another could not resist me and I didn't care. By the time I threw my head back and disengaged my eyes from the prize before me, letting those drums and the rest of the noise that followed finally have back the control of my body I knew the drums were not the only ones who could not resist me. I knew I had won.

"I threw my hips forward one side at a time, and rolled my stomach muscles in time, in love with the heavy feel of all the chains and belts, the draped ropes of gems and jewels and bells and coins, all the wealth my mother could display on my body. I shimmered and winked and I was dazzling and I knew it. I swung my long hair around allowing the weight of it to bring my body round with it and I felt glorious. Breaking every convention, I combined many styles and traditional dances into one and no one thought to stop me. No one condemned the mockery I had made of this night. No one thought at all, I think, they were as lost in it as I was.

"I came to my knees and threw my head back rather than forward on the floor before him and suddenly everything stopped. The drums, the bells, the steady clap of a thousand hands; all that was left was the heavy beat of my heart and the sound of my breasts rising and falling dragging the weight of my family wealth up and down my bare ribs.

"I heard him rise, but still I did not move, not even my eyes. I felt him move before me. Suddenly his beautiful face was over mine, even more striking up close and not seen through the veil of my black locks. Ah, just as I thought!

"As he bent, I slowly elevated my upper body to meet him halfway and as he placed his brooch above my breast, my mother's sharp intake of breath told me it was beyond worthy as far as she was concerned. I was more concerned with the fact that he had come to me, that he had bent, that he had met me halfway. There was something in that which meant more to me than a thousand brooches, no matter how extravagant, and any alliance, no matter how powerful, could ever mean. This felt like the difference I desired. This did not smack of the mundane, memory-like reality I had been living in since I could remember."

"See!" Genie exclaimed, "I told you! You want to be special to him this round, not only treated as an equal but loved by him above all else. Sounds like you and Jordan have been at this for quite a while, by the sounds of that dream that wasn't the first time you captured him and only to worry it was only partially."

"Well, if every dream of me in India is me in a life trying to change the way we coexist then I have yet to succeed, even in this one, in finding a balance in our relationships that pleases me," Aizlyn said sadly. "It's as if I knew, know, there is a better, deeper kind of love out there and want to

achieve it with him, and yet never can seem to. There is not a single dream of
me in India, that I can recall, in which I remember true satisfaction with my
state, or true contentment other than those moments like the dance itself.
Listen to this entry, it's not even a whole dream- just something I wrote when
I was much younger and had been dancing in my sleep again."

Aizlyn flipped back even closer to the beginning of her journal and
found the entry almost too quickly. It made Genie think it must have been
something she had read and probably brooded over many a time.

"Somehow I felt the dance itself was the real prize, not the husband
it had won me. No thrill of the win engulfed my ribs and made it hard to
inhale his beautifully spicy scent as he bent to place his jewel upon me. I had
more pleasure of breaking the rules, doing the dance my way, bending the
drums to my will, than capturing a prince who seems too easily captured, one
who had been captured before. Somehow I felt he had already been mine, my
destiny, my fate, and that I wanted to make that different too. I did not want
to be just another wife among many, another lover and mother to be lost in a
room full of them. Maybe next time I should not dance at all. What would
happen then?"

"You have felt this way too long, dearest," Genie said after a moment
of silent consideration. "Maybe that is what the dreams are *really* trying to
tell you and why they have become so adamant. Maybe you are trying to
show yourself that you have tried and failed enough, that there is no changing
who each of us is at our core, that no matter how many times you try he will
always be the way he is and you will too, nothing will ever change that.
Maybe these dreams want you to see, before you've wasted another lifetime
with the constant trying, that you've already tried it all and nothing works."

"Well, that sucks," Aizlyn replied, dripping sarcastic cheeriness.
"Guess I'll just stop loving him now. Voila, I'm done."

Aizlyn stood and walked toward the kitchen, as if by escaping the
room she could escape the hard realizations her friend was trying so gently to
make her see.

"I know you love him, honey," Genie said, following her friend into the kitchen and refilling her coffee cup as well. "But maybe you should consider that there are different kinds of love and this one may not be the healthy kind."

Genie paused while she stirred cream and sugar into her cup, looking closely at her friend, knowing this was very tender flesh she poked. "I mean, is it possible this is more like one of those obsessive loves. The kind that wants to possess, needs to *win*, a hold-it-and-squeeze-it-and-pet-it-and-keep-it-in-your-pocket kind, rather than the kind that wants to see the one they love happy, whether or not that means they are the one to hold it?"

"He's like that about me," Aizlyn replied quickly and a bit defensively.

"I know," Genie said carefully, "but what about you? You never wanted him home with you rather than out playing his piano?"

"Well, yeah, but that's different," Aizlyn tried.

"Not really," Genie said, putting her spoon down and heading back to the bedroom knowing Aizlyn wouldn't be able to remain too far behind. She continued over her shoulder, "You work in the same kind of place now, make your money the same way, and probably draw the same feelings from it. You should get this. Yet you begrudge him what makes him happy because that happiness doesn't always involve you, because it makes you feel less important to him by comparison. That's as much hypocrisy on your part as it is when he goes out with his boys but gets upset when you come out with me."

"I can't give it up," Aizlyn said pitifully, "I can't rely on him, obviously, and even back in the beginning I felt he needed to see what it was like."

"Yes," Genie agreed, "Win's penchant for lending karma a hand, *showing* someone how something feels rather than simply trying to tell them. I get it. But do you? The thing I think you're missing is the first thing it should have taught *you*, that it is good to be and feel free and beautiful and wanted, to find joy in each day. If you enjoy it why would you begrudge him that same joy?"

"The women," Aizlyn defended some more, "I don't encourage and collect guys at work and when we go out we don't go out with guys. He'd shit a brick!"

"Ahh, the thirteenth wife's perpetual dilemma! Well, he already shit a brick, dear," Genie said, poking just a bit more, "he left over two months ago, remember, unlike your other friends, I know! And so what if he had a couple dozen twittering chicks waddling after his tail feathers all the time, he came home to you. Did he ever cheat?"

"How would I know?" Aizlyn snapped. "He didn't always come home right away!"

And that was the crux of it!

Was.

Now it was more that she was just sick and tired of the constant fighting, of him always storming out, creating even larger gaps for doubt, with his longer and longer absences, perpetually creating more resentment and destroying more trust. She had vowed this would be the last time. She had even sold the ring this time but the sad truth was she hadn't really let go or it wouldn't have hurt so bad when Genie poked. She wouldn't have snapped. Sadder still was her own fear she was bound to give in and start trying again when he finally called her. It felt almost like a void inside her eating the hope out of every day, a great vacuum of helplessness that sucked up all her courage and told her not to bother to move on because he'd be back.

"You're still waiting for him to call," Genie said then, taking her friend's rudeness with a grain of salt and seeing it for what it was.

"What am I gonna do?" Aizlyn said, suddenly close to tears.

Not only were Aizlyn's senses short-circuiting but her emotions were a total wreck. One day the lowest of low, with a terrible headache and the memory of a musket pressed to her temple, the next waking up laughing and floating around like a well-inflated balloon that was too easily popped. It felt great a second ago to find solid correlation between her dreams and her current state, almost proof enough they were past-life memories to get her to start sorting them out in earnest and stop the doubts and her grandmother's tisking in her head from setting the task aside. But now she just felt defeated by it, like if she were to believe they were indeed memories, despite how wonderful it would be to have so many other questions answered, the one she'd rather it didn't was just as surely answered too. It was never going to work with Jordan and her!

"We're gonna figure these dreams out once and for all," Genie replied, patting her leg reassuringly. "So you can get on with finding those things in this life that make you laugh like you were when I woke you. I wanna see you laughing like that, and waist deep in the good kind of love, that makes you happy and *is* happy because you are."

The phone rang just then, so if Genie planed on waxing poetic about the kind of love she felt her best friend deserved and she wanted to help her find, she wasn't given the opportunity. Genie smiled to herself, though, as she watched Aizlyn go on the hunt for the ever-absent handset, because she felt she had finally won the epic battle of convincing Aizlyn to believe her dreams were her past life's memories coming back to show her something. Genie had always believed in past lives and the occasional memory of them, it was why she was so content to live the life she did, adoring a man she rarely saw but was madly in love with. It was why she had chosen, or rather not resisted, the friend she was so bound and determined to help.

"Who was that?" Genie asked of Aizlyn as she reentered the room and flopped down on the bed with a puzzled look plastered to her expressive oval face.

"Papa," Aizlyn answered. "He said he has something for me and I need to catch a ride over there to get it."

"So, what's got you making with the puzzle face?" Genie asked, not quite seeing what the dilemma would be.

"Why would I need to catch a ride over there?" Aizlyn pointed out, "I have a perfectly good SUV. He knows that. He just changed the oil two weeks ago."

"Ahhhh," Genie said, now just as intrigued as Aizlyn, "Good thing I drove this morning."

"Where's Nathan?" Aizlyn finally thought to ask, realizing her favorite nine year old was noticeably absent this morning as they walked out to her friend's little maroon four door sedan and got into the passenger seat.

"With his father," Genie said, smiling as she always did when she spoke of her offspring and her husband.

It was almost creepy to Aizlyn, how in love Genie seemed, especially now, as jaded as her view of such things had become over the last few years. Aizlyn was torn between jealousy and worry for her. Wanting the same thing but fearing her friend was bound to someday suffer the same disillusionment she had.

"They went to a ball game," Genie continued, still smiling as she put the car in reverse and got the trip to Aizlyn's grandparents' house underway, oblivious to the thoughts her grin was putting into Aizlyn's head. "They're gonna have a whole day of good old-fashioned boy stuff, cheering maniacally at guys swinging large whittled sticks at small balls of murdered cow, while stuffing their face with greasy burgers and nasty chili dogs and practicing new public belching techniques."

"Sounds fun," Aizlyn grinned at her friend as her joke pushed some of her glum mood back.

"You work tonight?" Genie asked sometime later.

It took Aizlyn a second to figure out what Genie had asked. Her mind had been running over a thousand different scenarios of why her grandpa might have needed her to "catch a ride" over to his place and some of them were terribly worrisome, having to do with her grandmother and news that he may feel she needn't be behind a wheel after hearing.

"Yeah."

"Your next day off?" Genie asked then.

Between her own thoughts and the sounds of the radio and wind blowing in the cracked windows they were ashing their cigarettes out of so Genie's husband wouldn't be upset by her obviousness when he found ashes in the car, this particular conversation was clipped. Genie was supposed to have quit smoking and everyone was pretending she had, including him. It was another thing about their relationship Aizlyn was both jealous and worried over.

"Saturday, of course,' Aizlyn laughed at her friend's total lack of subtlety. "I covered my shift for your birthday a month ago."

"Oh yeah," Genie said a bit distractedly, confusing Aizlyn and making her wonder why she'd asked if not for that reason.

"Why?"

"Oh, nothing," Genie said, restoring her grin perfectly and putting on her blinker before turning down Grandpa's street. "Tomorrow night?"

"Tomorrow night what?"

"You working?"

"Yes," Aizlyn was completely bemused now. "I traded it for Saturday."

"Okay, well, Sunday then," Genie said, making up her mind. "You're mine, so no making other plans. Straight to bed after we get home, no tipsy painting for you. No staying up so late you are worthless to me."

"For what?" Aizlyn tried again, reaching forward and turning down the radio. She had a feeling she was missing something in this conversation. The clock on the radio read three thirty-three, she didn't believe in coincidences, she knew the clock was telling her she was right as they pulled in the drive and Genie got out a bit too fast to pass for anything less than evasive.

"You'll see. Hi, Grandpa!" Genie ran forward and greeted Aizlyn's grandpa like he was hers, with a great big hug, successfully ending the conversation for the moment.

"Hey there, Papa," Aizlyn greeted him then, taking her turn in the great big bear hug he offered. Then stepping back, she looked up into his beloved face for a clue, and got right down to it. "What's up and why wouldn't you tell me on the phone?"

4

Papa

"I have something for you," Aizlyn's grandpa replied with a grin, "but first go in and give your grandmother a hug. She is always so worried you don't love her. Don't give her any further reason to keep me up at night with the eternal question of why you don't visit more often."

"You know why," Aizlyn said, grinning and winking at him as she cleaned her shoes on the front doormat and prepared to enter her grandmother's domain.

Indeed, Mr. Windell knew exactly why his granddaughter visited so rarely, but he was no more willing to discuss such matters as Aizlyn's very varied beliefs versus his wife's quite narrow view, at two in the morning, than Aizlyn was. So he mostly pretended he didn't understand such woman stuff as worry over depth of love measured in visits, and grunted as though he were too close to sleep to be bothered with more in-depth answers than the run of the mill, "She's probably painting some huge canvas and has lost track of time."

Grandpa knew a lot more about what Aizlyn did and felt than Grandma ever could. For instance, Grandpa knew Aizlyn quit her receptionist job years ago and was now a bartender in what Grandmother would have surely labeled a "den of iniquity." He knew because he knew how to separate church from state, how to love his granddaughter despite their differences and talk about said differences logically and calmly rather than citing them as proof he had failed somehow to raise her properly, and calling then and there for the good Lord's grace and patience to do better.

Grandpa understood Aizlyn and he understood his wife; loving them both he had become quite the phenomenal tightrope walker. He knew that Aizlyn had the same ability to separate herself from the work she did and where she did it from who she was, and it never lessened his faith he had raised her well. If anything it made him a touch proud to see she too had learned to walk the tightropes of life. The thing with Grandma was she was too dead set; one way was the right way, period. If you did it any other way you weren't doing it God's way, end of story! Grandma's way had lost him his daughter and so he took on the role of tightrope walker deftly and eagerly the day he got a second chance and a twelve-year-old Aizlyn thrust into his arms.

"Come give me a hug, child." Aizlyn heard hear grandmother's voice in the dim living room ahead of her before her eyes had adjusted. "You don't come see us enough!"

Aizlyn made her way around the coffee table and leaned down to hug her grandmother, who hadn't moved from beneath the pile of knitting on her lap when Genie and she had pulled up. She smelled homey, like pancakes, clean laundry and love. She was good to hug, just hard to talk to.

"You smell like cigarettes," her grandmother commented, screwing her face up into a grimace that spoke volumes of her distaste not only for the smell itself but the fact Aizlyn was "destroying the temple" still. "I see you haven't quit smoking those nasty things yet."

Genie followed her and hugged Aizlyn's grandmother as though she too were her own and ignored the huff she also received upon registration of the same smell on her clothes. Genie took it with a grain of salt, in fact Genie took most things with a grain of salt; the saying was made for her. Aizlyn wished she could, as she felt the old sting of guilt and hurt that always assailed her when Grandmother made that grimace of distaste over something she had done, not done, or done wrong. As usual, though, she said nothing in her own defense. Such action had long ago been trained to run with its tail between its legs at the prospect of another long drawn-out discussion of right and wrong which would see Grandma pulling out her Bible and Aizlyn mentally pulling out all her hair. Instead she went to the kitchen to distract herself by searching for something for Genie and her to drink.

"There is coffee made," her grandmother called to her, "and I made sure to have your grandpa get some half and half for you."

Again, Aizlyn was assailed by guilt, feeling like she'd just been caught saving her allowance for a pair of jeans she'd have to keep hidden in her locker at school. Her grandmother was a truly good person, who did love her dearly and cared deeply for her and her happiness; it just never occurred to her that maybe Aizlyn's happiness was to be found a different way than hers had been, that maybe Aizlyn didn't find peace in the prospect of blindly following another human's translation of a translation of what the Creator wanted for and from His creation.

It crushed Aizlyn that she couldn't be the perfect God-fearing girl her grandmother had tried so hard to raise. Some of it had stuck, most of it in fact, but there were still a great many things that Aizlyn couldn't blindly believe, and still more she did believe, which her grandmother would call heresy or even dabbling in witchcraft.

Heaven forbid she took any pleasure from reading her "horrible-scope," as Genie and she referred to their daily life's forecast via e-mail, once in a while, let alone relate it to her day or how she should proceed through it. That would be looking for guidance from somewhere other than God, consulting the stars rather than praying; never once would it have occurred to her grandmother that the Creator put those stars there for a reason and if He could use them to spin around the earth, just so, and ripen an orange, He might also use them to shape humanity's growth.

It killed her because she really did love her grandmother and knew her grandmother loved her, undoubtedly. Why couldn't they just agree to disagree and love each other in spite of their differences? Why couldn't they have a normal conversation that didn't in some way involve religion or point out how much of a disappointment the way she conducted her life was?

"You missed a wonderful sermon this past Sunday, dear," her grandmother continued, not looking up from her knitting as the two girls walked back into the living room with their coffee. "The preacher spoke to us about Lot and his wife, how she was turned into a pillar of salt for disobeying the Lord and looking back on the destruction He made of Sodom and Gomorra. He told us how seductive evil can be and that we need to turn our faces from it and avoid temptation."

Well, so much for talking about something other than religion.

"Aizlyn." Her grandfather's voice, the voice of the real salvation she had found living in this house, suddenly put a stop to the mental hair-pulling Aizlyn had just started doing. "Come out to the barn as soon as you have a minute, please."

"Go on." Her grandmother hadn't missed Aizlyn's readiness to be away and again made the grimace which caused Aizlyn to cringe inwardly. "I'm sure if you wanted to hear the sermon you'd have come to church with me Sunday."

"I love you, Grandma," Aizlyn called back over her shoulder as she and Genie escaped down the hall toward the back door. As ever it was the only answer she had for her grandmother.

"Coming, Papa," Aizlyn yelled too eagerly, throwing open the door and seeing him ahead of her, almost to the barn already.

As Aizlyn and Genie made their way across the back lawn to the old barn, Aizlyn was filled with a calming, beautiful nostalgia in welcome contrast to the weight of guilt she felt when in grandmother's domain. The old barn had sheltered more than one dream for her in her younger years, its gapped roof leaking soft light and illuminating the earthen floor where Aizlyn used to hide from her Grandmother's disapproving gaze and continue to try and master the dances she'd always dreamed she could.

Her mother was there too, or as close as she could ever be, sitting in the driver's seat of an old decrepit sixty-seven Mustang with bricks for tires and an engine that hung on a chain from the rafters for as long as she could recall. It was called a "California Special," her grandpa had told her once, and it was the only thing of substance her mother had ever bought, but the only thing "special" she'd ever known about it was that she felt her mother there. Aizlyn had been known to crawl into it, pull on her seat belt, and talk to her mother, as in her imagination they drove for hours, to anywhere but there, when she had needed her mother most.

Looking back, Aizlyn could see how that old beat-up red car with its cracked and torn, used-to-be-white leather seats was her mother's nose ring. The thing her mother wanted and found a way to get the first second she could when she had come of age. Only it hadn't been enough, hadn't gotten her far enough away from the oppressive love that sat knitting in the house behind her. Her mother had parked it here, safe with Grandpa, and run off to a whole other country to fall desperately for a man who gave her Aizlyn but, apparently, little more.

She hadn't been out to the barn in ages, not since Shanks had died and took so much of the life from the place with him. As she entered its cool dim confines, she wondered why she had forgotten and thus denied herself that wonderful peaceful feeling it gave her for so long. Something was different, though. Her grandfather stood smiling beside the old Mustang with a hand extended toward her, but the Mustang itself no longer looked so old. It had new tires and its engine no longer hung above it. Her grandfather opened the driver-side door and motioned her in, wordlessly handing her the keys, as she approached.

"She'd of wanted you to have it," her grandpa said, taking in the look of astonished wonder Aizlyn didn't try to hide as she rubbed the new leather covering the seats. "I just never got around to fixin it up for ya till now. But I met a guy who offered to recover the seats for that old horse trailer I hadn't used since Shanks died and that finally got me started."

As Aizlyn continued petting the interior, putting the key in the ignition and checking the lights and gauges, he continued as though the explanation needed making if only for himself. "I know you feel close to your mother here. But I do too. I think that's why it was so hard for me to get started fixin her up and give her to you."

He patted the roof of the car as though it were another favored old horse he was losing and a bit of moisture could be seen coming into his eyes. Aizlyn was overwhelmed. She couldn't think of anything to say as she climbed out from behind the wheel, smiling up into his aging eyes as hers too welled up. Aizlyn wrapped her arms around him and buried her head in her grandfather's chest, crying softly, tears that were both happy and sad.

Finally her grandfather had enough of the "girly moment' and patted her back, putting her gently back behind the driver's seat. "I put some of her things in the trunk for ya; you can take a look when you get home. I managed to save a few things from the great purging your grandmother tends to do every once and a while. Go on back in the house and tell her you'll see her again soon so she don't think ya hate her and I'll warm her up and pull her 'round front for ya."

So this was why she needed to catch a lift over here, Aizlyn thought jubilantly. She bounced back toward the house to the sound of the engine firing up and rumbling idly like a Harley, well-tuned but beautifully loud.

Genie elbowed her happily as they nearly raced for the back door. "You are so taking me cruising Saturday night," she giggled, "and we are definitely finding a drive-in for our next movie date!"

"You know it!" Aizlyn replied happily, sliding onto the porch just ahead of Genie and barely scraping her feet on the mat as she swung the door wide.

"You wipe your feet good?" she heard from the dim living room, cutting sharply into the feel-good moment.

"Yes, Grandma," Aizlyn called ahead of her as she came down the hall. "You knew Papa was fixing Momma's old Mustang up for me?"

Why she would have blundered into that trap of a conversation she would never know. Maybe just the excitement of the entire situation made her forget who she was trying to share her joy with. Maybe she held some outside hope her Grandmother had condoned, even encouraged, this great gift be made, but in any case it hadn't been a smart dialogue to begin. It had ended up with her having to hear a lecture on fast cars, fast women, the dangers of cruising, drive-up dinners and drive-in movies, the powerful lure of all things evil disguised as "good fun" and her husband's dangerous and sadly never-ending lack of foresight when it came to such things. The end result of which was another round of interrogation on when she planned on marrying "that boy" she was "living in sin with" and a warning that she didn't want to end up like her mother.

What was that supposed to mean? Aizlyn wondered while mentally pulling out the last little bit of her hair. As far as she was concerned, all her mother ever did wrong was get herself taken out of the picture and leave her with a woman she hadn't been able to handle either. If she ever was to become a mother she fully intended to do everything in her power to be exactly like her mother had been, less the absent the last half of her child's formative years part. Her mother had understood her, encouraged her in all things and above all made it possible for her to dream. If their views had not matched it had merely been a matter to keep them up past bedtime talking rather than a reason for a lesson on how she was wrong and her mother was right.

There had never really been a "wrong and right" with her mother, merely "how would that make you feel if it was done to you?" and if her answer had been something like, "I'd be upset for being left out," her mother would say something along the lines of, "then share the toys with them and apologize for being stingy, my love." Punishments were always fitting and only when truly necessary; she couldn't recall ever being grounded for a week by her mother simply for being caught with a wet pair of shorts that not only said she'd been swimming in the creek behind the property but that she'd been wearing something "skimpy" to do it. She could, however, recall being dragged up from the floor by her ear and being made to apologize to a cat!

Once when she was about four, she had been caught trying to get a cat out from under a bed in a none-too-gentle fashion; pulling it out by its ear. Its yowls of pain had brought her mother swooping into the room and down on her with a swift lesson. She'd been pulled up from all fours by her ear and while she'd squalled and squirmed her mother had asked her repeatedly how it felt, till she sucked it up enough to tell her mother it hurt between hiccups. Her mother had then taken her hand and walked her to the kitchen. Taking out a can of tuna, she poured the juice off into a bowl and sent her back to her room to apologize to the cat.

If only Jordan's mother had thought to instill in him that self-check mechanism which acted as a personal jiminy cricket constantly at the back of your mind asking how you'd feel if something was done to you. Maybe they might have been able to find common ground and establish a trust and understanding that could carry them through the smaller battles life presented every couple. Leaving the toilet seat up was nothing compared to leaving an entire meal that took hours to prepare growing cold while you ran off to play with someone else who was momentarily more important, no matter who they were.

She was saved, once again, from these mental wanderings she tended to go on when her grandmother really got started by her grandfather, as he was heard pulling the car around front. So giving her grandmother another hug and saying she'd be back, she escaped the house once again.

Sitting behind the wheel of her mother's car, feeling it hum all around her, gave whole new life to the feeling her mother and she were about to be off on another incredible journey. Her grandfather told her to drive safe, warned her to stay out of the gas and go easy on the brakes, but smiled knowingly even as he did, saying a little prayer that angels would fly fast enough to keep his granddaughter safe as he watched her drive away.

As soon as they hit the open road, Aizlyn put her hand up, waving to Genie in the rear view mirror, and pegged the gas peddle. The car jumped, sucked in a deep breath and took off screaming. Man it was beautiful! The radio had picked out an oldies station as if of its own accord and suddenly it was telling her "…let your hair down, girl." She could hear her mother singing with the radio, at the top of her lungs, outdoing even the wind in her ears. No amount of late night driving around the outskirts of town to wined down and leave her worries in the ditch, taking the long way home after work had ever came close to this pure, unadulterated feeling of freedom and endless ability to conquer anything. This was true "motor therapy," as she had labeled her occasional, late night, wined-down drives. She'd definitely have to do them more often now!

Aizlyn slowed down as she drew nearer the city and began looking for an exit that would take her by a drive-through on the way home. She'd decided she didn't want to make lunch and she'd just pick something up and have it waiting when Genie caught up and met her there. The prospect of getting ready for work afterwards seemed even more pleasant for the simple fact it would be another excuse to drive this wonderful car again and she didn't really mind she was going to have to work this night, as well as the next, which she would normally have off. She had traded it for a good reason, and Genie and she could drive this thing even more on Saturday when they went for her birthday dinner.

Aizlyn juggled the go-cups of soda and bags of sloppy barbecue sandwiches around and managed to open the door and let herself into her house only to be met by a ferocious sight. Angus stood in the arch between the living room she had just entered and the dining room beyond, hackles up, all teeth and no sound. She'd seen that look only once and it had not been directed at her but rather a man who had approached her unawares beneath her broken street light one night after work nearly a year ago. She'd left the door open and gone back out to the car, already barefoot, to grab something she'd forgotten from her car and been frightened near to death by the stranger's sudden appearance.

The man had scared her for reasons she couldn't rationalize, he had simply asked to borrow a phone. But then he had shown an angry disappointment when she had instinctively lied and told him her service had been temporarily disconnected. She wasn't sure at first why she had lied, she hated lying, but she was glad she had when the man had stepped toward her, unsettling her even more by reaching into his pocket, menacingly. Her heart had nearly jumped out of her chest when something in his eyes, suddenly illuminated by the light coming from her open front door, spoke to her of very ill intent.

Then Angus had appeared out of the dark from behind her, having crossed the threshold out into the front yard, where there was no fence, as he knew not to unless on a leash. She had thanked God the dog had somehow known there were times you could disobey and it be okay, as he put his nose in her shaking hand and nudged it to the top of his large reassuring head. He had then given the unwelcome man the same silent, unmistakable warning he was giving her, all teeth-no sound, and it had been enough. The man had left, hand still in his pocket, grumbling about women who preferred big dogs to cats and ankle-biters.

It only lasted a split second, the fear Angus had contracted rabies, gone mad, and was about to tear her viciously limb from limb. All tension suddenly left his body and he began wagging his tail twice as much as normal as though to apologize for such a rude greeting.

"What the hell was that about?" she sighed with welcome relief. Angus ran up to her and after accepting one brief pat from the hand she freed by placing the sodas on the T.V. cabinet, he pushed his head past her rudely and looked out the front door. Suddenly it occurred to her he hadn't recognized the sound of the car that had pulled up and hence had no clue who was entering his house in her absence and she gave him another pat and a "good boy" before closing the door.

Wanting to hide Genie's painting and clear a spot for their lunch, she made her way ahead of Angus, who seemed to want to remain by the front door a little while longer to assure himself nothing further out of the ordinary was about to occur. Aizlyn had just finished stacking all her paints and pots to one side of the table and hiding the paintings away when Angus began huffing at the door, letting her know Genie's car had turned down their street.

Genie let herself in to a much more normal greeting from Angus and made it to the dining room table just as Aizlyn finished setting the food out and tossing the bag in the trash.

"Ha, I knew it," Genie laughed and grinned, pulling up her chair and picking up her sandwich, "I almost stopped by there myself but something said you already had."

"Didn't want to waste time cooking," Aizlyn replied through a mouthful.

"Wanna get in that trunk, don't you!" Genie giggled at Aizlyn as her friend lost some of her sandwich to her lap and tossed the wayward chunk of barbeque toward the dog who had intelligently placed himself in the arch perfectly able to beg and watch the front door at the same time while appearing to do neither.

"I can't figure what Papa might have stashed of my mother's," Aizlyn said around another mouthful as she continued to seem to try to get lunch down for no other reason than to get past the task and on to better things. "I thought my grandmother had taken everything to Goodwill when we were notified my mother had died. I mean that's what she told me."

"Gawd, you're gonna make yourself puke," Genie said finally, unable to bear watching the vulgar attempts her friend was making at breaking the speed-eating record. "Or me! Just go get the stuff already and let's see it, the food will still be here to pick at when you're actually ready to eat it rather than wear it!"

Aizlyn laughed at herself as she tossed Angus another chunk of the escaping meat from off her leg and set the last half of the messy sandwich down. Damn, she thought, and she had been doing so well with not giving him scraps, but when they ended up on your lap or the floor, it was just pure habit, she excused.

"Be right back," Aizlyn announced, jumping up and heading out the front door again.

Genie followed her out to the car a few moments later when she hadn't returned soon enough to sate her own curiosity and found her friend leaned into the trunk holding what looked like a small porcelain statuette. There was a box there too, unopened, but it seemed that the little figure in her hands was all Aizlyn saw. Genie figured it most have been wrapped in the long length of scarf Aizlyn now had wrapped around her shoulders and neck, since the box appeared sealed still and the material had to have come before the all-consuming statue that held her friend's rapt attention.

"Grandmother would have had Papa's ass for this," Aizlyn fairly whispered after a moment, realizing Genie had joined her and was looking at her prize quizzically. "Grandmother would have broken this "idol" and then burned it and buried the ashes too. I haven't seen this since I left India. I wonder how Papa got it and how he managed to save it."

"What is it?" Genie asked, her attention now full on the small, delicate and distinctly Indian figure sitting on a lotus holding some sort of musical instrument in her friend's somewhat shaking hands. "Who is it?"

"Sarasvati," Aizlyn said in her same near whisper that said she was still in awe of what she held. "She is the goddess of all the arts and learning, some even believe that only through her worship can true liberation from reincarnation occur. I remember my mother spent half our groceries money on this for me when I spotted it at the market. I was seven. I don't even remember now why it meant so much to me. I just wanted it so badly, I begged Mom the whole time she was trying to shop.

"Honestly, I don't think we had the money for it but when she asked me why I just had to have that particular statue my answer must have been right." Aizlyn grinned, "Mom had set down the item she had been looking at and gone right over and finally looked at it. She had examined it closely for only a moment then she had bartered relentlessly with the old woman who was selling it until it was suddenly mine and she handed it to me."

"It wasn't your mother's, then," Genie asked wondering why it would be in the trunk.

"No, these are mine," Aizlyn said, holding the statue to herself and fingering the scarf. Then she reached behind the box, to the floor of the trunk and came up with a handful of old, melted and reformed eyeliner pencils. She showed them to Genie too. "Papa must have stashed them when Grandmother took them. I wonder how... Oh my..."

Aizlyn trailed off as she caught the glint of precious metal that had been buried under the eyeliner pencils and must have been wrapped in the scarf as the rest had been. Suddenly her eyes filled with unexpected tears. There, resting in the short carpeting of the trunk, lay a gold nose ring with a small green emerald set in a lotus flower. Aizlyn pushed the pencils into Genie's hands and scooped it up as though it were about to fade like a mirage created by her tears if she didn't do it swiftly. She held it to her heart with her statue for the longest time until Genie could bear the suspense no longer and finally asked her what she'd found.

"My nose ring!" Aizlyn cried, extending her hand and opening it slowly as though she were about to unveil and display a beautiful butterfly that might fly away too quickly for its beauty to be honestly enjoyed.

"Oh my...," Genie too trailed off, having little to say that would make more of the moment she knew this was to her friend.

Finally all she could do to express her understanding was to hold the statue along with the pencils as Aizlyn suddenly thrust it on her and began pulling her current nose ring out so she could replace it. They walked in the house so that Aizlyn could use the mirror in the dinning room and Genie freed her hands by placing her precious cargo on the coffee table as she passed it.

As Aizlyn continued to stare at herself in the mirror, thinking and remembering things Genie could only guess at, that one took her curiosity back out to the car and brought in the box and put it in the living room. She then went to make a pot of coffee before returning to the couch to wait for Aizlyn to come back to the present and go through it with her.

Aizlyn joined her when the coffee was ready, coming through the archway with two cups full and striking Genie in a way she never had before. Genie was suddenly met with the sight of a regal Indian hostess, at least from the shoulders up, and that's where her attention was suddenly focused. Aizlyn had arranged the beautiful scarf carefully and now wore it draped over her head and around her shoulders; she had placed a small gem between her eyes and put on her eyeliner. Genie had the distinct impression she was looking on a walking version of the statue she'd stared at till the life-sized one walked in and captured her full attention.

But then Aizlyn threw back her head and broke loose with a happy laugh that started off more like a bark and ended with a snort and broke the spell completely. "What do you think?" Aizlyn asked finally, catching her breath and wanting her friend to put into words what had been plastered on her face for those few brief moments when she'd appeared in the arch as she had. "Could I pass for Indian?"

"Well, other than the stained sweats that should be on someone twice your size and the donkey laugh, yeah," Genie laughed back, taking her coffee and nodding toward the box. "Now stop with the suspense, woman, and open those things."

Aizlyn set her coffee on the table and plopped down on the floor before the box and began plucking at the tape. "Oh for goodness sakes," Genie grumbled, leaning forward and handing her the letter opener she kept on the coffee table, "you're killing me here."

Aizlyn laughed at her friend's curious impatience and gave into her own, stabbing at the offending tape and slicing it free. Then tossing the letter opener on the table again she pulled open the box. Letters, lots and lots of letters, all addressed to her grandfather from her mother, postmarked from India.

She pawed through the layers and eventually came across an old pair of blue corduroy hip-hugger pants with cloth and rhinestone butterflies sewn on the hem and a little black, square-necked, sack dress shorter than even she would wear, with a yellow ribbon around it just beneath the breast and a daisy sewn right in the middle. There was a leather vest too, with little daisies cut out of it all up the front and tassels so long they'd have hit the backs of her knees had she the strength or will to stand up just then and put it on.

Then there was a photo album under those articles of clothing and beneath that was a short stack of records that included Janis Joplin, Jimi

Hendrix, Pink Floyd, Crosby Stills and Nash and even Credence Clearwater Revival. As she flipped through she was awestruck not only by the things her mother had obviously cherished but the fact her grandfather had kept them safe for her along with her car.

Suddenly she realized she didn't know much about her mother other than the "motherly" parts. She could seem to make all of her findings work as belonging to one single person. The clothes and music, to her mind, said her mother should have smoked marijuana and driven a VW bus, the stacks and stacks of perfectly penned letters never dated more than a few months apart and the choice of cars said she should have been a secretary and still tried to dress like Jackie O.

As she slowly began to flip through the photo album and Genie moved to the floor beside her to look with her, she began to realize there were as many sides to her mother as there was to her. Her mother, too, had a Miss Windell side, posed in family photographs, choir lineups and school photos. There was an "Aizlyn" side whose paint-stained sweat pants were bell-bottomed hip-huggers and shirts tied off just beneath her breasts, whose playground was muddy outdoor concerts and festivals with many guitars and bonfires, instead of a basement of a friend's house with tables full of every craft under the sun and an ever-changing stack of rented DVDs for the T.V. in the corner.

Then there was her mother, just Mom, captured on film, standing before a mirror in India with her daughter, scarves tied around their hips like they were the poorest of belly dancers as they practiced putting on their eyeliner. And then this must have been her "Win," dressed in ratty old jeans, her Greenpeace tee-shirt stretched over her slightly pregnant belly, earnestly talking to an old man sitting on his front stoop with a pipe clasped firmly between his wrinkled lips.

That tee-shirt had to have been her leather pants, the armor that made her job possible, as surely as that Mustang outside was her nose ring. The tee-shirt allowed her to be and do and feel on a different level, to escape her own problems by immersing herself in another's. She didn't have to feel inadequate and incapable because when she wore it, it instilled faith in others that she knew what she was doing; she could do it well and meant to help. The unwed single mother suddenly became someone to respect and pay attention to and it made her able to believe it too and do her job.

Aizlyn lost all sense of time as she flipped through her mother's life. She didn't know what more exactly she was hoping to find until she had come to the last page and still not found it. She stared at the photo of her mother and her out front of the airport, taken the day they'd come back to America, and felt more emotion than she new what to do with. She wasn't sure if she wanted to cry some more or if she wanted to flip back to the pages of her and her mother playing dress-up and laugh as she had back then.

"What is it?" Genie asked suddenly, breaking her reverie and forcing her to focus again on the photo before her. "What are you staring at?"

"He's not here," Aizlyn said finally, closing the book and looking up at the clock reflexively. Now that she was back in the present she would need to be aware when she needed to get ready for work.

"Who?" Genie asked, a bit perplexed by her friend's quickly shifting moods throughout this day.

"My father," Aizlyn replied, putting the album back in the box on top of the letters and pushing herself to her feet. She was pleased she had learned so much about her mother but realized only after the fact how much she had hoped to catch a glimpse of her father.

"Oh," Genie said softly, also getting to her feet.

She knew her friend well enough to realize they were done for the time being, having seen Aizlyn glance at the clock and noting herself how close it was to time for her to get ready for work. She was still very curious as to what the letters might reveal but also knew it was going take Aizlyn a good bit of preparation to get ready for work and be able to leave all of this behind when she did, so she wasn't about to push...much.

"Mind if I stop by tomorrow, go through the letters with you?" Genie asked as she rinsed her coffee cup and prepared to head home.

"Of course," Aizlyn grinned reassuringly, letting Genie see that the bittersweet of all she'd discovered, and not, today had been more sweet than bitter and that she was going to be okay with all of it.

"Then I'll see you tomorrow," Genie called as she opened the door and headed for her car. "Make lots of money because you're buying my drinks Saturday night."

Aizlyn locked the door behind her friend and wandered about for a minute; she refilled her coffee cup, emptied a few ashtrays and threw away what remained of the lunch she didn't have any appetite for. She put her mother's dress and vest on hangers and put them in the back of her closet, then refolding her mother's jeans started to put them under her own stack and paused.

She shook her mothers hip-huggers back out and held them up to herself, and then quickly, without thinking much about it, she jerked her sweats off and dragged them on. They fit like a glove. She smiled at herself as she looked at her reflection in the mirror before closing her eyes, hugging herself. For just that brief second she felt her mother was hugging her, that if she opened her eyes quick enough she'd be able to catch a glimpse of her in the mirror, but she could not bring herself to do it, to ruin the moment. She simply stood there a minute or so more, hugging herself.

She was very much like her mother, she thought briefly.

"Be careful what you sacrifice..."

Aizlyn's eyes flew open and she spun around. No one was in her house except Angus and her and that one made no sound as he lifted his head in curiosity at her sudden movement. Had she imagined the whisper in her ear just as the wonderful feeling of her mother's arms around her faded? It was as if the beautiful thoughts of her mother and being so much like her had been corrupted by her grandmother's words earlier that day, as she found herself suddenly thinking that she did indeed hope she didn't end up *too much* like her mother after all.

5

Mustang

Work was going to be difficult tonight. If the full moon, hanging bloated and proud above her as she'd driven, its blue-tinged self hinting it had mischief in store for the humans playing beneath it, had not been enough to warn Win of that, then her last glance in her mother's rearview mirror had. She realized, belatedly, that she still wore her first and most beloved nose ring and seeing it just then, sitting as she was in her mother's car, had brought out a bit of her true self in the parking lot of the Gentleman's Club. She caught herself smiling, really smiling, at the radio as she heard "…let your hair down girl" coming from it for the second time that day and wondered if her mother was trying to tell her something.

Coincidence or "cowwinkydink," as she liked to call it? Well, she didn't really believe in coincidences and she tried not to ignore it when the "cows winked and dinked." She simply couldn't figure out what it was exactly that the universe was trying to tell her. Just like with her dreams, it seemed she was constantly stuck in the position of knowing something or someone was trying to tell her something she just couldn't seem to grasp. The light bulb seemed to blow every time she flipped the switch in that corner of her subconscious mind.

Realizing she was slipping, she tried to put on the serious, somewhat aloof smile Win should display, the one that appeared friendly enough to ask for a drink but definitely not receptive to crude, drunken come-ons, and failed. She had meant to turn off the ignition, silencing the radio, get out of the car and head inside, but found herself sitting there still smiling as the song finished with, "come on come on, come on Sloopy..." Win looked up just in time to see the doorman, Gamble, approaching her vehicle and quickly rearranged her features as best she could. There was one she couldn't afford to mess up around; he saw too much as it was.

She grabbed her purse off the seat beside her and pushed open the door, stepping out quickly and pulling the leather mini-skirt down while still hidden by the door, since it had decided to become a super-mini during the drive. She looked down at herself, taking in the heels, the fishnet hose, the leather skirt stretched over her thighs and butt like second skin. She told Win hello and hoped it woke her up.

"Oh," Gamble said, coming to a dead stop halfway across the lot and staring at her.

She couldn't make up her mind what the "oh" had been about from the brief glance she allowed herself to give him in recognition of his presence, and refused to study his face to find out for sure. It could have been appreciation for the outfit or just the realization it was only the bartender arriving and not a dancer who would need assistance dragging bags of outfits and make-up inside. It could have been a little of both, but she wasn't about to make the same mistakes she had last night and get involved in a conversation with him by asking any questions. She was already more than a little off balance starting this night off and seriously wary of this particular person's ability to make it worse.

Besides, what did it matter? Why was she even wondering what the doorman's "oh" *might* have meant as she walked to the door of the place where she should be all business? Why was she suddenly self conscious of the fact he was now behind her and most likely watching her walk to the door in her suddenly too-short-for-comfort leather skirt?

Yeah, work tonight was going to be difficult.

"When did you get that car?" Gamble asked, running to catch up so he could open the door for her.

Oh hell.

"This afternoon," she said without looking back, unable to avoid answering without being terribly rude.

"Where?"

She was almost there, almost inside the place where Win worked. She was almost semi-safe. Then she paused beneath the bright exterior lights. God, his eyes were a beautiful blue.

"What?" she managed, realizing he was holding the door open and looking down at her patiently waiting. Waiting for what? For her to walk through it, for an answer, for her to stop staring at his eyes and move for God's sake?

He had to think her quite retarded, she thought when she began thinking clearly a few moments later, safely behind her bar. He had obviously asked her something, she'd figured that out long after she had jerked her eyes away from his and all but ran for the sanctuary of her bar to regain her composure and hearing. Catching herself staring, trying to figure out where she had seen that blue before, wondering if there was, in reality, any other thing that particular shade that she could match those eyes to, realizing she was staring at his eyes at all, had scared her stupid.

Her senses had gone completely haywire, her dreams were draining her, and now her ability to concentrate would make someone with A.D.D. look focused, which was just great! What next? She took that last thought back quickly and knocked on the wood of the bar. Last time she had asked the universe "what next," in accusation of poor treatment, a bird had flown overhead and pooped right on her shoulder. The cows had winked and dinked, she'd had her answer as well as a warning, and she had tried very hard from that day forward to take heed.

The ocean, at about an hour to sundown, she thought, dead in the center of summer but only when viewed from a decent height, where the greenish cast of kelp waving just beneath the surface gives it an ethereal cast.

That was it. That might come close. She wondered if she could recreate that blue and then she wondered how the hell she'd even know what the ocean looked like when viewed from up high, and finally, why all these thoughts were there in the first place.

Oh hell, Aizlyn had come to work in Win's clothes *and* it was a full moon, a blue one. She was in trouble now.

As the other bartender came up to her and handed her the shot they always had together, she heard herself say, "I probably shouldn't. I'm feeling a bit off and I don't know how alcohol will affect that."

"The doctor says you put the lime in the coconut," was Gina's only reply, obviously having nothing of it and pushing the oversized shot into her hand despite her protests that it probably wasn't a good idea.

"To money then," she caved.

Swallowing it down, she demanded Win straighten up and get to work and proceeded to count down the drawer and try to settle in. Even though random thoughts about the ocean and her mother getting stoned kept trying to butt in she managed to get slowly into the swing of things. She began filling what orders the girls were asking for to start their nights off and returning compliments to one or two on their outfits.

A few moments later she realized there was no music, no sound at all. She closed the register and stared at it, focusing on the noticeable absence of the ding. She told herself to listen and hit the no sale button, opening it again. She had always been a firm believer that her mind was the most powerful tool she had, that with concentration and honest effort she could overcome almost any problem it presented her, it had kept her close to sane this long so she put her faith in it again and told herself to focus and hear. If this was a concentration problem then she was determined to fix it right then and there, this zoning out at work business had to stop. She slammed the drawer closed, the ding sung out.

"So is it a secret?"

Gamble's voice cut in loud and clear and sudden as the ding still rang in her ears. She jerked her head up to see him standing directly in front of her register, those eyes and that strange huge grin almost taking apart all that determination to concentrate she'd just been working to gather.

"What?" she asked, knowing she had to somewhat resemble a deer in the headlights just then and hating it. Once more she saw herself coming up short next to someone with A.D.D. How many times was she going to have to ask this poor doorman to repeat himself?

"Are you gonna tell me where you got that car, or play like you don't understand the question," Gamble sighed resolutely, apparently thinking it was going to be the latter. "It's not stolen, is it?" he added, looking suddenly shocked at the idea that might explain her unwillingness to answer him.

"It was my mother's," she answered, sighing her own relief he had not only created a wonderful excuse in his own mind for her odd behavior but also because she had actually heard his whole sentence and though his eyes were beautiful she was managing to think still.

"Oh." Gamble went silent, looking down thoughtfully, and put it all together in his own mind, coming up with an even better excuse than the first. "She's gone? You don't wanna talk about her?"

He seemed abashed he had forced such memories to the forefront of her mind with his questions and for once seemed like he now didn't know what else to say. Once again she felt compelled to alleviate those kinds of feelings for him, and though she couldn't understand why, she simply did. Later she would blame the car, the nose ring, even the damn song playing on the radio when she'd pulled in to work but for now she simply let Aizlyn explain a little about herself to set the young man with the beautiful eyes back on his happy grinning way.

"No, it's okay," actually came out of Win's mouth, "I simply am not good at showing the real me to those I don't know very well or discussing the more personal aspects of myself at work. Yes, my mother has passed, but that was a very long time ago. My grandfather just took a long time to fix the car back up and give it to me."

Well, that wasn't so bad, she thought, seeing he obviously had a lot of questions for her but was politely refraining since she had just told him she didn't like discussing her personal life at work. In this particular case she didn't mind him being so astute and was glad for his "consummate doorman" manners. She was actually on the verge of deciding that the course she had just allowed the softer side of herself to take in the matter of this particular young man had in fact worked better than how Win might have handled things, when he made Win stand up and say "told you so!"

"So when can I take you out for coffee and get to know you?" he asked boldly, grin fully restored.

Win knew darn well he had to have been amply forewarned by everyone at this bar not to bother trying to get her to go out with him. She was usually pretty good at reinforcing those rumors about the futile nature of perusing her with her total lack of cooperation in conversations that could lead to a guy feeling he had a chance and risking it. Now she was suddenly stuck somewhere between awe of his daring, no-holds-barred approach and disgust with herself for letting them both come to this moment she knew she could have avoided indefinitely had she just kept her mouth shut last night. Now she was going to have to come up with a polite way to set the young man down gently and she hated that part.

Aizlyn, on the other hand was asking "why not?" and still talking about the beautiful shade of his eyes and that terribly cute inexplicable grin, ignoring Win's assertion's that it was never smart to play where you worked, saying things like "don't pee in the pool." So it was Miss Windell who handled the problem, or tried to.

"How old are you?" She heard herself asking.

"Almost twenty-two," he grinned.

"Well, I'm almost thirty," she rounded way up, in a somewhat motherly tone she'd learned from Genie, with a cocked head and eyebrow, which would have told even a deaf person that meant "never."

"And?" Gamble prompted, apparently unphased by what she'd said and oblivious to the answer it had been meant to be, standing his ground still waiting for her to give a time and date.

"Ugh." Win was in disgust of the mess that had been made so far this night, silently cursing full moons and having a seriously hard time keeping Aizlyn and that part of her amusement at bay. The noise she'd made came out part cough, part sigh, and barely masked the laugh that had tried to come out instead. Luckily a small party of men, obviously out early to excuse the night's revelry as a business meeting to their wives, opened the door just then and she was able to add, "door." to send him off.

Luck stayed with her the remainder of the evening, at least on a personal level. Whether Gamble spent his evening in the chair by the door, mentally reviewing her "ugh" as she had his "oh" for any hidden meanings, or not, managed to slowly cease being her problem as she got in the rhythm of bartending. This was work after all and Win was eventually able to take over, if only out of pure habit, stowing the rest of herself away properly to get through the night.

The night was a bit crazy as she had expected when driving in and catching sight of the moon. The full moon played havoc with her patrons and dancers alike and there was a good bit of drama brought before Win for her consideration. One of the girls accused another newer one of "stealing her regular," a scene as old and overdone as any long-running soap opera's grand coma recovery episode. The brief scuffle that had ensued ended with the new girl in tears and packing her bags while Win, using her be-as-calm-as-I-am voice, asked her to come in the next afternoon to speak with Gina about a different schedule. She then promised herself to have another talk with her girls about the difficulties they caused her, as that always proved the most profitable approach when asking them to straighten up, and hurried back to her bar.

She worked quickly to get the buildup of orders back down to a manageable flow and had it almost completely back to normal when a short slapping contest between two customers broke out. Both of them felt they hadn't gotten enough attention from the dancer they had been spending their respective mortgage payments on. She was grateful not to have to post the Jovan on guard between the register and the rest of the bar again so soon, as

81

she saw Jimmy and Gamble handle it quickly. She noted the two customers were actually buying each other drinks moments later and had ceased tipping the girl in question altogether as she had moved on to contestant number three.

Later there was a five-minute stint where her hair-holding services were required in the bathroom by a dancer. The girl, one she actually favored and hence berated with motherly love in the form of "what were you thinking" the entire time the girl was face down over the toilet, had brought a bottle of some ill-advised concoction to work in her bag. She had then proceeded to take two pills of unknown origin, that were promised to make her feel amazing, and been passed to her as a tip. Her quickly slipping state had managed to escape Win's notice until she was spotted tripping toward the bathroom, bouncing off the DJ booth on the way there, with her hand over her mouth. Win had, once again, been forced to post the Jovan by her register and go to see what new mischief was afoot.

She was quite sure, given the timing and the age of the guy who had given the pills to the dancer, that he had some wild dream she'd be all about him at closing time, a little less than an hour away. He probably actually thought they were going to help him get lucky. He was wrong. Win threw together a quick mental painting of the guy who had passed the pills to her girl, placing his face on a canvas in the back storeroom of her mind where she stored all the "creep of the weeks' likenesses. That storeroom was quite full, and stunk of mildewed canvas and cheap grease paints, but it had served her well and she went there when she needed to.

It wasn't until after close, when she sat at the bar counting the money and Gamble and Jimmy had seen to the overabundance of problem patrons and dancers and their safe means home, that had plagued this particular full moon, that her personal luck failed her. Gamble came up and plunked his large frame down one chair over from her at the bar and simply started to stare at her until finally she couldn't help but look up. When she did he immediately got that damn grin back on his face.

"What?" she asked, exasperated and tired of guessing.

"You don't look thirty." Even his eyes grinned!

"Well, I'm not," Win replied, quite unsure of how that comment should be taken, "yet."

"When?" he asked, his grin broadening if that were even possible.

"When what?" she asked, torn between curiosity, wonder that she seemed unable to avoid talking to this particular doorman, and mild annoyance that he'd just made her lose count for the second time.

"When's your birthday?" he asked, indulging in a soft laugh to himself, noting her disgusted sigh at having to restart the counting of the stack of fives before her yet again.

"July," she said absently, determined not to lose count again and consoling herself she wasn't really *lying*, twenty seven was almost thirty, in some countries, and he hadn't said specifically "when do you turn thirty."

"July…," he prompted leadingly.

"Ninety-five, one hundred, the twentieth, one ten," she answered, smoothly continuing her count and becoming quite proud of herself for managing yet another mind-over-matter feat this evening. No more deaf moments, she hadn't lost count, she was doing great.

"A Cancer," he stated, his tone conveying appreciation she didn't want to consider at any length as she triumphantly wrote the total for the stack of fives on a piece of scrap paper and began to count the tens.

Jimmy came up to the bar just then and caught her eye, making a motion with his head that was meant to ask permission to step behind the bar and grab his shift beer. She nodded back, wordlessly approving the free drink as she continued counting. After pulling his from the cooler, Jimmy twisted the cap off and raised it in a questioning salute toward Gamble, making a comment about the crazy night they'd just survived and asking if he too would like one. Gamble grunted his agreement with Jimmy's assessment of the night, muttering something about lunar eclipses of Pisces full moons, as he accepted his beer from his coworker.

Win was once again forced to concentrate and hush the curious voice of Aizlyn at the back of her mind, finding herself wondering about Gamble's

83

obvious interest in astrology and what more they might have in common when she should be finishing counting down this seemingly never-ending drawer. She just wanted to get it done and secured in the safe so she could go home, make a short pot of coffee and crawl into bed with her dog and her mother's letters.

The conversation of the two men at the bar with her slowly faded as she concentrated on the numbers on her scrap of paper, placing them into the proper columns on the night's bar sheet before her to resolve them into something the boss would be able to glance at and call a "good night."

As the two men's voices became a sort of low drone behind the numbers floating through her mind, she suddenly caught the scent of wood smoke again and something more. What was that sweet stench? Flesh? She looked up and around quickly, hoping to see some sign from the men present that they too had caught the sickening aroma, but they seemed far away and completely unaware of her dilemma. She was scared once again that her own senses were betraying her and more so that one of them would notice she seemed to be losing her mind right then and there at the bar.

Suddenly afraid that she was going to pass out like she had the other morning in the back yard, she tried desperately to pull her vision back, as the two men seemed to float further away from her, fading into smoke. She focused on Gamble, bringing his features back into focus by sheer force of will, telling herself to pay attention as she had about her hearing. Gamble looked up then, catching her eye and she saw his lips moving but his voice was too distant to make out.

"Are you all right?" Gamble asked, come unexpectedly into focus right over her and looking down into her face with a good amount of worry plainly displayed in his expressive eyes.

When he had moved to her chair, how he had come to be so close, what she had done that had prompted his obvious worry and caused him to do so, she wasn't sure. But he was too close now, his eyes too blue, his scent too masculine and appealing after the smell of burning wood, and more, which had just singed her sensitive nose. She pushed her chair back quickly;

it would have toppled over had he not been there to catch it. She stacked the money and paperwork hurriedly and headed for the safe, out of view of the two men, without responding. She stood before the safe, punching in the numbers reflexively while thanking God she had tomorrow night off and she had survived unscathed...mostly. At least she hadn't fainted.

It was when she came back from the safe and looked at the bar that she began to wonder if she had made that assessment too soon. Gamble was leaning over the bar looking at her expectantly, Jimmy was nowhere to be seen, plus her tip jars were still there, still full. Damn, she thought, not only had she somehow forgot to pull and count her tips, trading her take for larger bills, but she was apparently going to have to make some sort of explanation for her behavior to the all-too-observant Gamble, if his current look was to be any indication.

Or was she?

"Did I miss something?" she asked, resigning herself to this apparent inability she seemed to have to ignore this young man completely, but refusing to give anything more away and playing stupid.

At first he said nothing, just looked at her for a moment then started to grin again. He watched her dump her tip jars and try to straighten the bills out quickly but said nothing. She just wanted to get home and didn't want to have to go back to the safe so she simply stuffed them into a Crown Royal bag, like the dancers did. Pulling her purse from beneath the counter, she stuffed the bag into it, and glanced back at him to find him still grinning.

"Besides my tips, that is," she added, wondering if he had only been looking expectantly at her waiting to see when she'd notice she'd forgotten to grab them or if his grin indicated it amused him that she was blithely avoiding answering for her odd behavior a moment ago.

She hated the guessing business but refused to ask. It seemed for a moment that her tips could have been it after all as his grin faded abruptly and he sat back, seeming at a loss for what to say once again. She actually began to wonder if he even remembered what it was he had been waiting for as it now appeared he was searching his own mind and trying to organize his

85

thoughts, when with all seriousness and maybe a touch of precaution he leaned forward again.

"When?" he said, almost conspiratorially.

"When, what?" she asked, suddenly feeling like she had missed something far more important than her tips.

"When can I take you out for coffee?" His grin came back full force shining through even in those eyes that disturbed her, so obviously he was pleased he'd gotten her full attention once again.

Oh my gosh! Win was completely at a loss with how to deal with him. Aizlyn was laughing and Miss Windell was worried sick. Her face went quickly from dumbfounded by his brave and crazy determination to suddenly letting out that bark of a laugh that so amused Genie with its total lack of femininity, and back to serious in about the time it would have taken to pour a shot.

"I don't have coffee with people I don't know," Win answered, regaining her composer quickly and stubbornly ignoring the Aizlyn and Miss Windell portions of her mind that were screaming about 'how else is he gonna get to know us" and "that's rather curt and rude, he's quite sweet, you could do better than that."

She knew she had built a box, told him he must get in it and was showing him the hammer she intended to secure the lid with, but it seemed for the best. She had told him she didn't like to talk about herself at work with those she didn't know and now she was making it clear she wasn't going to give him the chance to get to know her outside of work. For one, she excused to herself, they worked together and that in and of itself, especially when work was a place like this, made anything more a no-no.

For two, she continued as Aizlyn demanded she take it back, he was a significant number of years too young for her to be anything serious for very long. Boys his age needed to run free and hard for a bit, stretch their legs and test their wind, not get saddled and kept in a corral, and she was not of a mind to break him in just right only to have another's apples lure him later. She'd tried all the tricks of that route with Jordan and was in no mood to try again. In other words, she wasn't the kind for a brief fling and couldn't see someone his age, who had chosen to come to work there, wanting much more. Hell, she wasn't sure she was even ready for a fling of any sort, she couldn't promise herself one hundred percent that she was going to be able to actually get past Jordan this time for it to even matter.

Besides, he wasn't even her type, she concluded, even if she was emotionally available, she liked them swarthy, built like a panther, ready to pounce. She like dark features that hinted of secrets, it seemed built into her genetic code, and despite the fact Aizlyn seemed obsessed with the blue of Gamble's eyes and that grin of his was growing on her, he totally didn't fit that description. He was large, imposingly so, she'd almost call it bulky if not for the fact that word somehow implied it was from fat and it wasn't. This kid was home-grown, corn-fed, made-to-run-a-football, white boy all the way. That was perfect for a bouncer but not for her.

His grin never wavered as she made these excuses to herself. He merely led the way to the door and held it wide for her to pass through. Win accepted the mental thrashing Aizlyn was giving her as she locked the club and got in her mother's car, she just kept telling herself it was for the best and refusing Aizlyn's requests to look at his eyes one more time so she could capture that hue for future reference when painting. She suddenly wanted to paint!

"You just let me know when," Gamble said as he pushed her door closed and stepped back so she could drive away.

Win didn't have the energy or inclination left to respond. She let him have the last word and simply drove. This was the very sort of night she had invented motor therapy for.

Some of the girls headed to Wal-Mart after work with their evening's take, to wander the aisles of the only place open that time of night. They'd soak in the light and softer music and ease themselves out of the mindsets of whomever they'd been the last few hours to earn their money by spending half of it on nonsensical items they didn't need. Sometimes she wondered, between the drinks they bought to put the facade on and the shopping they did to take it off, if the job was ever worth it.

She understood the compulsion though, she'd been there after work a few times after Jordan had taken his things from her closet and walked out the door of her place one of the many times. She had wandered the home improvement aisles a few nights as though her many late-night purchases could somehow change the way it felt to come home to the absence of him. All it had accomplished was improving a house that wasn't hers, and nothing had made it a home until she had realized it had nothing at all to do with the walls themselves or what hung on them.

The only problem that had remained after that had been the knowledge of her seemingly endless lack of foresight and spine when it came to him wanting to come back and talk about it. She still feared the next call from him, full of loving apologies and professed insights he wanted to share, which might somehow see her weakened and falling into his excuses again. She suffered the curse of seemingly endless hope that maybe the next time he would have truly changed. It lingered in the back of her mind, brewing up "what ifs" every day he was gone. It made her doubt her ability to send him on his way if he were to confess to some grand epiphany with just the right amount of sincerity. Because what if it was true, and what if he had finally seen?

She was tormented by the fear she would find herself rejoining the game indefinitely, wasting what was left of her youth, realizing repeatedly that his epiphanies never held up, the changes never stuck, and every few months he'd storm out the door to start the cycle all over again. She knew she was weak with regard to Jordan, she always had been. Something inside her felt they were meant to be together and it was just a matter of time before it snapped to and began to work, but then something else told her she needed to just let it go.

Back when they had first gotten together and she had still believed in soul mates she had tried everything to please him. She'd quit school so she could keep the house and laundry up, she'd supported his business ventures out from under his dad's wings and kept him still attending his classes. But slowly, through long nights of watching the clock and crying as his dinner got cold, she came to feel that was all she was anymore, a support structure. She didn't feel that she was getting any support back, no recognition, not even a thank you for the meal. His friends/business partners could keep him out to all hours, Lord only knew where, discussing "deals," and she was supposed to be fine with all of it. But she wasn't.

One night, when he didn't come home at all, it came to her; she was alone in this world, no one had to care how you felt and work to keep you feeling loved, not even those who professed to love you. It wasn't fair, but it was true, so if someone did care enough to do that, that was a blessing, not something owed you. It was a total Zen moment, come to her in the shower while brushing her teeth; you came in alone and left that way and it was okay, what made it worthwhile were the moments like that one, realizing it. The next time he stormed out, which was right after she confronted him about being out all night without so much as a call, she left too, marched right over to Jadin's house. Then she promptly got a dog, because it *chose* to *love* her, showing it in ways she could feel and not just hear, and she felt blessed as that brought her more of those kinds of Zen moments.

Now Win knew you could make alliances and friendships that lasted entire lifetimes but not because it was fated or deserved or otherwise preordained. She no longer believed in soul mates per se; that term implied that it was easy and it wasn't, you had to work at relationships and just because you did didn't mean it was guaranteed to work. She was very careful who she put that kind of energy into now and Genie was the first that it had paid off with, honestly Genie was the only one she'd put such energies into since the realization had hit her. But all those revelations had yet to hold up when she'd heard Jordan's voice coming over a phone after weeks of longing, asking if he could come by and talk. Jordan lived in an area of her heart where the different parts of her had never grown and blended or learned to apply the knowledge they gathered, through the rest of her life, with regard to him.

She felt it coming though, felt it move with the wind through her hair as she sped past Wal-Mart in her mother's Mustang. She felt the different aspects of her personality blending and thought that eventually they would stand in unison even when in the presence of Jordan. She felt those Zen moments all coming together to form a whole new view on life that she could retain and use to see through the next emotionally clouded moment she spoke to him. She was coming to a moment she felt she could love him, really love him, the way he was and even if he wasn't hers. She felt she could be okay with the fact he was okay without her. And maybe his knowing he had her love and acceptance even though they weren't together, he could then accept the thing about himself that couldn't settle down with her. Maybe he'd learn to love himself and then, possibly, how to truly love someone else. Now that was a Zen moment.

So now, Win saved her tip money and took the "extra special crunchy" long way home. She turned the radio way up and cruised the outer roads, singing too loud to carry any recognizable semblance of a tune and letting it all out before heading home to Angus. Every crude come-on or drunken insult hurled due to her lack of compliance, be it for another drink, a stronger drink, or her phone number, got blown off her shoulder on these drives home. She had promised herself she'd never blow another dime on something she didn't need from the four a.m. Mecca for the lonely that was Wal-Mart. Her days of Band-Aid shopping were done, she had motor therapy.

Win was still frustrated with a lot of what had transpired this night and arguing with herself as she took the exit and got out on the highway. She didn't like that she had found herself in the position of having to set Gamble back. More disturbing was that she couldn't begin to figure why it seemed to matter so much, other than she did think him a nice person.

All she had observed of him told her he didn't deserve to be treated harshly and she worried that she might have been unnecessarily rough. And yet she heard his voice replaying in her head, "you just let me know when," and knew he couldn't have been that put off or hurt. She couldn't have done

90

him much damage for him to have been so bold as to blithely leave the invitation open despite her attempts to shut him down nicely. She realized, to Aizlyn's cheers, that she probably had not heard the last of him and was reminded of the phrase "brave and crazy" for not the first time. She didn't see him giving up very easily and part of her applauded that quality she had recognized in him, while another part dreaded it.

"Cancer." She suddenly heard Gamble's voice in her head again, replaying his repetition of her sign in her mind, and something clicked. Maybe that was why she was how she was, if he knew as much about astrology as his mentioning of the fact tonight had been a lunar eclipse in Pisces implied, then he probably had discerned a lot more about her than she could currently figure out how to be comfortable with.

How else could Aizlyn have come into adulthood maintaining her inquisitive, open-minded search for inner peace and knowledge, having been stripped of her like-minded mother and sent to her one-track grandmother, had she not invented Miss Windell to sit down to dinners and say grace or sing in the church? How else could a Cancer survive working in such an emotional-rape-crisis-center as a Gentleman's Club but to create an alter ego such as Win? It didn't make her schizophrenic, she concluded, it made her a Cancer smart enough to survive in the outside. Right?

Briefly she wondered what his sign might be, if it might explain anything about him and that constant inexplicable grin. What had caused a young man, obviously straight, to take an interest in astrology? That seemed kind of unusual to her, all the guys she knew who took an interest were either gay or wiccan, but then how many guys did she *really* know? Was he wiccan?

Then she found herself wondering why he had sought employment at the Gentleman's Club, like so many other young men, but she had yet to hear one snippet of gossip from the dancers about him. What was the point of a young man getting a job at such a place only to waste his time flirting with the one employee well known for wanting nothing of it. Was he gay, just flirting with the safe one he knew wouldn't take him up on his offer? It was all a puzzle, he was a puzzle.

She caught herself and pushed those thoughts back quickly. It wasn't allowed to matter. They worked together; he was too young, he wasn't her type and she wasn't emotionally available or interested. She had no inclination whatsoever to start all over again with another green horse, she'd been thrown enough for this lifetime, and she would rather walk. So she shoved the inquisitive Aizlyn part of her back into bed, told her to go to sleep, and returned to analyzing herself.

So what was with the going deaf at random moments at work? What was with the scent of burning wood and worse, attacking her nostrils randomly? What was the mist or smoke rolling in and blotting out her vision all about? And for goodness sake why had the dreams become so much more frequent and real? This was definitely the worst round yet, far worse than when she had made the decision to move from the dorms and in with Jordan. She was almost afraid to sleep these days and yet couldn't seem to get enough of it. The self-analysis wasn't going well. All she was coming up with was that she was either going completely mad or the dreams, be they past life memories or not, were seeping into her conscious mind and taking on a life and reasoning all their own. Neither option was acceptable to her but both could explain her current state.

She got off onto another outer road and put the pedal down, letting it all blow away. She was good at tuning things out, turning things off, disconnecting from things that presented puzzles to her that she couldn't easily solve, shutting up the Aizlyn part of her that asked too many questions. That was the true power of Win. Things like motor therapy, a good novel, or getting lost in a new canvas merely made it easy. She thought her discovery of the ability and modification of it was just another aspect of her evolution into a creature that could survive. Her mother had been, at least to some extent, able to do it too. Hadn't her mother also been a Cancer?

Thinking again of her mother, sitting behind the wheel of her mother's car, listening to the same radio station she obviously had, she was suddenly compelled to switch lanes, take the next available exit and turn toward home. There was a wonderful dog, a coffee pot and a box of letters that might answer that question, waiting for her, and she suddenly wanted to get to them quickly. She had to actually put effort forth to convince herself to pull into the gas station just long enough to grab a pack of smokes and a fresh quart of half and half, but she was quick about it and pulling into her drive ten minutes later.

She let herself in and let the dog out, put the coffee on and hauled the box to her bedroom to sort the letters out and put them in order. Then she let Angus back in, locked the door, fed her boy, made herself a large cup and headed to bed to read the stack of pages that held promised such insights.

6

Jay

Her mother's words came up from the page and surrounded her with warmth as she read of her first time truly away from home, her first ride in an airplane, and feelings of overwhelming awe at the country she had arrived in. She spoke in comparisons; how it was nothing like leaving for college or going on a road trip to a concert, explaining how this time she felt she was going to make a difference.

Her mother had loved the flow of another language, difficult to learn but beautiful to her ears, surrounding her everywhere she went. She even mentioned overhearing a lovers' quarrel and how appealing and musical it had been to her even though she knew the words were hurled in hurt and anger. She was awed by all the new scents and sights of this strangely vivid place, all were totally foreign and completely alluring.

Aizlyn was swept away, finding herself seeing again, as if for the first time, the markets and shops she had taken for granted growing up. She found herself reexamining the complexity of a language she had grown up using and feeling the difficulty it must have presented to someone facing the task of learning it as an adult. She saw all of India, as never before, in all its grime and glory, flashing alternately bright and colorful then dilapidated and needful in her mind's eye. It all glittered though, through her mother's descriptive words, words written with much adoration to her father, Mr.

Windell, whom she missed "most of all" and wished desperately could have been there with her.

There was not a whole lot of explanation as to how or why she had ended up choosing to go to India, just a lot of loving apologies to her father that she had moved so far from him. Aizlyn took quiet note of the absence of such words as "miss" in regard to her grandmother, only the constant "tell Mom I love her." She saw then that her mother had shared the same bond and closeness she felt with her "Papa," and that her mother too had had much difficulty resigning herself to a life of loving her mother without being able to communicate openly with her as she could her father.

Her mother's words, in one letter in particular, seemed to be in response to some letter of his which Aizlyn had no access to, indicated their bond was due to an understanding between them which had been hard won. It seemed to Aizlyn that Papa had done much explaining and excusing of her grandmother's behavior over a period of many letters, that though he couldn't and wouldn't change the woman he loved, he understood the pain that it caused his daughter and sought a balance through his bearing all in honesty. Her mother was expressing her thankful understanding.

From what Aizlyn could gather, something had happened to her grandmother, a great loss, occurring in her youth, which her mother had been made to understand. This had left the love of Papa's life feeling that her complete and utter unquestioning faith in God was all she had. It became the only means for understanding what had happened and her only hope of avoiding such pain again; she clung to it and those who loved her had come to accept that, including him. Aizlyn got the feeling her grandfather was not the first and only love of her grandmother's life but that he had accepted that just as he accepted all things about her.

It seemed her mother felt great empathy for her father, Aizlyn's grandfather, as he had been made to stand by and watch, unable to do anything more for his love other than love her from the distance she kept him at. He had only been able to step in after this life-changing event had shattered the formerly happy-go-lucky and precocious nature of the woman he had fallen for, but had done so with mixed joy and sadness; sad for the cause, happy for the effect, and unable to do anything but love her no matter what it had made of her.

Despite the fact he loved and accepted her as she was, he was able to stand back objectively and see how it had destroyed their daughter's relationship with them. He had obviously made these explanations in an effort to repair the bridges between all of them, and Aizlyn could see her mother knew this, respected this, and loved him even more because of it. She could see he had, by the mere fact he had taken the time and opened his soul through his letters, asked that her mother find a way to do the same. Her mother was expressing a desire to try and the desperate wish they could just get past their differences. It seemed at that point she had even considered moving back to America to be closer to them.

But the next letter showed why she hadn't, when Aizlyn unfolded it and it brought tears to her eyes that made it difficult for her to even see to read. The photo fell to her lap and lay there a long moment while her stunned fingers refused to stop trembling and release the pages long enough to pick it up. When finally she was able to lift it and had dried her eyes on her sleeve enough to see, she understood instantly.

The photo showed her mother, Ozark beautiful, pretty as they come, smiling up at the camera as though someone had just called her name while she leaned over a desk, a book before her. A very handsome man stood behind her, one hand resting gently at her back, the other pointing to the page open before her. He had also looked at the camera, smiling happily. It was old; the whole thing was cast in a sort of brown hue, almost like she was seeing it through the eggs her grandmother used to send her to steal for breakfast from the chickens out back of the house. The corners appeared to have been shoved up under the rim of more than one mirror, there were water spots that somehow made her think of tears even though the two people pictured smiled like they'd never know the meaning of the word "pain."

The man was tall and thin, could have been scrawny but it seemed to her he had a sort of wiry strength about him, just thick enough in all the right places. He was beautifully dark, like a cup of coffee with just a smidge too little half and half, and his teeth shone brightly from under his black, well-trimmed mustache. His hair, too, was black, combed back in glossy waves that reminded her of the movie "Grease." She knew he was Indian, by just looking at him, but his clothes -the pressed button-up with butterfly collar, the fitted slacks with the high, thick waistband and the haircut -they said American.

Aizlyn went back to study his features and was assailed with an overwhelming sense of déjà vu. She knew him, he had made her mother smile and cry and leave her with a sitter many a night. Aizlyn suddenly saw herself as if watching an old home movie, standing at a window watching her mother and this man walk away from her hand and hand. There were tears in her eyes and she couldn't understand why she had been left there, why her mother had told her to sleep well and be good while she was gone and then dismissed her hurriedly when the front door opened. Her mother had always sat and talked her to sleep, rubbing her back. No true bedtime stories could she recall, just a constant companionship and endless conversations as she nodded off.

Aizlyn pulled herself back to the present, pushing back the very old ache of feeling left behind and unimportant. She turned the photo over, hoping to put a name to the face of the man who now seemed to float, hauntingly familiar, through random memories she couldn't organize. He was glimpsed around corners when she'd been told to stay in her room and draw or paint, and seen through cracked doors when she was supposed to be asleep. He was suddenly a part of her past, fitting into her memories like the painting that had always been on the wall above the fireplace at grandmother's house and she'd never missed when it had been replaced, until, coming home to visit from the dorms and hunt up some old paint pallets, she'd found it in the attic and recalled where it had been.

There was nothing written on the back of the photo except a date, 1979. The year before Aizlyn was born.

She set the aged photograph and the feeling of mild disappointment aside gently, turning to the letter that had held it so long. A slow ache began to crawl up her limbs toward her heart as she read, hoping maybe there would be more about it revealed by her mother's words.

The words were almost expected; her mother had met the man of her dreams and intended to stay just a little bit longer. But her father was not to worry, the fact that he was Indian would not keep her there indefinitely. Her father should be happy to know that he was wealthy and well-educated, that he had family in America and had just returned from there to apply his education to helping where he could here. She still intended to come home, soon, she was just going to wait and do so with him when they were done in India.

The "done" implied some mission, some task or other that when complete would allow them to leave there with a feeling of accomplishment. It was just never made clear what it was they had set themselves to do. She continued to expound on the wonderful qualities of the man she had chosen to spend her life loving, telling her father how he spent so much time teaching her not only the language and history of the place but how kind and gentle he was. She applauded his giving nature, his apparent lack of personal agenda in all that he was willing to do to better the lives of those around him. And then there it was, his name.

Duranjaya. She told her father it meant "heroic son," a name he made his family proud by living up to, but that he made her proud in that their pride seemed to mean little to him in comparison to the joy on the face of someone he lent a hand to. She called him Jay, apparently what his friends and family in America called him too.

So Jay was the name of the man who had meant so much to her mother. Jay was the name of the man who had made her spend endless evenings crying. Jay was that painting she hadn't missed until she'd discovered it in the attic of her mind. The letter told her little more than that but it was enough, now she knew why her mother had stayed in India so long. Now she knew the name of a man who had haunted memories she had apparently suppressed for quite some time.

Having recalled the feeling of being left out of something by someone who was supposed to love her more than anything, of her mother apparently preferring his company to hers, her perpetual self-analysis grew wings. Suddenly she hoped that she might have just opened the door to helping her come to understand those deep-seated feelings of inadequacy that may be the true reason for her dreams. As she went to refill her coffee cup she hoped that now, if she could recall the rest with any accuracy, she might be able to lay the memories to rest and thus stop the dreams. Her quest for personal enlightenment, the real reason for her interest in psychology, seemed more hopeful now than ever. She thought that maybe, just maybe, while she was younger she had repressed feelings that she might now reflect on and expel, thus achieving her goal of simple inner peace.

Aizlyn sat back down on the bed, moments later pulling the blanket up over her knees, and picked up the next letter in the stack she had organized by dates and began to dig in earnest. However, it was not to be as she had expected. The answers would not be clear-cut and easily attainable.

As she read, her mother's previously exuberant voice took on a sad note, her words unsure and at times almost helpless. She admitted to her father that she had become pregnant, begging him that if he must tell her mother that he find a means to do so that would not cause them further grief. She told him, and inadvertently Aizlyn as well, that Jay was the father- her father.

Aizlyn's eyes went again to the aged photo beside her on the covers. Surprisingly, she felt nothing new. No sudden breaking of some mental dam and release of further memories. She wasn't sure why that surprised her. Maybe she had simply thought she might recall something that she could say, "ah, yeah, he must have been my dad, that's what dads do." All she saw was an old photo, right then and there in the present with her. A snapshot of her mother and a man named Jay.

Then, slowly, she saw her eyes and then her cheekbones, she caught a glimpse of her straight smile in his. Her artist's eye blended the two skin tones of the people posed and smiling before her and suddenly saw her shade, the perfect amount of half and half. She looked back to the letter, hoping for more.

The reasons for those memories not having been there, the explanation why he was just a photo of a guy named Jay, whom her mother had loved, why he had never been "Dad," did not sit well. As Aizlyn read on, something akin to anger twisted her intestines into twitchy knots, as her mother, for reasons that made little sense to Aizlyn, said she was unwilling to tell him. Her mother confessed she hadn't the heart or words to tell Jay of the daughter she carried, she made excuses to herself for this decision and mailed them to her father as though having him hear them lifted some small weight. They did not, they created it, and it dropped like a stone to the pit of Aizlyn's belly to send the acids there into heaving rebellion.

Aizlyn's eyes blurred, but not with tears, as though her vision was now somehow tainted by the lies she read of her mother's telling. Her mother excused them with such explanations as she feared he'd feel trapped, like she'd done it on purpose to get him to cease his track down some hell-bent path he had chosen. She thought it better to try and make him see reason, and not get any further involved in what she felt was some nasty political mess, rather than be made to feel she had taken away his choices. Aizlyn had no clue what political intrigues her mother spoke of, she only knew she felt her father had had the right to know about her and that she had had the right to know him.

Aizlyn grew even more nauseous as her mother said she had made excuses, told little white lies and hidden the pregnancy during his visits. Then she had even began hiding her, after her birth, when he'd return briefly from wherever it was he went to do, whatever it was he was doing. She continued to try to make him get out while he still could and she had continuously refused to sight his offspring as reason, despite the fact Mr. Windell had obviously asked her to do whatever it took to get him to return with her to the States immediately. It seemed her mother wanted him to choose her over this insanity he had become embroiled in, and didn't want it to be because she suddenly sprung the fact he was a father on him.

Eventually the whole situation appeared to send her mother into a deep depression, as in later letters she spoke of how now it seemed beyond surmountable, that it seemed he'd never get out of this mess he'd gotten into and appeared to only be sinking in deeper. She wept on the pages as she lamented how she knew now that even were she to tell him the truth, the truth itself would be an unforgivable grievance between them. She should have never withheld the information, let alone for so long.

There were tear stains on the letters now as she told her father of her near inability to cope with his rarer and briefer visits, the fact she feared each would be the last. A little of the anger that Aizlyn had felt at realizing she had been denied a father by her own beloved mother began to fade, as her heart started responding with nods of understanding for the feelings she read had prompted her mother. So much of her life she had spent trying to feel how others would feel, treat them according to how she would like to be treated, that maintaining her anger, even righteous indignation, was at times difficult. Standing up and saying "what about me and how I feel," had been something Win was reinvented to do for her. Win was the part of her that had the strength to not only say "my feelings are equally important" but to hold on to that and do something about it.

Aizlyn, however, sat quietly and realized she had never really missed it. Not having a father had been more of a background noise, knowledge of yet another thing about her that was different, than an actual void in her life after all. She found she couldn't help but relate to the desire her mother had felt to have him choose a life with her of his own accord, without perceived coercion. She could feel her pain when it had become the nightmare of knowing that the one thing that might have worked, telling him they had a child to think about, was become the one thing that would also break them, the lie that would almost definitely separate them for good. Aizlyn had a deep understanding of how her mother could have spent so long trying to make him see that what he was doing was driving a wedge between them, hoping he would stop and smell the roses, so to speak, on his own, that she had found herself in a hole she could not seem to crawl out of. Her mother had taught her almost too well how to place herself in another's shoes, and she felt the anger drain out of her nearly as quickly as it had seeped in.

Aizlyn felt for her, more so than ever, as she saw in herself that same longing to be chosen above all else, to feel so important in someone's life, that everything would have faded in comparison and they'd have dropped it all to be with her, they'd have never thought anything worthy to risk one ounce of hurt. She knew such longing to be irrational, that no one ever lived up to such expectations, it wasn't even so much that they needed to really, only that they should be wanting and willing to try. Her father had obviously chosen to continue in what was apparently risking life and limb, oblivious to the fact it wounded the one he said he loved and slowly destroyed their relationship. She saw how it was that at some point, having seen the irrationality of her desires as Aizlyn too had eventually come to see, that telling him of their daughter seemed to have ceased even being an option. Aizlyn forgave her mother the small sin, because she saw the sinner in herself.

It didn't negate all the hurt, she still had wishes it had been otherwise, but she understood it and there was no point inventing a grudge now. Aizlyn sipped her coffee and lit another cigarette, since the last had smoked itself while she swallowed, stewed and spewed back out the anger. Her stomach slowly returned to normal and the angry butterflies fluttered back to fitful, wounded sleep.

In the next few letters her mother seemed to escape one despair only to be captured by another. Her worries over Jay seemed to fade into the background, like the baying of hounds on the heels of a deer who'd just come face to face with a bear; they were there but not nearly as pressing as what she currently faced. His granddaughter, she told her father, apparently had begun showing signs of a frightening inability to separate dreams from reality.

Aizlyn cringed mentally at the lines before her, as they shattered what small hope she had been cultivating of finding "normal" reasons for her mental state. Her mother's words chewed it up and spat it out, as she cried on her father's shoulder through her letters. She wept verbally over her new daughter, confessing she was growing to be a problem child in not so many words.

Aizlyn read about apparent endless rounds of her waking her mother at all hours, from the moment she had learned to talk, and asking questions her mother had no answers for. Questions like why she couldn't make her hips move the way they could when she was sleeping, or where all her jewelry was. It seemed the terrible twos had been nothing when compared to the insolent threes. Sometimes she would throw her food or purposefully tip over her drink and her mother would be shocked and frightened by such things as "I am a princess, this is peasant's fare," coming from her three-year-old's mouth with a distinctly British flair.

It seemed her grandfather had resigned himself to loving and assisting his daughter and granddaughter from afar. Her mother seemed no more willing to leave India and the man she loved than she was to risk loosing him by giving him the one reason to leave with her that could have worked. At some point thereafter her grandfather had obviously given his daughter more advice than the usual, about telling the father he was the father, begging his forgiveness for the years of lies, and all of them coming home and living happily ever after, because she said, in yet another letter, that it seemed to be working. "It," apparently, being that when Aizlyn would do something wrong her mother would show her how it felt to have the same done to her and Aizlyn would pause, digest, and straighten up.

Aizlyn smiled nostalgically, recalling her swift lesson involving a cat and a can of tuna. She was happy momentarily as her mother was happy, well maybe not *happy* but at least not unhappy. The following few letters were just more about her, how she was coming along, how her curiosity and aptitude propelled her through each day like a rocket ready for the stars. The questions she asked were often odd but her mother had become used to them, crediting them to her diverse upbringing and surroundings and ceasing to have a near heart attack when her five-year-old asked about such concepts as reincarnation.

Then there was a letter in which her mother mentioned Jordan. She spoke of a strange instantaneous feud they had begun. Telling her father how a wealthy, retired, Air Force man had come to India with his wife, a local he had met in the service, and their son, and had struck up a lucrative trade business. She had offered to keep their son for them, when they would take their business trips to and from those places dragging a six-year-old would have otherwise been an incredible nuisance, and had come to regret it very quickly.

Her mother said that Aizlyn had immediately become an unholy terror again, slipping back into her "I am a princess" mode. After nearly three years of settling down and considering others' feelings like a big girl, she begun to act out once again. She had actually begun yelling at her mother, screaming about trust and how they were supposed to help each other, telling her how she "wanted nothing to do with him," and "you can't make me." It had made little sense and even less when she had begun crying hysterically, digging in and fighting like a thing possessed when it had been time to leave for her dance lessons that first night.

She had pitched this horrible fit, refusing to leave her mother, accusing her of lying about something her mother couldn't conceive of, and could not be made to remain for her lessons no matter what she had been told. The whole thing had confused and crushed her mother, because the reason she had offered to watch young Jordan in the first place was so that they could continue to afford those lessons, lessons Aizlyn had begged for since the first time her mother had explained to her that she could teach her hips to move as they did in her sleep but that it would take patience and practice.

Apparently it had taken her mother the better part of the two weeks that Jordan's parents had been gone that first time to make her see how the way she was treating him made the poor young boy feel. Explaining how he was probably frightened enough with his parents away and not knowing them so well. Telling her that she wouldn't like to have been left with strangers and that she should make him feel welcome, not make it harder for him.

The letter said it had been a difficult task for her mother but she had finally managed it. Aizlyn had eventually begun to sit quietly through meals, actually eating some of her food rather than glaring at her unwelcome guest and stabbing at it as though she wished it were him. The next week she began allowing her mother to drop her off at her dancing lessons without further tantrums, realizing after all she enjoyed them greatly and that they kept her from him, even if they kept her from her mother as well. Toward the end of his stay she had even torn a page from her coloring book and left it near him, with five of her crayons, before escaping to her room to color alone.

Another letter indicated it took much more time for her to actually begin to share her toys, remaining in his company and playing quiet games, but eventually his visits were accepted gracefully. The dreams had apparently begun disturbing her again as well, during this time, and she had once again begun waking her mother with more questions she couldn't answer. She was obsessed with some jewelry she had in her dreams, her mother complained in the letter, and repeatedly woke her to tell her it was missing, pointing at her ankles. Once again she found herself having to explain the difference between things in dreams and what was real, encouraging her to examine her dreams for what life lessons they might be trying to teach her, without confusing the six-year-old as to their otherwise inapplicability to reality.

Aizlyn smiled sadly to herself as she remembered her early preoccupation with anklets and her mother finally buying her her first one. To this day she wore it, among many others collected over the years. She had not realized this had been the reason for that particularly expensive birthday gift but it made sense to her now. It made sad sense, she'd always been troubled it seemed, probably always would be.

She was taken aback and even somewhat amused, having not remembered the obviously rocky start to the lifelong friendship Jordan and she had created only to ruin with trying to make it more, and finding it strange to hear of herself behaving so meanly. She had obviously moved from that day forward with thoughts of "how would that make me feel" and her mother's way of teaching her by showing her how things felt, dictating her actions toward him. She frowned then, wondering what would have happened had her mother just allowed her to dislike him as had been her first inclination, and never forced the issue. They would have never grown to become fast friends, they would have never become lovers, they would have never broken each other either. It was too much to think right then, this whole evening was fast becoming more than she could process and put out to be any kind of quality product.

As Aizlyn picked up another letter, it seemed the same things had crossed her mother's mind as she mused to her father about the friendship she was witnessing them forge. She told him how odd she thought it that Aizlyn seemed to slip into a strange silent companionship with him, throughout his further stays with them. She began explaining scenes of Aizlyn simply passing Jordan the choicest toys, as though it was no use opening her mouth to fight it. Where once there was an irate six-year-old princess, demanding he be told to go home because she didn't want him there, now sat a silent ageless husk. She had observed them as she had cooked dinner, watching Aizlyn pass along whatever toy seemed to amuse him at the moment and quietly move to another, which would grab his interest quickly and she would once again pass it along. She said such behavior seemed to continue on other nights as he got the choicest crayon, and Aizlyn simply moved to another page that didn't require that color without saying a word.

Her mother tried to express how it was as if the right to ask for something she wanted had been removed from the equation for Aizlyn, and she feared she'd taken that out of her by making her be nice. Whereas Jordan never seemed to notice he was even doing it, so she didn't know how to approach him and make him see what she couldn't even put her finger on herself. Jordan seemed oblivious, as though it were simply the way of things and nothing about it was out of the ordinary. Her mother wrestled with the concepts herself, as she told her father how of course she wanted Aizlyn to cooperate and play fair but she didn't want her to be a pushover to be walked on later in life either. She had wondered then whether she had been right to squash her daughter's initial reactions to him, as it seemed when she was with him her spirit was dampened. She admitted to her father that such ideas were strange but that he'd just have to be there to see what she meant.

She then spoke of a dream she had had before Aizlyn's birth coming back to haunt her shortly after she had begun watching Jordan and Aizlyn and this new behavior pattern they had slipped into. She said that the dream itself was part of what was now causing her to question her wisdom when it came to her having hushed Aizlyn's angry pleas and apparent feelings of betrayal. It had obviously been a disturbing dream, and this intrigued Aizlyn, but she never described the dream to her father in a letter for Aizlyn to eavesdrop on.

All she said was that she had come in from the kitchen one evening to see her daughter, still wearing her dancing attire from class, sitting perfectly still and staring contemplative and somehow sadly at Jordan as he pushed his cars across the floor, running them over her Barbie speed-bumps. Aizlyn, she said, had looked for all the world the living incarnation of the statue of Sarasvati she had begged for at a market not long before, and just as hollow. Somehow this vision, in her living room, had recalled the dream she'd had to her mind and she questioned her dad as to why Aizlyn would have so much apparent difficulty coming to terms with this young boy's presence. She wondered if she should stop watching the child while his parents were away, despite the fact they had come to rely on the money.

Her father's answers must have been good enough to help her set these fears aside because her next letter was very thankful for his suggestions. She'd said that it made sense, after all, that Aizlyn be so attached to her and afraid of anyone being able to take her place in her heart, since her mother was all she'd ever had. She'd wished things were different and that Aizlyn

107

could also bask in the love of her father and grandparents, but sadly they were not. For now, the constant reminders that Aizlyn was her deepest, truest love and best friend seemed to steady Aizlyn, and yet another letter revealed Aizlyn had apparently come to even better terms with Jordan's presence thereafter.

Soon the descriptions of her behavior were the things she actually recalled. Soon she was reading of escapades she and Jordan had shared as two spoiled half-breeds wreaking havoc through the streets, pretending not to speak the language when it could get them out of trouble and speaking it all too well when it could get them in it. Of all the moments her mother shared with her father throughout the next few letters, she recalled all but one.

A recital of sorts, she and her classmates, led by their dance instructor, set to perform for some visiting American benefactors. The story seemed oddly placed among those remembered tales of her youth. Here was one that seemed to be about someone else, for she could not recall it ever having happened. And surely she should have. You shouldn't forget such an event, especially at nine.

Her mother recalled, as she could not, Aizlyn standing frozen in the doorframe, just beyond the colorful length of silken cloth they had hung to create the stage entrance. Her eyes had locked on her mother, sitting silent and proud beside Jordan and his parents, awaiting her daughter's triumphant debut. This was her daughter's time to shine, for all those lessons to pay off, here was when she would move her hips in reality as she had always dreamed.

The music had begun and the teacher tapped Aizlyn's shoulder, but Aizlyn's eyes never wavered from her mother. Her mother saw panic race through her baby. The teacher pushed past. The show must go on. The rest of the class followed and the show did. The music stopped and Aizlyn's eyes had yet to drop from her mother's as she seemed to silently beg to be saved. Her mother had feared she'd had some sort of episode, something drastic to have brought on this catatonic state, and the first second she could she had run to her and gathered her up, shaking her and asking her what was wrong.

Aizlyn had seemed unaware anything amiss had occurred, she had snapped to as if just waking and asked if she had done it right. Her mother hadn't the heart to tell her she had missed her cue and never even danced, so she had simply told Aizlyn she was beautiful and awarded her the anklet she had bought to give her after her first recital. Aizlyn had happily plunked to the floor and immediately put it on, seeming to never have become the wiser. Jordan's parents politely ignored Aizlyn's attack of stage fright and played along with her mother. Jordan himself seemed bored and completely unaware anything at all of interest had transpired, or rather not transpired, so the incident had sunk into the great forgetfulness of eternity until right then and there.

Aizlyn sat back, sipping her coffee and swirling around as she lit another cigarette and tried to think. She heard Genie in her head, triumphantly pointing out how that episode proved her theory, that her dreams were of past lives after all, poking her and grinning her I-told-you-so's, as she reminded her of the dream in which she thought she should refuse to dance for him next time and that in this lifetime that was exactly what she had done. Yet she argued back about how it could be just as likely that the dreams were caused by the episode and her subconscious mind remembering what her conscious mind did not. Boy, Genie and she were going to go round and round over these letters, she could hear it now.

Aizlyn tried and failed to recall the incident in full, to see it through her own memories and not her mother's words. She couldn't find it. She was recalling all the other things her mother had spoken of in the last few letters just fine. The time she and Jordan had gone on safari and captured all the lizards and toads, even a slug or two, that were silly enough to think they could freeze and blend in and escape their keen hunter eyes. They had caged their prizes in a shoe box and taken them back to the camp in the living room. They had lifted the lid with great gusto, proud to display their collected trophies of the day to her mother, only to have it unsettled by an especially heavy toad making its escape, and lost the whole day's find right there in the house. This memory was hers too and it made her smile, recalling her mother's squeaking levitation trick that had propelled her onto the coffee table to dance and squeal until everything had been recaptured and released back into the wild.

She couldn't seem to concentrate on what she should be, once again she felt she had flipped a light switch in an area of her mind that desperately needed cleaning and exploring and that the bulb had blown the second she did. She felt she had glimpsed something important and yet not only had she not been unable to make it out but she couldn't even remember now why she had thought it important.

She was getting tired, she knew, she hadn't been sleeping well at all, and desperately wished for just a good eight hours of dreamless, warm, comfortable oblivion. Looking over, she saw there were only a few letters left and couldn't resist. What was another thirty minutes after all?

Those remaining letters went through such a wide range of emotions that she felt her own recent short-circuiting pale in comparison. Those years before had been so much about her that what had been of him had merely related a sort of sad contentment, a resignation that said she had accepted the fact she was bound to be madly in love with a man whom she knew loved her back just not in the way she so desperately needed him to. Jay saw nothing wrong with the way things stood, he loved her, she loved him, what came in the interim was merely his obligation to his people and her understanding of it, it was all gravy as far as he was concerned. But in these last few letters something began to change.

Her heart went out to her mother with such empathy and whole-hearted understanding she felt her stomach knot back up, only this time with shared pain. Despite the fact that her relationship with her daughter had grown into a beautiful thing, that she no longer required four-page letters from her father to correct, her mother was truly miserable. She would write briefly about Aizlyn and herself learning how to put on eyeliner together and then suddenly pour her heart out about her missing love, staining a full page with pure pain. Aizlyn's father had apparently not visited in quite sometime, she had no idea whether he was dead or alive, married to another or still loved her as dearly as when last they spoke. Then she'd say something about how pretty and tall Aizlyn was growing to be, only to have that remind her of her missing love, sending her back into another few paragraphs about him.

It was heartbreaking to read. It was worse to feel.

Her mother wrote of much time and heart-rending energy spent trying to track down any information on him, and how she met and occasionally crossed many an unsavory in the process. It seemed the more she dug the dirtier it got and the harder it was for her to understand just what he had gotten into. Somewhere along the line, what had been a well-mapped plan to better the state of his homeland had ended up growing into a veritable catacomb with dangers at every turn, to which that map no longer seemed to apply. She began to fear the worst and talked about returning home and continuing the search from there, keeping Aizlyn and herself safe until such time as she was made aware one way or the other what had become of him. Something had obviously shaken her to the bone, and her bones where already brittle from years of stress.

Then, in another letter, she wrote a few lines about Aizlyn's joy over her first nose ring on her twelfth birthday, and then spent two pages going back and forth between despair and hope over the progress of her search for her love. She spoke of having enlisted the help of people she wasn't quite sure she could completely trust, and was scared she would come to regret it.

Then, suddenly, the decision was made. It was a short letter, informing Aizlyn's grandfather of a few of their belongings being mailed, begged him to say a prayer for her.

This struck Aizlyn beyond odd, her mother never mentioned religion to her grandparents, even her grandfather, with whom she was so open. And here she asked for prayers? Something had scared her near witless. As her frazzled letter ended with a flight number and arrival time, Aizlyn was sure her mother was nearing a complete nervous breakdown and unsure how she had avoided one so long.

The last letter was nothing like what she had expected, if you could even say she was *expecting* anything. She would have thought the one before to be the last, had she not seen there was one more waiting on her blanket. It was bittersweet and heartbrokenly apologetic. She begged her father to watch over Aizlyn and swore she would return as soon as she could, and with Jay. It seemed one week back in the States, trapped in her mother's domain, and she had come to a very hard decision. She was taking all her savings, returning to India to pay his ransom, tell him the truth and drag him home with her.

Aizlyn's eyes balked at the word, rereading it four or five times. *Ransom?*

She read on.

Her mother was resolute, he would forgive her, or not, for her twelve years of lying, but she would at least see him freed for her penance. His family had refused to pay it, saying he was already dead, that the money would only fund the terror that was enveloping their homeland. They had consulted the best, they were sure of their information, but then they hadn't opened the letter that had been mixed in with the rest that she had grabbed and stuffed in her bag as she left their house for the airport. They hadn't read the words and felt the pain contained in the unmarked envelope.

She had to try.

Her mother's fear was palpable, she could feel it through the very paper and see it in the ink. She was not as sure as she wished to sound that she was going to be able to return to India and make it out again, let alone *with* Jay. But she was still bound to try. Her mother's pleading instruction to her father as to how to handle Aizlyn's time with him and her mother reflected her fear that the care she asked him to provide her daughter might be for an indefinite period of time.

She begged that he not let the love of life and indomitable inquisitiveness be taken from her, she still had fears related to her dream and the hollow husk she had seen once of her six-year-old. She pleaded that he do what he could to allow her to explore herself and come to terms with who she needed to be, to be happy as best she could without her mother stepping in and redirecting it all toward the ever single-minded answer that was her

112

Bible. She asked that Aizlyn be encouraged to continue to write down her dreams as they had begun doing when she was young and had so much trouble separating them from reality.

In one paragraph her mother apologized with all that was left of her heart, as if to Aizlyn herself, though it was her father who had read it first all those years ago. She no longer held out excuses to the altar that had been her pride. She merely said, "If I could teach Aizlyn just one more lesson as well as I have so many others, I would have her know, truly know, to be careful what you sacrifice for love, because it may end up being the love you sought. There are times you stand back and allow those you love to run like hell is catching up, but then there are times you rein them in, tell them your bum is starting to ache, and turn their heads toward home. You tried to teach me that, somehow I think I knew and just missed that sign that said here is when and where you stop, until that time had long since passed.

"I have spent so much time having her check her actions for how they make others feel, I fear sometimes that she will lose sight of how *she* feels, as I did, and that it must be equally important. I let Jay take the bit in his teeth and run until he forgot I was along for the ride because I didn't want him to fear the bridle. I kept her stabled so long, with thoughts of how others might feel, I fear she will not know the first thing about taking the bit or how good it feels to just run. I would not have her make the mistakes that I have. I do not think she will, the princess in her still lifts her chin often enough that I believe she will stand up and take her toys back when the time comes. Still I have my fears I have done her a disservice.

"I have been my own worst enemy, lied to and tormented myself, I have played the martyr so long at times I even believed it was an unavoidable truth. Yet I reserved the cruelest tortures for the two I had sworn my soul to love. What I lacked was because I did not stretch out my hand and take it, what I have kept from them I never gave them fingers to grasp with or eyes to see the need. I feel the weight of it will burden my spirit for all of eternity. Sometimes I think it would drag me straight to hell were I not so stubborn and had so many years of practice digging in my heels and denying what should be done.

"I will fix this, Dad. I will be back."

But she hadn't made it back.

"Be careful what you sacrifice..."

7

The Sandman

Aizlyn had heard her mother's whisper again and this time didn't fight it or look around like she was crazy and hearing things. This time she knew it was all in her head as she stared at the final letter, the weight of it crushing her back against her pillows as though an invisible hand pressed right between her breasts was restricting her lungs. Her heart ached, her stomach hurt, her eyes were swollen and yet begged for more. She relived the sunny summer afternoon when Papa had taken her out beside the barn and told her that her mother had been called up to heaven and her world had darkened and the sun had died.

The invisible hand reached through her ribs and squeezed the slowly pumping vessel that tried to hide there. She was filled again with the confusion, the pain, the feelings of being abandoned, the being lost among people who said they loved her and would care for her but whom she barely knew, those whose ways she could hardly understand or why her own upset them so.

That was the day Little Win had finished shriveling beneath the loving torture of it and simply gone to heaven too and Miss Windell had taken her silent place at the supper table with the stern old woman who had taken her nose ring and then baked her cookies, and the nice old man who shared his horse and his broken heart. The aged and sleeping ache of it all suddenly woke and thrashed against her like waves, breaking themselves endlessly on cliffs that would never give but begged heaven through the ages with crumbling tears to let them.

She buried her face in the pages of her mother and cried.

Next thing Aizlyn knew, she was in terrible pain. Her entire body ached and for some reason she couldn't justify, as her waking mind tried to make sense of the idea, she thought she had been beaten. She would have sworn to it, in those first still half-leeping moments when she'd stumbled to the back door and let Angus out into the dusk to pee, and her mind had registered little more than the pain that throbbed and pulsed throughout her being. As for then, she simply limped from the now brewing coffee maker, down the dim hallway toward the warmth of a waiting shower and the hope the pain would leave her as quickly as the inexplicable idea it had been due to a thrashing.

She stood with her forehead and palms pressed to the shower stall wall for support, the warm water flowing from the adjustable spout just above her head, beating into the nape of her neck and loosening her spine as it flowed with her hair down to her tailbone, then continuing alone from there. Her eyes felt swollen and gritty, like it had literally been a sandman who had brought her dreams- dreams that had made her cry but that she couldn't recall. Her head still throbbed, though it had slowed to a dull thump, thump, thump that seemed to have settled in her jaws just under her back teeth to resonate only every third or fourth thump up to the back of her right eye. The stiffness in her body, the bone deep-ache that had made it so difficult for her to unfold from the fetal position she had been nuzzled out of by an insistent, almost worried Angus, was retreating as well, now almost out of the muscle and soon to escape the skin.

She lifted her forehead, but only for a moment, as though that took all the strength the water had yet provided, and allowed the warm steady flow to pound into the front of her face. She tried to open her eyes to wash away the sandman's gritty leavings but they fluttered with reflexes she couldn't control and she ended up simply sputtering and spitting, then dropping her forehead back to the wall, closing her eyes again. She relaxed into the water, the water relaxed into her, she could have fallen asleep again right there.

Suddenly she was again overcome with the feeling she had just been badly beaten. She jumped reflexively and reached for her ankle with a burst of energy and speed she wouldn't have thought she possessed. Her searching fingers found her ankle, as it should be, with multiple chains of gold and silver dangling bells and charms. They chimed and chinked dully, weighted and water-logged but still responsive to her movements and calming to her mind.

She caught herself, wondering where this terrible idea was coming from, why it wasn't gone yet, even after her telling herself it wasn't right or real, and why it should have made her feel her anklets wouldn't be there. She told herself she was silly and dropped her forehead back into the wall. She told herself it made no sense and must be just more forgotten leavings of the sandman. She told herself not to worry. She told herself she wasn't allowed to lose it, then she rolled her forehead on the wall and looked at her other ankle anyway. It too was as it should be.

She sighed, closed her eyes, turned her head back straight onto the wall again and waited, breathed shallow as the water trickled down her forehead, through her eyebrows and down her nose to tumble off her nose ring. Her heart rate slowly returned to normal. She told herself again that everything was as it should be, that she must have just had a terrible dream, and that she just needed to wake up completely. She heard Angus scratch at the door. She remembered the letters she had stayed up reading. She said a prayer of thanks that it was Friday and told herself she would take Angus and the letters for a walk down to Genie's, since Genie obviously hadn't been by yet, and they would have a nice evening of friendly argument.

Then it hit her she was working this Friday, tonight, she had traded it so she could have Saturday off to go out with Genie for her birthday. She had forgotten all about it. She even recalled having been thankful when making it through last night that she didn't have to return until Saturday.

That was her normal schedule, but for one week in March and one week in July, for the last two years it changed, Genie had changed it. Genie had changed a lot of things and this would be the third year she had done all she could to get a Saturday off to go out with her girlfriend and celebrate "being ageless."

Birthdays had not been so big a deal to her, whatever natural day off came closest used to suffice for dinner and a movie. But Genie, Genie liked Saturdays, no need to get up early, ever, as far as she was concerned, so you could drink as much as you wanted, dance as much as you liked and sleep as long as you needed to, recovering. With Genie at the wheel sometimes that meant all day. Movies were for every day. Sending Nathan to stay with her mother, putting on a brand new pair of earmuffs that had been marketed as shoes and getting silly-buzzed while dancing until your thighs and lungs burned, that was for "being ageless."

Aizlyn grunted and forced her aching arm over her shoulder just long enough and high enough to grab the toothbrush from the small ledge of the prefab tub and shower stall. Still supporting herself with her forehead, she squeezed some toothpaste onto the brush and told herself it was going to be worth it. She giggled as the toothpaste burped and suddenly shot out, filling the entire length of the brush just like in the old commercial. She didn't know why she'd giggled, where the inclination or even energy had come from but she felt better already. She brushed and brushed, swished then rinsed, then brushed some more and spit. The white foam landed on her maroon toenails and so she giggled again.

Jordan hated that.

She rubbed one foot over the other, rinsing the toothpaste down the drain, then she quickly shampooed and put in her conditioner. She had no idea what time it was or if she was going to make herself late but she didn't have the energy to move much faster, so she left the conditioner and scrubbed everything else. She turned so the water could rinse her hair as she ran a razor over the needful parts far too swiftly to have been efficient, but found she lacked the inclination to care.

Win would just have to wear a pair of her pants tonight.

Aizlyn pushed the shower curtain aside and judged by the light that she was indeed probably running a good bit behind. She rushed in her towels to let the dog in and feed him then poured her coffee in her thermal mug mixing it just right before she went to the bedroom to check the nightstand clock. She was right, she was behind.

She grabbed an old standby from Win's closet, it was an outfit that was always ready and waiting no matter how late she ran, kept on a single hanger so as to remain that way. Win's original outfit: a pair of comfortably worn leather pants given to her by Jadin and a matching leather vest she'd come across at the swap-meet that fit so snug it didn't zip all the way and made her breasts look great. She threw the outfit across the bed and began scrounging through Win's drawer for a thong and a bra that would hide inside the vest, secretly working to help do her chest justice.

Aizlyn didn't care much for thongs but Win saw their usefulness in that they left no room for the crude comments that would set her teeth on edge and leave her fighting a twitch that begged her to put her cigarette out on some dumb ass who thought himself amusing. Finally she found under-things that would work and pulled them on, then she danced and wiggled into the leather pants that seemed to want to stick to her still moist legs. She deodorized, perfumed and quickly dragged a brush through her long wet hair before spinning it up into a knot and sticking a set of short decorative sticks in it to hold it in place and out of the liquor. Then she grabbed her keys, thermal mug and purse, hit the kitchen to be sure everything was off and headed for the door, patting Angus goodnight as she walked through the dining room.

Aizlyn grabbed a quick look at herself in the mirror that hung there and stalled, took a second look and failed inspection. She ran back to the bedroom to put Win's face on. Another great night in the making, she thought sarcastically, as she got in the car a few minutes later. She had five minutes to get there and it usually took at least ten, the moon still shown hugely pregnant with promises of misfit children, and she certainly didn't feel settled into herself properly.

Hell, she wasn't sure anymore who herself was from one moment to the next. With parts of her seeming to want to blend and make war simultaneously at any given moment, she was at a loss to predict how she was going to make it from moment to moment. She wished this blending thing would finish more quickly in her regular life, wished Win would step in more frequently when dealing with her grandmother or Jordan, but wanted desperately for it to stop at work, for Miss Windell and Aizlyn to stop coming out there. She was comfortable with who she was at work, or at least had been until recently.

It was her real life that needed help. She needed Win's confidence and resolution, not just when it came to the littler things like keeping Angus and her job, she needed Win to make peace with Jordan once and for all. Those desperate eleventh-hour hopes brewed by the cruel witches that cackled in her conscious on "what if" nights were toxic. She was sure it passed for codependency; him, with a burning need to be reminded every few months that he was loved to the core despite his faults by her constant inability to turn away and she with a desperate incomprehensible compulsion to fight for the same loving acceptance from him.

Now maybe if she could just hold onto that, that moment right there, she'd be okay. All she had to do was make it through his next phone call and somehow she felt in her bones it was coming, he never stayed away much longer than three months. She shored herself up, at least the big bloated orb leading her mother's Mustang toward the Gentleman's Club didn't have a blue tinge to it tonight. At least the radio wasn't telling her to let her hair down. A bird had yet to shit on her shoulder again. She still felt poorly prepared for it all over again so soon and continued to give herself a pep talk the whole way, pushing thoughts of the letters and dreams and frazzled senses to the back of her mind, spitting more toothpaste in the shower stall in her head and giggling.

She pulled up almost completely confident, and even noted her oldest favorite nose ring still in her nose with a snort that said I can beat this. She smiled at her reflection then and put the car in park, turning it off. She paused a moment before grabbing her purse though, looking ahead to the door. Something was wrong, something was different. When she put her finger on it, it nearly blew her composure.

Gamble wasn't standing at the door to greet her, he hadn't noted her arrival and held the door wide or come out to see what was amiss while she'd dawdled and looked herself over in the rearview. She opened the door and shoved her boot down on the thought hard, then gave it a twist for good measure. What did it matter? So he was already helping another dancer in or assisting a customer to find a seat. She was a big girl, she could walk herself across the parking lot. She'd done it for years before he came to work there, no need getting spoiled now. But something still wiggled when she lifted her boot and started to walk in, there was still a small squirm left of the disappointment she'd smeared over by her car.

Win managed to take over the bar and the shift flawlessly, leaving everything at the door when the loud music tugged that final strap of her armor snug. She apologized for her lateness and made it through counting the drawer and passing the torch, despite the fact Gina's choice of shots that evening was a nasty concoction she could have sworn came from the bar-mat and she had to fight herself not to put it right back there. She made it through the first few rounds of shots for the ever-early regulars wanting just one more on their way out and the dancers who needed just one good one to settle them in.

Win sat back on the cooler and lit a cigarette, surveying her domain.

She caught sight of Jimmy, whom she noted was absent from his normal post by the stage but at least no later than her, he was leaning low and intent in the DJ booth, probably picking out some songs and listening to stories she could imagine from past experience that she wouldn't want to overhear. Jimmy laughed, a loud appreciative sound that rang in the semi-silence between one song fading and another taking up where it left off. He

121

slapped the DJ on the back, probably, she thought, congratulating him on another notch under the counter up there. She'd found herself in accidental range, and had not tuned out the bawdy tales often enough to know those grooves weren't accidental.

The guy who ran the music, Joe, had been up there so long, seen and done so much, she was surprised at times that he hadn't turned green over the years. She couldn't help but like him though, in her own detached sort of way, he had a playful smile and bouncy, energetic style. Most likely that was due in good part to the fact he seemed to live off energy drinks and papaya rum. He tipped her well though, for the annoyance the frequency at which he required them caused her, and even played a song or two he knew she liked now and then, despite the fact he found her tastes odd. She was unsure how he would be at his job otherwise, without the alcohol, couldn't swear she'd ever seen him sober to assess that, but he did his job well, rum and all. She had grown a measure of respect for him over the years, but she didn't talk with him anymore than she needed to because she hadn't ever been silly enough to forget there were probably quite a few little demons dancing on his tongue, hidden just behind those straight white teeth.

She realized her own thoughts reflected how jaded *she* had become over the years and it reminded her again why Win was here. She was thankful for Win, that Win dealt with the underside of her life and could slough it off so that she could relax and paint when the bills were paid and it not all be in blacks and greens. Win could rid her of it all through the simple processes of driving around the outskirts of town singing obnoxiously or on the easy nights merely by removing her armor and wiping off the leather before hanging it back in her closet.

Jovan came in, beautiful as always, sashaying in the door, ever the picture of current fashion. Win was sure a good majority of her earnings here went into her closet but saw how it only made those earnings all the bigger and better. Win liked that, it made her tip-out from the girl all the bigger and better too. Win stuck to mostly leather, failing that at least black or some shade thereof and occasionally a touch of red. Win would probably be

122

considered Goth or a "food court druid" by those not noting her makeup stuck much more on the natural side; some even likened her to a dominatrix. Win didn't rightly care what people thought she was trying to be as long as what she was, was supporting herself.

Win stowed Jovan's purse under the counter with her own, and listened with apparent interest as Jovan began regaling her with tales of her latest shopping adventures, pointing out with glee that she'd only paid fifty-six dollars for her comfortably stylish shoes. Win neglected to tell her they'd have only cost her four had they walked down the street from her home in India and bought them off the cloth laid out on the ground displaying that new style since she was a child. She didn't need to, soon customers began to arrive in earnest and they were put to work. The tales ended, both women knew the real reason they were there was to make the money that quick service brought them, not talk about shoes.

The other waitress, Pixie, arrived and a third named Jan who only worked weekends, followed close on the heels of the second doorman whom Win knew by dress and description but had not, as yet, worked with. From the proximity at which the final two regular employees arrived, and the instant parting at the door, Win guessed they had rode in together and didn't want it known. Much more guessing had been subject for the dressing-room gossip for over a week now, since such things were not generally discussed around her. She was known to enforce a few rules here and there.

Some thought they had gotten away with things merely because she had never made comment, which was not the case. Win was quite alert but usually disinterested, and here, as with many other things, she simply took mental note. She didn't rightly care, like she didn't rightly care who went to their car to hit a joint rather than retrieve a forgotten thong, or that the DJ booth had been a trysting spot for more years than she could count. As long as they did their jobs and didn't jeopardize hers, the things she noted remained just notes, good things to know. You wouldn't want to fire a waitress and lose a doorman the same night unless you were prepared. Win preferred to be prepared, she kept notes.

Jovan returned to place an order and Win asked her, "What's the new door guy's name?"

Jovan laughed, a hearty sweet tinkling sound Win knew she'd miss if this one lost herself in the bright lights and regrets, "He's not new, been here over two months now, started right after Gamble. They work together. I mean, you know, besides here. They do some contractor-type stuff together during the day."

"Didn't realize he'd been here that long," Win admitted, her mind whirling, "I just heard about him last week."

"Yeah, he's been filling in Mondays and Fridays for Gamble, pretty much since Gamble got here," Jovan said, unaware just how closely Win was listening as she arranged the drinks Win was making on her tray for better balance. "His name is Jon."

Jovan looked up, handing her the money to pay for the round. She probably mistook Win's look of dismay for her feeling bad she hadn't know the guy had been there that long because she added, "You just haven't ever worked with him is all, how are you supposed to know?"

Win smiled, gave Jovan her change and tried to organize her thoughts. She'd only gotten as far as, "those are my days off, the cows are winking and dinking again, should I be scared?" And then "so that's why he wasn't there to greet me at the door." These thoughts were likely to be the first few steps up a disturbing flight of stairs and she was thankful to be quickly sidetracked.

One of her favorite girls, Sunshine, a slight boyish creature with barely a curve to speak of but possessing long raven-colored hair which made up for it, hair that Win had held out of the toilet more than once, came up just then and slammed her Crown Royal bag of bills on the bar. She was gorgeous, *and* she could do her entire set on the pole. She was pure muscle due to the fact she often did, to loud applauses and fists full of hurled bills. She was also quite adorable when she was pissed.

"Hold this for me, would ya?" she said angrily, "Money keeps comin' up missin' from the dressing room and I ain't bangin' my knees to shit for no one else's tuition, damn it!"

Win took the bag and turned to put it under the counter with her own purse, trying not to laugh. If she continued to feed those lines about her knees and tuition to the men here all night, she'd be bringing a Crown Royal bag Win's way at least every two hours. Win couldn't let the girl see she was in any way amused so she put on her serious face, making another promise to herself about the talk she needed to have with the girls, before turning back to face her. She knew better than to ask for input as to whom Sunshine might think it was taking the money, despite the fact she loved the girl she knew her answer was always "that new girl." It often eluded Win how any new girls ever became anything else in this place.

"Wait," Sunshine said, turning back after only one step. "Buy us a round outta there first, would ya? I need to chill, put on my money maker mask."

"What ya buying me, sexy," Win said playfully, as she only was with a certain select few.

Had it been a few hours later she'd have found a nice way to decline but since it was barely eight and it would only be her second, she decided to give the girl the lift she knew her sharing a shot and a joke with her would be.

"What's that yumminess you make with all the flavored rums?" Sunshine's face lit up with a clean but somewhat crooked smile, realizing she'd caught Win early enough. "Mix us some a them."

Win winked and started mixing.

The rest of the night went as Win felt it should, less the appearance of quite a few regulars who weren't her regulars, and wanted the same treatment they got from the part-timer who covered Gina and hers days off. These assorted young men with a few women thrown in proved somewhat annoying but for the most part good tippers once they came to terms with the fact Win was in no mood to barter.

Win finally kept her promise too. At the end of the night, in the lull between the bar being cleared of customers and the dancers still changing and packing up to leave, rather than lighting her cigarette and checking her beer cooler, she headed for the dressing room. After her initial request for their attention had drawn a few flirtatious comments from some of the bolder dancers, comments which she had learned years ago to accept from the girls as a compliment and leave at that, she managed to get all their attention and break a few things down to them again.

Win encouraged them to work together, explaining again how there was generally a lot more money to be had from a table of girls all gently pushing a big spender to tip whichever of them was up next, by praising each others' skills and backing up each others' stories, than there was to be had by a single one spending all her time trying to convince the guy she was the only one who deserved his cash and coming off catty. One way made the man feel on top of the world, surrounded by beauty and the envy of every other guy there, the other left him feeling like he'd never left home and all you wanted was his money.

She also reminded them to make sure their personal stuff was stowed, their money was safe and their lockers were locked. That's what locks were for after all, and better to keep the temptations out of play and go home with all your stuff, money included, than be lazy. She offered again, as she had often, to stop and buy locks on her way in next time for any who needed them and store money for anyone who would have to wait until then to have a safer place all their own to store things.

"I love you!" Sunshine yelled, tipsy-happy and counting the cash Win had collected behind the bar for her all night as she listened with half an ear.

Win laughed and said, "I love you too, hun." Then she asked that they remember to help each other out, catching a few of the girls' eyes and requesting if anyone saw someone's stuff left out or locker open, push it closed.

Once again she talked to them about how not only was bringing their own liquor to work illegal, something that could cost her job or a pretty hefty fine, but that it endangered all of them. What if they were to get shut down, even for a week, how would they *all* pay their bills? Win knew this track would have them watching not only their own actions but also the girls next to them. Win was using all her charm and logic at this point, coaxing them to see things her way even if they cared nothing for laws and rules. She reminded them she didn't care or judge *whatever* they did outside of work, but like with the liquor, not to bring it in and risk all their jobs, keep it *outside of work*. She pointed out how if she didn't know how much they'd had to drink, by monitoring what she sent out via a waitress or made herself, she couldn't tell if they'd been slipped a micky or been sipping a bottle in the back. Win appealed to their sense of preservation as well as the desire of a good number of them to make her proud. She told them there was a guy who'd been passing misrepresented pills lately, even to those who weren't aware they were taking them, and she wanted them to be safe. She saw they were listening. She had worked long to earn their trust and respect and it paid well. They were taking her to heart for the most part.

"How much money do you really save if you lose the ability to earn for a week? Just save us all the trouble and the cash, do what you do before you enter the front door and otherwise get the customers to buy you drinks here. Then I can keep an eye on you and be sure you're okay." Win paused and smiled winningly around the room, looking for anyone with questions.

Win winked at a girl who begged for more than just her eyes to be on her and said, "Not in front of the children, dear."

Realizing they had no questions and were chomping at the bit to go home as everyone laughed, she said, "Look, I'll let you guys go, I know we all want to get home. But I know you guys know better than to ever buy your own, even from the liquor store where its cheap, that's what we were blessed with boobs for." They all laughed again and she finished, "I'm not trying to be anyone's mommy, I just want to make my money, just like you. So keep looking out for each other, that's what makes us the best. I love you guys."

Win left the dressing room to the sounds of happy cheers, a few more flirtatious comments about her love and how she would be welcome to show it, and the happy laughter of a dozen girls. For some reason these girls liked hearing she loved them and loved hearing she thought them the best. Her spirits were elevated. She felt she had done well this night. She had let things slip for longer than she normally would have, these girls needed encouragement and gentle reminding in this portion of their lives as much as any woman did in any other thing that involved their emotions. Despite how much they all tried, emotion was interwoven in all they did, part of their genetic code, and so it required a careful mending now and then.

Win got out of the bar quite late that night but felt it had been worth it. This time when she dragged her tired butt out of the bar chair and put weight down on her sore feet to put the money in the safe, she knew she really did have the next night off. It was truly going to be okay. She was going to go home, soak in a bubble bath, then get a good morning's sleep. She had much to do, including getting Genie's painting framed and wrapped. There was no need for a long route home, she headed straight there.

Four o'clock and all was well in Win's world.

Her senses reeled and for the longest time refused to pick apart the burning. Her nose was rebelling. It was all one scent; wood, cloth, camel dung and animal fear and blood; vomit, incenses, piss and stew and blood. Sickening sweet came the stench of singed flesh blistering beneath layers of stale sweat; then came sound.

A scream, a gurgle, a grunt, a laugh; all played to the background of snapping wood, broken by heat, and the dull roar that was the burning. She wished she'd have remained deaf when her mind tried to tell her about the sounds and her inner eye tried to conjure pictures to explain them. Hooves suddenly beat the sand, heavy, fast-paced, angry, abusive, they beat the ground and then, thankfully, faded to a dull distant thud.

At first she'd thought she had been mercifully blinded, but turning her head to escape the smell and sound and the visions inside it, she found it was only that the eye which could have seen was swollen shut, its slit view graciously narrow. Her other, horrified and working, had been buried in the sand that was soaking up the blood and vomit beneath her. Now it caught glimpses of demons and beloved dead, all part of the smoldering ring that had been her caravan. She had real visions now, not the pretty inventions of her mind but the true horrors of her good eye. Her mind revolted now, unable to comprehend, unwilling to accept, things burned into her mind to be viewed long after she turned that eye back to the sand.

Her slight moment brought pain to life in every fiber of her being, it shuddered awake and screamed at her for the waking. She found burning aches and blooming bruises, blood clots mixed with returning stew on her tongue and a piercing gash it found for prodding, checking on its cage of teeth. She found momentary refuge for her senses and her mind, hiding in the simpler torture that was existing inside herself. Layers of skin lay raw to the heat and smoke, where her wealth had once ridden proud. Chains ripped from ankles and waist and neck left angry evidence of their unwillingness to part with her flesh easily. A torn bicep spoke of a prized golden circlet that had known her line since the time of Leonitus, a bloody nose mourned emeralds and gold it had earned with first woman's blood. She was naked to her soul, covered only by the shifting heated sand, and she knew hell was coming. She remembered the devil.

An explosion of expelled air, a hard sniff as if from a dog's searching muzzle, sounded in her ear, shooting new pain into her head, then she heard, "This one breathes still..."

Aizlyn shot up from the floor of the tub, splashing water all over Angus who leaned over it, his large muzzle directly in her face as she tried to catch her breath. The water was oppressively hot, it had worked the long night's aches out of her only to coax her into a dream that brought them back many fold. She hefted herself up, afraid to try to relax in there again and risk sinking under the water another time. She had no great desire to accidentally take the forever nap. The dog stepped back from her and shook, then sat down panting hard as though the heat had gotten to him too.

Five o'clock in Aizlyn's world and all was not well. "Damn Angus, your momma broken," she sighed.

She toweled off and went to bed naked, the cool morning seeping into the house being just what the doctor ordered. It cleared her head a bit and put her firmly back in the here and now where she desperately wanted to be. She wondered briefly if she'd had a similar dream yesterday and if some of what she'd felt upon waking hadn't been due to that, and not all to blame on the poor posture she'd kept throughout. She was sure sleeping curled over, butt up on the pillows hugging old letters, had been a large part of her pain-filled waking but somehow she couldn't help but relate the events. She didn't believe in coincidences. The red ring around her ankle a few days past, after the dream where she'd been shackled, made her wonder about a lot more than she'd like to admit to her former fellow psychology students.

She lay there, eyes wide, skin cooling, breath growing shallow, and even though she wanted it she was fighting the sleep that tried to come. She was afraid, couldn't help but be afraid, every which way her mind wandered it found a question she couldn't answer or was afraid to because of what that answer might mean. *Every which way* her mind wandered, *including* when she dreamed. So she made her mind work on the afternoon ahead, write down a mental list of what she had to do that day. Go by the frame shop, stop and buy a card, repaint her nails, she went through it detail by detail as the birds chirped their lullaby.

She went over again what she intended to wear out that evening, patted Angus's extended paw where it lay close to her face, and nuzzled her head into her pillow. She smelled sleep there but told it to go away. She tried to keep her mind working as she pictured herself again in the new red dress with delicate silver chains for straps and sheer layers floating from hip to hem. Her eyes fluttered as she saw her fresh, painted-to-match toes slide into the strappy silver heels that laced round and round and up and up her calves and she was gone again.

There was about this day a sense of peace. She rode serenely in the covered cart, jostled gently over the occasional rut and watched dusk dance on the leaves of the trees she past. The horses paced quick but not hurried, the seats were well-padded and the road well-maintained. What bumps came, merely kept her awake despite the hypnotizing shift of evenings light through the wood surrounding her; they did not bruise her. Others here, in this cart with her, cried as their homeland fell further behind, long out of sight, swallowed by the gaping orange maw of dying daylight. Not her, she tilted her head to the frame of the cart, eyes forward, restful and easy in her soul, watching what came with the night.

The men of metal, that chinked and chimed on their heavy steeds, were red and sand, due to the sun of her homeland, but pale when stripped to bare chest and taking rest. Some rode with bits of cloth hung from poles like holy things to be held proud above the dust of travel. Some wore these same symbols larger than displayed on those bits of cloth over their mobile metal shells, honorably displayed mid-chest. All wore weapons. All wore scars. These were holy men, noble men, they did not have the same beliefs as her people but they defended them the same. She recognized them for what they did, why they did it, but more for how a single one had treated her, and she was at peace with her conquerors.

She had learned enough of men in her short life to know the man who had claimed her from the gutter, dug her from beneath the wounded and dead, had her cleaned and fed, had not taken her from her home for her flesh. Wide-eyed, refusing to weep for those loved ones that she'd lay buried under, he had found her, looked long upon her and spared her. She had known the kindness, the goodness in those eyes as they assessed her. She had lifted her chin, told him she was as good, without language, despite faith and skin, and he had believed her.

Slowly she had learned his words, worked them in her mind then pushed them from her tongue until they no longer seemed so foreign. She heard of his quest and his god, and slower still, came to understand the loss of a daughter many years before. When the time came for him to return to his wife and the country of his birth, there had been no question, she had grabbed what little she owned and followed him. The man who rode, straight and proud, on the heavy horse with the ever-present dog loyal at its heel, the one to whom her eyes strayed often, was her father now, the only family she had left until such time as coming night revealed a new country and mother.

Those who huddled moist-eyed and scared riding beside her occasionally glanced askance her way, but how to explain dreams that were more memories? How to convey to anyone the mirage- like knowledge of the needful future and hurtful past which had haunted her existence since first conscious thought? How was she to share with them a sense of wellness in one's soul that told her all was as it should be? She did not know their dreams, could not look into their memories and tell them this is what is meant to come or this is were you should break away. Each man's path was his alone. Each woman's chain her own.

She smelled the great open water, heard it beating against ageless unyielding earth, felt its cool comfort steal into her marrow and she knew only this: that for her, this path led home.

8

Karma

Aizlyn woke up alive. She couldn't have described it any other way. The day was cool and full of promises come like kisses on her bare skin. She looked to the other side of the bed where Angus snorted and twitched, still lost in his dreams, and felt amazing. She grabbed her dream journal and tried desperately to capture that sense of inner peace and calm. She wrote what visuals she could recall but mostly just sat and soaked it up, penning only what stood out without depleting the wonder of it by picking it apart.

Aizlyn set the journal aside and fell back lengthwise across the bed, head flopping into the covers and hair swooshing out around her. She laughed when Angus startled awake, "Good morning, Sleephound," she said, patting his head and scratching under his scruffy muzzle, "That's what you are, not a Wolfhound."

When Angus snorted and shook his head, she figured he disagreed.

Aizlyn sat up and said, "C'mon, let's eat and get about this wonderful day!"

She opened the back door and left it that way. While Angus wandered about, doing his business, she started a pot of coffee. She put his morning scoop in his magic bowl and made herself a bowl of cereal, then sat on the back step crunching the milk-sodden flakes distractedly, paying little attention to her breakfast and just soaking up the day.

133

She was almost out the door, painting draped in a sheet of plastic clasped under one arm and thermal mug and purse occupying the other, when she caught sight of her statue of Sarasvati and told herself she would need to find a better place for her than the coffee table. A small wall shelf was added to her mental list of things to buy that day and she turned again toward the door.

The phone rang. She almost didn't turn back, but something about the persistent burst of noise, sounding at demanding intervals, drew her hand back from the door knob and sent her back into the dining room. It could be Genie, she thought, about not showing up yesterday. Now, however, she just wished she'd kept right on walking when she heard her boss's voice come through the receiver.

Her whole beautiful day went right out the door like she should have. Her boss needed her to work tonight. The guy she'd worked for last night so she could have tonight off had broken down on his way back from visiting friends in the next state and couldn't get back in time for work. He'd prettied the prospect up by saying the guy had said that he had someone headed out to pick him up and would try to get there by eleven, but she knew better. It was a Saturday night. If the guy did make it back tonight, he wasn't going to run right to work to pull the last half of the shift.

She took the understanding comments her boss made about tonight having been a long-planned event for what they were, grease. She took his statement that she was the last resort and he had tried the others as she took the compliments about how she always came through for what they were, grease. She took his thankfulness for her covering things, once again, while he too was out of town for what it was, grease. We aren't talking about cooking grease either. She was reminded of a bumper sticker that had read, "if you're gonna ride my ass at least pull my hair." She hung up the phone feeling violated, like her butt should hurt.

Genie was going to be pissed.

She walked out to her SUV, deflated, the feel-good afternoon had fled with the phone call. She slid the painting gingerly into the back and closed the door, wondering why it was that she hadn't just said no. What was it that made her unable to leave them hanging? Suddenly she recalled an argument with Jordan, asking him for much the same reasoning she was unable to provide herself, and something inside her began the forgiving process.

Was it something to be blamed on her mother for making her always think how she'd feel if it was done to her, doing things that put her in the same position to make her feel what another felt so she would learn? She heard Genie in her head telling her, "If you lay down like a door-matt you can't be mad that people walk on you." She thought of all the excuses and even lies she should have spoken and bemoaned her silent tongue as she drove. Yet a small part of her was glad of the situation, it had made a few things come so suddenly clear, flipped the switch in that dark corner and the light had remained on long enough for her to make out a few things.

Her mood perked slightly while reading the various birthday cards and finally choosing one for Genie while the painting was being framed. But it darkened again when she spotted the perfect shelf for her statue and was reminded that the goddess of learning was failing to teach her the harder lessons. "It's one thing to be kind and understanding, but stand up for yourself next time," she told herself, "take your toys back, the way you feel is just as important as the way others do."

Present framed and wrapped, she drove back home to get ready for work. Her call to Genie to inform her of the change of plans and beg off till the following weekend went better than expected. All Genie had said was, "Right then, see ya later," as if distracted by more important matters. This week had been rolling steadily downhill for Aizlyn and she just knew tonight was going to hit bottom. The more of Win's Armor she strapped on the more upset she got, until finally Win was full-blown pissed off to have been called upon this particular evening.

Pulling up to work, she didn't even take that normal final glance in the rearview mirror, she didn't need to. She could tell by the boiling cauldron in her stomach, stewing up snippy comments for all the imagined

135

situations she would be likely to face, that Win was rocking in rare form this evening. Heaven help the first guy to tell her, "keep the change, pretty lady," when that change was just that, change.

She barely glanced at Gamble when he pushed the door wide after having seen her pull up, nor did she come up with any niceties to hand back to him when he greeted her good evening and complimented her new leather pants. They are nice aren't they? had gone through her head when reminded via the compliment of the new pants she had come across, that laced loosely from ankle to hip, hell to get off when you gotta pee though. None of it had made it out of her mouth though as, jaw clenched, she'd headed straight for the bar.

Gina met her, two large shots of something dark and smelling sweetly repugnant already in hand and apologies already flowing. "I'd have stayed all night for you," she'd began as Win took the shot and held it to the light, eyeballing it, "but my man-thing has already left for work and I don't trust those darn kids for more than an hour alone." Win took the shot and grimaced, appreciating the burn, while Gina, too, swallowed and continued, "Last time I got home they had invited half the neighborhood to stay the night and eaten every microwaveable item in the house. Walked in to seven scared kids, half of whom I didn't know, huddled on my couch watching a movie with some psychopath and a chainsaw, stuffing half the cupboards in their dirty faces. Took me two days to clean the place, a month to mend fences with pissed-off parents of kids having nightmares, and twice that long to get over my man leaving such a movie out for the boys to find."

"It's all good, girl," Win said, letting the rest of the explanation slink off unneeded. She liked Gina, just not her taste in shots, no use making her feel it was any of her problem. "Bife's a litch, get a helmet..."

Gina laughed at that and said, "...fuck around, get your feeler hurt."

Having been let off the hook and knowing she was not going to be blamed, Gina gathered her purse and tips to leave. She informed Win of the one open tab and who it belonged to, and nothing more of note, as she exited the bar, and Win merely glanced at it to show she had heard. Win counted down the drawer, lit a cigarette, and waited for her first victim.

Gamble eyed her contemplatively from his chair by the door and part of her realized she probably shouldn't have taken her foul mood out on him. There was nothing to be done for it, however, and it was soon forgotten as he stopped Firefly when she walked by and they began to talk. His quizzical eyes now removed from her, she went back to brooding over her cigarette.

Jazz, another of her favored dancers, slid into a chair at her bar and smiled cautiously, ducking her head to catch Win's eye.

"You ain't supposed to be here tonight," Jazz said at last. Taking in the snort she got in response as a "No shit, Sherlock," she added, "I'll buy us the first round?"

Win turned and started mixing in response.

"Count me in," Firefly said, sliding up beside Jazz and looking askance at her, "You got this one? I'll get the next," she added.

The first round went down smooth, almost too smooth. Win told herself she wouldn't want to shoot that mix too many more times. The two girls laughed and thanked her, also noting the well-hidden potency, then pointed at their empty glasses, indicating the next round could and should be right then.

"Gamble was kinda shocked by your mood, I think he has a thing for ya," Firefly said as she watched Win pour the next three shots and hoped for a reaction. Win didn't oblige so she just finished with, "I told him you're just burnt cuz you worked last night to have tonight off. You was gonna go out with your girl for her birthday, right? And Al screwed ya outta it. That's all, right?"

"Yep," Win said, telling her favorite little white lie, raising her shot and telling herself this needed to be the last for at least a minute.

She had great tolerance, she'd built it up well over the years, but she wasn't one to push her luck either. She remembered the bitter penance made to the porcelain god last March all too well, and the memory of Genie rinsing her hair with a Corona in the bathroom sink of a tiny, downtown, hole-in-the-wall bar they'd wandered into long after they should have stopped, always slowed her down.

The night got underway as usual, the slow influx of customers began right on cue, following the arrival of Jovan. Win tried to keep her bitterness in check but it was still something Jovan noted and also apologized for the cause, though it wasn't her fault either, telling her such things as if she could bartend she'd have done it for her.

Win was to be pleasantly surprised by the evening though, when she heard a customer ask for her most expensive shot and looked up to find a vaguely familiar face. She ran quickly to the storeroom of her mind and began flipping through the canvases she kept there, to find whether this face was remembered because it was that of a big tipper or a scumbag. The painting came clear quickly enough, it was still quite fresh and titled "scumbag;" he was wanted for the crime of tipping pills that made Sunshine puke two days before.

She went to get him the shot he'd requested, coming to a decision on two points at once. She couldn't call the cops on the guy. Though she knew they were likely to find enough damning evidence on his person to rid her of him for a while, cops were horrible for business. And not all the girls were going to be smart enough to avoid him on Sunshine and her words alone, they'd tell themselves she was a lightweight and they could handle it. No quick meeting in the dressing room was going to keep her girls safe from this guy, everyone was superman until they met kryptonite. No, Win would have to handle this one herself, as usual, she thought, choosing his whisky from the top shelf's furthest corner. This evening was going to be entertaining after all, she concluded sadistically.

As she poured the *gentleman* his shot, she put on her best smile and leaned forward seductively. "Gonna conquer the world tonight, handsome?" she purred.

"I'm gonna conquer something," he responded, smiling happily and walking right toward her trap. "Can I buy you one, beautiful?"

"Not this," she simpered, pushing his overpriced whisky toward him, "I like sweet stuff."

He fell in, hinting to her of sweet things he had for her while she tuned it out. She couldn't let him get to her, she had to focus on the plan, not happy little visions of snuffing her cigarette out on the hand he kept reaching across the bar toward her with. She grabbed the butterscotch schnapps from the rail beside her knee, making sure he was watching, and poured herself a short shot, then layered some Bailey's that she made a show of turning and pulling from the cooler, on top. She started him a tab and thought, "Let the games begin," as she allowed another crude comment about leather and what else must be sweet to slide off her armor and smiled prettily, sipping her shot down.

As the hour progressed, she got the guy to try this, and that which he might also enjoy, then this other thing she was proud to have invented. All the while she stuck to her favorite sweet stuff and tuned out his crude flirtations. She caught Gamble watching her, worry written all over his face, replacing his missable grin. She wanted to smile, put it back, let him know she hadn't lost her mind and knew she needed to have a care with this guy, but she couldn't take her mind out of the game enough to truly care. Win was in rare form, nothing really mattered now but winning.

She caught a look in Sunshine's eye a few moments later that said she was worried too, she probably hadn't been sure Win remembered his face until Win winked. Sunshine giggled, mouthed "I love you," then whispered something to Jazz who then whispered something to Firefly. Soon quite a few of the girls were watching the game progress, with sidelong glances and giggles hidden behind their hands.

Win tuned them out too so that she wouldn't be tempted to laugh herself, and flirted and simpered and ran up his tab. She got his home phone number, but got out of giving hers by simply saying her phone had been cut off, which earned her a twenty in her jar to help her fix that situation. She got his uptown address, on the wonderfully woven misconception she just might visit him after work, and got out of him learning her's by saying she lived

139

with an aggressively jealous ex she couldn't afford yet to leave, earning another twenty in her jar. She even got his My Space name and his email address followed by his cellular phone number, all of which she couldn't give in return due to the non-existent mean old ex she lived with.

The game was progressing beautifully.

Then there was a bit of a commotion at the door. Win caught an unusual burst of movement out of the corner of her eye. She turned and focused completely to see Genie waving and dancing around. Win waved hesitantly, fighting a sudden, unexpected wave of panic.

Gamble walked with Genie up to the bar. "This one says she isn't here for the titties, so she isn't payin for em. She says she's here for you." His bemused tone and raised eyebrow said those were not his words but Genie's.

His worried attempt to keep her eye said he still wanted to warn her about the guy she seemed to have developed an unhealthy liking for. Win almost lost her careful composure, too many ways she should react at that moment. One she was supposed to be drunk, two she should be happy as hell to see her girl, but her girl was at her work and that just posed a whole slew of problems. Three, damn Gamble for not knowing enough about her yet to just let her be, she couldn't explain herself now. He better not blow it for her.

"Happy birthday, my dearest," Win managed, breaking eye contact with Gamble, purposefully abrupt, and stepping out from the bar to hug Genie. She added a theatrically drunken sway for effect as she pointed to a seat in front of the register. "Have a sheet," she slurred with a grin.

The *gentleman* she had been steadily stringing up for the skinning heard her and swung his head heavily, trying to focus on who was her "dearest." On seeing it was another beautiful woman he broke loose with a happy drunken laugh and offered them both another round.

Gamble took the hug as sufficient evidence this particular woman was welcome at the bar and didn't need to pay, then leaned in to whisper a warning in her ear which he'd been unable to find opening to give Win. He wanted the sober one of them to know he suspected this guy slipped pills into the girls' drinks and he had been trying to catch him. Genie allowed him his worried moment in her ear before taking the chair he pulled out for her. Genie took one look at the shots Win was making, noting they were her "stay-sober mix," did a quick mental review of Win's obviously false drunken state, then patted his arm, telling him he was a good doorman but not to worry, they were big girls.

Gamble shook his head, resigning himself to watching out for the bartender and her best friend as well as the dancers this evening. He posted himself against the wall, between the door and the bar, able to see and get quickly to either, and proceeded to try and learn how to juggle.

"What are you doing?" Win leaned over and whispered to Genie as Gamble planted himself a few yards away. "You've never come here."

"It's my birthday!" Genie responded gleefully, "you ain't getting out of getting me drunk so easily. The better question would be *what are you* doing." She glanced sidelong at the drunken man beside her and raised a questioning eyebrow as she swallowed her shot, adding, "Cuz this ain't gonna get me drunk."

Her victim picked up on the demand for alcohol from the new lady at his side, through his liquid haze, and called for another round for the lady, she needed to catch up, he'd slurred. "It's her birthday!"

"Why, I'm lending karma a helping hand," Win had smiled beguilingly in answer as she made them yet another round, this time fixing Genie something a little stouter. "Your cell has a camera built in, doesn't it?"

"Why yes, my love, it does," Genie grinned. "Does karma need a hand that bad?"

"Why yes, my love, it does," Win replied, something terrible in her smile.

Genie smiled too. "You can be quite the evil bitch sometimes," she giggled long and low.

Their victim perked up momentarily at the mention of a camera and the drunker he got the more personal information he gave Win, trying to assure himself that she *and her friend* would be able to reach him when she could slip out from under the abusive ex's ever-watchful eye. She wrote it all down as though it were the most important thing she had ever learned, and the drunker she acted the more he offered her and her girlfriend more, not just alcohol. A few of the girls gathered around the bar not only to view Win's best friend, a very unusual visitor whose arrival had caused a significant ripple, but also to watch Win get drunk.

"I know that guy who stopped me at the door from somewhere," Genie commented as the drinks slowly loosened her up and she looked around the bar, feeling now that she could handle whatever she might see.

"Really?" Win questioned absently, following her friend's eye to where Gamble leaned pensively against the wall a few yards away. "Where?"

"Dunno," Genie giggled.

Win smiled, let it slip away, and got Genie everything she could possibly want to drink on her victim's tab at his request, and they laughed frequently but not for the same reasons the man imagined. Finally the *gentleman* pushed to his feet and swayed a bit, saying he might need to close his tab and get a cab, he wasn't feeling so well. She added it up, swiped his card and handed it to him to sign, leaning long and flirtatious over the bar, telling him she'd get the cab he needed to get home and get rested up. Win observed his one-eyed focus on the outlandish total and thanked him again, profusely, for such a wonderful night for her and her girlfriend. Then they both watched him scratch one hundred dollars on the tip line with wicked cackles sounding in their heads.

He pushed the tab back at her and swayed again. Win couldn't resist.

"Wait," she called as he swerved away, "you never tried my sweet stuff."

Gamble looked horrified from first the guy to Win. Was she serious? He cringed when the guy paused and smiled, his mind obviously coming up with a crude reply which his tongue couldn't quite wrap itself around, and flopped back in the chair. She reached down by her knees, purposefully repeating the motions the *gentleman* had seen her make all night, and pulled the wrong bottle up. Genie's eyes went wide seeing what Win intended to do, she looked away down the bar so he wouldn't note her sudden inability to contain her glee and caught Gamble's very disturbed look.

"We'll make it a good one," Win said sweetly, smiling at the prospect. "I'll buy this one for you."

She poured the lemon juice in a shot glass by itself and then turned and made great flourish of pulling the Bailey's from the cooler again and pouring a shot of it too. She then passed them to him one at a time. "I mix mine in one shot but I want to buy you a double." she said beguilingly. "Hold that in your mouth and add this one to it."

He held the lemon juice as directed then poured the Bailey's in too. It curdled instantly, as any good Cement Mixer would, and he tried to chew it down. It was a horrible drink, if you could even call it a drink, reserved by collage kids to initiate the young and stupid and she knew it too. His eyes grew wide as his stomach revolted and he flew out of his chair, sending it spinning and crashing to the floor. Jimmy, the dancers, hell, half the bar looked up at the commotion and Gamble watched in horror as the man pinballed his way through the tables toward the bathroom with his hand over his mouth.

Win laughed and held out her hand to Genie, who was already digging through her purse for her cellular phone. Putting the phone in her friend's hand, she whispered, "evil bitch," and cackled manically, letting loose the glee she had barely contained.

Gamble walked up just then, his face showing he was caught somewhere between horror and a need to puke as desperate as the man's he'd just observed. He said, "Your new boyfriend is face down in a urinal full of puke with his pants around his knees and his package airing."

"Wonderful," Win replied, dropping the drunken act instantly and getting back to the business at hand. "Watch my register, please. Oh, and call me that cabby you keep in your pocket, please."

She noted his surprise that she too had a good deal of observation prowess, and then she noted his features switch suddenly to shock and apprehension as he saw something in her hand. It seemed he might argue with her but then she heard Genie ask him his name and she slipped back to the men's room, camera in hand, while he was sidetracked. Gamble stepped behind her bar to answer Genies questions, which if she knew Genie, would keep him occupied for a good long minute.

She got what she needed then coaxed the guy to his feet, got him to pull his pants up without laughing, got him to wash his face without heaving up her own drinks, then walked him to the front door herself. She told him she'd see him later as she pushed him into the waiting cab then went to the dressing room to find the shop vac.

She was back behind her bar in five minutes tops, to the sounds of hushed applause and whispered avowals of undying love and adoration from the girls. This was the kind of thing that had earned her the girls' love and respect over the years. She watched their backs and they watched hers. Word had spread now that Sunshine had been justly avenged in an oh-so-appropriate manner.

Gamble had obviously heard or figured out on his own what she had been up to the better part of this evening, because he looked at her upon her return, with a new-found respect that hinted at a small fear of ever pissing her off. His grin was back in place full force now and she wondered briefly what all Genie might have shared about her and prayed it wasn't anything of import. But she was sidetracked from that thought as she too found herself looking with new found respect on someone. She saw she'd not really had to rush so much since Gamble had proved proficient at filling a good portion of the orders and this impressed her a little.

"I used your register," he admitted, then grinned, "but your girl here watched me like a hawk. So don't get mad at me."

"Thank you," Win replied, taking her place back and handing Genie her cellular back. "Email that to me, would ya?"

"Is it gross?" Genie asked, accepting it back like it was dirty.

"Yes," Win smiled.

"Is it disgusting?" Genie eyed her phone as if afraid to open it.

"Of course," Win giggled.

"Is it demeaning, disturbing, and in every conceivable manner horrible to look upon?" Genie demanded, still eyeing her phone.

"Absolutely!" Win laughed outright, her big barking laugh, and flipping open her phone and looking, Genie joined her.

"Remind me not to ever piss you two off," Gamble said, watching them carefully a moment as if fearing they might show fangs and lunge at him, then he too couldn't help but laugh as a few dancers gathered around the phone and the laughter became too contagious to resist.

Win's night progressed precariously from there, as she watched with one worried eye as dancers, doormen and customers alike gathered around Genie to hear tales of other such triumphs Win had pulled off, and not just here. Some had brief, more private conversations with her best friend that sometimes weren't brief enough. She assumed for the most part people just wanted verification of who Genie was, but Win couldn't help but worry some of her private life was being exposed when she caught a giggle or sharp inhale of disbelief coming from the other end of the bar her girl had claimed.

Win also couldn't help her defensive hackles rising every now and again when some gentleman or other meandered about a tad too long, not taking the subtle hints from Genie that she was uninterested in more than the drink they offered. Yet Genie always got through to them in the nick of time and Win was saved the need to intervene. All in all, Win managed to do her job and keep making the drinks, especially for the birthday girl herself as the orders kept coming and knocking her worries aside. Everyone adored Genie instantly, much like she had when first they'd met, and she found she only had to pay for one round herself as everyone who stopped by offered one to her friend. Genie was just so vibrantly alive, full of impish like energy that hinted of mischief, ever the little ball of fire she'd fallen in love with. She was simply irresistible to one and all.

Genie asked for water around one and Win gave her one of her rare real smiles, and obliged her, holding her coffee high in a toast. "To being ageless."

Genie giggled adorably as some of the water missed her mouth. Win was pleased, her girl looked happy, drunk and tired, but happy.

"Thank you," Genie smiled her amusement back, accepting a napkin. "Take me to breakfast too?"

"Of course," Win grinned, "can I take you home afterwards?"

"Of course," Genie giggled again, "I'm no tease, like some people I know."

They both laughed loudly again and Win smiled and winked conspiratorially before she was called away to fill another order.

Cleanup went as smoothly as could be expected too, with Win wondering what in the world Genie and Gamble had found in common that kept them chatting quietly in the corner while she tried to concentrate and get Genie and herself out of there. She stocked the cooler, cleaned the bar, pulled the drawer and started the paperwork. The totals were off by a good bit and she was about to worry, running quickly back through the night in her mind. Then she remembered to adjust the credit-card slip she'd put in her tip jar. She pulled her hundred-dollar tip from the till, counted the rest of her tips and traded them in, finding all the paperwork balanced properly then, she put the bar's money in the safe.

Win returned back from the back of the building and cleared her throat to get the attention of the two chatting in the corner. They jumped like they'd been caught doing something wrong and Win lifted an eyebrow at Genie in question.

"Come along, dear one," Win said, "I'm taking you away from this den of iniquity."

Genie giggled and picked up her purse and headed for the door. Gamble followed her at a slower pace that brought him closer to Win.

"Your friend is pretty cool," Gamble said.

Win refused to rise to the bait despite a part of her wanting to answer and pretty married too for some unexplainable reason.

"The way you handled that guy was genius, by the way," he added, undaunted by her silence, as ever. "Thought you'd lost your mind there for a minute. I had been trying to catch him so I could ban him. I'd pretty much pinpointed him as the problem, the girls are so closed-mouthed about some things and not at all about others, it makes my job difficult sometimes. I just couldn't catch him in the act. I doubt he'll be back now, thank God. Just one question though…" He paused as she locked the door and set the alarm, waiting for her to give him her attention. Win realized she had little option here and looked up into those beautiful eyes while hushing Aizlyn's happy applause. "Why the picture?" Gamble asked.

"Because he will be back," Win said more steadily than she felt while looking up at him. "And by the way, you banning him would only cost you a fortune in slashed tires and other unfortunate accidents."

She kept eye contact only a moment longer, just to prove to herself she could, and noted how his eyes darkened with the thought. Then she turned and walked toward her SUV where Genie was already standing in wait.

"What about you, then?" Gamble called, running after her as the thoughts progressed and he became suddenly worried for her again.

"That's what the picture is for," she said simply, without looking back.

Just then Genie started jumping up and down and pointing at the back seat, making excited squeaking noises that Win couldn't translate. Gamble rushed forward, not sure what the ruckus was about but obviously prone to looking out for the worst and wanting to assure himself it wasn't crouched in the back seat.

Win had figured it out just about the time Genie calmed enough to hiccup happily and say, "That's mine, isn't it?"

Gamble had the door open and the large present taking up one whole side was clearly displayed, a card marked "Genie" resting on the seat before it. A part of Win wanted it kept wrapped back there until she had Genie alone, and another didn't really mind if Gamble saw her art. It felt strange, those parts were too darn close for comfort. It wasn't up to her though, as Genie bounced forward and pulled it out, setting it on the ground before her.

147

"It's heavy," she griped, huge smile belying her tone.

Genie tore the wrapping open then stood back letting out an airy "ohhh" that said she loved it. Win smiled and watched her friend pace back and forth, cocking her head this way and that, then pace forward to squat close, like a child looking at a feral cat under a bush. She was taking in the details in the meager street lights and adding another oooo and ahhh here and there. Gamble took it all in, smiling to himself, acting as though a passing car caught his full attention as Genie stood and wrapped her arms around Win, thanking her and calling her "Aizlyn." Then he lifted the painting with ease, sliding it gently into the back seat and closing the door. Appearing to have seen and heard nothing unusual this night, he wished the two ladies a good evening and watched them drive away.

Safely away from her work, Win began to quiz Genie.

"You like it?"

"I love it," Genie answered, glancing in the rearview at the gift in question.

"You called me Aizlyn," came the gentle reprimand.

"You are Aizlyn," Genie defended.

"Not there," Aizlyn reiterated, "not in front of those people. I am only Win, there."

"Those people?" Genie questioned, "what's wrong with them? Some of them are pretty darn cool, especially that bouncer guy and that one dancer, Sunshine."

"Yes, they are," Aizlyn admitted, "but not all of them are. One wrong person knowing one relevant fact, even as simple as my real name, and guys like the one we played with tonight could find out more than I am willing to have known."

She gave up trying to explain the difference as Genie pouted and seemed to take her for being truly upset at her. Her need to maintain a separation was something they had discussed more than once and now was not the time to begin the old conversation again. Genie was still a bit tipsy and wasn't going to take well to anything that might be misconstrued as criticism.

"That's really why you wouldn't let Jordan talk you into quitting that job when you guys got back together," Genie said a moment later, "not just cuz it made you feel a bit more equal and was *showing* him how you felt. You need a place to be that person you can't be with him."

"It may have started as a means to support yourself better with him gone," Genie continued, when her best friend said nothing. "You may have even hoped it would force him to see how you felt about his job and why, by showing him how it felt to be told, in essence, that the job was more important than how he felt. But really, you discovered something in yourself there, and you are scared to death of letting anyone take it from you again."

Aizlyn said nothing, she was having a hard time thinking of anything worthy of being said. Except for maybe, "Amen sister, preach it!" Genie had hit it dead on, given words to concepts she herself had wrestled with for quite a while now. And Genie was half drunk, imagine that! The silence grew, not thick or uncomfortable, just the simple quiet of one friend understanding another.

"That bouncer, he's a cutie," Genie said a little later.

"Yeah, I guess, if you like corn-fed white boys," Aizlyn replied, not needing to ask which doorman Genie had taken a fancy to, "and I don't."

"Well, he likes you," Genie said to the window she rested her head against.

Aizlyn ignored the comment, it was no great achievement for Win to garner an admirer, because Win was Win. Aizlyn was thinking it was those who knew her, the real her, and loved all of it, that were the prizes of life, as she put on her blinker and took the nearest exit. She intended to find a little-known twenty-four-hour diner, frequented more by truckers than the after-bar crowd. She was looking to buy Genie breakfast and talk about a few things, such as the letters she'd read and what they'd told her, and her two most recent dreams, not beat drunks off with a verbal stick all night.

"Sorry I didn't make it over yesterday," Genie said after a while. "Dristy came over and I lost track of time. You were already at work by the time I remembered."

"It's okay," Aizlyn replied, "I way overslept, having a wonderful dream."

"What was his name again," Genie asked, her head still pressed, tired, to the window. "Something strange...didn't fit."

"Gamble," Win answered, after a moment of wondering what Genie was talking about and realizing it had nothing to do with what she was talking about.

"You should go for it," Genie said suddenly, sitting up and looking at her friend as she drove.

"I don't," said Win, then paused, needing to be sure they were talking about the same things. "Gamble?"

"Maybe you should," Genie said, seeming oblivious to the brief pause and taking the three words together at face value. "You just told me you're Win there."

Win laughed at Genie's play on words, but Genie wasn't laughing.

"You're serious?" Aizlyn asked incredulously.

"Why not?" Genie asked, with far too much serious in her tone.

"Well, let's see," Aizlyn said, spitting out the reasons she herself had been chewing on. "We work together. That's a big fat no-no all by itself..."

"Why?" Genie asked.

"Because it just is," Aizlyn said, unable to find words for how many pitfalls she knew and feared lay along that road. If Genie was still refusing to see how the two aspects of her life should never meet, especially in a place like that, she wasn't going to try and open her eyes to it again right then.

"And he is not even done with his twenty-first year," Win pushed ahead instead. "Boys are meant to go crazy..."

"So he's got a few more days," Genie said, cutting her off and not missing the shock that crossed Aizlyn's face. "Yeah, he's a Pisces too! And I know how much you love us fishies."

150

"I'm still too old for him," Aizlyn said, trying not to laugh, seeing her exit ahead and focusing on that instead, a little bit of Win still trying to keep things in check.

"Whatever," Genie said with a dismissive pout. "Any other excuses you wanna try and feed me?"

There were a few more but Aizlyn kept them to herself. Instead she found the diner and a parking spot and took the two of them to breakfast. As they sat sipping their coffee, awaiting the arrival of the food, Aizlyn changed the subject and told Genie a little about the letters and the two recent dreams. Genie soaked it all up. The food came and they ate distractedly, as Genie seemed to take mental notes while Aizlyn continued to relay the newest in her ongoing struggle to figure herself out. None of the expected argument was forthcoming, however, as Genie simply digested all she heard. The table was cleared and still they talked, then Genie yawned, and Aizlyn called it, paid the tab and took them home.

Aizlyn walked Genie up to her porch and placed the card and painting just inside the door. She patted Genie's little dust-mop-like thing she called a dog then hugged Genie, wishing her a good night's sleep, and turned to leave. She was almost back to her car when Genie called to her, "Don't forget you're mine when you wake up, go straight to bed and get good sleep. Then get your ass back here tomorrow. Bring your journal with you too."

Aizlyn was pretty worn out and didn't have the energy to turn back and question her as to why. She simply waved her hand over her shoulder, got in her vehicle and headed to her own bed.

Angus met her at the door, fit to burst, and she let him out then dragged her feet and legs out of her boots and pants standing right there in the kitchen. She wandered back to the bedroom and removed the corset, then wiped and hung the whole lot before finding a large tee-shirt and letting the dog back in to eat his dinner. She heard him crunching kibble from the kitchen just before her head hit the pillow, then there was nothing but sleep.

9

What's in a name?

The waves were ringing.

Aizlyn tried to make that make sense as she stared from the cliffs into the writhing blue depths that flung themselves against the rocks beneath her. From her vantage, when the water was calm, she knew she could gaze just a little ways out and see the green of life just below the surface. She knew there was magic in the waters out there on those days.

The water rang again.

Aizlyn turned her head into her pillow, trying to mute the intrusive sound, but in turning away from the hypnotic blue her mind was released.

She was reminded that water couldn't ring.

She rolled from the bed, thumping to the floor in a talentless crouch that required her hands to keep her landing from turning into a face-plant. She crawled to her feet in a few awkward movements that resembled the evolution of man reenacted in four steps, and then stumbled down the hall toward the bathroom.

She had already washed her hands and face and was just beginning to brush her teeth, quite sure something foul had crawled up from the depths and sheltered in her mouth through the daylight hours, when Angus showed up in the door frame. She squeaked when his cold nose pressed unexpectedly into the small of her back.

"Who was it?" she asked him, regarding the phone call, but he gave her no answer.

She rinsed her mouth and splashed her face again, then turning, she flicked water from her fingernails at him beginning to back him out and down the hallway. His tail was wagging furiously at her playful torture and the loud thumping of it against the walls of the short hall suddenly reminded her of drums in the distance; strange.

She let Angus out before heading to the dining room and checking the machine to see who had woken her. Just as she'd thought, it had been a you're taking too long call from Genie. How does that woman recover so quickly, she wondered. She would never figure it out, she supposed, so she just shook her head and went back to the kitchen and started brewing a single cup of coffee directly into her thermal mug.

Aizlyn fed the dog and went to find something worthy of leaving the house in while her liquid life brewed in the kitchen. She ended up in baggy jeans and a newish tee-shirt, figuring if she didn't know what was going on she couldn't be blamed for being underdressed. At least she'd picked things that were paint- and coffee-stain-free, she excused herself to Genie in her head, as she swept her hair up into a pony tail.

She mixed her coffee just right, then she went looking for her boy's leash. The sound of her digging for the right one, one long enough for him to get a bit ahead and sniff about, was enough to bring him bouncing into the dining room mid-meal. Too late she thought to let him finish his breakfast, he'd never calm down enough for that now. So she attached the clasp, made sure she had cigarettes, threw her purse over her shoulder and headed for the door.

Turning the knob she caught sight of Sarasvati, still sitting on the coffee table, still awaiting her wall-mounted perch. She glanced at the clock on the wall, it read three thirty-three, again. She knew Angus was going to shiver out of his skin if she didn't get him out the door, so she talked herself out of pausing long enough to hang the shelf she'd purchased before work yesterday. She simply told herself not to forget to do it when she got home and pulled the door closed.

She was halfway down her block when she recalled the dream journal she was supposed to bring along, and it was a disappointed Angus she turned and dragged back to the house. It seemed he was actually going to argue with her when they hit the porch and he balked, but after a second he merely dropped his head and plodded back inside behind her, pouting about the too short walk. She was quickly forgiven, however, when she led him right back out the front door, journal now tucked in her purse, and he bounded ahead of her happily, testing the length of the leash.

The walk was wonderful, her legs, tight from her extra long week behind the bar in heels for eight plus hours a night, stretched eagerly into the slow burn Angus's speed put in them. She let him lead and breathed deep of the cool moist afternoon. She smelled spring, knew rain was coming, and looked forward to it. As long as it was warm rain she never minded, it was the cold, often freezing rains that now lay behind that her Indian blood didn't take very well. It was as if the cold got into her bones and took forever to be shooed.

She gazed around her at the fresh blooming life everywhere, the soft puff of white and pink and yellow shrouding most of the trees lining the street, the occasional one with limbs laden with what looked from a distance like blood drops frozen all over it and hadn't realized yet that the thaws had come and gone and it was time to flower. Nearly every yard displayed some bright color besides the healthy hue of new grass that spread in dozens of shades of green until it met dull grey sidewalk. The flowers always caught her artist's eye, the colors themselves almost as much as the blooms that wore them. Even the smallest and most mundane of flower, that might actually be called a weed, caught her attention- tiny purple, yellow, blue and white, perfect miniatures, speckling the wonderful expanses of green.

Angus roamed both left and right and ever forward, ranging at the furthest extreme of his freedom, taking it all in, in ways she could only imagine, with a nose so big. She laughed a little at his version of homage to

154

the new beauty surrounding him, it seemed each new expression of life he met deserved he praise it by pissing on it. The only time he pulled his attention from the revival around him was those few occasions they passed someone. Those next few steps as a stranger drew near and then away, he drew back to her side as though she had actually trained him to do such things as heel. He remained there until he felt her again safe to be left unattended, then he'd continue sniffing and pissing his way to Genie's house.

Aizlyn and Angus arrived at Genie's house some forty-five minutes after Genie's phone call woke them. Aizlyn let them in and removed his leash as he was greeted by the dust-mop Genie had dubbed, appropriately, Scruffy. He promptly went to his belly to crawl around in a less intimidating greeting than he gave the bigger breeds, as she closed the door behind them and announced herself.

When Genie didn't answer she headed through the house, catching sight of the painting, hanging proud beside a curio cabinet full of fairies, next to one of her reading chairs in the den, as she made her way toward the basement stairs. Genie spent a good bit of her time in the basement, not only because it was where she did most of her artistic pursuits but because it was the one place she could smoke. Her husband rarely entered that part of their home, probably for that very reason. There was an ever-open window with an ashtray on the sill, right above the laundry table, in the corner she'd made into the walk-in-closet she'd always wanted. The ashtray was apparently made of some magical materials which he was somewhat disturbingly incapable of seeing.

Genie was sitting in an old recliner, which used to be blue, parked by the spinning washing machine, coffee perched precariously on the wide worn and stained padding of its arm rest. She was absorbed in a novel with some large tan brown-haired man on the front, a sword raised in one hand and a half-clad woman clinging to his thigh. She flipped a page, still unaware of Aizlyn's arrival, and exhaled her most recent drag out the side of her mouth in the direction of that open window. Obviously she had escaped into another romance novel, while awaiting Aizlyn's arrival, and was at an *entertaining* part.

Aizlyn flopped into the ancient padded rocker opposite her, giggling when that made Genie jump and splash a little of her coffee, adding to the stains on her chair. "Has he introduced her to the purple-headed love monster yet?"

"No, but he was worshiping at the mound of Venus when you so rudely interrupted him," Genie laughed, closing her book. "You certainly took long enough today."

"Sorry, dreaming about the cliffs again."

"Ahh," Genie smiled and set her novel aside, "you brought the journal?"

"Yeah," Aizlyn replied quizzically, "why?"

"I want a copy I can write on," Genie said. Picking up her coffee, she walked to the window and snuffed out her cigarette.

Genie came back holding out her hand and Aizlyn obliged her, digging through her purse, pulling out the journal, and plopping one of her most private possessions in her friend's care. She then rose and followed her back up the stairs to the den where a computer desk sat in the corner opposite her fairies, weighted down with all the gadgets and gizmos it could possibly hold. Genie paused, greeting Angus with her foot, where he lay sprawled in the center of the floor pawing the air playfully while Scruffy bounded around him, taunting him with one of her stuffed toys.

"Hello Monster, don't you let Scruffy kill ya," Genie said.

"You always say that," Aizlyn giggled, "but they love each other."

"Yeah, but one of these days Angus is gonna try to take one of her toys to play back, and choke when he swallows the toy and her both," Genie laughed.

Genie stepped over the dogs, and sat down at her desk while Aizlyn went around and sat in the reading chair, facing her. Genie proceeded to lay the journal open on her scanner page after page after page and Aizlyn quickly grew bored and got up to wander back into the kitchen.

"Why you want a copy?" Aizlyn called as she pulled open the fridge.

"Don't want me scratching notes all over your journal, do you?" Genie called back.

"What? Why?" Aizlyn asked, pushing some milk and juice around to see what treasures might lay behind them.

"I wanna try and put some order to them," Genie replied, "sorta like a time line."

Aizlyn didn't bother to mention, once again, that they we just as likely to be just weird dreams all from this one weird life. Instead she closed the fridge, having seen nothing that jumped up and said eat me, and turned to the cabinets.

"I baked brownies this morning," Genie called a few moments later, "they're in the oven still, staying warm."

"I love you," Aizlyn yelled, opening the oven and removing the treasure she'd sought and once again wondering where Genie got all her energy.

Aizlyn returned to the living room, one half-eaten brownie held between her lips and two more in her hand. "That all you wanted me for today?" she asked around her mouthful.

Genie stood without answering immediately and began collecting the stack of papers her printer had begun spewing. She was just finishing straightening the pages and had turned as if to answer Aizlyn when a knock sounded at the door.

"No," Genie said grinning, "I wanted you to meet someone."

Aizlyn suddenly wanted to run to the basement and hide. That grin spelled trouble. She couldn't imagine who Genie wanted her to meet but she was certain she wasn't dressed to be *meeting* anyone. Aizlyn felt suddenly self-conscious of the two-sizes-too-big and very loose-fit jeans that hung off her hips and the baggy tee-shirt with the faded beer logo on the front. She rarely cared what others thought, but if it was someone Genie thought she should meet, she felt like it might matter what they thought of her.

Genie went to the door and opened it wide, stepping forward and hugging a tall woman with short dark curls. As the woman came away, and was more visible, Aizlyn was relieved to see she also wore a worn old tee-shirt and faded jeans, though hers actually fit her right and the tee-shirt was a branded v-neck, not something given as a promotion at the bar years ago.

The woman also wore a large hazy purple crystal wrapped with wire so that it hung from a tarnished silver chain about her long sleek neck. Matching earrings hung long, accenting that swan-like neck all the more by peeking out beneath her short curls and still not touching her shoulders. She was thin, all legs and quite pretty. Aizlyn thought she finally understood what willowy meant as a quality descriptive. Part of her thought she'd make tons of money as a dancer with legs like that, but when she let out a happy laugh and a displayed a ready smile another part hoped the thought never crossed this girl's mind.

Genie introduced her.

"This is Dristy," Genie said, smiling big at Aizlyn's surprise. Then she laughed and added, "Dristy, meet Aizlyn also known as Miss Windell or Win, depending…"

Aizlyn had heard of Dristy many a time, she was a long-time friend of Genie's from back when Genie babysat for her entire neighborhood. Dristy was quite a bit younger, from what Aizlyn could understand, but had fit in and hung with the big girls just fine. Mostly they only got together for Renaissance fairs and such these days, or the occasional wedding or funeral of a mutual friend. That seemed to have a little bit to do with Dristy finally growing up, and Aizlyn had gathered that meant discovering serious dating.

From what Genie said, Dristy knew a lot about dreams and astrology and tarot and such, she was often the one Genie consulted on such things, Aizlyn was sure. Dristy was also very spiritual, and from what Aizlyn could understand, that meant she was multi-religious and somewhat pagan all at once. Aizlyn knew Dristy had been called upon to "meet the house," a few weeks back too. Aizlyn had long wanted to meet her on those merits alone, it had sounded like they would have a lot in common, but the occasion had never come up until now.

"I've been dying to meet you," Dristy said, stepping forward and hugging Aizlyn as though they were old friends just reunited. Aizlyn relaxed into the friendly hug quickly as Dristy added, "I have heard so much about you, I feel I've known you for ages."

"It's great to finally meet you, too," Aizlyn replied, stepping back and smiling up at the taller woman. "Dristy, very pretty name, it fits you."

"It means 'sight'," Dristy answered the compliment, "My mother was a bit of a hippy gypsy type, Genie can tell ya all about that, hell, she practically raised me. Mom was gone so much. Mom had grand *visions* of a fortune-telling daughter." Dristy laughed, adding, "There's much to be said about what a name brings the child it is given to, much like the placement of the planets and stars under which he or she is born. I like to blame my mom for pointing me in this direction every time I can't afford my car payment."

Aizlyn smiled again, and laughed, she liked Dristy already. Her opening sentences alone said they were bound to share many, many hours of interesting matches of theory ping pong. This was the kind of person to whom you could say, "so what if there were two lab technicians standing around taking notes and setting down criteria for their new experiment, one's name tag reads, Jehovah, the other's reads, Beelzebub..." and have a roaring good argument well through two pots of coffee.

"But those things only bring possibilities, maybe even probabilities, but not definite conclusions," Aizlyn countered comfortably.

Genie had begun leading them through the house to the back stairs and down to the basement, listening with a soft knowing smile on her face. Aizlyn found herself walking sideways down the back stairs to maintain an eye contact that told Dristy she was listening and wanted her to retort. This wasn't the feigned attention Win gave the woe-is-me customer, but honest interest, and Dristy sensed it as she continued.

"Well, I don't really blame my mom, it's just an old joke. I actually believe we come into each life with a certain amount of purpose in mind,"

Dristy explained more clearly. "Like we decide before returning that we want to be more outgoing and bold, maybe pursue a career we shied away from in a prior life which left us with a feeling we had missed something. So maybe we choose to be born under the sign of Leo; for a foot to be pre-placed on that path, which say, a less bold sign might have avoided again. I think I must have wanted this, constantly late on the bills or not."

They had all come to stand around the open window over the laundry table, back by the wall hung with shoe racks and dresses, hung under plastic, which Genie only wore on special occasions. They were in Genie's closet, and she caught a brief feeling of comfort seeing those things worn when celebrating with her in years past. Aizlyn stood facing Dristy, her back to millions of shoes, and "earmuffs" that passed for shoes, as Genie called her sexiest pairs that she collected obsessively.

"I can see that, in a way," Aizlyn said, feeling quite comfortable with this setting and her new friend as well as the conversation. "If we are to believe in reincarnation, then what of karma? What of the lives we *must* lead to repay our karmic debts for lives led poorly? You think someone would choose to come into a life knowing they were going to be poor due to a debt made in another life?"

"Of course!" Dristy laughed, "I am pleased with my life, just because I don't always have cash doesn't mean I am poor."

"That's not what I meant," Aizlyn tried quickly, but Dristy waved her hand as though no explanations were needed.

"I know what you meant, sweetie, all I meant was that I think it's all a choice." Dristy smiled and swayed slowly while talking. "That's the beauty of free will, I think I was and am *willing* to sacrifice one for the other, and peace of mind is more valuable to me than any car."

Aizlyn nodded her understanding and Dristy continued, "I think we choose each life, whether to pay debts, learn lessons, easy or hard, and walk in different shoes; we are not forced to. And I think we come into each life to learn and experience and understand whatever it is that we felt we hadn't the last time, which made us want to return. We choose to pay karmic debts to find equal footing on which to begin our real life's quest, that of achieving true inner peace, oneness with the universe. Otherwise we limit ourselves by feeling we do not deserve the good things we intuitively seek."

Aizlyn was about to counter when Dristy raised her hand, politely requesting she be allowed to finish before her statements were judged. Dristy appeared to be on a roll and afraid of losing track, so Aizlyn held her retort. She really liked this woman, she was intelligent, spoke her mind and wasn't afraid of how that would leave her perceived. It was one of the things she found so appealing about Genie. She also liked how Dristy fell into a slow sway, reminding her again of a willow, caught in a soft spring breeze, when she spoke. It was as though her words brought with them a comforting tune which only she could hear and dance to.

"Think about it; humans are the only things we know of in the universe that have such concepts as fairness, equality and justice; the only beings that *worry* about such things as what is deserved, worthy or earned." Dristy danced on, seeing Aizlyn was now fascinated and meant to let her finish. "Humanity has spent the entire history of its existence here on earth, fighting for these concepts; trying to project them from their hearts and minds onto everything around us, even others, with just as much free will. Problem is we see these concepts through our own eyes and our vision of fairness may not be another's. In trying to create a reality that can, as it spreads, evolve into *our* version of a utopian existence, sometimes we make awful mistakes, step on another's toes. It is part of what we are that we cannot help but seek to achieve these things, and yet we know that if they are not within they cannot be projected out; if we are not *worthy* we cannot *earn* them. Some take time accepting this natural intuition, wasting much energy making war with themselves, but mostly it is a part of us from the beginning. And it would be hypocrisy, which we could not bear and still seek fairness, if we did not pay our own debts. We must find equal ground by accepting the justice we demanded of ourselves by living as another might have had to because of us and our lack of vision in lives before, so that in future lifetimes we can be worthy of inner peace we now feel we have justly earned the right to."

"Wow." Aizlyn's head was spinning but Dristy lit a cigarette and just kept going, it seemed, since that inner chord had been stuck and she had found her rhythm and was dancing wildly away with it.

"My mother wanted me to have vision, foresight, to avoid problems she had stumbled blindly into throughout her life," Dristy continued, swaying slowly back and forth, exhaling her smoke at methodical intervals which were somewhat hypnotic. "She found all the names in all the baby books that even hinted at such ability and waited for one to jump off the page for her. Some mothers are further along, more in tune, they go with it when a name jumps off a page, taking the subconscious push the soul growing within them gives them, when it sees something that says to it what it is they wish to achieve when they arrive.

"Some mothers simply take someone else's lead and name a child after some relative or other they loved and respected, essentially asking that unborn child follow in that person's foot steps. Others still invent a name, give it meaning all their own and imbue it with all the hope and power of their own wishes for their offspring. You've heard of powerful names, though very used and often worn, like John or James, they have sent many a man down an amazing path. I'm sure you've even heard of cursed names too, like the surname Kennedy.

"Hopefully the name is well-chosen and it is not an unwarranted or unwanted path the child is then set to. See, we may have perfectly well-planned lives in mind when we decide to come back, but often what memories we have which made us decide on that path in the first place fade quickly from the moment we are born. We tend to forget and end up following what clues remain, our birth sign, our parents and what they teach us, and hopefully a well-chosen name. If we have set the plan in motion well, then all will come about just as we had hoped. We will have a life full of coincidences that are not coincidence and déjà vu moments because a small part of us is reminded by certain events of the plan we had."

"Yeah, like that," Aizlyn replied thoughtfully, lighting herself a cigarette now too.

"Take Genevieve here," Dristy said, snuffing out her smoke but never breaking the rhythm of the slow dancing in place, which she had begun while speaking, "She assures me, though she has yet to allow me to do a past life regression on her, that she has always been a woman. I tend to agree. I've known her since we were six and I think she has not only always been a woman but a darn good mother many times over. She's got it down, she'd comfortable with it, she exudes it and it draws others who seek the same easy peace from life. Did you know her name means woman?"

"Really," Aizlyn grinned at Genie, "yeah, it fits."

"You know what your name means?" Dristy asked then.

"No," Aizlyn answered honestly, still trying to absorb Dristy's whole theory and laughing at the sheer scope of that project, "I never thought that much about it until now."

"Well, I have spent a lifetime thinking about such things, and your first name means dream," Dristy said, watching Aizlyn's face for reaction. Getting the look of surprise she expected, she added, "Your mother did well, fits you good, doesn't it?"

"Hell ya," Aizlyn replied, only a little bit freaked out, the cows were just winking and dinking again and she was used to that. Apparently, if Dristy was right, that was a good thing, it meant she was following the path she'd set herself to before birth.

Aizlyn caught Genie's eye briefly and saw the bubbling happiness kept just barely beneath her surface. She realized this was the thing she had been planning, not just her meeting another of her oldest and dearest friends, but her being made to see a whole other world of possible explanations for her present state than her being merely insane. She was suddenly struck with how quickly Dristy had pulled her in, hypnotist to the core, her speech and slow sway had seduced Aizlyn into shutting down her ever argumentative side and simply listening. It felt right though, so even having noted it, she didn't fight it, she just continued, along for the dance.

"Here's the interesting part, though," Dristy said, smiling her pleasure at saving what she felt was the best part for last and having won Aizlyn's complete attention this afternoon, "Your surname, the name you most definitely chose by choosing the parents you did before your birth, means "walker." You are Dream Walker, I assume that means you sought to walk or journey through your dreams, and they are meant to take you somewhere or show you something."

"So Genie keeps telling me," Aizlyn responded, glancing again at that one's smiling face, and hearing "I-told-you-so's" in her head, which she meant to hush just for old time's sake. "One problem though, I got the last name from my grandfather, an unfortunate story I won't go into now, but suffice to say it's not from my real father. I don't even know his last name."

"I have heard the story from Genie. We spoke again this morning about your dinner conversation," Dristy replied nonplused. "Ever thought that's how you planned it, how it was meant to be?"

Aizlyn paused for a moment and remembered the swift way in which her hurt feelings about her lack of a father, and how that had come to be, had fled after reading her mother's letters. She hadn't really minded, just having his first name had been enough. Her grandfather had been all the "Papa" a girl could ask for, as far as she was concerned, and that still felt like the end of it. Aizlyn decided somewhat grudgingly that Dristy was probably right, if she had chosen this life, then she had chosen this family, and the last name it would get her must then have been chosen as well.

"So you don't believe in fate," Aizlyn asked of Dristy then, "like it was maybe just destiny I be born a Cancer and be named what I was? Like maybe the fates thought it an amusing game."

"I didn't say that, not really" Dristy replied, "just, each thing, your sign, your name, and the parents you choose, they are only parts of the bigger picture, things we choose to equip ourselves with at the outset of each life, to use as tools in accomplishing the tasks we set ourselves to that time around. I don't think it is required that I take anything from such concepts as fate and destiny with that belief. Both can be a part of the puzzle that is each lifetime's quest, even all of them as a whole. You could just as well say, '*it is my fate* to be destitute this life because I was greedy and hoarded or squandered wealth in the last one' as you could say, '*I chose* to live poor this life because in my last life I had it all and took it for granted, learning nothing.' The point remains that the quest for balance and inner peace is begun with certain tools equipped for the tasks in mind which we feel will help us attain our goal in the end. We outfit ourselves as best we can for the journey by choosing such things we can: parents, signs, etcetera, before we begin."

"But either way you are still saying that destiny is not really destiny as most people think of it," Aizlyn responded, thinking Genie and Dristy must have talked long and hard planning this meeting for Dristy to have so many answers ready on her tongue. She wasn't quite sure how to feel about that, adding, "You are saying destiny is merely the path we set ourselves to each life, not something beyond our control. Which, though that would explain such things as déjà vu or precognition, when we see things occur or feel they are about to because we chose them to before we were born, it does not explain the very first time."

"First time?" Dristy glanced inquisitively at Genie, as if to say, "what is she talking about?"

Aizlyn was proud she'd found something they hadn't thought of and prepared for. You'd have thought Aizlyn had spouted words in Indian that she couldn't understand and felt Genie could translate as Dristy's constant sway faltered. Genie merely looked back and forth between them, enjoying witnessing their debate but having no intention of joining in. Genie lifted a shoulder and looked from Aizlyn back to Dristy, effectively passing her turn.

Aizlyn ashed her cigarette and took a deep breath. It was hard for her to put the concept into words but she had to try, if she was going to display her puzzle she might as well explain how she thought they might help her solve it. "I want to know what caused the initial event or choice that sets us off balance in the first place. I want to figure out where the forever chain of questing to right ourselves is mounted and I want to rip it from the wall. I want to break the chain."

Dristy and Genie both laughed then. Aizlyn paused, casting a questioning glance at Genie, wondering what it was they found so funny. She had been trying quite hard to express a feeling, and they were laughing? Genie nodded her head toward the window and Aizlyn followed her gaze. She saw she had been smashing the butt of her cigarette into the window sill rather than the ashtray and it appeared she had been for a minute with quite a bit of frustration. It took Aizlyn a second but she eventually laughed too, seeing how her unconscious venting could indeed be amusing. She didn't laugh long though, for some reason she thought it very important that both of them, especially Dristy, understood what exactly she had meant.

"Would not that first wrong turn *have* to be *fated?*" Aizlyn said, wiping at the sill with beer-bottle calloused fingers absently and struggling with her words, trying to make that darn light in that corner of her mind work for more than just a second. "I mean, if on the first go-round you had no prior concepts of your destiny, no debts you needed to pay, no career you regretted not perusing, what sets the path, allowing for that first inevitable mistake? Why risk it, why come?" She looked up and back to Genie, as if, of the two of them, that one had to understand her. "I'm not saying I regret being here, by any means. I'm just wondering, if we know so much before we come why would we *choose* to mess up that balance in the first place?"

Aizlyn grinned then, adding sarcastically, "I hate to think that at some point, an eternity ago, I said to myself, 'Hey, let's go down there and make a big old mess so that hundreds of years from now we can be reborn, an emotionally fractured schizophrenic, haunted by the memories of a million screw-ups and completely out of control of our senses and then see if we can fix it. That ought to be fun! I love puzzles!' I mean, I understand what you are saying about one person's version of fairness versus another's and the stepping on toes and owing penance, but what I'm getting at is, where did it start? Wouldn't true fairness, something we are supposed to be born with the concept of, entail instinctually allowing for each to have their right to their versions of that fairness? That is, if we start off knowing so much. If so, when and why did I jump off the cliff with my friends and start making

166

mistakes?" Aizlyn smiled a bit bitterly. "Unless you are you a believer in original sin, a burden shouldered by all for the first. Can your theories tell me what started the chain in the first place and how the hell does one break it? That's what I *need* to know!"

"Good question," Dristy paused thoughtfully, rhythm completely broken, as if Aizlyn had stepped on her foot. "I had never thought about the very first time a soul comes through, whether what burdens they shoulder and lessons they are set to learn would be pre-ordained by some other entity or an event they hadn't taken part in themselves. Maybe a first-time soul views what goes on down here and says, 'I want to go and experience that love thing.' Well, that's a tall order. It would set them on a path all right, fated in a very wide way, not yet as defined by debts and lessons and regrets needing set to right, but definitely destined to experience much that leaves room for the need for penance to be made later." Dristy laughed suddenly, seeming to have gotten lost. "Holy cow, girly, what a tangled web you weave."

"Told you she would warp your noggin," Genie interjected, looking at Dristy. "The girl has a mind as convoluted as her problems."

"Well, I still say it's a good thing we all met this lifetime," Dristy laughed again, undaunted. "I'll take it as a sign that she has been able to stump me. Maybe she is meant to expand my beliefs and sharpen my vision as much as my beliefs and vision are meant to help clarify some things for her."

"Yeah, maybe, I don't believe in coincidence," Aizlyn said, smiling her amusement at Genie's assessment of her. "And it was three thirty-three when I left the house today."

"So you pay attention to the signs too, then?" Dristy asked, obviously finding another point on which she could expound upon for hours and beginning to sway slowly, hearing that inner tune again.

"You mean like when a bird flies over my head and shits on me right after I yell at the universe, 'what next?'" Aizlyn laughed at the memory and Genie and Dristy laughed with her, imagining the scene. "How could I not?"

"Yeah, something like that," Dristy said, still giggling. "The more common signs that *normal* people encounter are like what you just said, when your eyes seem inexplicably drawn to your clock just as it reads triple threes."

"Yes, I've seen that quite a few times," Aizlyn admitted. "Or triple fours."

"Threes are commonly believed to be the universe saying yes," Dristy said. "Triple fours are a way of it telling us no."

Suddenly Aizlyn froze. She hadn't even realized she'd been swaying slightly in time with Dristy's inner tune as they talked, until she did. Her breath caught and her heart jumped, she felt sure something was behind her, something that shouldn't be. She was afraid to look. She'd had so many strange feelings lately, like feeling she showered under a waterfall rather than her own prefab stall, her senses playing games with her. Normally she wouldn't have admitted anything out of the ordinary was occurring. She'd have tried to hide it, as she had tried and failed at the bar, when Gamble had noticed anyway, but this was Genie.

"What is behind me?" she managed to whisper.

"A three-year-old girl, I believe she died in the twenties," Genie said, nonchalant, then laughed at Aizlyn's shock. "She likes playing in my shoes."

"Damn woman," Aizlyn shivered, still unwilling to turn around, "you keep the oddest company."

"I know," Genie replied playfully, "you guys keep me amused."

Aizlyn would never get used to the way Genie drew things. Everyone loved her, *everyone*, and a part of her knew it was because of her easy acceptance of absolutely everything, her grain of salt way of bouncing through life, no matter what it presented her, leaving joy in her wake. Aizlyn tended to fade happily into her shadow and merely bask in the cool comfort when they were together. She enjoyed being with someone who could so easily outshine her. She had a deep distaste for being judged on her looks alone, they helped Win earn the money but Miss Windell preferred to hide out in sweats and slip through life unnoticed. Aizlyn simply loved being able to make a choice, she loved that she could be herself with Genie, that she had found herself with Genie.

"You are such the perpetual mother, everyone and everything is almost too at ease with you, Genie. You obviously are at one with you." Aizlyn said suddenly, "Why did you come back?"

"What?" Genie asked, bemused. She noted with no small amount of pleasure Aizlyn seemed to have accepted that she, at least, had lived before.

"You seem so settled and sure," Aizlyn said, looking thoughtfully at her best friend's ever ready smile, "it would seem you have no debts, no regrets, and no lessons knocking down your door. You float through each day and it is all good. You know so much, intuitively, almost like a damn mind reader, and you are so at peace with everything, what in the world did you come back for?"

"Because sometimes we don't come back for ourselves," Genie answered, smile never wavering and eyes returning Aizlyn's steady thoughtful gaze. "Sometimes we come back for those we love."

Aizlyn was considering Genie's words, dissecting them for every possible meaning. She might have actually formed a few questions had she not noticed Dristy had moved quietly around her and now knelt at her back. She was completely thrown off track when she heard Dristy whispering. It took some major self-convincing to get herself to turn around as she made out the other woman's words.

"Don't be afraid," Dristy whispered again.

"I'm good," Aizlyn whispered back now kneeling beside Dristy, facing all the shoes and seeing nothing scary except an extreme expression of a major shoe fetish.

"Not you, dear," Dristy giggled softly, "this beautiful little girl."

Dristy held out her hand as though coaxing a feral cat from beneath a bush with a can of smelly fish parts. Aizlyn couldn't see this "beautiful little girl" that apparently played somewhere before them, but she tried to make herself small and not the least bit intimidating as Dristy continued to talk.

""You can not wait here forever," Dristy seemed to tell the shoes. "You need to move on, choose the next path, dear one."

"She will, when she is ready, Dristy," Genie said from over their shoulders, looking down at a shoe which lay away from the others, with her hands on her hips, looking every inch the perpetual mother Aizlyn had just likened her to. Not coaxing really, just applying patient pressure toward the right, she said, "Put my shoes back when you are done."

"And you say I am odd," Aizlyn said, standing and moving back toward the open window to light a suddenly much-needed cigarette.

"You are," Genie said laughing. "What we mean to discover is why."

"What?" Aizlyn asked, feeling Dristy return to stand beside her and looking from one to the other of them.

"Let me hypnotize you," Dristy said then, "let's find out once and for all if your dreams are, indeed, past life memories or if this is your first time here and this puzzle is just the beginning."

"Whoa, wait a minute," Aizlyn said, taking a step back, subconsciously heading for the ever-open window, "I've seen that shit at comedy clubs."

"I would never," Dristy said seriously, but couldn't help but laugh as Aizlyn eyed her suspiciously. "No, really, I wouldn't. Genie wouldn't let me even if I would, and she'll be here the whole time."

"Oh yes she would," Aizlyn countered, switching her gaze to her best friend's now laughing visage. "She'd record it and play it at my wedding."

Part 2

The Past

10

Aizlyn: Dream

It took much pinky swearing and laughter, not to mention the placement of every battery in the house that might work in a camera in Aizlyn's possession, to be hidden by her, but they managed to convince her to submit to Dristy's mental ministrations. At some point the prospect of finding answers to questions Genie kept prodding and reminding her she couldn't escape outweighed the thought of some embarrassing footage held for later giggles at her expense.

They had joked and poked in good-natured jest for nearly thirty minutes, but then Dristy suddenly got down to business. She went upstairs and out the front door to return moments later with an antique-looking bag that reminded Aizlyn of those carried by old-time doctors on house calls.

Dristy had pulled a good many things from this bag, and before long Aizlyn was reminded of a good old-fashioned witch more so than a doctor. Dristy had pulled a few scarves from her bag's seemingly bottomless depths and draped them over the lamps and windows that lit the basement. This dimmed the whole area to near darkness were it not for the indirect light of late afternoon coming from the open window.

Dristy then pulled out a deck of large cards and handed them to Aizlyn, telling her to shuffle them while asking them for answers. Aizlyn shuffled the cards idly, finding that task was not a hard one at all. Her mind wandering quickly from question to question, wondering which it was she wanted answered first. Those cards were hearing questions all right, she thought, maybe too many.

Aizlyn was still shuffling when she smelled home, the familiar scent of Nag Hampa incense floating past her nose on its way out the window. She couldn't help but smile then, realizing this must have been well-planned in advance. Genie must have had this day up her sleeve for quite awhile. She was caught up in the scent and lost track of the thought though, she was back in India in dance class, her teacher lighting incense and starting the music. She shuffled cards and asked them questions as the other two women moved purposefully about her on another plane.

Dristy rubbed oils that also smelled familiar, only vaguely, down candles which also came forth from her bottomless bag. Blue, purple, white, each came forth and was anointed with what Aizlyn thought she remembered somehow was myrrh. Each candle was told its purpose and set to its corner. There was no music set to playing though, other than the drums which called to her hips from a memory her nose recalled for her of home. A blank tape was placed in the deck after Dristy and Genie discussed whether they should put on something or simply record. She smiled at the cows as they winked and dinked and thought to herself, "I have music already."

They spread a thick soft blanket that seemed furry over a bed-sized mat woven of thin straw. Aizlyn watched them as if from a distance, noting a small white label attached to the mat standing upright beside her big toe, that said, "made in Thailand." Aizlyn was amused when the words caught her focus, as so much that should be right then was seemingly incapable of. She kept shuffling, asking questions and dancing in her memories.

Suddenly Dristy was holding out a hand to her and without thinking she held out the cards.

"Keep one," Dristy said quietly.

Aizlyn drew one from the deck and left the remainder in Dristy's care. Then Genie was helping her from the old rocker. It felt odd when she came to sit on the floor, Genie and Dristy in front of her and to either side;

the world had quit rocking. Dristy lit the candle in the shallow bowl in front of her then went to sit behind her own, and Genie and she lit theirs in unison. Dristy reached up and removed the crystal from her neck, letting it hang from its chain before her, and Aizlyn was suddenly struck by the realization she had probably been mildly hypnotized all along by watching Dristy sway with that crystal around her neck the entire time they had talked.

Good thing these women were friends.

"One last thing though, Genie," Aizlyn said, forcing herself to focus and worriedly looking at Genie. "Please, don't let me get so deep I forget to breath or blow my head off. I don't want to know if my brain will believe it enough to shut down and stop my heart. Okay?"

Dristy began swinging the crystal slowly back and forth and the flickering light of the three candles seemed to reflect in its hazy depths a million possibilities. Aizlyn pulled her eyes away for just a second and smiled warmly at Genie, her eyes letting her best friend know she was trusting her with everything. Outside the open window the light spring rain Aizlyn had smelled on her walk here finally started to fall with a soft rhythm that matched the crystals' slow sway.

"I'll miss you while I'm gone," Aizlyn said, trying to make light of her fears and turning back to the crystal.

"No, you won't," Genie said, allowing herself a knowing smile as she reached out and hit the record button on the portable player she had taken from Nathan's room that morning.

"I want you to listen to me, Aizlyn," Dristy said, across the dimness, lit only by candles and shimmer and wink of the working crystal. "I want you to trust me and allow your mind to rest easy. I want you to take me for a walk, show me where you find your inner rest."

"Follow Angus," Aizlyn whispered, eyes already very heavy, a small smile on her face.

Dristy cut her eyes toward Genie in mild confusion, as if to say, "who is Angus?" and "never heard that before," but she quickly regained her composure and said, "Follow Angus, he is going to lead you to a peaceful place where your mind can rest." Dristy's soft monotone was lulling and seductive and Aizlyn saw Angus's tail wagging before her. "Keep following Angus but when you hear me say 'peaches' come back. Follow Angus. Follow Angus. Follow Angus."

Dristy repeated this mantra over and over until Aizlyn seemed to lose her spine completely. She slumped, visibly relaxed and completely at ease. Genie reached behind her and pulled out the stack of scanned journal pages and a notebook she had stashed under her recliner. Quickly she scratched "follow Angus" at the top of the first blank page of the notebook.

"Aizlyn, I want you to flip through your memories, see them like a photo album viewed from back to front. You are looking at the very last page, it is where you are now. I want you to go back, back a few pages." Dristy paused a moment then said, "Where are you?"

"At home," Aizlyn replied in a happy little girl voice.

"How old are you?" Dristy asked.

"Nine." Aizlyn made a small smile.

"You are happy?" Dristy questioned.

"Yes," Aizlyn giggled.

"Why are you happy?"

"I didn't dance," Aizlyn giggled again. "I did it right!"

Dristy glanced questioningly at Genie, and Genie too looked puzzled as she made a note of Aizlyn's apparent pleasure beside the words: Aizlyn, this life, age nine. Dristy waited for her to finish writing by the meager light they had left and set the book back into her lap.

"Go back a little further," Dristy said then. "Where are you?"

"At home," Aizlyn said in a small almost sad voice that Genie hardly recognized.

"Where is home?" Dristy prompted.

"India."

"How old are you?' Dristy asked, still trying to pinpoint how far back they had gone.

"Six," Aizlyn replied in that sad small voice.

"Why are you sad?" Dristy asked.

"I don't want to dance," Aizlyn said simply, 'but I am afraid I will anyway."

"Why?"

"Because Jordan is here," Aizlyn responded, drooping her head.

Dristy glanced again at Genie and Genie nodded, writing another short note in her book. Then Genie nodded again a short jerk of her head which said, "farther."

"Where are you?" Dristy began again.

"Home," Aizlyn answered in a much more normal voice.

"Where is that?" Dristy prompted, made hopeful by that familiar sounding adult voice that they had gone back to a past life that might hold answers.

"India," Aizlyn answered, revealing no emotion that Genie might note.

Dristy was thoughtful a moment, looking to Genie again, then said, "How old are you?"

"Seventeen," Aizlyn replied.

Genie smiled and winked at Dristy. They had done it! Genie knew Aizlyn had left India at twelve and never returned. She made an excited motion with her free hand for Dristy to start pumping her for information before bending to see by the dim candle light to scratch another quick note.

"What are you doing?" Dristy began.

"Watching the other girls practice," Aizlyn responded, still pretty much emotionless.

"Practice what?" Dristy asked.

"The dance," Aizlyn answered.

"You don't dance with them?" Dristy looked confused toward Genie as if to say, "I thought she danced."

"No," Aizlyn replied, the answer short but again betraying no hint of how she felt about that.

"Why not?"

"I can't," Aizlyn said, "I broke my hip over three years ago."

Dristy arched an eyebrow at Genie. This wasn't meshing very well with the dreams Genie described as disturbing her friend. Genie shrugged a shoulder, telling her she wasn't sure what was going on either, then scratched something on the page before her and held it out for Dristy to see.

"Have you ever been away from India?" Dristy asked her then.

"I could only dream," came the cryptic reply.

Genie gave up and leaned into Dristy, whispering in her ear, "I know in at least one life, she danced, won the prince, and was unhappy and then, maybe in a different one, she somehow ended up in Europe. In the one she was a man she went to Europe, presumably, if we are dealing with a karmic loop, to find someone or something there again which had made her happy the first time. She dreams those things too much and I remember her, I was drawn as much to her as she was to me. I know I've never been to India, she is obviously a woman..." Genie stopped dead, struck by an idea. "Find out what year this is, there may be even more lives we don't know about."

Genie went back to making her hasty notes by the dim light, and Dristy did as she was asked as best she could.

"What else do you see, besides the girls dancing?" Dristy questioned.

"I see Jordan," Aizlyn replied as emotionless as before.

Genie's head jerked up and again she glanced at Dristy giving her the "get me more" signal with her free hand.

"What is Jordan doing?" Dristy stumbled blindly, not really knowing at this point where to take the conversation to get what Genie needed.

"He's leaning on that new contraption of his," Aizlyn said in a monotone, "watching the girls."

"New contraption?" Dristy asked, truly confused now.

"He calls it an automobile," Aizlyn explained thoughtlessly, finally showing some emotion, as she said the word like it tasted bad, then added, "I call it stinky and noisy, when he tries to impress me with it. He has offered to take me for a jaunt in it.'"

"Do you know what kind of car it is?" Dristy prompted, hopeful she'd found a means to date this life.

"A Model T Ford," Aizlyn replied in a put-on man-voice that said that was how she'd heard it and probably too often.

Dristy looked at Genie again; there was their answer. This couldn't be the right life, Genie had said the dreams seemed to be set in a time when there would be long houses in use and Crusaders, knights on horseback. She leaned into Genie, interrupting her furious note taking.

"I think we have stumbled onto yet another life here, dear," Dristy whispered in Genie's ear, "and I think we now know for sure that Jordan has been a part of more than just this life. If you are right then we know they've known each other at least twice before, once when she danced and regretted it and this one, when she broke her hip and couldn't.'"

"But how does she feel about him then?" Genie wanted to know, "when he is not her husband?"

"Do you like Jordan?" Dristy asked then.

"We talk," Aizlyn said nonchalantly, but then suddenly she smiled a small smile, adding, "really shouldn't, but we do, Father is lenient with me. He says a man shouldn't share such time with a woman, not his wife, but I am not really a woman now, am I? I am a cripple with a woman's ear, enlightening to him at times, and he says I make him laugh. Father likes that Jordan looks well on our family, Jordan's family has wealth and influence. So he allows him to come with gifts of coffee and sweets and borrow my ear when his women confuse him. It is enough for Father to look beyond convention."

"But do you like him?" Dristy tried again.

"I would call him a friend, if it were not so strange a thing to think," Aizlyn responded, thoughtful now. "I think he treats me as one. He has gone far beyond merely making amends, though I still feel that it was meant that his horse was spooked by that over-large mongrel and ran upon me that day three years ago." She gave a small laugh. "He says he is going to go over my head and have my father *make* me try a ride in his noisy new motor car saying, 'I should know the feel of wind in my hair again since *that* horse took from me the ability to ride.' As if he needs my father to make me, does he forget who he is when he is with me?"

"So you are happy with your relationship with him?" Dristy clarified.

"I like it far better than were I one of those he beds eagerly but never thinks to have a decent conversation with." Aizlyn said with another small smile. "I feel I have the better of his company."

"Take her further back then," Genie said, after nodding and making a note on the page before her.

"Where are you?" Dristy began again, after pushing Aizlyn back to what she hoped was yet another life.

"Home," came the now usual reply, only this time a bit breathless and with some liveliness about it.

"Where is home?" Dristy asked again, intrigued as she saw Aizlyn seemed to be trying to catch her breath.

Genie looked up, vigilant now, remembering Aizlyn's fear of forgetting to breathe and thinking she needed to keep a close eye on this conversation. Hyperventilation would be no better, she thought.

"India," Aizlyn answered. Again the reply was short and breathless.

"What are you doing?" Dristy didn't need Genie's hand signals to prompt her, she couldn't help but ask.

"Washing clothes," Aizlyn fairly huffed now.

Dristy cast yet another questioning glance at Genie, Genie returned it and they leaned their heads close together. "She is supposed to be a princess, why is she doing laundry? You know, she actually sounds happy about it too," Dristy whispered.

"I dunno," Genie whispered back, "that's your department, ask her."

"You seem happy," Dristy prompted.

"Because I am," Aizlyn said. Then growing thoughtful, she added, "To some degree."

"Why is that?"

"Because I didn't want to marry him," Aizlyn said with a small smile.

"Marry who?" Dristy felt she knew the answer but wasn't taking any chances, too many things weren't what she had expected after her many conversations with Genie.

"Prince Jordan," Aizlyn replied.

Genie wrote a quick note and shuffled through the pages she'd copied. Genie was just becoming annoyed that neither of them was speaking to her when some part of her realized Aizlyn's heavy breathing had stopped. Genie looked up and was shocked to see Aizlyn had straightened and was looking toward the stairs. For a split second she thought Aizlyn had somehow woken until she saw her eyes seemed a good way off. She moved her hand in front of Aizlyn's eyes and got no response, then she too turned and looked toward the stairs. She knew she would not see what Aizlyn was seeing off in the distance of her memory, but she was unable to stop herself from looking anyway. She nearly fell over when she suddenly saw Angus descending the stair.

Genie would have laughed had it not been so damn weird and felt so inappropriate. She froze instead when she noted the dog's posture. Angus *stalked* toward them, obviously aware something was wrong with his human, as Aizlyn stared toward him with unseeing eyes. He paused stiffly at the edge of the blanket, took in the two women with his human and seemed to try to decide if they were responsible for her state.

Genie was actually on the verge of fear as the huge dog she had been comfortable with for years seemed to take forever to make up his mind about Dristy and herself and what needed to be done about their presence in this situation. Dristy had simply frozen, this was her first view of the dog and it wasn't a comforting sight at all. Genie was just about to holler "peaches" to save both their skin, as the dog's unwavering stare slowly eroded her composure. But suddenly he simply stepped forward onto the blanket and lay down, slow and gentle, resting his head in Aizlyn's lap and looking up at her, worry written on him as plainly as any human could wear it.

Dristy sucked in a deep breath of relief in perfect harmony with Genie, but neither had time to exhale. Aizlyn's eyes dropped to her lap and her hand came up and rested on his head. Again Genie questioned whether Aizlyn had woken and was playing some game with them. Genie raised her hand slowly, cautiously eyeing Angus as she waved it before Aizlyn's eyes again, and again, no one flinched but Dristy, not even Angus, whose eyes remained faithfully glued to his human.

"Hello, Angus," Aizlyn crooned, scratching the head that rested in her lap.

Dristy and Genie both let out explosive exhales they hadn't even realized they'd been holding onto, eyes flying impossibly wide. They looked quick askance at each other, as if the other were going to explain what was happening. Genie was the first to find and make her voice work.

"How does she know he is here?" Genie demanded in a loud whisper that betrayed her near panic of moments before. "Is she awake?"

"I dunno. I mean, no," Dristy stuttered, still scared half-witless the dog was going to lunge and kill her at any moment. She exhaled heavily again and tried to calm and order her thoughts, "She is definitely still under. She can't *know* he is *here* but maybe she senses him on a level. Or maybe...oh my..."

"What?" Genie demanded.

"He may be there with her now," Dristy whispered, as though the thought were taboo and should not really have been spoken aloud.

"You mean he just walked up to her in the past too?" Genie asked trying to grasp it. "Dogs have more than one life?"

"Hell, I dunno, this is some uncharted shit for me, on so many levels," Dristy admitted.

"Well, just ask her," Genie said, determined to figure this business out for her girlfriend and see her laughing someday as she did in her dreams.

She refused to be deterred by the unknown or some freaky incident with her monstrous dog.

"Will he hurt me?" Dristy asked, nodding at the huge dog that lay a mere two feet from her now, eyeing the two of them as they talked.

"I don't think so," Genie said, not as sure at that moment as she'd like to be but trying to sound it. "If anything, her talking to us should make him more comfortable with us and this situation."

Dristy took a deep breath, noted that Aizlyn now stared blankly ahead as though searching a distance they couldn't see again, which, though far more unnerving than her posture of head down and eyes closed of moments before, was still better than her looking at her dog as though she saw him. She plunged, "Do you have a dog?"

"No," Aizlyn replied, appearing to have caught her breath completely now but still sounding inexplicably pleased.

"Is there a dog there with you?" Dristy tried, letting out a sigh of relief when the dog *there* with *her* turned his head back to Aizlyn and seemed to nuzzle in her lap to fall asleep.

"Yes."

"What is his name?" Dristy said, slowly finding an acceptable heart rate and putting her bravery back to work for her.

"Angus," Aizlyn replied, destroying her composure all over again by looking down and scratching the dog's head again.

Aizlyn's eyes were still very distant, yet she seemed to see Angus was there, head resting in her lap, in another lifetime. It took another few moments of paced breathing and a whole lot of prompting from Genie, but eventually Dristy was back in control. Genie was still putting something together quickly in her mind; something about bleeding gums and reddened ankles but it wasn't quite finished yet so she said nothing about it.

"How do you know Angus?" Dristy asked finally, earning herself a winning smile from Genie for it.

"I fed him," Aizlyn said smiling, her gaze still unseeing of the present but cast down at her dog's head.

"*Why* did you feed him?" Dristy queried, still very confused why someone meant to be a princess, whether they got out of marriage to a prince or not, should feed dogs and do laundry. "Because he was left behind, when his master set sail," Aizlyn said, appearing almost evasive.

"Who is his master?" Dristy prompted.

"I am not to speak of him," Aizlyn said a little worriedly.

"Why?" Dristy was now intrigued more so than freaked out. The dog had fallen asleep it seemed, and that helped.

"My father was very angry when he saw me in his company. Very angry!" Aizlyn said. "He wanted to have done with me for shame but my mother begged him for my life."

"Why?" Dristy was shocked, a life-threatening offense, being seen with another person?

Aizlyn looked very worried still but she answered softly, as if confiding in a trusted friend, "He said I am too bold, that I should have averted my eyes from the foreigner, that I brought shame on our house by staring as I did. He will not forgive me that the prince has retracted his proposal now, that people still whisper. He says the foreigners brought dissention and sickness and nothing good and now they have tainted me. I am to be as a slave now and be glad I have breath."

"Angus's master is a foreigner? From where?" Dristy pushed, her answer as to why Aizlyn did laundry only prompting more questions.

"Britain," Aizlyn whispered, as though she were frightened someone might overhear her.

"Why is he there in India?"

"He returned three months ago with the trading company," Aizlyn said, her worry pushing her voice up a notch as she added, "now he closes his trades, and ends his business here, the fighting is grown out of control. He means to take Angus home now they have been reunited. I only meant to say goodbye to Angus, he was merely thanking me for having cared for him." Aizlyn's features and voice fairly pleaded for lenient understanding, then her expressive face drew closed. "I can speak of him no more."

Genie looked hard at Dristy when their eyes met again, in confusion and no small amount of worry too. She whispered, "You need to get a name."

Dristy stared at Genie a long moment. "You said not to push her, we both know she feels these things too well. If she stops breathing in her dreams…" Dristy bit her lip and added, "There is something terribly wrong with this whole regression, she offers too much, gives too expressive of answers… She is too in the moment, you'd think she feels she is talking to someone she knows."

Genie's look said she refused to budge.

Dristy sighed her resignation, hoping she wasn't pushing too hard, she said, "Just tell me one last thing and I will ask you no more of him. What is Angus's master's name?"

Aizlyn's eyes flew wide with fright. "I cannot dare speak his name! I should not even know it!"

"Please," Dristy said, cutting a condemning eye at Genie who looked pained but determined, "I just need to know that and I will leave you to your laundry."

Aizlyn's head jerked up again and once more she stared toward the stairs, though her memory showed a far different view. Her eyes became impossibly wide and her face suddenly registered fear and heartbreakingly recognizable pleasure in horrifyingly beautiful contrast. Genie noted this on her friend's face and held her breath, the word "peaches" hanging on the very edge of her tongue. She wanted desperately to know what Aizlyn was seeing that brought that pleasure, but was frightened as hell of what brought the fear with it. Genie's arm shot out and gripped Dristy's, unconsciously, in frightened anticipation.

"Sir Rune," Aizlyn nearly cried, "you cannot be here!"

Genie exhaled sharply, hand twitching the pencil it held, torn between writing it down and her unwillingness to tear her eyes away from Aizlyn's as she watched them fill with tears right before her. The moment stretched so long the spell had nearly broken on its own, so when Aizlyn spoke again both women jumped reflexively and quickly looked behind them to where Aizlyn focused.

"Please, you must stop, you must let me go. I can not...," Aizlyn cried, a single tear running down her cheek as Genie and Dristy hastily turned back to her, now unable to look away again. "He will hunt us, without mercy. He will kill me, if not you too."

Genie felt her own eyes well up and looked at Dristy, about to tell her to take her further back, that they had tortured her with that life enough. They had stumbled on still another life, tellingly sad, but giving no true answers to the dreams Genie held photocopied in her lap. She had yet to find any correlation between what she heard and those pages, no single glaring clue with which to solve their mystery. She'd neither heard nor read anything of Aizlyn ever dreaming of being in India at any point during the time the East India Trading Company had occupied it. Genie would write down what they had already learned, in case it was later useful, but she was unwilling to torment her further or watch another tear fall.

"Go farther..."

Genie's choked whisper to Dristy was cut off and swallowed, in Aizlyn's terrified, quiet yelp. The dog flinched and bared his teeth for an endless moment that shattered what composure the women had barely begun to regain. Then suddenly Angus began to growl, a thing Genie had never heard, a low warning rumble that made her want to scream, yet he never moved his head and her mouth never opened. It seemed he still slept and the growl was directed at a dream adversary. Genie and Dristy both began to shake. Aizlyn had gone stiff and was obviously as terrified as they were.

Aizlyn cried, "Go, take him and my love with you. Go, before..."

Aizlyn screamed, Genie and Dristy screamed too. Angus let loose a low terrifying growl that built and built and built and then Dristy demanded, unbelievably calm, "Leave this place, go deeper into your past and find somewhere safe to speak to me from."

The dog flinched again, the candles flickered warily as a sudden gust threatened them from the open window, Aizlyn slumped, hand lax on

Angus's head. The rain stopped and Angus didn't seem to notice any of it. Genie worked on her breathing, fighting to find that calming rhythm that forces heart and mind to follow. Dristy just started shaking violently. The candles slowly ceased to sway and flicker so roughly, the air seemed to clear and Genie reached out a hand, patting Dristy's shoulder reassuringly.

"Don't," Dristy said, shaking it off, not exactly bitter but just not wanting to be consoled. "We play with fire here, someone may get burned. That was too much and you knew it. We cannot push so hard."

"I am sorry," Genie said, not exactly contrite but very aware, "but..."

"I know, I want to help her too, Gen, I do," Dristy said then. "I know that all things have purpose, all lives, direction. I cannot believe I have made honing skills that fit her needs my life's path by some freak accident..."

Both women's attention was suddenly drawn to Aizlyn as she sat up tall and straight and incredibly proud. Here was a princess before them, if ever they had thought bearing alone would say so. Aizlyn closed her eyes and tilted her head, chin up, as though some beautiful scent came to her on the wind that had just come in the window or a lover whispered something sweet in her ear. Then she opened her eyes and focused straight ahead, seeing nothing of the two women on either side or the washer and dryer behind them.

"Let's be about it, then," Aizlyn called in an impossibly deep voice, not at all sounding like her own.

"Be about what?" Dristy stumbled, completely unsure now of how to handle this regression with any semblance of normalcy.

"This voyage, you oaf," came the good natured reply. "I've been promised a show of this famous Britain. I am itching to be off."

Dristy glanced at Genie, unsure, as had become very uncomfortably common this afternoon. Well, she had told Aizlyn to find a safe place from which to speak to her, this wasn't at all what she had expected, but what could she do? Genie lifted the photocopied pages which she had separated from the rest and written the word "man" in a red marker across the top.

She held the pages up for Dristy to see, then raised an eyebrow that said, "maybe?" Dristy took a very deep breath, having heard how that life had ended from Genie already and eyes wide, jaw set, she gave Genie a look of both worry and warning. They would have to tread very, very carefully here.

"What has you chomping the bit so, son?" Dristy said in her best man-voice, assuming the role it seemed had been thrust on her with many guesses and hopes and crossed fingers.

"Lord Windell, you would think me mad," Aizlyn joked, turning her head as if addressing someone in front of the dryer, every bit the self-assured prince but showing good humor even if it was about himself. "And I just might be."

Dristy raised her eyebrows at Genie, indicating she was pleased with the unexpected name she had been called. Genie cocked her head, more puzzled than pleased, and wrote herself a question before looking back up. Neither of the two women missed the fact Aizlyn's hand was again stroking Angus's head, nor the need to wonder if there was a dog there with her in the past again.

"I doubt that," Dristy replied, fine-tuning her role and adding a Hollywood accent and seventeenth-century turn to her manly reply. "You really must share.'

"Honestly…," Aizlyn took a deep breath, her face turned thoughtful, and she plunged. "Have you ever felt that there was something more, something just beyond the next horizon just waiting for you to come find it? What is that? Ahhh, compelled! I am compelled to see this foreign place you speak of, I cannot help but believe I will find many wonderful things there. You have given me this dog, and if he is any indication of the things I may find there, I go ahead of myself in a joyful spirit."

Well, that answered the question about the dog. This was getting entirely too strange for even Dristy's open-minded tastes.

"You have all the wealth you could need, have you not?" Dristy pried carefully, needing to be sure they dealt with the same Indian royalty of Aizlyn's dreams of herself as a man and not an entirely different life. She

187

began pushing the discomfort of the unknown aside. "What more could you want?"

Aizlyn sighed wistfully, "All the gold in the world does not buy peace of mind. I want what definitely cannot be purchased, a chance meeting with a new life long friend, an unexpected enlightening conversation, a view from a never-before conquered cliff of a sea that cannot stop me. I must be mad, yes?"

Aizlyn laughed a happy, non-self-conscious laugh that said as much as the words themselves had and turned her head again, with her eyes closed and chin up, as though another breeze had come to whisper sweet attainable things in her ear. She grew distant, and somehow Dristy felt the voyage had gotten underway. Dristy was silent, allowing her the moment.

Genie hadn't intended to dawdle in this particular life, she knew all too well what it came to, but that was only if this one was truly it. She quickly wrote out the question which she hoped would answer that for Dristy to read, wanting no more than Dristy did to say anything to interrupt Aizlyn's brief moment of peace. Dristy read it, then Genie made a motion indicating that was to be the last question and they were to leave it at that. This conversation was slowly breaking her heart and she wanted it over. There would be no risk-taking this round. Dristy thought a moment on how to word the question she'd read into the conversation she was having.

"Have you no wife or children to miss you while you are *compelled* to do this exploring?" Dristy asked at last.

"No, my friend," Aizlyn grinned, obviously a happy young man full of adventurous spirit and carefree hopes, not yet bound by anything but his own sense of something more just beyond him which needed chasing, "but maybe she too will be found."

Genie waved her hand, telling Dristy to end it there, and released a painful exhale. She mourned the young man in a whole new way, after having felt she'd just met him, a deep sadness settled in on her. She was no longer merely sad for Aizlyn, that she had to be tortured by his, their, memories. She was sad because she knew from the dreams that three years or so from arriving in Britain, dreams in hand, and pockets packed full of hope, this happy adventurous boy was going to take his own life. She was sad because she couldn't help but feel for this passionate young man, fueled by such beautiful vision, who would come to be so blinded by pain he would put a musket to his own head.

11

Jordan: A River, Flows Down

"Where are you?" Dristy questioned when she saw that Aizlyn, still sitting, back straight, chin up and regal, suddenly bowed her head in a posture of submission or reverence. She couldn't decide which it was. All she knew was Aizlyn's body language had indicated much to her through this session. If she had learned to read it, as she felt she had, she could assume it indicated she had settled, in her backward flipping through the photo album in her mind, on another particular picture. One in which she sat before someone or something that required she bow.

"The temple," Aizlyn replied regally. "The prince has restored it for me, here on the palace grounds."

Dristy glanced at Genie, her eyes questioning and hopeful. "Have you danced?" she questioned their hypnotized friend.

"Haven't I always?" came the almost bitter reply. "What has it done me?"

"Have you ever been away from India?" Dristy tried, wanting to understand Aizlyn's mood and get a grip on how she felt. Obviously she had won her prince, she had danced and was at the palace, but was this the lifetime they sought to revisit and examine or yet another in this unexpectedly long chain?

"In my heart, I am not even here," Aizlyn replied with bitter wistfulness that said a thousand more words as the silence lengthened. "Perhaps he knows this and that is why he used some of the trading company's silver to rebuild this temple, rather than allowing me to travel to the other?" she added thoughtfully into the long quiet. "Or perhaps I am unkind and he has done it because I am old and mayhap would not have been able to return. He knows I always longed to visit with my goddess."

Dristy leaned toward Genie, telling her she felt it odd that Aizlyn seemed to have managed three lives in the span of time the East India Company had occupied India, three lives in little more than twohundred and fifty years. Genie pointed out, however, that maybe it wasn't so odd since they knew for sure at least one of them she hadn't lived anywhere near a full life span, and most likely the one in which she had been doing laundry had been cut short too.

Dristy was considering the sadness of that when Genie held out the notebook to show her what she wanted to know of this life. Dristy's eyes told Genie she was uncomfortable, that she found something unusual about the way Aizlyn had opened up yet again and seemed so comfortable pouring herself out in a one-sided conversation, but she only questioned Genie briefly. Genie, it seemed, had come to some conclusions through what lives they had already traversed and meant to test her theory.

"You are not happy that you are a princess?" Dristy asked.

"Should I be?" came the biting response that still smacked of a heartfelt and honestly posed question.

"Many would be thrilled to be married to a prince, to have wealth and servants to tend to your every need," Dristy said hoping she was going about this conversation the right way and taking Genie's nod in her peripheral vision as encouragement.

"So the other wives have always told me," Aizlyn replied, dripping sarcasm. "But you have not answered my question."

Dristy turned her shock on Genie, nodding profusely in the negative, eyes wide again, indicating this was definitely becoming very wrong yet again. It was no more normal a response from a regressed patient than her speaking to Angus had been- demanding answers in turn from the hypnotist?

"Only you can say whether you should be happy or not," Dristy stumbled, when Genie's eyes said she wasn't letting this be stopped by oddities, no matter how often they were occurring. "It is not my place to tell you whether you should feel you have attained what was meant, or learned what was destined this life. Only you know what your spirit tells you was meant."

"Then my answer is as it has always been, and you have taught me nothing," Aizlyn said, downtrodden, "This temple has been rebuilt for nothing."

Dristy flinched at the bitterness that now lacked any hope or want to disguise itself, her emotions were pricked, her answer unintentionally personal. "Who am I that I should teach you anything from where I am to where you are?"

"Are you not meant to smile on those who seek to learn and guide them?" Aizlyn said, now retreating from bitter back into nearly begging. "I come near the end of this great corridor now. My beauty and health have fled; there is no hope in me, as there used to be, that somewhere just around the next corner lies a corridor I have yet to run down. I am old, even unto my spirit, my legs would not take me down a new path with any speed nor could my heart bear it, were such to suddenly appear."

Dristy sucked in a breath of realization as the conversation made sudden and perfect sense. Aizlyn must have come to sit before a statue of Sarisvati, in a temple Jordan had repaired for her, and bowed to have a conversation with her goddess in her old age. Dristy was awestruck by the possibilities, and humbled by the concepts. She was afraid to say another word.

Genie had her answer as she watched and listened to her theory prove itself. Aizlyn had definitely been living in a kind of karmic loop, fighting the same battles over and over, no wonder she suffered such *real* dreams and frequent déjà vu, no wonder she felt the cows were *always* winking and dinking. Somehow she knew, obviously not just in this life, that there was something more she had wanted to attain and it definitely wasn't marrying Jordan. She seemed to even hint at feeling Jordan somehow kept her from the things she knew deep down were waiting just beyond her reach. Such had been indicated, too, by the dreams and such thoughts as that maybe next time she should not dance. Genie just had one more question to set her theory in stone. She leaned into Dristy's ear again.

"What more do, did, you want?" Dristy said after much coaxing, feeling more than a little blasphemous for it. If Aizlyn felt she spoke with her goddess, then Dristy was sure she was going to pay for playing with that.

"Seems there should have been more sound, more smell, more sweat, more fur and fire, not silk and incenses," Aizlyn said thoughtfully, as if having a hard time focusing on her answer, maybe even getting a little sleepy. Her head bowed lower, "More communion, more friendship, more laughter, more life! Not gardens but glades, not baths but pools, I have felt them with my soul, when my soul wandered where I could not, and they were good to me. I should have traveled to your temple… I should have fed my sweetmeat to the dog at the port that day… so long ago… I should have found that cliff." Her breath grew shallow as though she stood on that cliff in her mind, saw the waters beneath it in her mind's eye, and it brought her peace. She whispered now, "Seems…seems there was more love…"

"Oh my god, she stopped breathing, do something!" Genie yelled.

Angus started twitching furiously but didn't wake and Dristy demanded Aizlyn go further back, not forward into the times between. She demanded she go right then and speak to her again, *take a deep breath*, and tell her where she was.

Aizlyn sucked in a huge breath and so did Genie and Dristy. Genie was still in shock and it was her turn to shake, and begin making excuses to herself for not having seen it coming. How was she to know Aizlyn had gone to the temple to have one final argument with her goddess rather than make peace? How was Genie to know Aizlyn had gone there to die? It was strange and fitting that they should witness the end of a life where she wished for freedom to travel, right after leaving the one where she had done just that by coming back as a man. It was scary as hell too, knowing how closely they had come to the cliff's edge themselves this afternoon.

"I am here," Aizlyn said. "You wanted to speak to me?"

Dristy still hadn't gotten her heart to stop thrashing wildly at her rib cage and was definitely not prepared to play a goddess that was supposed to lend wisdom. She could only guess that because Aizlyn had seemed to speak to her as Sarasvati in the temple that when she had demanded she go further back and then speak to her again that is exactly what Aizlyn had done. Dristy surmised Aizlyn probably sat before a statue in her mind, expecting it to speak to her as it had moments before. The whole blasphemous idea of it was messing her rhythm up incredibly bad, and she wanted desperately to call a halt to it right then and there. But Genie still hunted for a particular life, Genie had a list of things she wanted to know for sure. Genie was not about to let her give up until she had what she needed to help Aizlyn with.

"Are you happy?" Dristy asked at last.

"Should I be?" Aizlyn replied.

"Am I to tell you when to be happy and when not to?" Dristy questioned, hating herself for literally playing goddess again. She was just sure she was making some seriously bad karma for herself maybe even galloping happily toward hell.

"Mayhap only indicate that I am on the right path to finding happiness?" Aizlyn queried cautiously as though she had taken Dristy's words as reprimand.

Dristy knew the particulars, or felt she did. She had heard Genie's ideas that Aizlyn was only happy when she avoided dancing for or ending up wed to the prince, that she had entered a loop of avoid or be unhappy. But Dristy felt she was getting hints of more, and she meant to pursue her clues too. So it was a strange look of confusion and grudging appreciation that she got from Genie for her next question.

"Did you feed the dog?" Dristy asked.

"Nay," Aizlyn said, bothered and apologetic, "I tried though. I would care for all creatures, but the palace guards, they shooed him, cruelly and..."

"It is not your fault then," Dristy said, halting Aizlyn's obvious feelings of guilt but not her own as once again she played goddess, forgiving her. "I know you would have, given the chance."

The silence lengthened as Dristy considered the answer she had gotten and began to stir her thoughts on Aizlyn's problem. She felt sure the dog had something to do with Aizlyn finding happiness; the thought had started stewing when she began the hypnosis and Aizlyn had said to follow him toward peace. It had been an odd thing to hear, but was almost making sense as he kept coming up. She knew Aizlyn had come into at least one life with foresight; armed with a deep knowledge some might call premonitions, she had even broke her hip, long before her time to dance, presumably, so as to avoid dancing for the prince. Though she had said "mongrel" in that life and Dristy had to wonder if she had come to resent the dog for spooking the horse and causing the hip to be broken, somehow missing a point she had pre-planned herself to get? Aizlyn had apparently known the dog, maybe not this one in particular she amended, but a dog named Angus, in another life too and had cared for it then. Aizlyn had seemed to be very pleased, though also frightened, to see the dog's owner in that one life too, and then, later, in yet another life regretted not feeding the dog. What if she was coming into at least a few of her lives with foresight to know the dog would lead her to happiness?

If she could just get her ideas to congeal, she knew she would have an answer. She leaned over and whispered these thoughts to Genie, hoping her old friend would have some cornstarch or something in her mental cupboards to help her finish thickening what she had begun cooking up. Genie obliged and said she had been thinking something along those lines just then too.

Genie said, "What if the dog leads her to happiness, by leading her to his real owner?"

Why was it always a love thing?

Dristy sighed, "Do you love your prince?"

"Should I not?" Aizlyn asked.

"I am not judging the right or wrong of your feelings," Dristy said carefully, "I am merely asking you what they are."

"I do," Aizlyn replied after a moment of careful thought, "but I think I must love him wrong."

"Why is that?" Dristy asked, brow furrowed and puzzled by the response.

"Because when he visits his other wives and is not with me," Aizlyn said cautiously as though fearing her honesty would bring anger and yet dishonesty would bring worse, "it is difficult for me to love him. My love must be wrong, to be so selfish, I think."

"So you resent him sometimes?" Dristy asked then, cocking her head but almost sure she would know the answer already.

"I know he provides all I could ask, and I love him that he loves me in that way. He has made this temple, because I made mere mention I longed to see the face of Sarasvati. He has never raised his hand or his voice to me, he plays for us often, beautiful music to sooth and entertain us," Aizlyn said sadly, "but what I cannot ask and he cannot provide, is that he love me, as I am willing to love him. I hold no special favor in this place, I am but one of many wives, oft visited, but…is it wrong that I should want *more* from him?"

"That is an age-old quandary, dear one," Dristy said, a little sad herself, and thanking God women had at least come far enough to be able to leave a relationship if they felt somehow cheated.

"I want him to be passionate about me," Aizlyn said, pouring her heart out before a statue only she could see. "Passionate, in that he cannot walk away without one last caress and another's kiss could never suffice to carry him through the coming day, passionate in that each day is made perfect because it can end with seeing me, slipping into my bed. I need him to want to speak to me when we wake because he cannot help but wonder what I dream. I need him to show me weakness, share with me hope and tell me *his dreams*, because I need to know he trusts me with them. I need his passions,

196

even unto yelling if I anger him, because I need to know I can stir him to anger. I need to know I stir more than just his flesh, I need his mind and above all his heart."

"Doesn't every woman?" Dristy said, too empathetic to remember to remain in character.

"And what do they do?" Aizlyn asked then, surprising her.

"They either settle for the servants and silks and incenses," Dristy answered as honestly as she knew how, not knowing what else to do, "or they take the risks of being a dreamer, chasing the forever dream, and hope someday they wake to find it real."

"How do I do that?" Aizlyn asked.

"Feed the dog," Dristy replied, desperately hoping she would be forgiven for any cosmic karmic messes she might be making for herself, by playing goddess, and hoping there wasn't really a hell waiting somewhere in her future.

Genie patted her leg and got her attention and they slipped up stairs unnoticed by either Aizlyn or Angus. They refilled their coffee cups and made Aizlyn a fresh one in her thermal mug. Dristy assured Genie she could drink it without being woken by simply being told it was there for her to do so if she wished. They spoke a little more in depth about the life they were searching for versus those they had found, and again Genie assured her it would be found, citing once again that the dreams were too real, and though she had never been to India in any life, she knew Aizlyn from at least one as surely as they too had known each other.

Genie was also sure that particular life had to hold answers; why else would they come together again in this one? Why else would she so obviously always seem to be seeking her "more" on European shores?

Dristy complained about her role as goddess, telling Genie, "I am sure I have reserved a seat in hell at Hitler's table."

Genie just laughed and assured her, "You won't be alone at least, we will just have to offer him some hot hemlock tea sweetened with acid sugar cubes and enjoy questioning his sanity together."

197

So they were still giggling when they turned to head back downstairs.

"I can't wait to tell Angelica about all this," Dristy said, suddenly thoughtful, "She has been so desperate for information on past life's lately. She has to be writing again. You know she came and raided my books last week, then called twice to see if she'd missed any. Whatever it is that has gotten her started on this new bit of researching, it's got her wound pretty tight."

Genie never got a chance to respond, the view she'd just caught of Aizlyn, as her head cleared the steps, left all other thoughts scattering.

Aizlyn sat staring forward sightless; tears running down her face, sobbing silently as she pet the dog. All thoughts of Hitler, laughter and other friends, died in both their mouths to be spit out with no small amount of coffee.

"What is wrong?" Dristy asked cautiously, walking slowly back to the blanket and taking her seat again.

Dristy had not thought this regression could get any stranger but it just had. Aizlyn had obviously moved forward without her prompting and that could have been very, very bad. Terrible things could have occurred while they joked about going to hell. It wasn't funny anymore at all. She kept hearing "peaches" running around in her head, thinking to get out now while the getting was good, before something went even more wrong and it was Hitler questioning her.

"I fed him, just as you said," Aizlyn cried, still petting Angus's head and shoulders, rubbing them, massaging them. "I found him again by the rear gates, sniffing at the garbage the servants discard there. I made sure the guards did not see me when I brought him the platter of fish to pad his ribs." She cast her eyes downward as though speaking to the dog now, sounding heartbreakingly apologetic. The two women couldn't help but follow her sightless gaze as she continued, "I have always made sure, I don't know how they knew or why it should have been such a transgression in my prince's eye's, never have I heard my prince yell before…"

"What will they do?" Dristy asked.

She was deeply disturbed by the endless possibilities as she watched Aizlyn's hands knead Angus's back and ribs worriedly. Had her suggestion caused the act or was the act a thing that would have occurred regardless, and she merely bore witness. Had she just happened to say the same thing Aizlyn would have heard in her heart from her goddess? It seemed if ever a moment begged one to believe in coincidences, this was it. Because she had no idea how it could even be possible to have created an event in the past through hypnosis. Dristy was, however, quite sure that they had been from the beginning, and still were, playing in dangerous and uncharted waters.

"They have killed him," Aizlyn sobbed now, "and planted, within my soul, hatred for my prince."

Dristy watched the slow rise and fall of Angus's chest as he slept, saw his feet begin to twitch, head still resting in Aizlyn's lap, and prayed he was just dreaming. Yet she couldn't help but feel a deep dark fear begin to thread through her. After everything she and Genie had seen and experienced so far this afternoon, she was afraid to ask but was compelled to anyway.

"How?"

"They have poisoned his fish," Aizlyn cried.

Angus began twitching in earnest and Genie suddenly remembered again, Aizlyn relaying the incident of his bleeding gums a few days ago. She wondered if the dog felt his dreams more real than he should, as Aizlyn did, and had been chewing a bone in his sleep which hadn't really existed. Genie recalled Aizlyn's worry over her own red-marked ankle after waking that same morning and realized it couldn't get any weirder, she leaned to warn Dristy.

Suddenly the dog's twitching became convulsions and Dristy and Genie really freaked out. "Go back!" they yelled in unison.

"And take Angus with you," Dristy added just in case.

"Where are you?" Dristy asked when she saw Aizlyn smiling, petting Angus again, and the dog's breathing had returned to normal.

"On my way home," Aizlyn replied happily.

If they had skipped lives in their slow backward progression to arrive at one where Angus and Aizlyn were together, alive and well, Dristy didn't care. She knew that through her demand Aizlyn take Angus with her when she go back that they may have missed some, because the dog was not with her in all of them that they had visited so far. However, she felt missing one or two was worth not being murdered by Aizlyn when she awoke to find they had allowed her beloved dog to die. And weren't they working under the assumption they needed to follow him anyway? Wrong or not, at least all seemed happy for the moment in Aizlyn's world.

Genie was still thoughtfully wandering in her own head trying to put it all together, but nudged Dristy, fully aware of the moment and hopeful, maybe the fact she was with the dog and traveling meant she had escaped the dancing for this link in the chain of her lives. Maybe they had hit the right one finally. Genie wanted to know where home was.

"Where is home?" Dristy questioned, also hopeful.

"India," Aizlyn smiled.

"Where did you travel to?" Dristy asked, now thoroughly confused. Wasn't she supposed to be unhappy with her lives in India? Why should she be happy to be *returning* there? Unless in this life she lacked those precognitive kinds of foresights she seemed to have had in all the others.

"I have been to the temple," Aizlyn replied, smile widening, "and I have found a beautiful beast."

"Will you be able to keep him?" Dristy questioned, a suspicion growing. "Will your husband allow you to have a dog?"

"I am not married," Aizlyn giggled. "I belong to, and will return to live at, the temple, I have decided."

"And your family," Dristy checked further, "they do not mind that you have found this beast and mean to keep him or that you have decided to live at the temple?"

Aizlyn's smile wavered slightly and she became thoughtful and pensive. "I had not considered that. Mayhap they will not notice the beast with the all the festivities."

"What festivities?" Dristy prompted.

"The prince has said he will choose a new wife from among the people, it has ever been this way, when peace needs be made." Aizlyn's brow furrowed as though some thought had disturbed her suddenly, but she pushed it aside and continued, petting the dog, smile returning. "It will be a great honor to the family whose daughter is chosen."

Genie nudged Dristy and leaned in close to whisper. She wanted to know what was bothering Aizlyn, she said she could see it hidden in the way she concentrated on petting the dog as though it might shut out the worry, the simple pleasure of running her fingernails through his wiry coat.

"What is bothering you?" Dristy asked, taking Genie's word for it.

"I feel I should not join this dance," Aizlyn replied cautiously, "like something is not right."

"Do you have to?" Dristy wondered.

"All those of age, and unwed, will," Aizlyn answered.

Dristy knew that meant yes and leaned to ask Genie if there was anything more she needed or wanted to know before they moved on.

"Yeah, what happens to Angus then?" Genie answered Dristy.

"What happens to Angus?" Dristy repeated Genie's question in a whisper, unsure as to how such a question was to be handled but Aizlyn surprised them both by apparently moving forward in her time and answering as though it had been asked of her already.

"The Walker, a large man from far-away lands, eyes blue, skin red and gold, known by reputation and merchandise, came to our people to sell his wares," Aizlyn replied. Sudden sadness overtook her smile, her dialogue had become monotone. "He had heard of the grand event our prince was making and came far off his normal way. He seemed happy in his aura, generous in his exchange and genuinely kind. I felt him a good man, until he spoke words that meant the beast, which came to view his treasures with me, had been his before I lay claim to him. He called to it, saying "Angus," and it went to him, proving the man did not lie. Many times while the merchant remained among us making much profit of silks from Asia for my wedding, he came upon *his* beast lying happy in *my* company. In a great offer of generosity he made word and gesture that I should keep this Angus of his. As the beast was well pleased by me, Angus was to be my wedding gift. I was pleased beyond words, as my soul had been much burdened since the time of the dance, and Angus set my mind at ease. But my prince refused this gift as too kind, having no fondness for beasts. I watched the walking merchant and the beautiful beast depart after my wedding, and found a small hate had bloomed in my heart for the man I was to lay with that night."

Aizlyn fell silent and Genie and Dristy followed suit. It seemed no one wanted to speak after that. But Genie's mind couldn't stay still for long and suddenly she leaned in close, grabbing Dristy's upper arm in her eager excitement.

"Didn't you say Windell meant Walker?" Genie demanded, barely containing her voice and managing a whisper.

"Yes?" Dristy said quizzically, then her eyes widened also, making the connection.

"That's the second time," Genie said.

"Yes, she spoke to me as though I were a Lord Windell when she was about to begin her voyage as a young man," Dristy said. "And that Lord Windell had given her a dog. Again, there is this Walker and the dog."

"And don't forget the dream we search for, where she is with the knight and his dog, happy to be heading to a new place," Genie said, terribly excited. "Presumably some place with a longhouse and answers."

"But the dog belonged to Rune in that scary laundry life," Dristy said then, a little thrown off, "and I got the distinct impression she loved that Rune fella."

"Either way the dog leads her to happiness," Genie replied nonplussed.

"And," Dristy added, her own excitement building, having jumped that small puddle, "you have here before you a woman who stood up, went out on her own, and found Angus for herself, after arranging to be born a Walker. She seems to be making strides. But…"

"But what?" Genie said, not wanting to hear bad news.

"Let me see those pages," Dristy whispered, fairly jerking the photocopies from Genie's hand. "Yeah, here, these guys sound like Crusaders, the ones she travels with who wear tabards and ride with penants. Which at the rate we are going we should be getting close to that far back in time, but I don't think there were active Vikings still striking in Europe then. I think that's like another three or four hundred years back even beyond that."

"Vikings?" Genie asked. "Where you getting Vikings?"

"Knights didn't live in longhouses with bearskins draped to make doors," Dristy said, surprised she even needed to. "You know this. They lived in castles, and rode horses. Do we go to the same fairs, darlin'?" Dristy giggled. "Vikings are the ones with boats that steal women and, maybe," she paused for dramatic effect, "chain them in front of fires…"

"I knew that," Genie said sheepishly. "I just got it all wrapped up in my head in one pretty little package that I could hand to her and say, 'here this is the problem, here is where the chain is mounted, now fix it, break your chain!'"

"Well," Dristy said, smiling, "we are getting there, even if it ain't exactly pretty yet."

Genie laughed and Dristy took a sip of her coffee, thoughtfully. Suddenly she remembered they had made Aizlyn a cup and been sidetracked, she had yet to get a drink of it. Poor Aizlyn hadn't had anything to drink this whole time! Good thing they'd put it in her thermal mug. She leaned forward, careful not to disturb the dog resting so peacefully under Aizlyn's left hand. Dristy took Aizlyn's free hand in hers and placed her mug into it, wrapping her fingers around it and closing them tight.

"Here," Dristy prompted, "drink this."

"Ahhh, that is too wonderful," Aizlyn said appreciatively, looking right at her in a very unnerving way, as she sipped it. "It seems it has been forever. Where did you get such a treasure?"

Dristy tried looking to Genie for any kind of guidance, because she had no idea what was going on. Damn it if Aizlyn wasn't determined to make this hard as heck by taking everything she said as some cue to find a life and situation that matched and then talk to her as though she were there with her in that moment to respond. Well, Dristy thought stubbornly, I'll get the answers one way or another and if the coffee was a treasure then it was hard to come by. Wherever Aizlyn was currently in time, the coffee was a find and Dristy just made her best guess as to how to handle that.

"I saved it for you?" Dristy tried.

Aizlyn wasn't following any rules of thumb that Dristy had ever learned, and she reminded herself to be careful what she might step in with this girl. Her mind was indeed as convoluted as her problems but as long as she and her dog kept breathing she was going to keep going. Now it was she who was *compelled*.

"You are a treasure, too," Aizlyn smiled.

"Where are we?" Dristy asked, once again assuming a role she was, as yet, not sure of.

"Somewhere in route to the Caspian slave-trader ports, I would assume," Aizlyn said, eyeing her suspiciously. "They do not hurt you when they have you serve their meals, do they?"

Dristy looked at Genie, eyes widened, as Aizlyn tended to keep making them do. Genie looked just as shocked. They put their heads together once again.

"I am so lost," Dristy admitted in Genie's ear.

"Well, are we before the Crusades still?" Genie said reaching for the only obvious question.

"I don't know," Dristy said frowning, "and I don't have the faintest clue how to find out."

"Just ask," Genie said.

"And how do I work that in?" Dristy said, frustrated.

"That's your department," Genie grinned.

Dristy threw caution to the wind, shrugged her shoulders and said, "What year is?"

"1302." Aizlyn looked worried now. "You are certain they haven't knocked you about and hurt your head?"

"No," Dristy said quickly, not wanting to know what Aizlyn would have done in this particular life if someone had hurt someone she cared for, and obviously she cared for the person she felt she spoke with. "I have just lost track is all." Dristy hoped she was convincing; she'd heard stories about the defensive and protective Win side of Aizlyn's personality from Genie.

"Well," Aizlyn said, "know they will not come near to me and Angus here, and we welcome you, have you the need." She patted the dog's head, indicating to the two women watching that he was there with her again.

"Why?" Dristy asked, thoroughly confused and trying very hard to figure out how Aizlyn and her dog had come to be traveling with what she now figured were slavers using the old Silk Road en route to the Caspian Sea.

"They have not forgotten the man they buried by my blade," Aizlyn grinned caustically, "or the scars Angus gifted a number of them. I gave them my wealth freely when they attacked my goddess's temple, I did not mind they covet my jewels but I would not let them have *me*."

Aizlyn looked thoughtful and far off a moment then added, "I imagine were it not for the fact Angus will bring as much gold as myself they would have killed him and overpowered me with sheer numbers. But that was never meant and I put my blade away after their lecherous comrade fell and my stance was understood. I think they sense the sight in me and fear things they cannot grasp." Aizlyn sighed, "They are content, for now, that I follow even without their chains, and they keep their distance when camp is made."

Dristy looked at Genie, awestruck by the story.

"You travel with them willingly then?" Dristy was fascinated. "Have you no fear of what will come of you once they reach the Caspian slaver ports?"

"No," Aizlyn smiled peacefully and looked down to rub her dog's ear, "it is what was meant, I feel it in my soul. I traveled to the temple, but knew I went to meet my destiny."

Dristy again looked at Genie. What an intriguing life this one was! She said, "Have you always had a feeling you needed to visit her temple then?"

"Among many other feelings I have followed my whole life," Aizlyn grinned. "Tis why I sneaked away when first I heard of the prince's great dance, why I made the great journey to the old temple, why I cannot help but look out for you and why I know that I will be purchased by a kind master and someday if I stay true to my soul I will see magic water that sings to me of peace."

"You have visions?" Dristy asked her then, unnerved as hell that Aizlyn still seemed to be speaking directly to her. "You do have the sight?"

"Someday you will too, and it will serve you well," Aizlyn said, seeming to truly see her, if not all the way through her.

Dristy's heart stopped for a second, then suddenly jolted back to life, determined to break loose from her ribs this time. She all but fell on Genie's ear. "Was she talking directly to me? Did you hear that? She was looking right at me..."

"Easy, woman," Genie said, trying not to laugh, "You are the one who tells me she can't see the present right now, she was speaking to whomever it was she saw back then."

"Ya, ME!" Dristy started shaking.

"If you say so," Genie said, letting out her laughter, she couldn't hold it anymore anyway. "I suppose it would fit."

"Too well!" Dristy said then, furrowing her brow thoughtfully, "I didn't know I had ever been a slave..."

They sat in silence for a long time, Dristy considering the fact there were very, very many things, even about herself, which she had yet to discover, and Genie thinking things far more difficult for her to define. Genie was desperately trying to grasp what it was that would make Aizlyn happy. She had witnessed her try just about everything now and knew damn well none of it worked because she was sitting right there in front of them, scared but hypnotized anyway, still trying more. Finally all Genie could do was coax

Dristy into asking her one more question before they moved her even further back down the chain.

"Are you happy then?" Dristy asked at last for Genie. "Has avoiding so much you saw coming brought you any peace so far?"

"Moments," Aizlyn replied after a thoughtful pause, "like this one, talking to you over a priceless cup of coffee; Angus here, when he begins twitching in his sleep, dreaming as I do; seeing the temple with my own eyes." But Aizlyn turned pensive, even somewhat stricken when she said, "But I am become hardened. I have killed to accomplish my goals and achieve my visions and I feel to my core I will be made to pay for my self-serving pursuit this life. Be careful what you sacrifice."

12

William: Desire, a Helmet, Protection

"Where are you?"

"The palace gardens."

"What are you doing?"

"Listening to the prince, he plays for us tonight," Aizlyn replied mildly, sounding half asleep.

Genie sat up straighter. Last time she'd thought Aizlyn merely sleepy, she had quit breathing. She put a warning hand on Dristy's leg but it wasn't necessary, as Dristy's next question eased her mind a little.

"Are you tired?" Dristy asked.

"No," Aizlyn replied, "just tired."

"What does that mean?" Dristy prodded.

"We do nothing," Aizlyn said, suddenly a bit out of sorts. "Day by day I waste away here. I requested we travel to the temples and pay homage to the gods but my requests are lost among so many others. I request he take me to the port and allow me to purchase a pet beast and he laughs, saying that mongrels are not meant for such as we. He tides me over with dress-makers and baskets of beads and beautiful threads but I long for more. I thought it might be different this time."

Dristy glanced at Genie and their eyes told each other they were still not where they needed to be. Dristy made yet another comment about how many lives Aizlyn fit into such short spans and this time Genie too had to admit she felt it odd. They considered that maybe Aizlyn had died young in even more of them than they knew but were unwilling to try to find out. Then they considered it was possible too that she was so hell-bent a soul she just turned around and came right back after every try, jumping right back on the horse every time.

"Where are you?"

"He calls it England," Aizlyn answered with a soft smile, followed by a shiver. "I call it wondrous and a little cold."

"Who is 'he'?" Dristy wondered, glancing hopefully toward Genie.

"Lord Windell," Aizlyn said, pleased. "He says we will travel up the coast and I will see many cliffs. I have told him I long to see cliffs and he smiles as though he understands."

"Why will you travel up the coast?" Dristy pried, trying for as much information as she could possibly get.

"We return to his wife," Aizlyn smiled. "He assures me she is wonderful and I will come to love her as my own mother. He thinks I will help her too, he says she has not been herself since a great tragedy he does not speak of."

Dristy was thankful Aizlyn was being so open and free with her information again, she had no idea who she thought she was speaking to this time or was just being verbose with the hypnotist, but Dristy was glad of it either way as she searched for what she needed. This was their first time with her in Europe and she wanted to search ahead for answers, but was frightened of bringing Aizlyn into a sudden deadly situation and wasn't sure how to do so safely.

"What do you think of Lord Windell's wife?" Dristy tried, hoping desperately that the question brought her to a safe reflective moment from which to answer.

"She is cruel," Aizlyn replied very quickly. "She sent me to be scrubbed by heavy-handed servants as though I were filthy and took my jewelry and clothing; she had me covered in this shapeless thing. Then I heard her when she began to yell at the patient Lord Windell about bringing vermin home. Can you believe, me, vermin? I am a princess, granted a princess without a kingdom, but a princess born and bred."

Dristy had a hard time picturing a woman of that time stealing jewelry from a guest her lord and husband had brought into their home, especially if she was to believe what she'd heard, and he wanted her become as a daughter to them. She felt there had to be more to it than what Aizlyn had relayed in her obvious indignation.

"What jewelry did she take?" Dristy asked.

"All of it, all my rings, even those from my nose and ears." Aizlyn was quite bent out of shape. "My chains from my ankles and from my waist and neck, even the bands from my upper arms, gifts from my betrothed before the slaughter. She said she is only taking them for safe-keeping when Lord Windell came upon us, but safe from whom in their own castle? And I saw with my own eyes when she gave one of the arm pieces to the man in her temple, as if to pay for the favor of her god despite the presence of the infidel. Does she think by giving my gold she buys my salvation? Surely she cannot think stolen gold buys her own or dragging me before her altar made me any more blessed by the Creator than I already am?"

Dristy flinched when Genie smacked her, pointing at the note she had just scratched out hastily for her to read. Dristy read it, an eyebrow arched and the eye beneath searching her friend's face when that one displayed a huge grin.

"So you have religious differences with your new mother?" Dristy said stating the obvious for the conformation Genie asked for.

"Clearly!" Aizlyn huffed as if pouting to an old friend.

"But Lord Windell has the same religion as she, does he not," Dristy said, taking it the next step, "and yet you seem to get on quite well with him."

"Lord Windell has seen much," Aizlyn replied, tone softening, "as have I. We know first-hand what atrocities men commit upon each other in the name of their gods. I think it is that we both understand, no matter that we call to our Creator by different names, we accept that He is Divine and can hear them all. It is not so much that we have come to agree on what He should be called and how it is that we should do the calling but more that we both seek to attain that same divinity by accepting all for what it is, reverence for that which gifts us with every day, and not judge, any more than He, the manner in which that reverence is offered."

"Some might take that as blasphemy," Dristy said, after thoroughly enjoying the fact she felt much the same. Aizlyn's responses were giving her the distinct impression she was being viewed as a confidant, a friend Aizlyn had really had back then once again, and it made her rest somewhat more easy in her prodding quest for answers. Answers came easy this way and at least she wasn't feeling sacrilegious for playing Sarasvati again.

"Yes," Aizlyn said sadly, "Lady Windell."

Genie leaned into Dristy and they whispered back and forth for a moment before a plan of attack was settled upon and the next question was ready to be posed.

"You have the dog with you?" Dristy began.

"Of course, he is right here," Aizlyn replied, happy again as she rubbed his head. "Has been from the moment he found me for Lord Windell among the dead. And better still, Lord Windell says a man with another of his kind comes to bring him a mate. So I shall meet one of my wonderful Angus's kin soon."

"When?" Dristy said, hopeful it was the right push, noting Genie's hasty note-taking on a photocopied page meant they were indeed finding something important in this life and desperate to find more.

"They come now," Aizlyn responded as hoped, eyes gazing far off. "I love this cliff you know, this one is my favorite, of all I have seen in this beautiful place. One can see forever here. And out there, below, the most beautiful shade of blue with patches of green life just waving under the surface, it is magical. There," she added as though whomever she spoke to should not miss it, as Genie scratched furiously on another page, "the boat comes now, it is small but very sleek and well-built, it flies like an arrow beneath three sails and waves a deep blue flag."

Dristy could suddenly see, through her mind's eye, Aizlyn, standing tall at the edge of a cliff, arm looped through Dristy's own, avidly describing the beautiful scene below. She could almost feel a light breeze on her skin, and goose flesh rose on her arms in answer.

"So Angus's mate is here now," Dristy prompted, after a moment. "Who else?"

"Lord and Lady Rune," Aizlyn said.

Genie pulled Dristy to her, unable to contain herself and merely write her thoughts. "I thought she and this Rune fella had a thing. He was the dog's master in that scary laundry life and that was the name of the estates where, as a man, she saw the woman she loved fall to her death."

"Yes, but Lord Windell owned the dog this time, and the other time the walking merchant did. There have been times we met no owner at all. Maybe more happens we don't know yet, between meeting the dog and it leading her to peace," Dristy said, a little irritated her friend had stopped her when she was just getting so well into her role of inquisitive confidant. "Her lady love at the House of Rune was engaged to another and killed herself that horrible night of the dream and it didn't seem that she or Rune faired well in scary laundry life." Dristy sighed, trying to be patient and answer her friend rather than rush back to questioning Aizlyn. "We don't know what the struggle is just yet with this Rune and her, but there may be another loop here too. We can't do any more than just look for a pattern like the one we found with her and Jordan and see what answers it might give us to apply to her current problems."

Genie huffed, mildly annoyed, and lit herself a cigarette, trying to be patient as Dristy suggested. She was usually quite good at being patient, she had been exercising the ability for years but tonight just wasn't going fast enough for her.

"Lord and Lady Rune have no children," Dristy said getting back to her puzzle, "or servants with them, just the dog?"

"Lord and Lady Rune?" Aizlyn giggled happily. "They bring no children, they are the children, you ninny." Then Aizlyn quieted and became apologetic. "I forget sometimes you were blinded. I am sorry. I did not mean to hurt you. You are not a ninny. Mayhap, I should have said 'young lord and lady' and told you they are unwed like us. Sometimes these forms of address for your people still cause me difficulty."

Dristy didn't know how to take all of that at once. It was almost too much. Finding out Aizlyn was indeed thinking she spoke to a friend was one thing, it explained the openness of her conversation completely, considering how she spoke when Dristy felt she addressed Sarasvati. But having her, once again, speak of sight or lack thereof almost gave Dristy palpitations. She wasn't nearly as freaked out as she had been when Aizlyn had looked her dead in the eye and spoke to her of having sight in the future. Something about having someone, lost in her past but still conversing as if with an old friend, and then speaking to you about your future was just creepy. This was less personal and yet more, and Dristy found she was actually unbelievably comfortable exploring this particular life in this peculiar manner. The fact Aizlyn seemed to be in the habit of explaining things in detail, and with so much description because the friend she felt she spoke to was blind, only served to make it that much easier to dig for information.

A part of Dristy actually accepted the thought that maybe they had shared that life as friends and that was why it felt so right. She had always felt she had lived in a castle once, she had not, however, ever thought she was blind, but then maybe she had not always been blind, and with such a friend whispering descriptions in your ear your mind's eye might not seem so blind.

Dristy recalled her thoughts from before the hypnosis even began, thinking maybe she and Aizlyn met not only for her to help Aizlyn through her use of her vision, meaning unique views and the opportunities and insights they provided, but also that Aizlyn was meant to broaden her vision. Well, that was exactly what was happening, she realized, as she caught herself dawdling on her own revelations rather than those things truly relevant to Aizlyn herself and the many issues they were doing all of this to solve currently.

Dristy was trying to put herself and her thoughts back on the right track when Genie, who had been doing some thinking of her own, pulled her close, whispering, "You know that is you, right?"

"Yes," Dristy replied, possibly a little calmer in accepting and running with the idea than she should have been.

"Blind in one life," Genie mused, "gifted with extreme vision in another. Fitting, I like it. I like it a lot, as a matter of fact, so use it."

"Use what?" Dristy queried, not as quick on the uptake as Genie felt she should be, apparently.

"The fact you are blind," Genie said, a bit put out to have to explain. "Ask her to tell you what they look like."

"Tell me," Dristy said, playing herself quite naturally, "what do they look like?"

"They are beautiful in contrasts," Aizlyn said a bit awestruck. "He is tall and thick, she is short and small. They both have pale skin but his is golden where hers is cream. They both have the sun in their hair but his is more honey morning, darker where it meets his skin, and hers is more red sunset. Both have blue eyes but also different in their hues, his more like the ocean he came from and hers more the sky. I can see they share parents but I can't point out why."

Dristy couldn't help but look at Genie when she was given this familiar description and she didn't miss the small, nearly sly smile when she did either. A wiggling little feeling nudged at her spine and she turned back to Aizlyn.

"What is Lady Rune's given name?" Dristy asked, holding her breath.

"Genevieve," Aizlyn answered, smiling. "Isn't she wonderful, she has such life and energy. Don't you just love her?"

Dristy whirled on Genie, face full of accusations that swiftly turned to consternation when she saw the almost cocky grin her best friend couldn't help but display. Dristy answered Aizlyn's question with, "Sometimes, but then sometimes I want to throttle her," in a whisper directed to Genevieve herself. "You knew?" Dristy accused when Genie only began to laugh even more at her indignation.

"I told you I knew the *both* of you," Genie said, not the least bit apologetic. "You think it's an accident we love the fairs? This is our favorite time. When will the two of you begin to listen?"

"You never said you knew us both in the same damn life, though. What else do you know?" Dristy demanded, feeling suddenly this whole event had been as much about her finding out things as Aizlyn, as far as Genie had been concerned when planning it, and not sure how she felt about being led into it blind to some very important things that she, Dristy, should have foreseen.

"Not much," Genie said then, "no, really," when Dristy seemed to challenge the truth of that assertion with a raised brow. "Just a lot of gut feelings and intuitions is all, like you guys, only I seem more adept at reading my inner map is all."

"What about your brother, this Rune," Dristy prodded. "Wouldn't happen to know where he is right now?"

"No," Genie said honestly, as Dristy looked closely to be sure, "I have an idea or three but I have yet to feel confident enough with them to want to say much. Even this meeting, there in her mind, was just a hunch till she described me so well, so really, just let me stew it. I don't want to mislead because I say something out of turn and I am still looking for answers here too."

Dristy eyeballed Genie for a good long minute before letting her go and doing what more digging she could with Aizlyn. She hoped to uncover clues as to how to help Aizlyn find this Rune fella, should they establish her need to in a manner that caused her to attempt another meeting with him in this life.

"What about Lord Rune?" Dristy asked then. "Have you learned his given name?"

"I never asked," Aizlyn said, seeming a bit surprised and almost embarrassed, "but he tells me to call him Rune and I do."

Dristy considered that statement from many angles, the first of which was her Renaissance Fair background, screaming in her head, "Well that is a bit familiar for a young unwed woman to be calling a young unwed male, especially at his request." Another was her primal woman's natural instincts, saying, "Hum, sounds like he wants her comfortable speaking to him and has taken the mister, or rather, in this case lord, out of their conversation to accomplish that." Then there was the thought that seemed to come naturally into the moment that said maybe they were just all too young and open to have set themselves behind the standard walls of convention.

For some reason she suddenly felt that she was the blind servant awarded to the unwelcome daughter by the tyrannically religious lady of the castle, and that last angle she considered seemed to fit just right. The two visiting young nobles, the displaced princess and the blind servant, keeping constant and contented company in the castle gardens, the vision came to her and it felt right. Dristy paused, considering that little bit of intuition and eventually just went with it, no use beginning now to question her instincts. In any case, she had better things to consider, she felt she was truly onto the beginning of the something more which Aizlyn perpetually sought on foreign shores from the confines of many a life in an Indian palace.

"You like Rune, then?" Dristy poked playfully.

Aizlyn again seemed to blush. "He is to be wed."

Genie glanced at Dristy as Dristy simply cinched up her confidant's combat boots and pried away, saying, "I didn't ask you if he was betrothed, I asked you if you liked him. Everyone of any high parentage is betrothed, they practically come from the womb that way. One lord declares, 'I have here a cleft,' another yells, 'I have here a dangle,' and they yell in unison, 'Let us make an alliance.'" Dristy laughed at her own humor and Genie couldn't help but to chuckle too. "But things happen. You *were* betrothed once, were you not?"

"I was, but...," Aizlyn paused, seeming to become upset for a moment before she put those thoughts that bothered her aside to be replaced with those more comforting, "he is quite the most wonderful man. He speaks to me, not only as a woman but an equal, gentle in his speech but eager for my opinion on matters a man of my people would never discus with a female. I have to tell you something, but you must keep it close to you and never tell a soul."

Dristy glanced at Genie as though she were debating the bad karma of accepting the burden of a secret meant for her ears alone when another was known to be listening in. Genie rolled her eyes at her as if to tell her to grow up, and the decision was made with a little giggle.

"Of course," Dristy replied, "I wouldn't utter a single word."

"I came here last night, as I often do," Aizlyn began quietly, as if for Dristy's ears alone. "I sat with Angus and stared at the moon, longing that it were rather my Sarasvati's face, needing guidance as is so often the case. For the longest time I merely bemoaned the lack of her in my vision but then I realized I kept her in my heart. So I began to talk to her, here in my spirit, wanting desperately for any sign that I was on my proper path, that following the call of my soul to this foreign land had not been in vain…"

"And…," Dristy encouraged, as Aizlyn seemed to fade into the memory and grow quiet.

"Rune came into the garden," Aizlyn said, and then went silent again as though that should be answer enough for her friend.

Dristy sighed deeply, understanding the answer completely. "Did he see you? Did you speak to him?"

"He did," Aizlyn replied, "yes. He came and sat next to me, our hounds content between us, and simply gazed up at the moon with me in silence for some time. Then, as though no answers came to him, he directed his questions to me instead. I should have returned to my quarters, were I still among my own I'd have been stoned to be found in that state. I know even among your people a proper lady, according to all that Lady Windell so frequently tries to instruct me to be, would not have remained unescorted in the company of a man not her kin, but something seemed to compel me to remain."

"What did he ask you?" Dristy pried.

"If I had been woken by a bad dream," Aizlyn said, a small smile coming to light her features as if from within.

"Had you?" Dristy asked, wondering if even in that life Aizlyn had been plagued with dreams.

"No," Aizlyn answered, same small smile saying more than her words. "As I told him, I had been woken by the good dream and I had walked in it every day for over three years now."

"What does that mean?" Dristy asked, feeling she knew but wanting some confirmation anyway.

"That is what he asked," Aizlyn giggled. "His face is such a reflection of his heart, he makes no attempts to hide his feelings. His eyes told me I had confused him greatly. I must still be sadly lacking in skill with regard to some of the finer nuances of your language."

"I think I understand," Dristy said. "You meant you had always felt that was where you belonged, in that place, in that moment, right?"

"Yes," Aizlyn said, sighing happily, "I knew you would understand, you have always understood."

"But he could not?" Dristy asked then, taking quiet pride in the fact she had been a good friend as far as that life went and Aizlyn was concerned.

"No," Aizlyn replied, "but he will see it in time, I hope."

"Did you talk any more than that?" Dristy asked hopefully.

"Yes," Aizlyn said, now thoughtful more than wistful, "he asked about my betrothed. How I felt when he was killed as were so many others. How strange to ask me my feelings for someone who is moved beyond this realm but who once held such sway over my future. I think he has many worrisome emotions with regard to his upcoming wedding. He wanted to know if I had loved my betrothed."

"What did you tell him?" Dristy prompted eagerly. Now they were getting somewhere.

"I told him that I was glad to be free, to be where I am, but saddened by the manner in which the freedom was awarded me," Aizlyn replied. "I told him the marriage was arranged long before I could dance, the dance was a mere formality, our parents had plans for us long before we thought to make plans for ourselves. I felt I was blessed though, after a way, since I knew the prince from childhood and knew him to be kind. He spoke to me again of love, though, I think wanting more to know how I felt about *love* and mayhap the impending absence of it in the marriage *I* was able to escape. I told him a loveless marriage may not have been my first choice of paths but I knew there were worse things the fates could conjure were I to tempt them. I do not wish to sway him out of turn, you see?

"I think I do," Dristy said, cutting an eye at Genie, remembering that same phrase from her lips moments before.

"I think Rune is still wild in his blood, not yet tamed to the thought that some things are requiring sacrifice." Aizlyn said then, "I think his people are not so long from savage that they have forgotten the sweet taste of free will on their tongues. Genevieve and he both seem not so adept at taking orders from anyone, let alone faceless kings on far-removed shores. The fact he has been told he is to marry a woman he has yet to meet to maintain peace within his homeland is seen as more a threat than an offer of that peace and does not sit well on his shoulders. He spoke to me of a volatile heritage and the blood of a proud sea-faring people, singing to him in his veins, of raw strengths capable to take and hold what they want close within a tangible grip, not words or women to bind ideas to themselves."

"So he doesn't want to marry this woman he is betrothed to?" Dristy said then, eyeing Genie sidelong and winking.

"No," Aizlyn said, now smiling that small smile again. "He says he always felt marriage was for love, he says his father never married because he couldn't have love, and he complains that he does not know this woman to love her. When I asked him why he must love her, why he could not marry her to secure this alliance and then take a second wife for love, he explained that your people and his people only take one woman to wife at a time. I told him I had thought Lord Windell quite special in how he loves his lady but asked if mayhap that was how you Europeans love?

219

"Rune conceded that Lord Windell was quite special and that many men take mistresses, but he feels that is a lie somehow. He does not want to marry if not for love, like his father and Lord and Lady Windell, and feels anything less makes mockery of marriage as he believes it should be if it should be at all. He thinks that if one cannot be true to the marriage then one should not enter into it, and cannot fathom why it is fallen to him to be faced with such hard choices. I see it must weigh heavy on him, for him to share this burden with me.

"I felt honored that he should tell me all these things that are so close to his heart. It seems he is torn between securing his lands and the people's well-being or losing what he sees as a piece of his soul for a lie before his god. He laughs that these English kings would be so lax as to take mere words to signify allegiances to their god but want solemn vows and marriages to believe allegiance to themselves is truly secure. I can only offer him hope by suggesting he may yet find a peaceful resolution.

"I questioned him again why it weighed so heavy on him, wondering why he cannot offer false vows like false words to their god. I was hoping to help him find peace if only for the remainder of the evening, asking him, if he was left without choice would his god not see that? Then he tried again to explain the difference between loving a woman enough to make her soul one with yours before Odin for all time by marrying her, and lust for a wench at port, sharing ale and flesh but no promises of love either verbal or implied before any god, but I think he embarrassed himself." Aizlyn giggled, suddenly happy as if the memory tickled her. Genie couldn't help but feel her hair rise at the sound, as Aizlyn added, "If he only knew what we Indian women are taught with the dance when we go to the temple, he'd have never stumbled himself to silence."

Dristy giggled too, suddenly reminded of something her mother had said about what every man wanted: a saint at church, a chef in the kitchen and a whore in the bedroom. Rune was in for a few surprises, she thought. Soon she was back to the problem at hand though, thinking back to her history lessons and the changing political climate of Europe throughout the

Crusades. She had it in her head that a proud sea-faring people would be from Iceland and couldn't recall there ever having been issue between Iceland and England during that time, but it seemed something had been asked of at least one ruling party in Iceland, if Aizlyn's memories were to be believed and she had the right sea-faring people in mind. Dristy was suddenly ready to move on and find out more. Genie, however, was still scratching notes to herself.

"You are falling in love with him?" Dristy said insightfully, using knowledge gleaned from having just born witness to many other of Aizlyn's lives. "He speaks of the kind of love you have always secretly longed for, the kind of marriage you know deep down you could have never had with your Indian prince. He shares himself in ways you have only dreamed a man would share with a woman."

"Yes," Aizlyn replied wistfully, "but now I wonder what can come of it if he cannot take a second wife and will not take a mistress. This is not at all what I thought it would be when I first saw him come from his ship." She sighed heavily, adding, "He may never be mine."

"But if he could," Dristy said pointedly, "if he did, he would not be the man you have come to know and therefore love. He would not so embody nor be providing the life and love you seek if second wife or mistress was what he made of you. You would not be as happy with him were you to have him any other way but as he is now, a dauntless dreamer who still believes in one man, one woman, in love, in marriage."

"I know," Aizlyn said, a bit forlorn now.

"Did you talk of anything else?" Dristy tried when the moment grew long in its silence.

"He merely asked me again how I felt about love, now that I had been freed of my betrothal," Aizlyn sighed. "It seems my answers had not satisfied him and when his gaze remained on me, awaiting a better one, my heart wanted to stop beating and my tongue certainly could not formulate any coherent or proper response."

"What did you do? What did you tell him?" Dristy begged.

"I held his gaze as long as I could, even though the moon was so round and bright it lit his eyes in such a manner I just knew I was going to drown in them. It seemed a challenge I should not back down from."

"And?" Dristy pleaded when Aizlyn stalled again.

"Then I merely said, 'We have this life,'" Aizlyn said dreamily, "'and in it, anything is possible.'"

Dristy looked back at Genie, who was still scratching furiously at her notebook, then she leaned close and whispered, "We have got to find this Rune fella for her, you sure you don't know where your brother is this lifetime?"

Genie merely arched an eyebrow that said, "what did I tell you about me needing space?" and went back to writing, still listening as she was quite adept at doing. She was a mother, she could write and listen *and* chew gum all at once.

"So what do you think he will do?" Dristy asked after a moment. "Do you think he will marry this woman for the peace treaty or risk a weakened position come war?"

"I don't think even he knows yet," Aizlyn answered. "I think it is the dream that wakes him, for I do not think he has slept much since he arrived. I think this proposed wedding of his more a reason for his visit than for Angus to breed his bitch. I have come to understand that the Windell and Rune houses share a long and happy relationship that goes back hundreds of years. It may have began with these Wolfhounds themselves but somehow has grown far stronger than merely sharing breeding stock. I have seen them sit often over a board game which they do not really play. I think they push the little people around and hope they will reveal a route by which all parties can be made happy. Lord Windell speaks often of Rune's father, whom I think must have been a beloved friend to him, and how that one would have had the wisdom to move the pieces just so."

"When will the decision be made?" Dristy said, hoping that question would propel them forward to a moment when Aizlyn could give her more information.

"Soon," Aizlyn said, a bit forlorn, "some important lord or other has sent his son to retrieve the documents that will serve to bind until the Church can bear witness. We shall see what comes."

"Are they here yet?" Dristy prompted when Aizlyn was silent for a moment.

"He comes now," Aizlyn said, a bit awed. "They are all so shiny and awe-inspiring, their horses so large and beautiful, like young gods on the march they come, can you hear them? The one at the head, he brings the sun on his helm. Oh, poor Genevieve, she looks like she is going to faint. I think I am contagious."

Genie looked up at that and Dristy looked quizzically back at her. It seemed both of them were at a loss as to what Aizlyn might have given her that was contagious. Genie finally shrugged her shoulder, as if to say, "You got me," and motioned for Dristy to find out.

"What have you given Genevieve that is contagious?" Dristy asked, somewhat worried. "Why would she be about to faint?"

Aizlyn giggled. "Love, I have given her love. He is so very large, this lord's son, she had to practically lay her head on her spine to see his face when he dismounted. Quite handsome, he is, pure gold, the moment he removed his helm I think she caught my sickness. After all the poking fun at me when Rune wasn't listening she is made to suffer the same. Sweet karma has come to visit her with the flutters." Aizlyn laughed again, "She stuttered, did you hear? Ge ge ne vieve, she said. How sweet he is, he politely ignored her stutter and lowered his head for her to see his eyes when he told her she could call him William. Maybe he caught it too? He did seem almost unwilling to look away when Lord Windell addressed him. I shall have to poke her later in the garden tonight."

Genie started laughing and so did Dristy, and then Aizlyn began to laugh again, either with them then or in her memory didn't rightly matter to any of them at the moment. Finally Genie whispered, "I do that every time! That's how I always know." Dristy just looked at her longingly, wishing it were so easy for her.

"We will meet in the garden tonight?" Dristy asked then, when Aizlyn's last comment finally hit her.

"Don't we always?" Aizlyn asked.

Dristy looked at Genie as if for confirmation of the sudden feeling she got, that yes, they did. Genie nodded with a soft smile that said the thought felt like a memory or the other way around. They both felt they'd all been sneaking out to the gardens since that first fateful conversation Rune and Aizlyn had shared beneath the full moon, playing quiet games, or just sitting and talking, but making fast friends every night from then until now.

"What will we do until then?" Dristy tried for more.

"We wait. Lord Windell has taken Rune and Lord *William* to his private quarters where they shall discuss what is to be done." Aizlyn said the name as though teasing an old friend and it made Dristy recall the way she had poked at Gen when they were younger, telling her, "There's *Billy*, looking over here."

"Well, what has been decided?" Dristy prompted, hoping to propel things along.

"We shall know when Rune comes," Aizlyn sighed pensively. "He gave me no sign at supper, seemed to not even want to look toward me, in case his face should betray him as it is always wont to with me. I saw more telling things pass between Genevieve here and her Lord *William* than Rune risked sharing with me."

Dristy knew by her mood and comments they must have moved forward to the gardens and were awaiting the arrival of Rune to learn their fate. She glanced at Genie, now also pensive. She was almost afraid to try and push it along again. What if it wasn't good and Aizlyn threw herself from the parapets or something horrible? Genie nodded at her, eyes also betraying a small worry, but both were aware they needed to know and she had a good feeling about this life that she was willing to go with.

"Well," Dristy said, more than a little frightened and with "peaches" ready to fly off her tongue. "Where is Lord Rune?"

"He came and gathered Genevieve and took her for a walk, he barely glanced at me when he did," Aizlyn said, also sounding small and frightened. "I am afraid. What could be happening?"

"I don't know," Dristy tried. "What did Genevieve say when she returned?"

"Rune has presented a plan to her and she has agreed to it," Aizlyn fairly shouted, sounding triumphantly pleased suddenly. "Can you believe how sweet and kind he is? He would not choose his own happiness over hers and has left her path up to her. Never have I known a man like him."

"What plan?" Dristy begged.

"We shall *all* spend the next two weeks here coming to know each other better, then come time for Lord William's return to his father, if he has found favor in our Genevieve's heart, as he has her eyes, she will return with him and his father will have the alliance he seeks in a much more pleasing way for all those concerned."

"What?" Dristy said, taken completely by surprise by the twist. "How?"

"Lord Windell had noted our Genevieve's gazes and William's returning of them, so he approached Lord William man to man, asking him what was really needing to be accomplished for his father to be happy. It seems all his father really wants is some alliance that might bring him ships come a need for them, and when Lord Windell asked him, he revealed his sister had no great desire to wed some sea-going barbarian. They came to see that Lord William is a younger son and so long as an alliance was made it would matter very little which offspring made it." Aizlyn laughed happily, "Lord Windell suggested Lord William make the alliance himself, marrying Lady Rune, saving his sister from our Rune, the sea-fairing barbarian, and Lord William agreed quite quickly that the plan was a good one. I think, more so, I was right and he has been afflicted also with the love I carried with me from India and desired a way to make our Genevieve his in a manner that her brother would readily agree to. I do not think he had realized that was not to be the end of it though, that man to man talk. I think it shocked him when she was not simply told she was to be wed to him to save her brother from a marriage he obviously did not want either, but rather asked if she would agree to the plan. Neither do I think he realized that he might have to earn her love, but I think the idea has captured him as surely as she has and he is up to the challenge. I think he has begun his *conquest* already."

"And you and Rune?" Dristy asked as Aizlyn seemed to gaze far off, as though watching the two she was speaking of. Dristy realized she was holding her breath. "What of you two, now there is nothing to come between?"

"He has asked me if I could love him," Aizlyn said, now completely dreamy. "He says he offers no great palace, not even a castle so fine as Lord Windell's, just a proud old longhouse, a bunch of flea-ridden dogs, and a lifetime full of love and companionship."

"And?" Dristy said impatiently when Aizlyn seemed to become lost in the memory.

"I have told him it sounds like all I could dream," Aizlyn said giggling again, "and that I had been unable to resist. I had always loved him."

"Will you go to live with him then?" Dristy asked finally, to confirm the happy ending.

"You are coming too," Aizlyn said excitedly, "pack your things, Lord Windell said I can take you with me, he has not missed the bond we have made this last three months. We leave right after the ceremony. He gave me my jewelry back, here, feel," Aizlyn said as if she meant for her blind companion to see it through touch. "I suppose he managed to recover my things from wherever Lady Windell had hidden them away." Aizlyn became nervous, adding, "You think Rune will like it? He has never seen me in my own dress and jewels."

"I don't know," Dristy tried, pushing her forward a little further, "What did he say?"

"He was awestruck, I think," Aizlyn said, a bit bemused. "He didn't say much at all at first, just kept looking very long at me. Then finally he said

I was amazingly beautiful. Then later, when I asked him how he liked my clothes and jewels, thinking mayhap they overwhelmed, he waited until no one could hear, causing me to worry I had been right and it was too much for him. Then he told me," Aizlyn paused and laughed, again causing Genie to sit up and take notice, "I'd be lucky if I made it through dinner with all of it on."

"So you are happy then, old friend?" Dristy asked after laughing too.

It was meant as one last question and a goodbye, to that life and someone she felt keenly that she had known and loved, before moving on. She had not expected her words to draw the kind of response they did but she was glad later to have heard it.

"I have been nothing if not pleased with this life my oldest, dearest, friend," Aizlyn said, sounding aged and tired, "even my regrets are minute. I have oft times missed the face of my goddess and mourned the deaths of all those that saw to it I left her and my country behind all those years ago. I would sometimes that it had come about differently but..."

Aizlyn sighed deeply, and then moved on, "I have sometimes even regretted that the Lady Windell and I never had any reconciliation. I think at times she even blamed me when Lord Windell went again to the Holy Land, where my people and I had traveled and first came upon him that fateful day, and never returned. I think she felt until her death that he was somehow drawn there again because of me. But I think he has always been drawn there, something in him is bound to wander..."

Aizlyn then smiled, a small smile, bittersweet. "I have even, at times, wished I could have given Rune a son or even a daughter, though he tells me I have given him all he could have ever dreamed, I know it must weigh on him this old longhouse has no sons to carry it into the next life, to keep its roof and tend its fires. But there is not a single moment that I think I would sacrifice for any of those things to be different. I have fed dogs and gazed from the cliffs, I have bathed in springs and slept on fur and woken to a man who desires to know my dreams. I am well in my soul and I will keep that with me always, even unto the next life."

The darkening evening outside the ever-open window sent a gust of wind to threaten the candles again and Dristy remembered, said goodbye to an old friend, and sent her further back.

13

Angus: Special Choice

Dristy was quick to tell Aizlyn to flip a few more pages back in her mental photo album, she was not about to risk another slow recollection of life at the end of it which would find Genie screaming about Aizlyn having stopped breathing again. But she was glad she had heard Aizlyn's thoughts come the end of that one. I gave her hope they were getting to the bottom of things.

Genie had a wonderful little smile playing with her entire face, even making her eyes twinkle, when Dristy was finally confident with Aizlyn's breathing and took the time to glance at her old friend. Dristy could only bear the self-satisfied visage for so long before she had to wipe it away with some good old-fashioned schoolyard picking.

"Yeah, yeah," Dristy whispered at last, a bit peevish, "Aren't you the lucky one? *Gen Gen and Billy sitten in a tree, k-i-s-s-i-n-g.*"

"Oh hush," Genie smiled, "let's finish this, wake her up."

"Wake her up?" Dristy queried, taken by surprise by the request. "Why?"

"We're done,' Genie said, now a bit puzzled herself that Dristy seemed to think otherwise.

"No, we're not," Dristy stated.

"Sure we are," Genie disagreed. "We've seen where the wall is, a chance meeting of her people with the English that put her on a path where she discovered a whole other world of possibilities, a love which took her to a longhouse and has sent her searching endlessly for it again throughout a dozen or so more lives thereafter. The Crusaders and the longhouse were in the same damn life after all." Genie returned the school yard taunt, "Na na na boo boo!"

"Really? And if that was the first time her life's train was thrown off track," Dristy interrupted, "where do you suppose she got that deep-seated feeling she was meant to go with Lord Windell that time and search for a cliff from which she'd later see her destiny making his pre-ordained arrival?" Dristy paused dramatically then added, "And at what point did that particular version of our elusive Lord Rune strike you as the kind to chain his *love* in front of his fire?"

Dristy preened when Genie pouted, "All we have discovered so far is why she feels so strongly about her 'something more' to be found on what we'd previously assumed were European shores. I think, personally, it was probably some cliff-lined coast, more closely narrowed to Scotland, some close-ish to Iceland, but that is neither here nor there." Dristy said, getting down to business, having successfully made her point, "We also have an ever growing and changing list of regrets which presumably send her back each time as surely as, as you so deftly put it, 'coming back for those we love.' I intend to chase this down if it takes all damn night and you, my dear, are in it with me since you have been so kind to reunite me with an old friend I intend to repay a favor to."

"Repay a favor?" Genie said, confused again.

"I have always believed in past lives," Dristy explained, "you know that. I have never trusted another to do a regression on me, probably because I have seen first-hand what can go wrong and only trust myself enough to do it, even at that, look what narrow misses we have had. Since I can't regress myself I have simply had to be tantalized by visions of a few happy lives. Or so I thought, until tonight. But I think maybe, at least in my case, they were indeed all of one, a castle and an old longhouse but the same, single, happy life. One in which, I know now, I was quite likely spared the sad life of a blind scullery maid by a visionary princess who felt completely natural being the eyes for an otherwise unwanted servant she called dearest friend. That life obviously stuck with me as it has with her, the happiness and vision have been enough to compel me to seek happiness through vision in this one. So I will find her damn wall for her, I will be her eyes tonight, and damn it, you better start looking real hard for your brother if my hunch is correct."

"What hunch?" Genie said, thrown for a loop by her friend's determined rant.

"Ask me again when we find the real wall and I'll tell you if I still think I am right," Dristy said, relishing in her moment of mild karma, "unless you want to tell me now what other hunches you're still stewing."

"Bitch," Genie grinned, accepting it.

"Yep," Dristy said. Taking one last look at Aizlyn and Angus's breathing to be sure it was steady and normal before pushing to her feet to refill her coffee, she added, "Want a refill?" as she left Genie to stew.

"Where are you?" Dristy asked after settling back in, in front of Aizlyn, with her newly refilled coffee.

"The palace pavilion," Aizlyn replied, sounding winded.

"Have you danced?" Dristy asked, afraid she knew the answer already.

"Of course," Aizlyn said, excitement lacing her breathless voice, "I made it back in the nick of time, the drums had stopped but they began again for me."

"Got back from where?" Dristy asked, confused, glancing at Genie.

"I saw the beautiful beast again, slinking just beyond the tents and fires, I was drawn away and followed it thoughtlessly," Aizlyn responded, "but I heard the drums quicken before they would fade one final time and I recalled myself as I wandered after him and raced back to the pavilion to meet my fate."

Dristy was confused, she thought Aizlyn didn't want to dance, didn't want to win the prince, wanted to follow the dog. She asked, "You are pleased to have won the prince's favor? You do not wonder if you should have followed the beautiful beast and seen where he might lead you?"

"Seems to me I have done all I could do." Aizlyn sounded befuddled. "I have tried to be true to the inner wisdom I have been given. I know I was born to be a princess, destined to dance. I think I have done well in that I have set a different tone, done the dance my way by arriving late and making the drums begin again just for me and at least for now, I do not feel less in that I am not the first to have won his eye. I grant you, I feel a great loss not having laid my hands to the beast's head and told him my secrets. I even had a sweet meat I had saved for him but I can see no means by which to have had the two things at once this night."

Genie and Dristy exchanged puzzled looks and leaned in to discus this seemingly new outlook on life. Dristy said, "Seems she is trying to make happiness with her prince. She seems to be drawn to the dog but not more so than the dance."

"I think she realizes it will be one or the other," Genie replied. "She mentions not being able to have both and knowing it, and it seems she chose this life to try to change her state with Jordan. It won't be till later lives that she gives up on Jordan and begins to long for the dog and the ability to follow it."

"Why would she regress from then to now?" Dristy asked. "Why come into this life after having spent so many before with it pre-planted in her soul to avoid him, seek a dog and cliffs and choose to go after him and try to change their fate as she had obviously stopped doing so many lives ago. I mean this is the first we have come across that desire in her."

"You're a dork," Genie answered after a long moment. "This life is before the one she just married Rune."

"Oh yeah," Dristy said, taking the "dork" on the chin with a grin, "but she still senses there is more. So I was right about the wall being still further back!"

Dristy thought for a long moment. There seemed no quick answer. Genie huffed, Dristy sighed, Aizlyn was told to go back a few more pages.

"Where are you?" Dristy asked again.

"In my chamber," Aizlyn sighed. "I await my prince."

"So you have wed your prince?" Dristy wondered, "and are you pleased?"

"No, not completely," Aizlyn sighed, "but I am willing to work toward my peace. All good things take time and effort."

Dristy knew damn well Aizlyn was willing to work toward her peace, knew damn well she had done so for countless lives they had visited. She also knew damn well she was not going to find it in that life. So she pushed her even further back, still looking for the wall with the chain mounted in it.

Suddenly Aizlyn screamed and began thrashing wildly as though she wrestled many invisible hands. She screamed again, yelling words neither of them could understand. Dristy yelled "peaches" but it brought no change as Aizlyn weakened, her screams became yelps, short and clipped. Then just as suddenly as it began, it ended, she fell limp over Angus's still-sleeping head.

Genie and Dristy had both lunged forward, when screaming peaches had failed, trying to pin her thrashing arms as she threw her coffee and rocked the dog's head on her jerking knees. Angus remained disturbingly fast asleep in her lap, unaware of their presence- shocking in and of itself, but Aizlyn made no response to them either and that was much worse. She, too, still seemed unaware they were there and had been deaf to their safe word which they yelled over and over.

Then the dog began breathing very hard, rocking Aizlyn from the torso up where she lay limply draped over his head, her breath disturbingly shallow. Genie felt for a pulse. Dristy said peaches, over and over in her ear, to no avail. The two women sat back in shocked silence, completely at a loss. Genie was on the verge of dialing 911, though she hadn't the faintest clue what she would tell help when it arrived.

They stared, horrified as the dog's steady, heavy breathing kept rocking Aizlyn, it seemed to set her body to a wicked unnatural dance and be the only life about her. The candles fluttered as another chill gust found the ever-open window and brought the eager hand of death close again. Dristy started crying, chanting prayers she hadn't prayed since she was a child. Genie did the only thing that seemed to work in her mind after all they had witnessed tonight. She begged Angus to wake Aizlyn up. When Angus suddenly let out two huffing snorts and Aizlyn jerked as though waking, the two women watching nearly screamed again.

They all smelled the burning as it left on the wind, whipping back out the open window into the now dark night. A chill calmness settled about the three candlewicks but the women watching were not fooled. There was no safety to their present circumstance, never had been, and certainly wasn't now.

Genie saw red marks had appeared on Aizlyn's upper arms, saw her lip swell slightly. She might have convinced herself it was due to Dristy and her trying to restrain her had she not smelled the burning too, had she not recalled the burning dream. She glanced at Dristy and knew by her wide frightened eyes that Dristy too remembered the second dream Genie had warned her most vigorously to avoid.

Angus huffed again, and again Aizlyn twitched as though she had heard him.

"Where are you?" Dristy tried. "Go someplace safe, talk to me."

Aizlyn made no response except that she began to shiver. Genie jumped up and ran to the large chest where they had withdrawn the blanket they sat on now and pulled forth another of the heavy faux fur blankets she layered on the beds in winter. She came behind Aizlyn and wrapped it around her gently, careful of the angry welts she saw had risen beneath the red rings encircling Aizlyn's biceps. As she glanced down on her friend's blank visage, while tucking her warmly in the blanket, Genie couldn't help but notice that Aizlyn's ears and nose were red and seemed irritated as well where her many rings looped through the flesh.

Genie recalled reading the terror of the burning dream, and knew Aizlyn had just relived it again, knew her body had just lived through it again and believed what her memory was playing for her enough to supply the pain. Genie whispered in her ear, "I am so sorry..."

Aizlyn twitched as though she heard, tilted her head as though she didn't understand but wanted to escape the words anyway.

"You can hear me?" Genie whispered then. "Can you understand me?"

Again Aizlyn moved her head slightly and made a face that was all the answer Genie needed. Genie looked at Dristy, near hopeless, and said, "I don't think she understands us, maybe she can't understand our language, maybe that's why she didn't respond when we said the safe word."

"It shouldn't matter, her mind is here *and* there," Dristy said, trying to sound confident, "She has understood and responded in kind in every other life whether she had been taught to speak English in it or not."

"Maybe because it made sense to?" Genie asked. "Maybe because it fit the moment to, because she either felt she spoke with an old friend or her goddess. Hell, maybe because it wasn't so real that she was lost in it. But I sure as hell don't think she understands our words at all, let alone our safe word."

Aizlyn was listening, they could tell because her head had begun to tilt this way or that every now and again and she would look in different directions as though looking to where she thought the words came from. But Aizlyn was definitely not at their disposal as far as giving any discernable directions to at the moment, and the two women who were supposed to be helping her felt they had made a terrible mess.

"What are we gonna do then?" Dristy said nervously, beginning to bite at her lip and try hard not to freak out. "I don't know how to direct a regression if the regressed doesn't understand me. Hell, I don't know how to bring her back either."

The two women stared at each other for the longest time, apparently hoping the other would have an epiphany at any moment, but neither one was having any luck. Dristy, finally, in desperation, began to dig through her bag as though she might come across something that might give her an answer. Genie took her lead and gathered the photocopied pages from Aizlyn's dream journal out from behind and under her, where they had ended up in the commotion, and began laying them out before her, hoping one page or another would offer a clue as to what to do next.

Aizlyn stared blankly ahead as silence descended upon the basement while Genie and Dristy looked for a means to communicate with her. Dristy eventually found herself thumbing through a worn book of baby names and their meanings, knowing, even as she did, she wasn't going to find a way to make Aizlyn understand her, but she just kept flipping through it anyway, at a loss for anything better to try.

Genie pushed the pages around, organizing them for the third or forth time into what she felt was the right order and feeling, once again, that she was missing something. Suddenly she grabbed the journal itself and began to flip through it, wondering if, in her haste that afternoon, she might have missed an important page or two. She had gone through it completely, twice, before she gave up and sat it, too, down in front of her and began wishing she had the letters.

Hadn't Aizlyn said she was going to want to read them? Hadn't she hinted there was even more information in them that would fuel their never-ending argument about past lives and her and Jordan's destiny? Maybe there was something in them that could help her now, some means her mother's words might reveal. Genie was just about to get her butt up and run over to Aizlyn's house right then and there to get them when she noticed Aizlyn seemed to be looking at her journal, seemed to be really seeing it.

Genie picked it up and held it out in front of her and sucked in a deep breath that drew Dristy's complete attention when she saw Aizlyn's eyes follow it. Genie was suddenly struck by an idea, spawned by the explanation she had received from Aizlyn years before when she had asked when and why the journal had come to exist. She took another deep breath and hoped desperately that she truly was the perpetual mother Aizlyn had proclaimed her to be.

"Aizlyn," Genie said putting the journal in her hand, and tilting Aizlyn's head up to meet her eyes, "this is for you. You need to separate your dreams from your reality. Write them down and study them to see what they mean to teach you." Genie prayed her *mother voice* was getting through, as she saw Aizlyn seemed to actually see her as she continued, "You must remember they have nothing to do with your current reality, in reality you are safe, you are here with me, just write the dream down and we will figure it out together."

Genie's heart leaped when Aizlyn tightened her grip on the journal and she reached around behind her, patting desperately around on the blanket for a pen or pencil, unwilling to remove her eyes from Aizlyn's and risk breaking the spell. Dristy planted a pen in her hand, holding it tight for half a second as though passing all her hopes into her hand too.

"Write this dream down, Aizlyn," Genie said while praying her heart out, "just like all the others. Write this dream down and then let it fall back into eternity with every other dream and be at peace with it." She placed the pen in Aizlyn's hand and squeezed, adding, "Then we can go back and figure this out. *We can talk* after it is written."

Genie and Dristy both sat in further shocked silence as Aizlyn began flipping through the pages till she reached the back of the journal where some clean pages still remained. They seemed afraid to move until Aizlyn began writing quick sure strokes that ate up the page, then they both moved in unison leaning forward quickly as if needing to be sure the pen was working, the words were in English, and that what they were seeing was truly happening.

Aizlyn's words began eating up page after page as she seemed determined to get it all out and let it go as the perpetual mother had told her she could. Genie finally tore her eyes away and told Dristy she would be right back, to watch her closely. Genie ran up the stairs, jumped in her car and drove the two blocks to Aizlyn's in a rush. She flew through the small house straight for the bedroom, where she found the letters filed neatly in the now half-empty box they had come to her in.

Genie was home and back in the basement in under ten minutes, flipping quickly through letters while Aizlyn's hand slid endlessly left to right filling in what space remained in her journal. Genie's track through the letters was much swifter than Aizlyn's had been, she spent no time snooping through her friend's grandparents' lives as shared between father and daughter, she only paused on those lines that spoke of Aizlyn herself or occasionally Jordan. She knew Aizlyn had intended for her to read them and wouldn't mind, but for now she was intent on what she could learn of further use to the current situation.

Genie was only interrupted occasionally by a low growl or huff or sudden twitching from Angus accompanying Aizlyn's steady scrawl. She glanced at Dristy the first few times but that one just raised a shoulder that told her it was nothing new in this life and nothing she could explain either. Since it obviously hadn't yet been a problem, eventually Genie quit letting it bother her too. Genie was just putting the letters away when Aizlyn closed the journal and put it down. Genie raised an eyebrow at Dristy as the cows winked and dinked and both watched Aizlyn relax visibly.

Dristy lunged for the journal, desperate to know what had just happened.

"Out loud?" Genie asked.

Dristy read, "I came screaming from the bloodied womb of fire, was swaddled in the stench of death and suckled the tit of fear. I only began when I survived the burning. I would not know it for many years but the night of the slaughter of my wedding party and my people is the night I was born. I am the only one to start my life as so many others were ended, I can see that from here, while viewing this dream, but for then it seemed those marauding thieves took everything from me, including my life.

"A huge beast's intrusive nose shot cold, wet agony into my burnt and bloodied ear as he sniffed for life within my damaged shell, and I remembered, I lived through that fateful night. I heard words from a distance I couldn't measure and longed to escape their masculine creators, but from here, while dreaming, I know it was a kind voice announcing, "This one still breathes." Strange to know now, things I couldn't have then; even being so utterly in those moments, a part of me knew I should not have understood him.

"Weeks I stay in the company of these large men whose red and gold skin is foreign and frightening enough in and of itself without having been stretched so taut over such massive muscled frames. For weeks I see them pointing and speaking and I know I am the subject of their heated debates. I see them gesture to parts of their body and then to me and I know they feel the marks made by my large amounts of stolen jewelry, torn from me with such violent force, means to them what it would to any observant man, that I was a woman of great wealth. Their arguments, loud and sometimes brutal in their ferocity, terrify me. I think sometimes that the man who calls the beast 'Angus' shall lose one of these harsh debates and I fear I shall not fare well come a time such as that.

"These men show respect for him, undeniable that they fear his wrath, but sometimes I hear them call him 'Wi-n-dell' and their tone tells me it is not a reverent title, they would not say it so were he able to hear them. I know this man, this leader, keeps me safe because he feels my person is worth more to them as well-kept as can be accomplished while traveling as shabbily as they do.

"After weeks of kindness, from the man whose words were then foreign to me but kept a fate at bay I cannot imagine, I made my escape into the night, fearing his power over them was bound to fail. This future me who sees what I cannot see, screams I was not to leave their company, I only prolong my journey. I slip away from the Walker and his men, and make my way to distant smells and lights that seemed familiar to me and just beyond my sight. The Walker's shaggy, small horse-sized beast came slinking behind me, at a distance I know now was meant to provide comfortable ability to care for me and yet keep from being shooed. I had spent weeks trying to be rid of the 'Angus,' as they called him, when the huge hairy beast approached me. I was ever throwing morsels of the sad fare his master provided to sustain and replenish me at the furthest distance I could manage with my sore arms to make him leave my company. It seems this Angus has no sense whatsoever, as he has only become more enamored with me despite my best efforts to be rid of him and his cold searching nose.

"I make my way silently as I can, not wanting to make his master and the men with him aware of my departure, afraid that he might try to stop me, though he has taken no action that should warrant this fear. I am merely frightened by these huge men, with red and gold skin, so different from my own and all I have known. I kick sand behind me and make angry motions but this Angus is persistent or daft, I cannot be sure. He pauses and I hope, but when I look back, still he slinks after me, head down as though he were merely following a smell and not me.

"I am suddenly glad of his company though, when I see the camp, whose smells had been so promising, so close at hand and suddenly as foreign to me as that I had left. The watchman notes my approach. The man's jeering calls to his comrades that a woman comes toward them alone, frighten me, but at least I can make out some few words, their dialect is different than my own but close enough that I can gather their meaning. I fear I may have done a very stupid thing as they gather close around me, studying me in a mean way. I become terrified and stumble on words they seem to barely understand, telling these men I am a princess and that Prince Jordan will pay a healthy reward for my safe return. It seems at least 'Prince Jordan' is recognized if no other words, and they form ranks, apart, and begin to argue amongst themselves. Finally it seems they have made a decision, they point me toward a tent and give me food and drink, but they say nothing to me of their plan.

"Come a few hours before the dawn they wake me with the sounds of breaking camp and I come out and watch as they prepare to depart. There is another argument as I am given a mount but I convince myself that I am safe as we travel, that these men mean to return me to my prince, if for no other reason than to receive his gold.

"It takes many weeks to reach a city, they travel quickly but in a direction that seems not right to me. I try to make them understand we move in the wrong direction, but they merely laugh and continue on. I suppose I am not to say what men should do so I hold my tongue and watch the shaggy beast that still follows me, trotting easily at the small horse's side. I come to see quickly they are not good men, and I harbor a false sense of safety while among them, when one of them comes to me while everyone sleeps and places his hand over my mouth so I cannot scream.

"Angus wakes as violently as I, a few feet from me, where I had tossed food to make him go away, and his teeth are a welcome flash as they lash out to drag the man from me when all I can do is squeak and try to breathe. I know I am only spared because the dog delays him until his comrade can come to see what the commotion is about. I know the man is only dealt a swift death for risking their payment. I am always terribly frightened to sleep now. I give the dog a portion of my food, close to my side; I do not want him to leave me alone. These weeks drag with terrible slowness, a true rest has not been mine in a very long time, but at least they bring me to a port from which they say they send a message to my prince.

"I did not know whether my prince simply did not send a swift enough response or they demand too high a price for the return of a wife he may have deemed damaged beyond redeeming. Maybe the trader offered more or they simply did not wish to wait, all I know is I was not sent back to my prince. I was taken to a woman who bathed and clothed me, not so gentle as my own servants and in nothing so fine as my own attire, but I am thankful to be clean and think I am soon to be headed home. Then I am passed into the care of a merchant whose belly pushes me up a long plank laid from dock to ship and when the plank was pulled away and the anchor hefted I knew something was terribly wrong, my home lay far inland. I scanned the faces on the dock and knew no one I could call to for help, and then I saw Angus and cried out for him.

"The dog broke loose a great gallop, evading those who tried to keep him from me, and come to the end of the pier he made the distance between us in one great leap that a horse could have made no better. The men on the ship fell back from him, frightened by his sudden appearance and powerful display, as he came to my side and I hugged him and kept him there. Again, I resign myself to have no rest as I was taken far from everything I knew by men whose language I could not understand with only a huge scruffy beast to maintain safe distance between them and me.

"I listen from corners, hidden behind Angus, trying desperately to begin to make sense of their words. I have a small hope if I might learn to communicate with them I might make some bargain with them that will see me sent home. I have seen some of these men whose motioning combined with rough words and mean looks might have meant they wanted to toss Angus over the side of the ship to be rid of his constancy between my person and their lecherous desires, but the man who rules this ship always hushes them. It seems the large gold coin he hefts to shine before their eyes bids them be silent or see what man risks Angus's teeth first, and none has yet to try for it or me. Still I have no peace. A woman does not belong on a ship, she is never safe. I find I hate that I am a woman.

"Life on that ship is hell itself as weeks drag into months and I am covered with filth and vermin from finding what rest I can so close to Angus. Then we come to a port where I see people whose face and dress reminds of home but who seem unable to comprehend me when I beg them to send word to Prince Jordan. The fat merchant smacks the back of my head to hush my pleas and Angus shows him teeth which cause him to back away from me.

"Again I am thrust into the care of a none-too-gentle woman who scrubs me, ridding me of Angus's crawling gifts, and then clothes me in finer things than I had been given before. She brushes my long hair and braids it, then she turns me to a looking glass as though I am meant to praise her work. I am staring at this person I have become when I feel her place a heavy band on my ankle; my mind did not work right for a moment then. Somehow I was thinking my jewelry was being returned to me but then I felt her lift the length of chain attached to it, handing the end of it proudly over to the merchant who hands her a few small coins. It seems all hope has abandoned me now, I am no princess, I am a slave.

"We leave this woman and come to stop before a place where men sit and drink and fall from their chairs. The merchant signals to a large man who sits straighter than most and has a large sword across the table before him. He points at Angus. The man shakes his head sharply, gives the merchant harsh words and turns back to his drink. The merchant pulls out his purse and calls to him again but the man does not turn back. The merchant raises his voice, addressing all of those men present, but none of them rises to his challenge.

"I am still trying to steady my heart; I know what the merchant had meant to pay the men to do. I have come to love this beast, for the love that it has shown me. My heart has come to fear the loss of him as much as my flesh has; both rely on him far to keenly now. The merchant huffs angrily down the docks dragging me by this length of chain and Angus follows, as ever, stuck to my side.

"I am placed in a room with many other women from every walk of life and in every state of dress. My heart stops for a long moment before it lurches to terrible life, meaning to beat its way free of my chest. I am scared near to tears as another merchant, this one thin as death and just as pale, comes and begins to argue with the fat one that brought me there. They make gestures toward me and then Angus who has proven impossible for the fat one to keep from me, short of finding someone brave who will bring a sword against him. The thin man seems to want nothing of Angus but everything of me and the fat one seems to tell him it is one in the same. Finally he has made a bargain with the thin man and is given a key and the end of my chain. The thin one leads me away while the fat one laughs and pats his pockets. I try to communicate with this merchant too, but he too does not seem to understand nor care what words I have learned so far.

"I am led to another small room where a few more frightened young people huddle. I begin to see what has become of me. I have become a slave of a sort I can only imagine as my fears begin to run away with me again. I find a corner of my own and crouch behind Angus, willingly retrieving my vermin from him. We in that room are brought food and for many days see nothing of the thin man, but then one day he comes with others, a rough gathering that remind me of the crew of the ship I was prisoner on for months.

"They round us up and shoo us down to the docks like so many cattle and again I am forced onto a ship. The men try to leave Angus behind, blocking his way up the plank bodily and then removing it swiftly. He seems unwilling to fight or bite them, only wishing to be close to me but not wanting to harm can it be avoided. I am frightened if he will not fight to come to me I shall be left to these men's mercies and I have seen nothing of mercy from men. The men who remain on the pier begin to laugh and pat each other on the back as the anchor is pulled up. They turn to wave to the thin man, casting him proud farewells, but I hush them quickly when I yell in desperation for Angus and again he makes the leap easily as they are busy congratulating themselves on a job not yet done, and again Angus comes to stand before me. The thin man is angry and lifts a large gold coin to the men on board but none of them finds it worth a limb and all turn and quickly to find other business to attend to.

"This journey is far longer than the other but somehow more acceptable, for I am not alone, and slowly I begin to find words that work among the young men and women with me in the bottom of the ship. There is among us a young woman I recognize now, but for then I merely come to know her slowly, when she pats her heart and tells me her name is Jade. Her language is clipped and harsh on my tongue but I am determined to learn to use it. When the water becomes very restless for many nights and we huddle together beneath Angus so as not to be thrown to and fro, she speaks to me of pride, a thing I have nearly forgotten. She tells me again her name is Jade, patting her chest above her heart, she tilts her chin high and I know she tells me more than her name again. She tells me to keep *my* chin high and hold who *I* am close to my heart no matter what might come. But I no longer know who I am, if I am not a princess, I am only a slave.

"The ship is damaged and we are forced to make a stop in our journey, something that has made the thin man very angry. I follow Jade's lead and keep my head low, my back turned, my mouth closed, as the ship is being repaired. The thin man has men bring a tub from the shore into the bottom of the ship and tells everyone to clean themselves and rid themselves of vermin. Jade draws the women together and makes of us a wall as we do as we are told as privately as we can, her chin is up and her eyes remind me to hide inside my heart and lift mine too. When all are cleaned, Jade points to Angus, and the men leave the tub that he might be cleaned too. I actually smile for the first time in over a year as we clean him and rid him of vermin too. The tub is removed, the workers depart, and again we set sail.

"We are brought to a harbor then some weeks later and at that harbor some of us are taken from the boat and others are not. I am happy they have left Jade with me as again we feel the anchor lifted and our lives propelled forward into the unknown. Finally it is our turn as they come and shoo both of us up the ladder and onto the deck of the ship. Jade tells me again to keep my chin up as they take us through a large dirty city and into a small dirty place where I am again bartered for briskly and again the dog is thrown into the bargain, with much amusement on the part of the thin man.

"I have come to understand enough of the words to know that my new master means to have the dog sold separately at another time and does not mind the deal as the thin man thought he might. This new man with ill intent living in his eyes feels he has gotten a wonderful deal, I hear it as he talks to himself about a man he knows who owns a female of my Angus's kind. He is the one laughing when he puts the key to my chain in his near-emptied purse and lifts the end of it in his thick grip, pulling me behind him and further into the great getting lost that has become my life. I look back over my shoulder as Jade disappears from view and I see her mouth words that meant she would see me again. I can only hope.

"This new man means to be rid of the dog quickly, since when he reaches for me Angus shows him teeth that frighten him. He wears his desires so close to his surface it seems to sweat them and this terrifies and nauseates me simultaneously. I see he will not be so easy to dissuade as others have been. He loads us both into a wagon and begins a long journey inland. The land around me is green and lush, but cool and often shrouded in gray haze that reminds me of smoke and death and fear. It is good to be on land but I am afraid my knowledge of *fear* is just beginning.

"We travel for many, many days and he stops in a town and speaks to an old woman who sells him something in a small pouch he tries to keep hidden. I am wary now when he approaches, with false smiles and pretend kindness. I see things boiling in his eyes and I am sure he has grown willing to lose what gold the beast might bring to have his way with me. That night he carries two separate platters of food, and offers one to Angus as though he means to make of us friends but I knock the food to the ground, suspicious and angry he would think to woo my hound. I feed Angus from my own plate and hug him close to me to sleep.

"The man grows more and more angry at me and his leers become meaner as the days pass. I begin to think of trying to get the key to my shackles from him when he sleeps and slip away in the night, of stealing this large fat horse he hitches to his wagon and running for my life, but I can think of no safe place to go and find each evening that my courage lags with the thought of leaving a known danger for an unknown, perhaps worse one.

"We come to another town and there is a man there with a beast that looks very much like Angus only much smaller and the man I traveled with approached him. This man gave him words but not coins and did not try to take the dog from me. The man I travel with is very frustrated and becomes cruel with the horse as he travels even further inland in search of the one he was told would be willing to pay handsomely and take the hound off his hands. I pity this man, in some strange fashion, as he grumbles to himself frequently now. He mumbles things I have come to understand meant that he felt he should have purchased the other woman, the one that did not come with a dog. Reminded of Jade, I am sad, she is brave and proud; I cannot help but worry for her, hoping she manages to keep hold on that.

"It seems another few weeks passed before we came finally to a place where someone was found who pointed the man down another path. I smell the ocean again and fear another ship in my future but we do not come to a port by this path's end. It brought us to a large open flat space with a long

246

low structure in its center, surrounded by a low row of sharpened timbers. Here I saw many dogs very much like my Angus and they began to make much ruckus with wagging tails. There were pens with other animals, and a small group of horses running in the distant waving grasses. There were many people milling about, some practicing swordplay, others doing other labors, but none paid much attention as we drew near this great house. The smell of the great open water was strong and I heard it but I did not see it.

"The man came down from his seat beside me, leaving me alone with Angus. I thought for the briefest of moments to take up the reins of the tired horse and turn it and run. But somehow my heart felt for the beast and simply let it stand. The man was quite pleased with himself and announced his presence as though he would be met with great joy. He pointed to the wagon and the dog as a man came out from this structure to see what it was that his own hounds told him.

"This new man seemed unbelievably large to me, even at such a distance. The dogs, which he called to his side and quieted, though I knew were matched in size to my Angus, seemed not so big beside him. He was golden in a way I could not explain, it is merely the only thought that came to me.

"This golden man looked intrigued but wary, calling over his shoulder for others to come and look at the beast this man had brought. From the structure came two more large men and a woman. The woman was sunset and cream, she seemed to bounce out the door before these men, inquisitive and carefree. She looked toward Angus and me and said words directed to me and not the man who'd brought us.

14

Genevieve: Woman

"I had no understanding, but desperately wished I did. It seemed to me that here, for the first time in nearing two years was someone who might care what words I gave them. She tilted her head impossibly far back, said something to the golden man beside her. He nodded, seeming to disagree with her. She stomped her foot, looking at him for a long moment then turned and stepped toward me. He grabbed her arm and spun her back to him, speaking quickly but not unkindly when she swatted at his hand and pouted up at him.

"I was amazed at the freedoms this woman was being allowed, that he had not beaten her already for even having exited the structure to greet a strange man. Now, even more unheard of to me, this golden man seemed to fold under her continued pout, dipping his head and shoulders when she replied to his reprimand with her own swift decisive words. She showed no fear her words would bring his anger down on her and I squeaked in fear for her safety when she suddenly drew back and smacked him on his rear like a horse and sent him walking toward me and the dog.

"The man who had brought me to this place stood proudly next to the wagon as the golden man approached. He had not seemed as surprised by the woman's behavior as I, he had not flinched when she had smacked this golden man's posterior like a slow horse. The man merely stood in wait as the golden one came to *my* side of the wagon and looked up at *me*, gesturing and asking *me* something I knew meant he wanted to know what name I called *my* beast. What manner of people were these whose women were spoken to as equals and their slaves allowed ownership of beasts? I stare at him and he looks patiently at me for some time before he addresses the man who brought the two of us to him. The man seems to not give him an answer he likes because the golden one's brow furrows with suspicion again. Again he turns to me, this time he puts out his hand toward the dog and a sudden fear assails me. I throw my arms around Angus and Angus shows him teeth as he is ever doing when I am afraid.

"He drops his hand quickly and calls something in the direction of the two men that had remained behind with the woman. The woman begins to come forward, even before the men, but he raises his hand and she pauses, pouting again, as the two men come toward us alone. He tilts his head as though he cannot understand how or why his actions had frightened me and again he asks me for a name to call the beast. But I am suddenly afraid to tell him. I fear the dog will feel kinship with another who knows his name. I fear the beast might be coaxed from my side and leave me unprotected from the man who made this plan.

"Suddenly the golden man sees the shackle on my ankle. He looks angry and addresses the man who brought me in a new tone, one that I would have thought would have been more readily used on his woman for her actions before. The man shrivels beneath the golden one's words and draws out the key to show him proof, professing ownership, bought and paid for, for both the dog and myself. I know these words that mean "ownership" and "paid for." So too does this golden man. What I do not understand at first is why they do not seem to calm his anger.

"Then it begins to make sense, through certain repeated words, that the golden man cannot see how he had come to *own* a woman that *owned* a dog. It seemed I had misunderstood the reason for his approaching me; it had only been that way because he had not known I was a slave and couldn't have owned the dog. He had thought the dog was mine and I was here a willing participant in the sale of it. How, the golden one now wondered, his continued suspicion withering the other man to near shivers, had I come to be with the dog that this man now wished to be rid of to then be able to better own me. The man explained that the purchase was made that way and that to own me he had had to take the dog as well. The golden man had laughed at him then, a loud frightening sound that had no mirth, asking him how then was he to purchase the dog and not the woman? He pointed to his woman, saying he already had one.

"I am astounded yet again by these people. The man who brought us here seemed to have not thought of this and stumbles into silence. The golden man's woman had come unnoticed by any but me to a distance at which she could hear this conversation, which I was desperately trying to follow, and now she stepped forward causing me to fear for her again. She said something quietly to this golden man which gave him pause. He then turned his withering gaze on the man who'd brought Angus and me to that moment and asked who had *sold* the two of us to him. Who had *owned* us before him?

"I knew the man relayed all he knew of my great journey, as heard from the thin man, as told him by the fat one, as told him by the people who told the first lie, when I heard words I remembered for places I had been, names I remembered for men who had bought me, and then I heard the name of my home. I could not help that my face betrayed me then or that the woman saw this. It seems I could not shrink enough to escape her gaze then, as she began to study me while the men conversed amongst themselves. I tried to focus on their words, despite her clear eyes that spoke of free skies and a life the person I had become could only imagine.

"Again I heard words meaning 'ownership' and 'belonging,' words I had come to abhor, but I tried to make them make sense within the sentences being spoken hastily between the men. What I began to see, what it was this bold woman had brought to the attention of the golden man, was that these people prized their beasts greatly and they might need fear purchasing a dog that might have been stolen. The golden man did not want to bring trouble to his home for taking possession of another man's prized beast, that beast's owner might be somewhere wanting it back. It seemed his woman had pointed out to him as well that *the beast felt it was mine* and that somehow meant I too might belong to the true owner of this dog who they may not want to anger.

"She seemed to have an idea who might be the true owner of the beast, I heard the name of my homeland from her lips as she told them I too might belong to him and he might be wanting both of us back. She gave a name for the man she felt owned us both, a name she felt the golden one should respect because when the golden one laughed, she smacked him again upon his posterior and he silenced suddenly. I recalled the kind man, both red and gold, then, the man who had found me and fed me and brought me back to health. I searched my mind for a name and it came to me suddenly, nearly tumbling from my mouth.

"This woman, whose gaze seemed to miss nothing while studying me, saw my mouth snap shut when I had caught myself about to speak. She stepped closer to me, demanding I say what it was I had stopped myself from. The men had paused in their talk, turning to see what it was that had the woman suddenly thinking she could get words from me when I had yet to say a word to any among them. She was not unkind, I think, merely determined. Again she told me to speak and I feared the word would come out wrong, but as she put her hands on her hips I tried do as she asked so as not to anger her. If these men were not willing to resist her will, neither was I.

"Wind-dell," I stumbled.

"The woman jumped and clapped, smacking the back of her hand into the golden one's arm, demanding he take note of what I had said. It appeared my words had pleased her but not the man who had brought me there. His face fell as he too seemed to recognize the name as much as they did. There was a brief exchange in which the man who had purchased Angus and me said very little, merely nodded his head a lot and soon I watched in awe as this little sunset and cream woman lifted my chain and put out her hand to the man. She offered no gold and he demanded none of her, he said nothing, merely dug in his pocket and placed the key to my freedom in her waiting palm.

251

"The golden man put his hand up toward me, I know now that he merely meant to assist my descent from the wagon, but then, I shied back from it, pushing into Angus, afraid still of any male hand that reached toward me. Angus, who had been looking far off toward the others of his kind running happily about, took instant note of the push and spun. Suddenly his massive jaws closed next to my ear but in front of the man's hand and not into it, in three quick, snapping warnings. The man again jerked his hand back and looked to the woman. She put her hand up then, offering it to me to grasp, and again she spoke, not unkind, merely determined. She told me to come down.

"I was led into this great, long, low structure, and was placed before a great fire they had made inside. Their was much discussion as to what was to be done with me, the woman it seemed wished to remove the chain but the man spoke in low tones with eyes darting about to all the other men of this place and the woman was made to leave it in place. I was left chained then close to this fire, and she brought two skins of animals I couldn't name and a large length of some heavy multi-colored cloth that was coarse, to my mind, placing them in my hands. I stood holding them, not knowing what more I was meant to do, until she sighed and took them back, laying them upon the floor and motioned me to sit. She returned with food, a strange smelling and thick but wonderful stew.

"Then she sat before me.

"She patted her chest and told me she was called 'Genevieve.' I stumbled to repeat the strange word which my tongue did not like and she encouraged me with a small smile, one a mother would give a child who had tried but failed at a difficult task. She repeated her name and again I tried and failed. She sighed and said, 'Gen,' and smiled indulgently again when I managed this. She seemed to note I had not touched my food, I was desperately hungry for such wonderful smells but I did not wish to insult this new woman who held such power in this house. She pushed the bowl closer to my face and told me, 'Eat.' She did not have to give me permission twice. I ate quickly and again she smiled a small smile and watched me devour my portion before giving the better half to Angus.

"She frowned then, not unkindly, just as though a thought had not sat well in her mind. She left me, but quickly returned with another bowl, and again I ate only my portion then gave what remained to my wonderful beast. Again she left and returned, bearing another bowl, again I ate but much less now, as my belly was filling and I gave the rest to Angus. Once more she left and returned with this delicious fare that had been so quickly filling. I began to wonder at her motives, had she not seen I was full? I am suspicious as I taste the food to see it is not now poisoned and meant to remove Angus from my side. I hold it for some time to see that it does not affect my senses, and only when it does not do I give it to my protector. She smiled then, a bright smile that said she was truly pleased and got up again. She did not return this time, she merely approached the man she seemed to enjoy smacking like a lazy horse, the golden one who had called her *his*. They speak for some time with many looks directed my way.

"He does not give her answers she likes, for she comes to me again with a look that tells me she wants to speak to me instead. She pats her chest and tells me she is Gen and then she points to Angus. I cannot guess why they might want to know his name, why it is that this should be important to them that they should ask me again, accept that it might give them power over him and so I clamp my jaw. She sees I do not mean to answer her, her face darkens and I await the pain I know will come. I lift my chin as Jade has taught me and close my eyes but no heavy hand crosses my cheek, Angus is not made to defend me. I open my eyes, she is smiling. Again she gets up and goes to speak to the golden one.

"When she returned and sat before me some time later, the same smile was still on her small, pretty face. She pats her chest and tells me she is Gen. Does she think me daft? I know her name is Gen, I repeat it, to her to show her I have learned this. Her smile broadens slightly and she points to me. I am confused. Why does she wish to know a slave's name? None have asked before. The thoughts that ran wild in my head made time stretch endless before me. I saw myself, as I had been, a woman on the cusp, stood upon a great dividing wall, a destiny to either side. Behind me lay the life of a princess, before me the life of a slave. The princess had a name, the slave did not.

"The name I was given at birth seemed a foreign thought, a thing belonging to another life now left on the other side of this great wall in my mind. It comes to mind due to her question but it does not belong there. I wonder what she wants of me. Was I to sit there and give her a name that no longer applied, that spoke of a royal bloodline that was now ash like so many wagons, a station in life I no longer held, a right of birth in a life I no longer led? Was I to tell her a name that was no longer *my* name? Her face grew thoughtful as mine must have, watching me, waiting for my reply. I had none to give. I had been given no name, I was born in the previous life's all-consuming flames and no one else had survived the burning to name me.

"She pats her chest again, again she tells me her name is Gen and I see she is determined to know a word to call me. I cannot fathom the need, but I am weary and do not wish to anger her. To keep my Angus close to me is worth risking this oddly powerful woman's wrath but not this, not the matter of what I was to be called. I name myself, as none had been able to do it for me. I tell her I am Ayesha, meaning she who lives, she who survives, meaning simply, alive. I felt it fitting; I felt I had named myself well. I had survived. I was alive. It said what I was and I was nothing more. She stumbles over the name, as I had hers, and I smile, showing her it is well done. I do not care how she has said it, or if she has said it right, how she said it is how it would be said.

"I am left then again and she does not return until the sun has left, she takes me to a sheltered place to relieve myself and when she returns me to the fire it has been made huge. I cannot help that this frightens me, the flames send a chill through me I cannot control that has nothing to do with cold. She notes this and brings another of these skins, draping it over my shoulders kindly. I do not shake it from me, though I begin to sweat beneath it. She glances at me frequently, seeming to see into my soul, as many men and women come in from the darkness and all begin to eat. She brings me much food, enough for both Angus and myself who she frequently says are too thin while shaking her head and looking at us as though we somehow disappoint her. I feel she is truly kind despite the fact we are not pleasing to her, and begin to rest easier under her gaze.

"A man comes toward me from among all those who have come into this great structure to eat, he says things to me I do not understand as though I should. He becomes angry quickly when I do not respond how he feels I should and draws his hand back. I flinch reflexively and Angus comes to vicious life as is his way when I flinch or squeak. He lunges snapping the air in terrible warning but this man is not like all the others have been. This man turns and in two great strides retrieves a huge, deadly looking, duel-bladed weapon which leans against the wall with so many other weapons. He turns back, a terrible rage in his face, hefting this evil looking weapon with a strength I know can easily cleave Angus in two.

"Angus crouches low before me, his fur stands straight and his size seems to double, a terrible rumble begins deep in his chest and he shows this man all of his many frightening teeth. I have never seen or heard such violent defense of my person from Angus, always those short snaps and mere show of front teeth have sufficed. His rumble becomes deafening to me and the closeness of the fire and the depth of this sound build a terror in me I can make no sound to express. Suddenly I hear a scream but it is not mine. I jerk my head with the realization that it is Gen who has done the screaming.

"The man lowers his weapon as she stalks toward him angrily and Angus slowly regains a more normal posture. I am in complete awe now of this woman's power, I cannot begin to fathom how she has managed to attain such a place of authority among men so powerfully made they could have snapped her small frame like a twig. I cannot grasp why they have not stoned her for her brazen ways. She comes to a stop before him, and jams her hands, which she has balled into fists, down on her hips, she gives him angry words. Then she points at the chain on my ankle. She tells him even more angry words, I recognize among them 'Wi-ni-dell' and belonging and I watch his face fall as he allows his weapon to come fully to rest on the ground held loosely in lax fingers. I hear him mumble the name under his breath, again with a note of derision I had heard from others before, but not for her to hear.

"I recall the men who had traveled with the man called Wi-ni-dell, I remember the deference they had showed him, the fear they had so obviously had of him. I remember how they had said his name in such a manner too when he had not been able to hear them but this memory leaves me quickly chased away by more important things. I begin to see clearly now that these people must truly believed I belong to that man, that I had been *stolen* from him. They had known the dog, known the dog's owner to have gone to my home and now they thought since the two of us came together we must both be his. I begin to see that the woman has taken me and the dog to care for, only to return me to him, perhaps to keep his favor. I think maybe some of her power comes from the fact she acts in his name. I think then that this Wi-ni-dell must be a truly great man that his name is so widely known and so greatly revered. I am glad that these people believe me to be that man's slave and do not know *I stole his dog* if only by accident.

"As the days progress into weeks, this powerful woman comes to me frequently and she teaches me many, many words. I learn Gen calls the golden man William but sometimes they say 'husband' and 'wife' instead when he comes to speak to her while she is with me. I learn more than just the words she gives me for objects as I see she calls him *hers* as he called her *his* and I wonder at this. How strange that their ownership is mutual and he seems as pleased by this as she is. I begin to see that her physical abuse of him is a gesture of love and symbolic of her claim on him. I see him return these gestures in his own more gentle-looking manner and I begin to see why she always has a ready smile and bright outlook. I see also that her power here comes not from acting in the name of Wi-ni-dell, but rather from their union. He is the prince of this place and she is the only princess.

"I begin to use these many words she teaches me with some small skill and much stumbling as she also begins to put me to small labors that involve them. She is often bemused by my inability to do tasks she seems to think should have been the most easy for her to ask of me. She is patient and thoughtful as she shows me how to mend clothing with needle and thread and how to peel and chop vegetables for stew. I become quite skilled at these tasks, putting my entire mind into them for it is a better place for it to be, and I see that this pleases her. All these tasks she puts me to she brings before me, before this fire I am forced to deal with night and day, constantly fighting the terror it reminds my bones of though I know in my mind I should not fear it, for it is tame.

"The fear of the fire is one my bones remember, but the fear of men, the men who still look sidelong far too often to where I am chained, when I seem to sleep, but barely find rest between the wall and Angus- that fear my heart knows. I begin to say small prayers of thanks, on a nightly basis, to a man-god named Wi-ni-dell and the fear or respect or reverence that his name, linked to me by a chain on my ankle, created in their minds and thereby was keeping me safe. This chain was not a burden at this time, not a thing I even noted much anymore, other than as a symbol I was relatively safe for the moment. At least until this Wi-ni-dell returned and demanded reparation for the theft of his beast, a grave mistake and terrible crime, I see now, these people took quite seriously.

"I was coming to see that my thinking these large beasts were prized was a grave understatement. They were brought in at night and from cold or rain as surely as Gen's own son and all these people's children. They were fed well and groomed to be rid of vermin as frequently as their masters, which to my mind was not often enough by any stretch but telling none the less. My prayers to the man-god Wi-ni-dell were often followed by prayers to the Divine. I often dozed, still begging Him that my death be swift and painless when it came, as I was sure it would, when the man-god returned or received word from these people and finally came and retrieved his beast.

"I had nearly forgotten the binding quality of this chain when one day Gen came and released it from the wall by the fire. Taking up the end in her small hand, she led me and Angus out from this structure and around

257

behind it, down a path. This path led through a short distance of thick trees and out onto another open flat place where suddenly the sound and smell of the great open water was everywhere, no longer muted by this screen of woods. I fought a small surge of fear upon hearing and smelling that which had conducted me so far from my home, that other fear which had raised me after I had been born and weaned of fire. Gen took note of my brief pause, saw the moment I thought to balk, and she smiled as though she understood and wanted me to know I had no cause to fear.

"'Come,' she said kindly.

"We came to the edge of this small space of land and looked out from it to a distant beauty far below. The water rolled and boiled and flung itself endlessly upon the many rocks that had given way, from where we now stood, over the ages. There below, great stone tears had gathered for centuries, falling from the earthen eye of the world from which we now gazed, making of themselves a gauntlet for the waters that tried so valiantly to re-approach the lover they had been forever parted from by the Divine. Beyond, out in the distance, there was a calm. A calm that was still waters, glittering a brilliant, deep blue, purer than the clearest sapphires, something so awe-inspiring that it could never be related to the words fear or loss or longing.

"We stood and gazed out and it seemed she was as much awed by the view as I, though I was sure she had stood this very spot and took it in many times. She was silent for a long time before she pointed down to where the water met the land, and then at her feet and the long house behind us hidden by woods. Then she said, 'Gen' and 'William,' holding out her arms as if offering a welcoming hug to the very air around her as she spun in a slow circle. I knew she meant that this was *their* land and she loved it. She pointed to the south and then waved her hand once, away from her, indicating a good distance out past the water and what I could see. She said, 'Windell.' It seemed she was then telling me that the lands of Windell lay beyond the water, to the south. She watched my face for reaction, but I gave her none. Then she pointed across the water and waved her hand three times, indicating a much larger distance. She hugged herself, and said, 'Home.'

"I think of my home then, and wonder in which direction it might lie, but I cannot even begin to guess, as I do not even know where I am. So I think then, instead, how it is that I might find some measure of the joy as she has obviously found, knowing now this is not her home either. We stood silent for a long period of time and then finally, as though she had received some sign that I had missed, she led me along this cliff and to a wide rock path that led down to a shore line I had not been able to see before. We came around a great huge rock and there below me stretched a long wide track of sand filled with people and boats and the boisterous noises of busy people. I suddenly knew where all those who came only to dine and sleep spent their days, why for the last fortnight or better so very few had come. It was not a comfort to know now where they spent their days and how they labored.

"These were no mere honest fisherman, led by an indulgent man and his kind wife, working the land and sea for their livelihoods, breeding great beasts to hunt their red meat. These were the great marauders of the water, and like their counterparts upon the land who had taken what they wanted of my people and left the rest to burn, they took from others to fill their needs. I had heard the stories. I knew by the ships. The mere sight of one prow, of one ship, of which there were many before me, and even those of the lowest intelligence ran. It was much the same as the sound of a million hooves upon the land; one did not wait to see who led, one simply fled.

"I was torn between a desperate inexplicable fear, which had my heart racing madly ahead of me, and a deep calm rooted in a sudden understanding of a thing that had chewed at the back of my mind like a rodent. I thought for the briefest second that Wi-ni-dell had come to reclaim me and his beast and that was why Gen had shown me the direction of his home. But that great man was nowhere to be seen, he did not lead the men of any of these boats, and as I watched these men go about the care and unloading of them, I made an incredible connection. That was why, though they had obvious fear for that great man I had met in my homeland, they still said his name derisively- he was not one of them. I found I suddenly had to revise my opinion of why his name gave those men pause when they sought to approach me. I could not now see *these* men as fearing anything or anyone and I thought it now better to think they merely respected him.

"There seemed to exist a grudging respect which explained why the derisive laughter and mumbles were always beneath one's breath, why these brave people might indulge but were still careful who heard. I had no idea why or when he had come into his standing among these people, but I saw it was mayhap not a right of birth. The man I had met traveled by land, and was called 'the Walker,' which was far from a compliment among *them* but they were careful how they said it and in front of whom. He may not be one of them, or if he had been, wasn't considered to be any longer, but they still held him in much regard. I could not imagine what deeds a man must do that those people before me, whose reputation alone caused mothers to quake, would give deference to me because of the mere knowledge I was his.

"I could not help but try to turn my ideas into stone by pointing at the ships and turning to Gen and saying 'Wi-ni-dell' with an exaggerated quizzical look. She had turned and looked long at me before making a cutting motion with her hands and saying, 'No more.' She said, 'He began walking,' as she moved two fingers as though walking them across invisible land, then she made a motion of giving and receiving and rolled her eyes to heaven in an exaggerated sigh. 'He is a merchant now,' she sighed. I thought I understood. I lifted my eyebrows in response, also finding it as crazy a notion as she did. A Viking had stopped raiding to become a merchant? I paused to think of his behavior upon discovering me, of his kindness so unlike what I had heard was to be expected of his people. I began to think I understood what his plan had been. Return the woman whose many marks and traveling accommodations said had been obviously quite wealthy to her wealthy people and make an instant equitable partnership through the kind act. I saw why those with him had argued and called him Walker under their breath.

"She gazed at me for a long moment but said nothing more before leading me back up this rocky path to the cliff. I could not help but to wonder what it was she had taken me to see all this for but my wondering made no answers of itself as she led me deep into those woods that kept her home from being viewed from the sea. We came out into another open place where water pooled, clean and clear, before making the bumpy decent to the ocean I could still hear below and behind us. She looked around briefly then bent and removed the chain from my ankle, putting the key beside the chain on a stone, and pointing to this pool. Then she simply began to remove her clothing and walk into it, not even looking back to see what I would do.

"I stood dumbfounded by the bath offered to me and soon the desperate want of it overcame me. It seemed a part of me should be thinking of escape, that I should take this beautifully wrought opportunity to take Angus and simply run. But where would I run to? Of all those I had met since all my own had been slaughtered, here before me wading calmly into the deeper center of this pool, trusting me, was the kindest. Even were I to reach one who could get word to him who was to have been my husband and prince, how was I to know if he would even respond? He had not before. I stripped off quickly and waded in feeling more naked for the loss of the shackle than the clothing I had shed. My breath quickly exploded from me as my foot, feeling oddly off balance for lack of weight, slipped and I was suddenly submerged in the cold clear water.

"Gen laughed a bright happy sound as I came sputtering back up to the surface. I stood back up, hip-deep in this pool and patted my leg, pointing to the chain on the stone behind me and then my ankle. I told her I couldn't walk right without it after over two years. Her eyes widened with happy surprise and she giggled giving me a bright and well pleased smile. It took me a moment to realize I had told her this in her own language with a skill I hadn't known I had come to posses. It hadn't been perfect by any means but she obviously thought it a wonderful start.

"When we came out from the pool she did not immediately put the shackle back on my ankle but rather allowed me to dress and bade me walk around awhile. She watched me as I paced in slow circles about this clearing and after some time she asked me a question I think had bothered her mind for quite a while. She pointed to the discolored rings encircling my upper arms and asked me what had marred the skin. I found it easy to be honest, I pointed to a bracelet she wore and then my arms and she smiled a sad smile of comprehension. I said nothing, I knew her imagination would tell her how the marks related to jewelry and she never asked about it again. I noted her glances as she studied the empty holes in my ears, the one in my nose and all the many other places my flesh still remembered jewelry it had worn its first fifteen years. But she never said a word, so neither did I.

"She did not bend to put the shackle back on until we were nearly clear of the wood and the long low structure could be glimpsed at a distance between the thick trunks. Even then, she placed it on the other ankle and laughed a little telling me it might make me more balanced. It seemed her eyes told me more though, they told me she would not even be putting it back were it not for the knowledge we both had, that it kept my person marginally safer by acting as a reminder that I belong to another, very powerful, man.

"As we returned to the longhouse she was still smiling and giving me more words, she had yet to pause in her instruction from the moment she had seen it was indeed paying off. Everyday thereafter she doubled her instructive efforts and I came to learn a great many things. I learned all she could show me within the structure, how to make teas and stews and clothing, most often for the small children including her own son. I learned how to care for the crying, sniffling, even fevered ones, through watching her loving actions toward her own child. I found one day, when brought an especially sickly child by a woman who seemed to have taken no notice, that I had a way with the sick ones. I saw I could hold them wrapped close to me beneath layers of fur, allowing them to sweat and shiver the sickness loose while sitting close to the fire whose creeping fear I learned to push slowly from my bones with my mind. I seemed well-made for this as my body accepted higher temperatures with less sweat, and more than once thereafter a child was brought to me by a mother who thought this ability a gift of gods I didn't know. I would find moments then, wrapped tightly to another's needful soul, where my own found quite peace.

"Gen and the other mothers contentedly tended gardens, now knowing their children were well tended, and brought me those things I needed to do what I did. It seemed all came to accept what I had found out so accidentally. Mayhap it was a gift, for these women began to look at me differently, offering me kindnesses one would have never thought a slave would receive. But I also learned these people did not keep slaves in the manner I was used to, they integrated them, made them comfortable, gave them jobs and praise until eventually all forgot they were slaves. I, at least, saw I was forgetting, at least when it came to the women.

"I still kept my head very low when the men came in, especially if they had been gone a good length of time. I learned to look forward to those times Gen came and unchained me from before the hearth and took me for walks that often began as lessons and ended in a bath. She began to take me with her more and more often when she would go to visit other woman whose men were also gone. I began to take note of the variety in coloring about these women and one day I asked how many of them had been taken from their homes. Gen smiled a sad understanding smile and began to show me that most of them had. I then asked her if she had been taken, wondering at her place among them, the power she had come to have and about the home she had spoken of.

"Gen explained that she had chosen her husband, not the other way around, that it had been a matter of love and good enough reason to leave her home of her own accord. She told me her family was greater even than his and she had, it seemed to me, made a step down, to have love over power, but somehow the love was a greater power. She pointed out to me that her man was kind and loved her and that was worth more to her than anything else she might have attained had she made a different choice.

"Gen then pointed out to me a woman who I had seen often, who moved about freely with a pleasant smile. She had recently brought me a gift of pretty-smelling soap to wash my hair, *thanking* me for having spent a day mending clothes for her while she gathered the herbs to make it. I had not known why she seemed to view my deed as a favor to be repaid in kind. I had merely thought it what task I had been given that day. But Gen explained to me that woman had been stolen, just as I had, but had come to love the man

263

who stole her. She had long since given him children and won his heart, earning his trust and love over time and in return she had been given the freedoms I had witnessed and both were made happy.

"Gen then pointed to a woman far out in a field, behind a small hut, tending a small garden. This woman, I recalled, had brought me the child who had been fevered and very sick many months before and hadn't seemed to have cared enough to have noted it. Neither, I recalled, had she been thankful when she came to reclaim him three days later and found him well, happily sharing a bowl of stew with me. Gen told me that woman had also been stolen, but she was not so lucky as the first. The man who claimed her was neither kind nor gentle. I could tell Gen was saddened for the woman *and* the man because neither would find happiness or love.

"I asked her then about this Windell whom I feared would inevitably come to reclaim me and take me from this place and people I was coming to make peace with. I thought I remembered him as kind but feared that had only been because he meant to trade me back to my people and that his manner would change once he found me again and with his dog. I suddenly feared the loss of Gen now near as much as Angus who was ever at my side.

"She did not immediately answer me, staring long and thoughtful toward the sad woman pulling weeds from her small garden while a child she had not wanted played in the dirt at her feet. Then she said, 'I think the fates are three terrible children, playing rough with human dolls, marching them over harsh continents and sending them across stormy seas to play house in separate rooms when they are pouting and not speaking to each other. They play queens, prettying-up, pulling the wings from butterflies to paint their eyes with their enviable color. I do not think they have yet earned the right to be called old crones, because being old would require some wisdom that comes naturally with age.' Gen looked at me long and hard then added, 'We are all intertwined through time and do as much to help as to hinder each other, but I believe you have come cross my path for a reason.'

"Gen saw this answer had done nothing to calm my fears so I think she was doing her very best when she finally said, 'I think him a visionary man in an very admirable way because he said he smelled what was coming on the world's winds and then looked to secure the future of his clan by changing the way it survives, despite the light this puts him in among some of the other clans. I have not seen him since he made his sudden strange decision to give up the way of life our people have always led and try another. So I cannot tell you who Windell has become and I will not frighten you further by telling you who or how I was told he was when I was a child. Only know that I grew up to revere the name that was given on a whim to a great lord's first born son, by a woman who pleased him so well he let her have her way for the laughter it gave her. Later, when the name proved prophetic in nature, he rued that laughter, from that day to the one he died, two winters past."

"I considered her words, trying to make sense of these beings she had called the Fates. She spoke of them as though they had the power of gods but not the wisdom, and I found no comfort in thinking such beings had any say in my destiny. 'So I am choice-less, as a human doll,' I had whispered, 'left to be the plaything of petulant graceless god-children?'

"Gen had smiled sadly then, seeming to understand my confusion and worry. She spoke of the fact that though they were *her* people she often could not help but see how their ways were frightful to outsiders. She admitted to me that sometimes she felt the world's winds spoke to her of needful changes too and that often she followed its whispers. She led me again to this cliff she had shown me the first time she had ever taken me away with her from the fire for longer than to relieve myself.

"'I can only say that I have come to love you and mayhap he will as well,' Gen had said thoughtfully. 'We are sprung from the same place,' she said, pointing again to the north and waving her hand three times, 'from the same great man many lifetimes past. My great uncle has much love for me *and* my brother, perhaps I can speak to him on your behalf.'

"I was not positive who she spoke of when she spoke of her great uncle or her brother, I was not even completely sure what 'great uncle' meant, though I knew uncle was something said of elder blood kin. I was simply thankful that she had come to care for me, as I had her, and that it meant she would do what she could to speak with those people who apparently lived far out across the water on my behalf. I gazed out with her, far past the bubbling closeness of it out to the calm water I found so beautiful, and as the sun weakened, I saw life beneath the surface, floating green, changing the glittering hue of this perfect spot for the eye to rest and making of it magic.

"We had returned to the longhouse in silence then, as the light left the land and water, neither of us having much more to say. I returned to the fire and she attached the chain, once again leaving me to my thoughts. I was torn in a great many directions at once and found myself settling for the more comfortable torment of my body and bones by wrapping warm, leaning into the fire, and fighting that small fear my bones were always wont to recall rather than deal with the larger fears my heart was wont to bring me. I found myself inside a calm moment where I recognized envy within me. I envied Gen for the many aspects of a simple happy life she had been able to choose.

"That evening one of the boats returned bringing her William home bearing all the many gifts of his victories abroad. There was much celebration as there always was when the men came home, and I kept my head low as I had learned was best for everyone, including Angus. There had been a time, not long past, that I had to take my needle and thread to a long jagged gash on Angus's chest which he'd received in defense of me. I had not forgotten the terror that had taken over my fingers as I fought to steady them and bring his flesh back together, and the long sleepless nights, guarding and tending him, had me not wishing to risk it again.

"There had been much yelling in the longhouse that night, as there was this one, only then it had been angry, as Gen took her needle and thread to the man who still wore many patches of pink puffy skin. Angus's marks of anger returned. I recalled the terror of knowing only her words and her William stood between that man and me, as I tended my now-weakened protector and I shriveled into the wall as the revelry continued around me. Gen came to me with a great gift that evening, she brought wrapped in a new blanket two matching arm bands. They were nothing so grand as my prince had sent for a wedding gift but they meant far more. She had smiled knowingly as I put them on, covering the skin of my upper arms which had never recovered completely. She had bent then and kissed my forehead before running back to her William, who had given the gift to her for me, and jumping into his waiting arms was happily swung around like a child.

"I had wrapped my new blanket around me, covering myself and my gifts from her, and sunk back behind Angus to hide in the wall again, remembering envy in my soul. They did not leave by the end of that week but seemed to await something coming to them, with much excitement building around my head, as I tried to shrivel still smaller. By the beginning of the following week another boat had come and by that week's end still another.

"I couldn't shrink small enough to remain unnoticed."

15

Rune: Hidden

"One night, soon after all these many boats and their occupants had come, as I lay behind Angus pressed to the wall, I felt a shadow move over my face and a hand press suddenly over my mouth. My hands flew quickly to remove them as my fear redoubled, realizing Angus's teeth had not flashed and his chest had not rumbled. Gen's words stopped both our protests almost before they began. 'I pray you have learned my words and come to trust me. Hear me well,' she began in a swift whisper in my ear. 'I cannot keep you safe here any longer. William's own brother has taken a keen liking to you and will not be dissuaded for long by the mere thought you *may* belong to Windell. Even I begin to doubt this assertion the more times I am forced to use it to keep you safe. I do not think you have yet belonged to any man, let alone a Viking the likes of Windell, no matter how passive he may have become. And my William's brother said this very evening that come the worst he will simply say he had no idea and hope it suffice. Some think Windell grown *too* soft, you see?'

"I nodded my head in the affirmative beneath her hand and her voice became pleading that I understand what she had decided to do for me. 'You remember the woman who brought you the sweet-smelling soap for your hair?' Again I nodded, hoping I was indeed gathering the proper meanings from all of what she said. 'Her husband has agreed to take you with him.' I jerked and she hushed me, pleading for me to hear her out, adding, 'He travels to my home tonight. I have begged him to take you to my brother that you may be safe in his care. Even those who would not fear Windell alone and may think him grown weak will not risk Rune's wrath.'

"She placed her other hand beneath my shoulder, applying a gentle pressure which was meant to aid me in rising as she reached over my head with the one she removed from my mouth and slowly, quietly, released the chain. She then let loose the shackle from my ankle and wrapped the entire chain in the blanket she pulled off of me silently. I then found myself clasping my soap to my chest, the only thing I had besides the dog that followed of his own accord as she led me on silent feet over and around all those sleeping bodies that covered the floor. The flickering light of the dying fire was barely bright enough for us to make out the many breathing forms needing to be avoided, but we managed it quickly and were soon out in the night, running for the woods.

"My heart raced before me, chased far ahead by all the many fears the unknown once again presented me. Angus loped on silent pads at my side as Gen led us deftly through the dark wood to the clear slope of the cliff. There she stopped and handed me a leather strap which had a buckle like it was a thin man's belt. Then she held it to the moon and showed me that the part of it that went through the holes to hold it in place was a key, the key to my shackle. She pointed to Angus and told me it was for him. I bent and put this belt, which hid my freedom, around Angus's neck and looked at her bowed head as she unwrapped the chain from the blanket and attached it again to my ankle.

"Rising, she peered at me closely in the moonlight, trying to be sure I understood her clearly. She said, 'None know how well you have come to understand our language, use that wisely. As far as the man who delivers you is concerned, you are the property of Windell to be kept safe by my brother until Windell can return for you. He thinks he does this for me, to prevent Windell's wrath from coming down on all of us. He does not know what else I have come to know or that I have come to love you as I have. I send you to my

269

brother for my sake, for I would not have you as William's brother's.' She paused in her speech, thoughtful and long, leading me quietly down the rocky, treacherous path with careful, silent skill. But before my feet touched the sand she spun one last time, adding, 'We shall see what comes when I warn the butterflies away.'

"She kissed my forehead again and then both my cheeks before pushing me roughly around the huge boulder and out onto the sand where all the many boats could be seen. Many men moved quietly about and she said not another word as she handed the end of my shackle to a man I had never met. He stood back, allowing me to fight my own battle with my fears and pull my own way up into the boat, and then he watched silently as Angus leaped to joint me. He said not a word either as he pointed to where he meant for me and my beast to sit and be still while they got underway. Gen stood quietly on the shore, watching as the boat was pushed out and glided silently away. I lost sight of her far too quickly, when the moon was unkind, hiding behind a cloud for too long, as the boat was pulled quickly through the still waters by many a quiet and skilled pair of hands.

"I knew the moment we hit that calm patch of water, the one whose beautiful blue and green glittering life had said so many things to my soul that hinted of calm inner strengths I too could achieve. I felt the blanket wrapped 'round my shoulders slip and a chill set into the silver metal that encircled my upper arms, my gifts from Gen. I knew in that moment that my strength would not be found in those arms, but rather in love and gentle caring. That was the true power of Gen, of any woman, one they could wield easily, no matter their physical strength. I had seen now how my having fed Angus for years, though it had begun as a means to shoo him, had been viewed as a kindness and brought Angus to love and protect me even unto risking his very life. In my observation of her, Gen had taught me far more about her people than their language, she had shown me the power of respect, kindness and love. I held that knowledge close to me as my only hope, knowing it was what had sent me on this next step of my great journey.

"I was determined then that if and when Windell came for me, I would do all that I could, to be, through kindness and gentle caring, a woman to whom he could not help but be kind and gentle. I was not so brazen as to think of love, love was for Gen and Angus, not men, but I knew how to care for children and dogs, I could learn how to care for a man. And in caring for the man mayhap he would care for me.

"The men on this boat paid me no mind and I lost track of time as I spent my nights rocked to fitful sleep beside Angus and my days under my blanket to escape the harsh rays of a sun that seemed enamored of my long black hair. I tried tying it up in a knot to keep its thick sticky weight from my face and shoulders but it just became an impossible mess of tangles and I had no kind Gen to bring me a comb. When we made land I was pleased to see more pleasant faces like those I had come to care for among Gen's people. These women came down to the shore with happy smiles and warm hugs given in greeting to the men they had obviously missed, receiving the many gifts these men returned to them with, with nary a thought as to how it had been won for them. There was much joyous dancing and bouncing about of not only these women but many children who came running from every direction. I found myself sheltering a hope of recreating among these women the easy companionable days of trades I had come to enjoy while the men were away. Some few men stayed behind with the man to whom Gen had handed the end of my chain. Those that remained waved happily to a few people in greeting but seemed to await some cue to disembark they had yet to receive.

"When that cue came it nearly stole the breath from my chest. There came down from the rocky slope, atop which perched another long low structure I knew now was their home, an impressively large man, quite close in height to Gen's William. Only this man seemed larger and more intimidating by means of width and mass and girth. He was not gone to fat in the middle, as the merchant who had purchased me first was, in fact he was somewhat smaller than one would have thought normal through the torso. It seemed to me as he came with agile grace, on strong legs, over the rocks and

271

across the sand, that he was merely made very thick with too much muscle and meat.

"I found myself staring at this huge man as he came closer, waving for those that remained with me to come ashore, trying to think what was so scary about him and I could not at first put my finger to it. He was golden too but not in the same ways as Gen's William. His skin had been well-loved by the sun but his hair was not the burnished gold that would have matched it as William's did. It was dark at the root and on his brow, which furrowed now as the man turned to watch me come down from the boat but did not offer to assist me. Angus followed swift on my heels, watching the men with a keen eye, to see that they did not touch me.

"Suddenly I knew what frightened me about him, as his voice cut sudden and deep into my ears, causing me to spin to face him. 'Help her less she break something,' his booming voice demanded, unleashing a mere fraction of the power he exuded with a swift angry force. I had seen, unmistakably, this power, as it lay locked just beneath his skin and it was a frightful thing. Angus grew stiff watching the man as I began to tremble. When the man who'd brought me said he could not touch me lest the dog attack him, the huge one then demanded this man explain why he had brought such a vicious dog with a woman in chains to his shore.

"The man fought to explain quickly as this huge one seemed to be building up a great rage, giving him little time. He wanted nothing of a woman in his house who could not even be trusted to remain there of her own accord, he said those were the ones you couldn't trust to cook your food and had to sleep with one eye open around, let alone the viciously protective dog the man had said was bound to attack if anyone reached for me. He told the man to take me and give me to someone who was willing to play such stupid games for so little reward.

"The man beside me shrunk only a little as he held to himself the knowledge he had been sent on a mission that should excuse him as swiftly as he could explain it. He made quick work with his words; the moment this huge angry man paused to breathe, he said Gen had sent him, a name which calmed the huge man if only minimally.

The huge man's brow cleared only for a moment as he said, "My sister has given me this *present*?'

He looked at me then, rather than the chain the man held, and his eyes consumed me far more quickly than I could remember to fear the flames. My mind was spinning trying to see this huge angry man, whosse very being screamed of raw violent power, as the brother of the very small and kind Gen I had come to cherish. This was Rune then? I could see how she would think men might fear him, if not Windell, but I could not see how she thought he would keep me safe. It seemed to me he might as likely break me in half just to save himself the trouble of having to look at me any longer.

"He turned back to the man quickly, suspicion taking control of his expressive brow, as he said, 'She knows I've no taste or need for an unwilling wench.'

"The man was quick to explain I belonged to Windell, as well as the dog, and the chain was merely a deterrent Gen had left in place to remind hungry men that this meat was meant to sate another man's hunger. I hated that they were speaking of me as though I were not there, especially in such a manner and about such things. I may have escaped the trying hands of men to this point but I had born witness with terrified eyes what those women with no huge hairy beast coming between were made to suffer when a man grew *hungry*. It had not nearly resembled the fine art of pleasing one's husband which I had been schooled in at the temple with the dance, and it made my knees tremble to think those thoughts these men's words put in my head.

"Rune threw back his head and laughed then, a huge sound that matched the man it came from. 'Some men still have regard for my crazy great uncle then?' he asked the man.

"'Some,' the man had replied, 'but not William's brother, he hasn't the good sense to fear even Odin when he is hungry.'

"Rune had grown thoughtful, a look that sat odd upon his face after so much anger but gave me hope I would not be broken and cast back into the sea. For a long moment he said nothing and then, as though he decided he didn't like the weight of the thoughts he was having, he shrugged his shoulders, shaking the thoughts loose, and bade the men come and drink. We were all led then up to the great longhouse that perched atop this rocky shoreline. When we came into the dimness I noted many more men, all large and hungry-looking and became terrified again.

"Then Rune took the end of the chain from the man and held it high, his voice booming out again as he announced to one and all, 'This is Windell's, as is the beast.'

"He looked about at all the faces that turned at his words and when no words came back at him he led me to the far end of this structure and pushed aside a large skin that hung on the wall, revealing another smaller room with a smaller hearth. He took me to this hearth and, gauging the length of the chain with a careful eye toward the furs that lay piled along the wall, he attached it there with only half its length available to me. Then he knelt, glancing at me briefly, and checked the shackle where it encircled my ankle, assuring himself it was secured. Then he simply left.

"I remembered his comment about sleeping with one eye open and realized he was assuring himself I could not reach him when he slept. I shivered then, realizing it was I who could be reached and this shackle meant there was nothing I could do about it. I thanked what gods still listened for Angus and sunk to the wall behind him, pulling my blanket close around me.

"Much later a woman came in; timidly she poked her head past the bearskin and found me in the dimness with her slowly-adjusting eyes. She came forward with a large platter of food which told me that someone had informed someone else that Angus and I dined together. She sat it before me and then hastily began taking logs from the small pile on the other side of the hearth, looking at me as though I were daft to have not done so myself, and she tossed them on the dying embers and blew till they bloomed new life. I had seen those small bits of wood, but I preferred to wrap tighter in my blanket and curl up close to Angus for warmth as the hours grew cool. I had no desire to stoke a flame when the flames still so reminded my bones of the night of my birth.

"I heard a voice rise in anger just beyond the skin and the woman flinched and tossed the last bit on the fire before spinning and bolting back out the door. I heard her swift apology to the man who felt she had tarried too long and felt a sudden sting of guilt as I heard her say, 'fire dead,' and 'cold,' followed by the sound of a heavy hand meeting what I could only imagine was her small round cheek. 'Then Rune should tend his own fire better or find his own woman to do it. You were only told to take the food.'

"I ate my meal in as much peace as my conscience would afford me as no one else entered this room. No one came to retrieve the platter, even as the hour grew late. I began to worry when I realized I needed to relieve myself and that Angus most likely did as well and no one had yet come, as Gen would have, to take me to a safe place to do so. I began to wonder what I was going to do without her.

"I looked about my surroundings and saw nothing that might help me with this new dilemma. There was a large stack of skins and blankets, even some few pillows piled up against a wall to my left, and to either side of this, two large, leather-bound trunks with varied containers meant for various drinks, and random small items piled atop them. There was a large dual-bladed ax leaning against the trunk farthest from me and a pair of large discarded sandals against the wall beside it, one of the straps, obviously broken and now far too short, beside it. There were other weapons in the other corner across from me, stacked as randomly as were the discarded articles of clothing piled along the wall opposite the bed.

"It was late when Rune came in but I had kept the fire high and his eyes found me instantly, curled into the corner behind Angus. I knew he'd told the other man he had no taste for the unwilling but I couldn't help but feel some small shiver of fear when his eyes stayed on mine a fraction too long. He walked to his bed and looked at it, then looked at me again and my heart stopped. Then he bent and yanked a number of skins from the pile and tossed them toward me without saying a word. I had closed my eyes when he'd looked from me to the bed and had not opened them when the skins landed atop Angus and me. I only dared to open them a few moments later when I heard the sounds of him falling across his bed and heard his breathing grow shallow. He lay silent and breathed slow, beneath many blankets, and I eventually made my heart calm as, moving silently, I worked these skins beneath Angus and me and sometime near dawn I closed my eyes again.

"The dawn couldn't come soon enough and I was actually thankful when Angus's insistent dancing and huffing woke the man asleep on the bed before us. I had been standing there, legs crossed, trying to get the nerve to say something, trying to convince myself he could not be too evil if he was Gen's kin and wake him before I pissed right there on his rug, when he opened one eye and looked at the dog. This Rune then crooked up his lip in a strangely childlike grin and asked Angus if he needed to pee. The dog and I both nodded a hearty yes, but Rune seemed to take no note of my nod, only the dog's hearty piss shiver. He stood, causing me to gasp and look quickly toward the fire as I had been suddenly shown his entire bare backside.

"I finally made myself turn back toward him when I heard him say, 'come,' but found the word had been for Angus. He stood there, paying me no mind, now wearing some long length of coarse-looking material I had seen on the floor, wrapped around his middle and belted, then thrown over his shoulder. He held the bearskin aside and motioned the dog out again, but Angus merely danced anxiously back and forth between me and the opening. Rune finally lifted a brow at the crazy hound and watching it closely he came toward me slowly, taking note that the infamous hound paused its constant dancing to watch him just as closely. I stepped out of the way as he slowly released the chain from the wall, using a key hung round his neck, never even looking at me as he eyed the dog. There had been no fear about his actions, merely a kind of inquisitive caution, and I got the impression this man did not even know what fear was but found the fact others felt it existed intriguing.

"He held the end of the chain lightly as if it were an afterthought and walked back to the opening. Turning back to the dog, he said, 'come,' and grinned his boyish grin again when Angus danced back to my side and walked with me out the door. He took us to a place behind the longhouse where water ran by on its way to the ocean and then turned his back to me, walked to the furthest extent of the chain and immediately started pissing on a tree. I had no more time to bother with propriety; I lifted the hem of the shapeless sack I'd worn since the night before Gen took me to the boat and stepped into the shallow flow and proceeded to enjoy a small bit of heaven's relief. Angus sniffed about my little area for only a second more, before deciding Rune's tree was as good as any to stake his claim upon. I heard Rune tell Angus he was 'a good man' before he asked me if I was ready without looking back.

"I simply stood, stepped out of the stream and dropped the dress back around my ankles in answer. He led Angus and me back into the longhouse, long before anyone else had risen, and reattaching the chain he left the chamber to me and my loyal hound again. I was left again to stare at the four bare walls and the mess about the floors, wondering what these strange beings Gen had called Fates meant to do with me. I was bored, to be honest, as for nearly a year I had come to spend my days trading duties with the women of Gen's house. They had brought to me those things I could do from my place by the hearth, freeing them for other things and in turn they had brought me those things I could not get for myself-my meals, my water, my precious soap. Gen had been the most giving and generous, but she had also had the most that needed doing that she would bring to entertain my hands. I found I missed Gen and her son desperately.

"Now I sat for many idle hours with only the random frightening thoughts about the Fates to occupy my time. The woman who had brought the food for Angus and me the night before came bearing another platter, a bucket full of fresh water with a large ladle hung inside it, and a nasty bruise. She left bearing my empty plate but refusing to take my pity. She had lifted her chin hauntingly when she had glanced at the fire out of habit and then at me, only to see my sympathetic look. She had clenched her jaw and raised her chin another notch before leaving quickly, as though she wanted none of my pity and would not remain if that was what she would receive for staying. The action reminded me sharply of Jade and I resolved to withhold such feelings from her view when next she came.

"Still many more hours later I heard Rune's unmistakably deep voice coming from just beyond the bearskin. It was low but I still made out his words. 'Are you sure they are Windell's?' he'd said.

"'Gen seems certain enough, thought it might cause Windell's wrath to descend on her William's kin where I not to leave in the dead of night and bring her to you for safe-keeping. She said the girl came with the dog along a path of many terrible twists and turns but that the path began in India and that is where Windell had gone.' I recognize the voice that responded, adding, 'She is definitely of Indian blood and the hound is undeniably his stock, only his grow to be so large, I do not know what else can be thought…' The man who had brought me to Rune paused as though the question had finally struck him as odd, as it had me, worrying me right off. 'Why? Have you a notion 'tis otherwise?' he'd asked then.

"'I have a notion something 'tis off that any Viking's woman be shocked by the sight of a bare backside,' Rune laughed.

"That man had laughed then and told Rune mayhap I was not used to seeing a backside so small, something that both men obviously found quite amusing because their laughter could be heard for quite a good distance, even as it faded, telling me they had departed. My mind went round and round this conversation, wondering if I had done something that would give me away, that would let Rune onto the fact I was not his great uncle's woman and therefore nothing to be protected. I was once again assailed by a whole new set of fears to occupy my otherwise idle time. Another meal came but no further opportunities to eavesdrop on a conversation that might give me some small peace.

"I knew when Rune returned that night, I woke from a fitful doze filled with fearful thoughts of being unshackled in the middle of the great common room beyond and it being announced that I was no one's woman, that I was ownerless. I had terrible visions of Angus's swift decapitation and my own body being torn limb from limb to be feasted upon by hungry men. I heard the sound of his steps nearing the skin and my eyes flew wide. He lifted the drape and immediately his eyes found mine, gazing out fearfully at him from beneath Angus's hairy chin. He said not a word to me, to indicate he had found out my secret, but rather asked Angus if he needed to piss. Angus stood, but didn't move, then I stood too, timidly, and the dog danced a few steps back and forth until Rune removed the chain and led us both out to seek relief.

"The days continued like this, with two meals brought by a woman who never spoke and never stayed longer than to be sure of the amount of fresh water remaining in my bucket, and two brief ventures out of that smaller chamber within the larger whole, to seek relief with a large unknown man a few feet away, his back always to me, only talking to my dog. I was pleased by this place of relief behind the long house, it provided me a means to clean myself, at least my lower half, but it also brought me uncomfortably close and made me feel very exposed to this huge man. He, on the other hand, seemed not at all bothered by my presence, in fact he seemed to ignore my being completely, but that did nothing for my sense of wellness. In fact, it made me almost more leery of him. What game was he playing? Why was he always talking to Angus? I got it in my head for a moment that he meant to befriend my hound slowly and leave me guardian-less but then wasn't he also my guardian, at least until Windell came and told everyone the truth, I was not his and I had stolen his hound?

"Two weeks passed in this manner, with my only means to entertain my hands being keeping a fire I abhorred fed to a high happy life and trying desperately, one handful at a time, to work my fingers through the knots of my hair as though untangling the mess that had become of my life. It was useless though, I had not bathed fully and been able to wash it in more than a month, the sweet soap my mending clothing had earned me had lain hidden, a priceless but useless gift, wrapped in the corner of my blanket since before I had come to this place.

"I resolved that I must find a way to convince Rune to let me bathe, but that presented a whole new set of imagined difficulties. I stared at Angus as though I might find some answer from his behavior, but he busily gnawed a bone that Rune had tossed to him one evening before falling into his bed and that told me nothing I could understand at the time. That bone had only gnawed at me, too, leaving me constantly unsure of how I should see this man, as guardian or clever fiend. When Rune's steps came unexpectedly toward the chamber in the middle of that day I saw it as a sign. I focused on the moment I had been provided, the opportunity I had been given, and told myself I needed to put my chin up and take it.

"Rune entered and again found me with his eyes too quickly, as he always did, but as ever, he said not a word and looked away far too swiftly for me to see if any had even come to his mind. I stood slowly, my heart jamming up in my throat, words failing me. He paused in his stride to the chest that lay furthest from me, on the side of the bed where he fell to sleep. He looked at me hard and I felt I would wither before words would come to save me. Angus stopped his constant gnawing and looked up at me and then at Rune, apparently unable to decide if he should stand and take action against the man who had given him that bone.

"I managed to make my trembling hands lift the dirty sack that covered my form to my nose and make a face that said it was unpleasant to smell, then point at the pile of discarded clothing Angus now rested upon. I meant to offer that if I could wash mine I would wash his but apparently the idea was shocking. Rune seemed taken aback, I feared I might even have angered him, but then he cocked his head and gazed thoughtfully at me for far too long for me to handle with any grace. My chin started to falter, my knees began to tremble. Then he turned and walked to the chest opposite the one he had just been headed for and swiping the many items that covered the lid onto the floor, he lifted the lid of that trunk. He pulled out three articles of clothing, one white, one a deep blue and the other a faded green. He turned with them in hand and in two strides dropped them into my still shaking hands.

"I stared at these things, my mind flying in so many directions at once I was unsure where I should try to make it land first. I was thinking, no wonder he was taken aback, he thought I had demanded fresh clothing because I felt mine smelled as bad as those he had discarded. I was thinking I did indeed want to change my clothes, and these he'd given me looked clean and soft, but I really wanted to wash my hair and how was I going to make that clear without using the words Gen had hinted I should hide. Then I was thinking the woman who owned these clothes, which he'd kept on that side of his bed that he didn't use, might be very angry were she to find me wearing them, and then suddenly I was wondering where she was and what terrible things might have befallen her.

"Rune stood before me expectantly, as though I was meant to respond to his kindness in some manner I had yet to, as I simply stared blankly at the clothes. Finally I managed a small smile, hoping he would see I was thankful and not grow angry that this kindness hadn't been enough. I bent and retrieved my precious soap from my blanket and showed it to him while hugging those gifts of clothing he had given me close to my chest. I prayed he saw I was thankful and that I only asked some small bit more in return for washing his clothes too. I raised the hand to my head and made a scrubbing motion, then pointed again to his clothes which Angus still lay upon.

"He looked quizzically at Angus then and said, 'Your mistress is spoiled, methinks my sister plays some game with me. So she wants to bathe...better run, seems she means to bathe you as well.'"

"Angus's tail thumped the floor as it tended to do lately when Rune spoke to him and this always made me uneasy. Rune sighed then and took the key from around his neck, and turned to release the chain from the wall. I bent then and tied the underskirt of the thing I wore between my knees as I had seen other women do, then squatted and began to pull his clothing from beneath Angus. Angus, who had stood, now bounded off of them to watch me with as much interest as Rune now did. Rune looked askance at my dog as I stacked my new clothes on top of the tidy pile I made and gathered it into my lap, lifting the hem of my outer skirt and making it into a basket. Rune said not another word as he led Angus and me behind the long house and far up the stream. I walked gingerly, the shackle had not switched ankles in over a month and was wearing hard on my bones as the path seemed to not end soon enough.

"Then the path suddenly ended in a beautiful, wide clearing, where the stream became a pool and I forgot such trivial things. This pool was fed by a small fall of rocks and my heart was awed by the beauty and calming music of the waters before me. I gazed about me for quite a long time, forgetting for a moment the large man who had brought me to this place and the fearful journey of many years that had brought me to him. I turned to Angus, wanting to share my joy, a smile I could not suppress coming to my face, and met the clear inquisitive gaze of Rune. He continued to study me as I dropped my eyes quickly and went to do as I had said I would, but I did not let his sudden change in demeanor detract from this day. I was worried, yes, he had ignored me so completely that to have drawn his eye twice now this day set a tremor to my pulse I could not calm, but the day itself held more sway over my thoughts.

"I perched on a rock that bordered this pool and scrubbed the clothing against it as I had seen the women of Gen's home do and I repeated it until I saw no color of filth wash free into the waters clarity. As each article was cleaned I rung it out, again as I had seen other women do, then hung it over the many branches of the tree Rune sat and leaned against. I avoided his eyes when I had to turn to do this hanging and tried not to let the larger fears creep in on me again when I saw Angus had come to lay some few feet from him, as though awaiting another bone like he had done when I used to toss his food away from me. I tried not to be terrified when Rune looked to Angus and said, 'Seems it was a trade she wanted, and I sweetened the pot with my mother's things for no reason. Suppose you're safe, good man.' And my Angus thumped his tail in happy answer.

"When the job was done and it was time that I felt I could reap the benefit of my task, I realized I still had this large man and his now far too interested eyes to deal with. His deep blue eye's seemed to see too much and I worried they would find my secret. I said a small prayer, thanking the gods that had listened for their kindness so far and begged of them one small favor further. I called Jade to mind, held her in my heart, remembering her proud chin. I raised the soap and looked at Rune as squarely as I could. Most men respected this action when Jade made it, they turned their backs and allowed her the moment of privacy her bearing demanded of them. Rune only began to laugh and looked at Angus as though I had made the grandest jest ever and my hound should be laughing with him.

"He said, 'I am not washing that mess for her, clean clothes or no.'

"I sighed heavily. Was he daft? I didn't want him to wash it, I wanted him to give me privacy while I did it myself.

"Rune looked back up at me suddenly when that exasperated sigh escaped my lips and he caught the look I hadn't been able to keep from my face. It seemed he was nearly embarrassed, if that was even possible, as he realized his mistake and said 'oh' to the dog, as if admitting only to the hound that the joke had been on him. He spun on his backside, facing the tree, and then laughing even louder he told Angus, 'I am going to kill my sister.'

"I wasn't sure what Rune was going to kill Gen for, but since it sounded like he was only amusing himself with the thought and not seriously debating her death, I let go of the worry his sudden announcement shot through me. I watched his laughter shake his broad shoulders for only a moment. Assuring myself he wasn't watching, I bent and untied my under-shift from between my legs and quickly pulled the whole stinking contraption off from over my head. I then waded quickly into the pool, soap and chain in hand, and once I had reached a depth that I could sink to my shoulders I made my way slowly to the far end, where fell the musical flow which created this magical place. I was careful with my footing and managed to come up close beneath this waterfall, finding a large stone with my shackled foot to stand upon. Then I stood with my back to the man who'd brought me, and letting the chain drop, I raised both hands and began vigorously scrubbing the soap into my matted nasty hair. I rinsed quickly and then scrubbed it again, and then I used the lathered length of it to wash the rest of my upper body. I rinsed again and scrubbed my lower half beneath the water and then I simply stood there allowing the water to run over me, allowing the magic of it to clean me far more than the wonderful-smelling soap had.

"I glanced back often but always found Rune looking at the tree and conversing with Angus, telling him things I could not hear to which the hound would thump his tail at random intervals but never take his eyes off me. I enjoyed the water as long as I dared, not wishing to wear Rune's surprising patience thin. It seemed my actions this day had shocked and amused him enough that he was willing to allow me this, but I was not going to press my luck. I lifted my weighted leg and found the end of the chain, then made my way back to the side of the pool where I had washed the clothes. I grabbed the white under-dress with the long soft sleeves from the rock I had perched upon, and then I stepped quickly from the pool and pulled it over my head. I then shook out the other two pieces, recognizing that one was meant to go over the other. I pulled the blue over my head and down my body then looped the other over my neck and tied it about my waist. Rune still had not looked back and I was thankful that he had returned to ignoring me as I moved to gather the clothes that hung from the trees. I washed the sack-like thing I had worn there just as well as I had his things, I wasn't sure why except that I kept thinking that there might come some unforeseeable need for it again.

"He did not move until finally I came to stand behind him, clothing already bundled in my apron and held before me. Even then he didn't look up, he merely turned, saw the clothing, and stood, scooping up the chain and leading me back to the longhouse. Once back in that small room, I felt stifled, the fresh open smells of where I had been made the close scent of wood and skins and man almost too much. I watched with a pang of regret as he replaced the chain and turned to leave, but I reasoned with myself that I had made a big step that day and that mayhap I could make another the following.

"I lay the wet dress I had worn to that wonderful place on the stones before the fire, then hung those few thicker pieces of his clothing that hadn't dried fully over my chain. I then walked to the end of it, stretching it taut to hold them to dry, as I busied my hands if not my mind with folding the others into something that resembled order. I stacked them on the end of his bed where his feet would be. Only then did it occur to me he had left me more slack than before. He had attached the chain much closer to its end than he had each time these past weeks.

"By no means could I reach the various weapons stacked in the far corner or the axe that rested near where his head fell to sleep, or even for that matter come too near the part of the bed he slept upon. I could not help but think this more than a mere accident as I found I could easily reach the mess he had made by clearing the top of what I had learned had been his mother's trunk. Having nothing more to do, I went to examine this pile and slowly began picking through it. I gathered the drinking vessels and stacked them with the platter that I knew the proud woman with the bruises would come to retrieve later. There was a small polished silver mirror, which I didn't bother to look at since I knew I wouldn't know the person. I wasn't sure who would be there but I knew I wouldn't recognize her. There were some items of jewelry and a small delicate pincer of bone, the kind the Egyptians used to pluck their eyebrows nearly away. I looked at this for some time, wondering about the woman who had owned these things and how she had come to be there, thinking it must have been a similar game of the Fates as had brought me there. I had no sure answers though, as I simply stacked everything neatly back in place.

"There was a bit of cloth with small rust-colored stains that I didn't know what to do with, so I folded for lack of a better thing to do. That was when I found a needle, which had been stuck through it, and moments later some thread which had rolled near the bed. I set these things aside, thinking they might come in handy to occupy my hands in days to come. I remembered folding quite a few articles of clothing that could make good use of those items. The small task of organizing the mess he had made was done far too soon, and again I simply looked around me.

"I gave up once again, trying to work my fingers through my hair and set about repairing the clothing, at least that labor seemed worthy, at least those things came together for my work. But again that task was too soon done. I returned to the work that was my hair.

"My hair had proven so unmanageable I was ready to simply cut it off. I began to eye the various weapons in the corner, wondering how I might get close enough to make use of one of their many sharp-looking edges. I suppose it was my labored breathing and the force with which I lay on my belly, stretching with all my strength toward one of those weapons, which caused me not to hear Rune's approach as I always had before. Suddenly I looked up to see him standing over me, looking terribly angry. I realized with frightening clarity what it was he must have been thinking. I jerked my hand back and away from those weapons but then he laughed, a sound not nearly pleased, and kicked a small blade from the corner into my reach.

"I was confused by his actions, he had seemed angry, his laugh was not the happy laugh I had heard by the pool and yet he gave me what I had needed, what I had reached for. I watched him closely, something like butterflies sent to fluttering chaos waking in my stomach, as he came close and crouched down before me, watching me just as closely. I had no idea at first what it was he meant for me to do now but I feared, whatever it was, I wouldn't have the strength to do it.

"Suddenly it came clear to me, as it seemed that he dared me by his very closeness to take the weapon and turn it on him. My face fell, my ribs constricted, I had only meant to rid myself of this terrible mess attached to my head and now I saw I had made a large backward stride after the improvement I had made of my life this morning. My heart slowed to a dull thud as I thought then that I might as well take the blade and do what I had intended, so that at the very least he might see what it was that had been my true intent.

"I reached slowly for the blade and he made no move, the only life about him the slow flexing and un-flexing of the muscles at the right side of his jaw as he stared at me intently. His eyes reminded me of the ocean then, whipped to a terrible rage, which had broken a ship I had lived in the bowels of, with a woman named Jade. I felt I knew then what men had felt when catching sight of Angus's teeth. I began to tremble under his unwavering gaze, his eyes were suddenly too much, the bone-deep fear of the ocean come to swallow me up. I nearly lost my nerve completely.

"I remembered Jade then and her proud chin, in the bowels of that ship, and I forced myself to sit up and took hold of my hair, raising the blade. He grabbed my hand then, staying it in a viselike grip that cause me to yelp more from fear than pain. Angus stood then, having watched this encounter with much interest but little movement, and Rune turned to the dog, saying, 'I'll not harm your mistress, good man, we've only had another misunderstanding, stay yourself.' Angus stood stiff, still, no more sure what to make of things anymore than I was. Both of us watched as Rune took the blade from my limp fingers and stood.

"He looked at me then with a strange expression I could not read, the ocean in his eyes calming slowly as the sun returned. He turned toward his mother's chest. I knew the moment when he saw the clothing I had folded and the order I had restored to the surface he had swiped clean earlier that day when I saw him pause to stare at it. I wasn't sure then whether I wanted to laugh or cry, I had done what I could to show I appreciated his generosity in the trade that morning and then made a terrible mess of it, *still* trying to rid myself of the mess of hair I had *still* ended up stuck with.

"I scurried back to my corner and put my head onto my knees. I heard him as he moved all those things I had set to order about and I thought then he must have thought I had taken something and searched to see what it might have been. I had replaced the needle and thread after I had used it but had no hope that would show me in any better light as I began to see I had done nothing right this day, nothing that those being called Fates would allow to bring me any good. I rubbed at my sore ankle thoughtlessly, I had chafed it terribly that day and worsened the mood of the angry skin stretching for a blade that I hadn't been able to use. I wanted to cry and fought hard to remember all that Jade had taught me.

"I felt his shadow fall over me and was afraid to look up, afraid Jade's memory would fail my chin and the butterflies would betray me. I felt his fingers brush mine where they rubbed at my sore ankle and froze. I couldn't have looked up then had I tried. I heard Angus stand and leave his bone, felt him move beside me, and I could only wonder if Rune had been shown teeth when he left suddenly. I began to breathe again, only to have the breath stolen when I heard his steps returning heavily only a few minutes later. I had a sudden all-consuming fear he had returned ready to kill Angus for the teeth I imagined the loyal hound had shown. I jerked my head up then, meeting his eyes pleadingly as they found mine instantly when his head ducked and cleared the skin.

"I had been ready to beg him to spare my beast, only to see him come weaponless straight toward me and drop a small bundle at my feet. I could not read what it was I had seen there when his eyes had met mine, it was written in a language I had yet to learn, but as he turned and left again I had remembered the ocean again. It was I who had to pause and reexamine a situation and realize I had misunderstood something. This bundle was a small furry skin of some soft-coated beast, the dagger he had taken from me, the needle and thread I had returned to his mother's chest, and a comb. I studied these gifts for quite sometime before I built the fire up to high, bright life and set myself to make use of them.

"Food was brought and I paused to eat some before giving most of it to Angus, wanting more to finish what I had begun than to eat. By the time Rune returned late that evening, I had cut the skin and sewn it so that the softness of the fur lay against my skin and the leathery side wrapped about the shackle. My hair had taken much more time but I had seen he did not want it cut so I had worked for hours, beginning from the bottom up and in sections, but I had removed the tangles from my hair. I lay still, close to the wall behind Angus, and closed my eyes again when he turned to prepare for sleep, after meeting his briefly to give him my thanks.

"The joy of looking ahead to the two brief jaunts to relieve myself paled in comparison to the longer track up the path to the pool I managed to convince Rune to take me on once a week thereafter. I began with some of his bedding as an excuse the first week following that day and more of it the week after, and by the time I had finished with all the cloth bedding the pile of clothing had grown sufficient to be used as an excuse to bathe myself again. It was not nearly so frequent as I would have enjoyed had my life not been turned so sharply down this very different path it had originally been set to, but I didn't think overlong on such things anymore.

"My worries had become simple now, for instance, my bar of soap had grown small and thin and Angus seemed to have come to a gracious understanding with Rune that still bothered me from time to time. I couldn't say I blamed him though, for I too had come to feel strangely comfortable with this huge man who held such sway over my life. I think I was more disturbed that, though he still ignored me for the most part, when he did look at me he seemed to see something that disturbed him because he would look away quickly. I think I was more disturbed by the fact that the last two times he had brought me to the pool he had wandered off, as if distracted by better things when it was time for me to reap my reward and bathe, leaving just Angus to watch over me.

"By the sixth week of this I couldn't help but wonder if somehow I displeased him on some base level, that though he was willing to keep up this trade agreement we had come to, he no longer felt I was worthy of his full attentive protection. I came up beneath the water's flow and turned to watch as he walked away, kicking a stone ahead of him. I was thinking that mayhap he felt I had been intentionally lost or his great uncle wanted nothing more of me and wasn't going to return for me, so watching over me, for him, had become a useless endeavor.

"I had just begun to push these unwelcome thoughts aside and enjoy the feel of the water rinsing them, and the soap, from my head, when I heard a heavy splash behind me. I couldn't get the soap from my eyes quickly enough to see what had hit the water but I saw it move beneath the clear surface toward me. I looked to the shore, sudden fear clogging my throat, and saw Angus standing at the edge of the pool, eyes searching the surface and then turning to me for a sign as to how to react. I wasn't sure myself until I felt the tug on my shackle pull my foot from of the rock I stood upon and jerk me beneath the surface.

16

Windell: Walker

"I tried to suck in my breath to scream but found my mouth filled with water. I felt rough hands crawl up my legs and pull me close to a hard chest beneath the surface, far from air I desperately needed. I opened my eyes and suddenly saw red water fading to pink, saw a flash of tarnished silver fur and one of Angus's huge paws sweeping through the discolored water. I heard the water-muted sounds of Angus's anger and I felt the hands about me loosen for a fraction of a second. I began to kick furiously for dear life, trying desperately to reach the surface. My ankle felt abnormally heavy, as though someone or something held the chain far beneath me. My head broke water and I glimpsed Rune, running hard toward me, I tried again to scream and again I was pulled beneath the surface, dragged down by the chain. Last thing I remembered seeing through the red haze was my own shackle which had done so much, and for so long to keep me safe, hooked around a large fallen tree. What Angus had fought escaped me.

"Next thing I knew I was lying across Rune's thighs as he knelt holding my upper body close beneath his chin. I was naked as the day I came screaming from the fire to be woken by a blast of hound's breath. My eyes fluttered open, my mind not yet fully taking this knowledge in, and he hugged me tight, thanking gods I didn't know and causing me to cough and spit water all over him. He tossed my clothing over me, damning the chain he

291

swung round his forearm, and then pushed to his feet, drawing me up with him in his arms. I gasped when I caught sight of the dead man floating face down in the red and pink pool that fell behind as he carried me back to the longhouse. Angus danced along at my head, as wet as Rune, paying no mind to the huge man who carried me, just watching me. At some point I thought I could have walked but there was no energy in me to argue the strong arms that hauled me to the relative safety of his chamber.

"I was placed gently on the side of the bed closest the fire, holding my clothing to myself. I started to tremble. I sat there, saying nothing, as he looked down at me with those unreadable eyes. Then he turned and went to the other side where rested his evil-looking dual-bladed axe, and taking it in hand he stormed back out into the large common room to face all those hoots and hollers that had descended upon his head when he'd entered with me. I heard his voice rise loud and terrifying, silencing the jovial congratulations his men still hurled. I knew how incredible he must look then to those men, covered in blood they had not seen when he carried me, and now holding that evil axe.

"'There floats a dead man in the washing vale's pool,' Rune bellowed. 'I think him *your* kin; *you* might wish to retrieve him.'

"I had no idea to whom he had directed those last words to but I knew there must have been much spoken with eyes, because the verbal reply was short and hoarse when it finally came. 'You killed him?'

"I began to shake in earnest as I tried to drag my clothing on in the silence that lengthened. I could just see these men who had seemed so pleased moments before, leaning whispers into each others' ears and gathering around Rune to exact their payment for a dead man. Somehow I felt I needed to be clothed and ready for what would come next were they to overcome him. I heard chairs scooting and a few voices raised just enough at times to catch 'Windell' amongst the words. I tied the apron snug and walked on shaking limbs, dragging my chain behind me to the corner where the weapons leaned. I called Angus to my side and waited.

"'I care not that some of you lack the sense to respect my great uncle and what *was* his,' Rune announced brazenly. 'He has been gone from us near five years now and you are filthy opportunistic beasts.' There was grumbling and another chair slid heavily back as I began to pray. 'And I would have you no other way.' A few cheers rang out then at this and I saw myself being sacrificed for his skin. 'But,' he added, again bringing the men to silence, 'any who hasn't the sense to respect *me* come now.'

"There was a long silence in which my heart thudded so hard in my ears I doubted I'd have heard them had words been spoken. Then the same hoarse voice that had made response before said, '*You* have claimed her then?'

"'Aye,' Rune replied, 'She is *mine*.'

"My face went suddenly cold, my knees weak, and the butterflies exploded to life, fluttering every which way. I saw Gen, in my mind's eye, chasing them through my abdomen screaming at them to fly before te Fates took their wings from them. I was Rune's now? What did that mean? I was to have no quick answer. When he returned some long moments later, followed again into his chamber by the cheers of his men, his eyes found me instantly, huddled and shaking in the corner where he kept his weapons. His eyes seemed glazed and I couldn't decide if it was leftover anger from confronting his men or new anger at me that I had brought him to it.

"I forced my legs to work for me and I picked up the chain and walked back to the hearth, not wishing to risk a repeat of the misinterpreted occasion when I had been too near his weapons. He turned and stepped to lean his axe back in its place, then took three steps slowly toward me. I held out the end of the chain and he paused, looking down at it as though he didn't know what to do with it. The high color of anger was draining from his face to be replaced by some shade that did not look right on him. He stood so still, seeming to think too hard and then waver in some decision, that I began to worry he might take his claim back and leave me to the men beyond his chamber. I feared he would not chain me and keep me. Then suddenly he sighed, took the key from his neck and locked me safely to his hearth. I let out breath I hadn't realized I'd been holding and followed his hands with my eyes as they replaced the key about his neck, only to be caught again by his eyes that were set on me too acutely again.

"I could not read all of what was in those deep blue depths but I suddenly recognized one word, pain. He wavered again, and this time I knew it was not thoughts alone which caused him to falter. His eyes broke from mine and looked down at his belly. I followed them, wanting to find answers for what I had read in his eyes and that is when I saw the cut in his shirt just beneath his ribs and knew the pain in his eyes said all that blood was not only from the dead man floating in the washing vale's pool.

"I gasped then and Angus jerked his head up, but he laid it back down with a low whine I had never heard before, when I reached up to try and pull the shirt away to be sure. Rune pushed my hand away and started to turn toward his bed. 'tis only a scratch woman, leave it be.' He spoke the words directly to me and the shock of that was lost on me for the time being. 'I just need to rest.'

"He turned then and began to walk away from me. He was going to make it impossible to be sure he was well and could care for me, by going beyond the length of my tether and falling into the fur beyond me. 'Rune.' His name escaped my terrified lips before I could think to stop it and he spun back to face me just as he reached the place his feet usually rested, just when he was almost beyond my reach. His brow furrowed with confusion, again a thousand other things were written in his eyes, again I could read only one word, pain. 'Please,' I stumbled, trying to remember how to make my tongue use the words, 'let me?'

"I could only wonder later whether the way he fell so heavily to a seated position right where he stood had been due to the shock of hearing me not only speak his language but say his name, or the loss of blood. I walked to him quickly then, finding strength in my limbs despite his keen but glasslike gaze, desperate to assure myself he had not been mortally wounded. I knelt and pulled the shirt away, my breath catching then as I saw the cut was not so long but seemed very deep. I turned then and ran to retrieve my things from my corner, the things that he had given me. I cut the shirt away with the small dagger and began making strips of the dress I had abandoned six weeks before. I dipped one of these strips into the bucket of fresh water the proud woman always kept filled for me. I wiped the area clean, and seeing his muscles jump involuntarily, I met his eyes despite myself. He stared beyond me, seeing things in the far wall I couldn't see, as he flexed his jaw over and over.

"I looked back to the wound and could see three very different layers, the taut golden skin spread wide, separated by a softer-looking center, very red with the return of seeping blood, then a layer like thin pink skin beneath. I began to tremble again. When I had sewn Angus, the gash had been long but I had not seen this second layer. I feared what damage might lay beyond my sight. I looked up at Rune again, and again he did not look at me.

"I threaded the needle with shaking fingers but I could not think how I was going to hold this inner layer together to be sewn, though I knew instinctively that it too needed mending. Then I remembered the pincers and prayed they might work. When I returned with them and Rune finally took note of me and what I meant to do, he stayed my hand again, pressing it to his chest where it had hovered as I tried to make my body obey me and be steady. He looked long and closely at me, as though trying to decide how much I could understand and mayhap even how much he could trust me.

"Rune cut his eyes toward the bearskin drape and sighed heavily. The decision made, he said, 'They cannot see me weak.'

"I knew how desperately all things hung in the balance, I knew now that shackle and the name Windell did nothing for me in this place, probably never had, my safety lay with the shackle belonging to Rune. I knew he needed to know I did. I pulled my hand, which had suddenly stilled, from beneath his, as I made my eyes return his steady gaze. I touched his cheek as I had seen Gen do for her son in a gesture of gentle understanding when telling him not to fear. I said, 'You are not.'

"He had long since passed out and by the time I was done a part of me wished it had been the other way around. I was stretched to my limit in more than one way, everything about me hurt, including my eyes and mind. I had been forced to lie across the bed, blocking most of what light the fire gave with my own body, unable to reach the wound any other way once he had slumped back onto the bed and into the blackness of pain. I remembered that blackness and thought it far better than what my body felt now. Every muscle I possessed was tight and ached to the bones it covered.

"I had no sooner begun to push myself back up to my knees to try to stand and stretch than I heard the woman who came to bring the food. I could not let her see his freshly sewn wound. I lay back down quickly, draping my arm gently over him for my hand to cover it as her head poked timidly through the curtain. I lifted my head slowly as though she had woken me, and looked to the floor at my feet. She placed the platter there, giving me a slow smile. Rune moaned, she turned and left quickly and I removed the weight of my arm from him as soon as the drape had fallen back into place.

"I stood and stretched, rubbing my back, thinking about that smile and the proud woman who'd worn it as easily as she usually did bruises, and it came to me, that must be the smile I had worn when I had seen Gen with her William. The smile was pleased to see someone as happy as you wanted to be, something like envy, but kinder. I realized then that I was pleased, I liked the man who had risked his life and claimed me, he was gentle and kind in his own way. He had cared for me and now I found I cared for him. Had I not determined that was the only route I could take? I was simply surprised to find it had gone both ways.

"Did it matter that I had taken it with Rune and not Windell? I did not know what more lay in store now that he had told his men I was his, but I found a small hope blooming within me. I knew now why Gen had chosen to send me to her brother, and suddenly knew why he had laughed and happily threatened to kill her. She had meant for him to come to feel for me as she had, he must have seen that long before I, but had she known I would come to care for him? That must have been what she had meant by, 'let us see what

296

comes when I warn the butterflies away.' It was a dangerous game she had played with both of us. What then did that mean she truly thought of Windell, the man whose hound I had inadvertently stolen?

"I had no answers for these thoughts for now, all I had was a sleeping protector I couldn't question nor allow to be seen in this vulnerable state he had trusted me with. I turned then to build the fire back up and heard him moan again and move about on the bed in a fitful sleep full of dreams I couldn't imagine. When I turned back, thinking to whisper and wake him, warn him to get beneath the blankets in case a fever tried to set in, he had rolled beyond my reach. I lay across the bed again, stretched as far as I could, and flipped a blanket over him. I was resigned to stay awake all night to be sure he remained covered as he wrestled inner adversaries I could not help him with.

"Some time in the dead of night I woke from a fitful doze full of frightened images, my head rested on the foot of the bed. This groan hadn't been like the others. I stood so that I could view his face and saw him pale and sweating. He had thrown the cover off and now I saw that the wound had seeped a bright red splotch into the wrap of my hem I had managed to tie around it. He groaned and shivered, thrashing again and causing me to fear he would tear the wound open anew. He mumbled words that sounded like they included 'Windell' and 'no' over and over. I couldn't reach him to cover or help him. I built the fire as high as I dared, my own bones screaming remembered terror at me as the flames leapt high. Angus stood then beside me, also watching the man on the bed fight death. Angus whined again as he had the afternoon before and I looked at him. Suddenly I realized if ever there was going to be a time I needed to use the other gift Gen had given me, it was now.

"I took off Angus's collar and let loose the shackle from my ankle before replacing it around his neck. I gathered blankets and skins from the side nearest the fire and layered them over Rune as he continued to shiver. Then I crawled behind his head, moving discarded pillows out of the way and pulling my blanket up round my shoulders. I lifted his head and crossed my legs beneath it, his fevered forehead pressed into my ribs as I leaned forward and pulled those many covers up beneath his chin. I bowed my back, releasing the tension out and away from my spine, steadying his shivering shoulders between my forearms where I rested them on my knees. I remembered this posture, as it came instinctively back to me from when I had been someone else, and I tried to recall the peace that other woman had found in it. Then slowly I allowed my head to be led by my hair, to follow my spine, and curl over this man I had come to care for, bringing the blanket and my healing warmth with me. I found prayers I had forgotten to gods I'd thought had forgotten me. I found a small measure of peace as my forehead touched down on his blanked chest and we shared breath in the space between my breasts.

"I woke to the difference in the man in my lap. The skin of his shoulders pressed to my arms was warm but not sickly, his breath was slow but steady and deep, his body still but for the breathing. I raised my forehead, bringing my hair with me, realigning my spine with heaven and the gods that had answered me. It would be quite sometime before it would come to me that it was the first truly peaceful sleep I had had in years. I looked down into his sleeping face, seeing in it that he had come to share the peace I had found in the night. It seemed to me that he was young, too young to have suffered the things his trembling mumbles in the night had spoke of, but then, how old was I? As I lifted his head gently and unfolded my limbs, his eyes fluttered open and caught me. I remembered the magic water when the ocean was calm and the green of life waved beneath it. It seemed he had thought it a dream, seeing me above him, for he closed his eyes again and a slow smile took his boyish face.

"The morning was not yet come completely when I took my new spine and lifted my chin and walked with Angus out behind the longhouse to relieve myself. I had taken the key from over Rune's neck and taken my shackle with me to remind any who might see me that I belong to Rune but no one stirred or noted our passing. I could not deny the joy in me that I had done this thing, my feet steady as I replaced the end of the shackle then returned the key to Rune's still sleeping person before attaching the part which I controlled once more with Angus's well-guarded key. I sat on the edge of the bed and poked pieces of wood which Rune had kept in good supply back into the fire with the tip of my toe, debating fear. When the woman came with the first meal of the day, all she saw was another woman tending a fire while a man still slept peacefully. She had smiled again, and still saying nothing, left me to my thoughts.

"Rune woke near midday and grunted, drawing my face to his with worry. He pushed upright slowly, wincing, causing me to wince as well. He sat then facing me, many questions seemed to fight to be the first to have answers. His brow furrowed thoughtfully as he looked to the hearth and saw the chain was attached, and he seeming to make that an answer for at least one of them as he touched the key that still hung on the chain at his neck. Then finally he seemed to set his mind on something with which to begin this new day and threw the blankets from off himself. He pushed slowly to his feet. He looked to the wrap around his middle and back to me, then paused thoughtfully again. 'How much was a dream?' he asked. I had no answer. How was I to know what he had dreamed? When I said nothing he merely turned and gathered some things from his trunk, putting his arms into a shirt to cover the wrap gingerly. He looked again at me, then simply turned, taking these things with him as he left.

"When he returned he had bathed. I was pleased to see his clothes were fresh as seemed his skin, as I knew this would help him to heal. He had done nothing to care for his hair again, though, it seemed he never did when he bathed. I knew he bathed, if infrequently, he just had no care for that part of his person. I did not understand why this suddenly bothered me, except to think that maybe more of the memories that belonged to the woman I had been, who had reminded me how to sit and find healing peace, had come back and remained. Yet I remembered the comforting smell of him through the long night and though it had not been the clean of spiced masculine soap it had not been dirty either, it had simply been him.

"He came to stand before me where I now sat against the wall near the fire, and then he sat on the edge of the bed and merely watched me. I became uneasy under his gaze and began to study my toes. When his voice came deep and cutting into the silence I couldn't help but jump.

"'You said my name,' he said at last. 'How did you know it?'

"I stared a long moment into the flames, again debating fear and what good it did me. After a long moment of questioning how much I should let him know of her great gift to me, I decided I must trust him as he had trusted me. I said, 'Your sister.'

"'She taught you our language before sending you to me?' he asked then, a bit awestruck, 'Then you have understood *everything*?'

"I was confused. '*Everything*?' I asked.

"It seemed he took my repeating the word to mean I hadn't understood rather than my simply not fully grasping what all he meant it to encompass. He looked around the room as if searching for a better word and his eyes came to rest on Angus. He pointed to the dog and changed the subject, perplexing me. He said, 'This hound, you understand?' He looked at me then. Of course I understood Angus was a hound, I nodded, then he said, 'How did you come to have him?'

"I wasn't sure what this was about but it seemed very important to Rune and if we were to trust each other and care for each other, as I had seen Gen and William did, I felt I needed to be honest. I took a deep breath and said, 'He followed me when I left Windell and his men.'

"I had just admitted to stealing the dog, whether meaning to or not and my heart froze awaiting his response. It was not what I had expected because he cursed then and said, 'So then you do belong to my great uncle.' He sounded almost angry but also disappointed. 'I have debated that for some time, thought my sister played some game...' His words fell off, becoming thoughtful again, and I watched him as my own confusion grew.

"'I belong to you,' I stumbled at last, hopeful I had misunderstood. How could the dog having merely followed me somehow mean I belonged to Windell? I had stolen the dog, Windell had never laid claim to me. Windell had not placed this chain of ownership about my ankle. He had never claimed me in any way, only fed me and kept other men from me with angry words and much pointing to the places where marks remained in testament to much absence of jewelry.

"Rune only looked at me with something like sadness about his face and eyes and said, 'He is my blood. He raised me when my parents were killed, taught me everything I know, made me who I am. I have much love for him.' Then he stood again, not waiting or looking at me any longer to see if I had understood. It seemed to me it had not mattered to him if I had comprehended his statements; he had made these explanations to himself. He turned then and left the chamber.

"I did not ask to go to the washing pool that week nor the week that followed, either with word or gesture. Rune continued to take me out behind the longhouse twice a day, but come the days I would have gathered things to encourage him to lead me further up the stream, I did not gather them. I was suddenly at a loss, the small measures of peace I had slowly been reclaiming for myself seemed to escape me. I did not wish to return to the washing pool after what had happened that fateful day. I was not sure if Rune would still wander away after what had occurred the last time, but if the way he reverted to ignoring my presence after that short confusing conversation was any indication, I was not wont to risk it.

"Come the third week though, he made the offer to me. He gathered the clothing into a pile and took the chain from the hearth, pointing to my blanket for me to retrieve what was left of my soap. I did not resist, though I was not sure I was ready to return there, and tying my under-dress, I gathered the washing into my apron. He went to his mother's trunk and took from it more clothing which I assumed was for me to wear, but he said nothing and neither did I as we walked up the stream toward the clearing. I faltered before the path widened, suddenly not wanting to see the dead man floating there in my mind's eye. Rune paused and looked at me then and said, 'You must not fear.' I put up my chin then, thinking he was right and I would not become less by finding new things besides fire to cause my bones to tremble.

"When the washing was done and it was time for me to bathe and wash my hair, I was suddenly fearful again. I did not want Rune to leave me alone there. I did not want him to wander off again as he had begun to do rather than turn his back and wait. I walked to where he sat beneath the tree while I did the washing and gathered the end of the chain. He looked up at me then, and when I did not immediately turn to bathe but I caught his eye, I saw it was pained. I thought then that his wound must be bothering him still and knelt to check that it healed well and had not begun to fester, since I had not been allowed to check it, but he stayed my hand. He said, 'It heals well woman, go about your bath.'

"I stood then, wondering what bothered him if not the wound. I stepped back toward the pool, still facing him, and when my heel touched the water's edge I said, 'Please...do not leave.'

"He spun on his backside in answer, facing the tree, and as I removed my clothing and entered the water I heard him begin talking to Angus again as he used to before he had learned he could speak to me. He said, 'Your mistress saved my life only to torture me slowly.'

"Understanding dawned on me then. I suddenly knew why he had begun to wander off when I would bathe. He meant to place space between himself and what he hadn't, until two weeks ago, been sure was another man's woman. I saw then that he fought his own hunger as much as he fought other men's. I was torn then between a strange new bloom of joy that it was not something in me that caused him to look away so quickly when I would catch his eyes on me, and a near disappointment he thought me another man's and there was in him a thing that made him unwilling to look then. It was something in him, which I knew was good, though it seemed a problem now, something I thought had been called honor once.

"As I bathed and washed my hair with what soap remained, I wondered what would happen when Windell came- if Windell came. Would I be given to him, whether I had been his before or not, simply because it is what everyone seemed to think was right because I traveled with his hound-everyone including Rune? What if Windell did not come? It had been over a year I had been with these people, in their care, kept safefor a man that was yet to show his face again, a man who could now be as lost somewhere in my homeland as I was lost now in his. What if he did return? I did not want to be given to Windell, though he had not been unkind. I wanted to remain where I was. I wanted to be with Rune.

"I stumbled then, nearly losing my footing on my rock beneath the fall, as the knowledge struck me hard in the belly, setting the butterflies to fluttering again. Somewhere along my great journey my actions had begun to take root in more than mere caring for a man because he cared for me. Somewhere in holding his head as he fought death, my actions had become less to save my protector's life and more to save the life of someone I had come to love. Doing his laundry today had not been so I could bathe... I looked back and saw him facing the tree still. I wondered what it was that had made him waver in thinking I was his great uncle's originally. Suddenly I was thinking if I could make him again begin to question that, maybe he would then cease fighting himself and claim and keep me for himself.

"I had not yet decided how I was going to do this thing I had determined to do, as I put on the clean clothing Rune had provided me and began washing the other. I remembered Gen saying *she* had *chosen* William and thought capturing a man, even one of her kind, must be possible if she had done it. There was deep within me the memories of a woman who had been trained her whole young life to capture a man's attention, though not this kind of man. I thought then I must find this womanwithin me and ask her for help and maybe some of it would transcend our different races.

"I returned to Rune's side and tugged a large leaf free of the tree he sat beneath, using it to wrap the small sliver of soap that was now barely worth saving. He looked up as I did this but said nothing even when I held his eyes, hoping to bring more words from him. I went then and gathered the clothing into my apron, then returned again and touched his shoulder gently. 'I am ready,' I said to both of us, handing him the end of my tether.

"That evening I listened from the shielded chamber as he gathered the men together and knew something new was in the wind. I forgot my plan to capture him as I heard him giving many orders. I heard many hurried feet and by full night knew the men were leaving. He came into the room and immediately found my worried eyes. Again he told me not to fear, that the men who would remain were old and trusted, and the women would care for me. He said he would return but could not bear to spend any more idle days waiting for his great uncle. He said that the men grew restless, as did he, and the water beyond the house sung a terrible alluring song to their souls. He said he meant to visit his sister and allow the men to re-supply. It seemed again that he made these explanations to himself, as he didn't wait to see if I had understood them or if I would make response. He walked to his corner, retrieving his axe, then walked to the door and paused. He turned back to me then and I had so many hopes for what his face might mean he was about to say until he walked to Angus. He paused before the dog and it stood, it was as close as they had come to each other and I held my breath as he reached and removed the chain about his neck, putting it around Angus's.

"He said, 'Keep her well, good man,' scratched his large snout and left.

"The men took out that very night and I was left then with my confusion and fear to try to make plans I couldn't begin to make work out in the end in my head. I found myself walking myself and Angus behind the longhouse without the strangely comforting presence of a man when and where it should have been least comforting. I found myself, after two days of trying to do this mental cleaning and organizing, releasing my chain from sheer boredom. I began cleaning the entire chamber, taking the layers of rugs up from the floor and wrestling them out to beat and air as I could not do my worried mind. I cleaned the blackened hearth and walls, and then set myself to the bed, cleaning and airing it layer by layer, all the way down to the lowest skin. By the first week's end I had begun polishing weapons and still had not escaped or cleaned or organized my thoughts into anything worth viewing.

"The woman who always brought the food stayed a moment one day, looking about the place. She smiled again and I couldn't stop myself, I asked if she knew how I might get some incense. She looked at me and I knew my word had not been from her language but I didn't know a word for it in theirs. The room was clean and free of dust and soot, but it still smelled of wood-smoke and skins and a man I found I missed- not bad, just not pretty on the nose. I tried to explain the concept of burning sweet-smelling things to cover those smells and she smiled then. She had not taken my ability with her words in the same shocked manner as Rune had, she merely turned and gestured I should follow.

"She glanced a few times at the chain I carried with me. I was still unwilling that any should know I had Angus's key if I needed it, still wanting it to show that I was Rune's just in case. It seemed she could not understand why I still wore it and I did not try to explain. Angus and I came down a path behind her to a hut placed deep in the woods the stream ran through, and she pointed to long racks of drying herbs that sat outside of it, her face questioning me if that was what I sought. It seemed to me then that it was she who did not speak this language I used as well as I did. I looked long at her face but it gave me no clue what language she might use better.

"An old woman came out from this hut, crooked under the weight of many years, eyes white with the film of great age and unseeing. She looked toward us a long time before speaking. When she spoke I was frightened by her words and the deep knowledge they revealed. 'The Fates have played havoc with you, princess,' she cackled, 'but 'twas you who tempted them to, no?'

"I was fearful and for a long time I made no answer. Finally I said only, 'I seek a sweet smell to burn in *my* chamber.' I would not let this strange old crone unsettle me with her hints at seeing things she could not have.

"'You would,' came her unsettling rasp, 'but what have you brought for me?'

305

"I remembered these people's strange notions of fair trades amongst themselves, even if a good portion of those items traded had been taken unfairly from others. I had no idea what I had or could do that she might take in trade for what I wanted of her. I tried to think but nothing had come to mind by the time she began to cackle again and told me, 'Another life then,' before pointing to the racks and adding, 'Take only what you need, I suppose I owe that much.'

I watched as she hobbled back into her hovel and wondered if her concept of reincarnation was very much like mine or if she merely believed man returned repeatedly as man and her kindness now could be repaid by me in another life. Then I wondered what she felt she had done to me in other lives that made her feel she owed me this kindness now. It didn't seem to matter for long though, where or if our beliefs split ways, since the belief had gotten me what I wanted, right now, in this life. I went to the racks, examining the dried things until I came to those bundles that had a sweet smell to them. I took only one bundle and glanced back only briefly before returning to the longhouse with it.

"By the end of the second week I had begun to come out from the chamber and join the other women as they gathered to cook the two meals they made each day. I would see them look questioningly at the chain I kept with me, but none of them voiced their questions to me. I knew at some point that what men were there were not likely to have forgotten Rune's claim, but I still couldn't bring myself to lose that link to him. One day, in the third week of the men's absence, I heard two women speaking as though they thought I could not understand them. We had all come to sit in a circle cutting vegetables for a stew and one said to the other, 'Why does she wear that thing still if Rune has given her the key?' The other said, 'Mayhap he only has the key to the one end and his great uncle really did own her and still has the other in his possession.' She'd laughed then, adding, ''Twill be Hades in this house, come Windell's return, that be the case.'

There was sudden silence then as if the thought were not nearly so funny once they had paused to consider it, and I found a new worry to occupy my mind. 'Is Windell really so fierce as the old ones whisper?' the younger one asked the other as I had just been wanting to. 'It is confusing to me how some speak of him as gone mad and mayhap soft and yet others seem awed when they speak of his fierce deeds.'

"'Windell was the greatest among us at one time, girl, never think him soft, even if he has gone mad.' The older woman said a bit harshly, 'You want to know him, watch young Rune. Some simply can not ken why he would take to trading fairly with *all* men is all, they are daft to think it makes him soft though.'

"That night boats came as though the women's words had summoned them. I returned quickly to my chamber to reattach my shackle and await the man I wanted it to belong to, as the other women went to meet their men on the shore. Rune did not come, however, even as I heard many men's voices raised in happy greeting and cheerful talk to the older men who had remained. When the skin was finally swept aside and I turned to see Rune, I saw Windell instead.

"His sharp gaze found and pinned me instantly where I sat on the edge of the bed, poking the fire with my shackled toe. I squeaked unwittingly, drawing Angus to his feet at my side to stare toward the intruder who had caused my uneasiness. 'What is this?' he demanded, turning to someone behind him I could not see. The answer must have been timid or whispered or both because I did not hear it and it did not please him. He ducked past the entry and came fully into the chamber, returning to his full impressive height and looking around him angrily. I began to tremble.

"Angus grew stiff as my trembling redoubled under Windell's inquisitive gaze when it settled first on my ankle then on the beast before it returned to my face. Angus watched this man who had owned him before me, I watched this man who had never owned me but from whom I had taken the prized beast. He looked back to the smaller, older man who had followed him slowly into the room and said, 'Aye, 'twas my hound, seems he's worthless to me now though, he thinks he's the woman's.' He studied me further before adding, 'But this was never *my* woman. She is a princess of her

307

people that I came upon in the wreckage of a burning caravan and thought to return to them for a healthy trade relation to begin. She ran away in the night and the useless beast followed her. You say Rune keeps her *for me*?'

"'Aye,' the other man replied, 'until one day one of the young and foolish thought to claim her, thinking you would not return...'

"'And...' Windell had prompted, when the man trailed off.

"'Rune claimed her himself then," the man stumbled, 'said any man fool enough to have no respect for you would have to go through him, said she was his now.'

"Windell let out a big hearty laugh that scared the blood from my face. What would he do now? Now that he thought his nephew had claimed me despite him. His laugh did not seem angry, but hadn't they said he was mad? I thought that I desperately needed to make him see that the claim had only been in show, but I didn't want to say such things in front of this other man. I was not given the chance as Windell turned and took the other man with him as he left.

"There was much drinking and revelry in the common room that night, and I huddled in the corner fearing *everything* again. I didn't even risk going out to relieve myself while so many unknown men wandered drunkenly about. I dozed only moments at a time. When Windell came back to the chamber in the dead of night, I thought I would die. I huddled into the wall behind Angus and buried my head in my knees. 'Why does he keep you chained then? Do you not yet accept you are his?'

"I was not sure if he spoke to me but his tone was low and thoughtful and when I made myself look up he was looking right at me, eyes betraying no hint of the drunkenness I had heard going on beyond the bearskin. He seemed to expect no response, much like Rune, he simple went on as though speaking to himself. 'Has he been cruel to you girl? I'll thrash him for you...'

"'No,' I nearly cried, 'do not harm him...'

"My voice and the power it had come out with suddenly faltered as the man before me looked shocked. Suddenly I had no more words but I pulled Angus's head to mine and showed this man who had shown me kindness once both of the keys, then looked toward the skin that shielded my view from the many drunken men. He followed my eyes and threw his head back again, laughing long and loud.

17

Dristy: Sight

"'So that is the way of it then?' Windell said at last.

"I found my voice then and began to answer his many questions, we talked long into the night and by dawn he had but one question left for me. 'So were I to offer to return you to your betrothed, you would not wish to return to that life, the life of a princess?' he asked, watching my face closely.

"I was thoughtful for a very long time before giving him one last bit of honesty. 'Even were it to have been some strange misunderstanding which kept my prince from reclaiming me before, I do not think I could want him now, not as I want Rune. And I do not think he would want me, not as I believe Rune does.' I paused then, knowing this man would understand. I said, 'I think it worth the trade.'

"'Aye, love would be,' Windell agreed, gazing back at the fire. I caught his eyes then straying to the trunk where Rune's mother's things rested and something occurred to me.

"'You loved her?' I asked carefully.

"'Aye,' Windell replied, 'but she had eyes only for my brother.' He sighed deeply then and said as if to himself, 'Sometimes you win, sometimes you lose.'

"I was silent. I could only imagine how it must have felt to love a woman who was in love with your brother. With the sense of honor I had seen Rune display which he seemed to have learned from this man, I could only guess at the torment it had been to then raise their children after their deaths.

"'I propose another trade,' Windell said then, grinning broadly, and shaking the moment loose, 'Your language for the beast you stole, no matter how innocently.' He looked then at Angus who slept silently beside me, paw over the bone Rune had given him, 'I think a better understanding of your people and their language will better serve me than a hound who doesn't believe he's mine.'

"We spent the following few days talking, as I began to teach him my words in payment for his hound. I had removed the shackle at his bidding, when he said it annoyed him to watch me with it and I moved freely amongst his men, knowing he would see to them and their manners as he had assured me. I was pleased with all things now, all except the absence of Rune. It seemed it should be an easy thing from here, the plan I had never been able to formulate seemed to be working itself out without my prompting. It seemed that he should return, see I was not his great uncle's and then take me as his own. I was all butterflies every time I thought of him, not because I couldn't see it going wrong, but because I could see it going right.

"I sat before the fire with Windell, giving him more words as he sat on the edge of the bed the fourth evening when there erupted a great commotion in the common area beyond the skin. There was much excited greeting of friends and family and much more loud conversation which included the name 'Windell' frequently. Rune's head came silent and sudden through the covering and I saw him as his eyes met mine, then turned to meet his great uncle's. Windell turned and faced him fully and I saw many things pass between them. Then Rune merely withdrew his head and left. Windell stood and followed. I kept my place, frozen there as surely as if I were still chained and had no keys at all.

"Rune had not looked pleased to see either of us.

"Rune did not return that evening nor was he back by dawn. I did not risk moving from my place, suddenly I did not know my place. I thought

311

for just a second of the feeling of relative safety the shackle had provided and was even half-tempted to put it back on but stopped myself when I realized I didn't know what it signified to anyone anymore, including to myself. If Windell had made it clear I was not his and Rune was not happy with that, had not returned to me eagerly having learned that then...

"The bearskin moved and I jerked my head up from where it had rested on my knees. I still held the chain and shackle. I had dozed while debating them but had not put them on. Rune came silently toward me, holding something in his hand. He squatted before me and I lifted the chain and shackle to him in hopeful offering. He ignored them, looking steadily at me. My face and heart fell as I tried to make my eyes hold on to his despite the fact he'd refused to claim me. I lifted the chain and shackle again and he took them absently, almost angrily, and tossed them toward the weapons in the corner. 'I do not want those,' he said simply.

"I wanted to cry then, when he took my elbow and pulled me to rise on unsteady legs. I was terrified now as he turned me toward the skin and I tried to stop. I could see me, left unclaimed beyond this room, and it was not a pretty vision. He looked down at me then and said, 'Not going to go small girl fearful on me now?'

"His tone said he had expected better of me so I put up my chin and allowed him to lead me through the longhouse and then behind it. I was confused again, as he took me further still, up the path toward the washing pool, while Angus trailed faithfully behind. What new game was this, I wondered? I was suddenly consumed with a new fear that though he did not want me he didn't want anyone else to have me either and meant to drown me. It was irrational, it did not fit with what I had come to believe of him but then neither had I expected he would deny me when I had offered myself to him. We came to the edge of the pool and he turned to face me, holding out the thing he had held in his hand.

"A new bar of soap.

"He pointed to his hair and then looked at the soap, offering the trade straight-faced. I couldn't help it, I began to laugh, the stress of the whole damned journey to this moment let loose. He started laughing too and it was a wonderful, happy sound. I realized he had no more use for the chains to lay claim to me than I had for any on Angus who now sat beneath the tree looking at both of us. He had me as surely as I had him.

"'You want me to wash that mess?' I asked finally.

"'To begin with,' he said, turning serious, 'I was not dreaming was I, I remember your hair falling around me every night when I try to sleep.'

"I knew he referred to the night I had held him through his fever and his eyes had fluttered and it seemed he had seen me. 'No, 'twas not a dream,' I said. I read his eyes then, saw many words there I suddenly understood, including hunger and love, and I did not fear either. Rather I took the soap and said again to this man, 'I am ready.'

"That night and every night thereafter I slept on furs, not silk, without regrets because they came with the arms of a man who shared his dreams and weaknesses as readily as his flesh. We shared laughter and happy conversation as eagerly and frequently as arguments over misunderstandings. I taught him as much as he taught me and we loved equally. We made trades with Windell, and Angus was brought a beautiful bitch, made for us our own hounds to continue to care for me and the other women when our men were gone. I sewed more wounds and held him through more fevers and as the years passed and my ankles came to know the weight of much new jewelry, my fingers and ears and nose again held many rings he brought me with each return from the sea.

"Gen came to visit us at least once a year and on one visit brought with her a daughter. Then on another she brought with her a friend. Jade stood on the deck, chin up, taking note of none till her eyes found mine. Gen had laughed then and told me she had been right when Jade had come to her home with the men upon their latest return, she had thought she'd recognized something in her chin.

"Then one day there came a large ship to our shore and I came down without Rune, who was away at that time with his men. I saw my own kind on the deck, afar, and in the small boat approaching. The dogs and Jade and

313

the rest of the women and the old men stood around me as those of my race came ashore and bade me return with them to the prince who had searched long for me. I asked them why he had searched so long and they seemed not to understand my question. I asked them what had compelled him to come in search of a woman he had not yet wed or come to love. They had looked at me as though I had gone mad. They had asked me what love had to do with this matter and told me again that my prince awaited me on the deck of the ship.

"I looked long at that ship, at the many beautiful women covered head to toe in the most priceless of gems and jewelry, draped in silks and sitting under great fans set to waving by servants. I saw the prince standing tall and proud amongst his many wives. I found myself pitying them that they would never know what I did. I found myself thinking if Rune and his men were here, it would all be mine. I giggled then, seeing I was thinking like these people I had made my own. I smiled to myself as I looked back to these men whom the prince had sent to retrieve me like some lost trinket. I was not some trinket to be retrieved, I was a free spirit there happily of my own accord, I had been taught much along my journey to this moment. I had chosen this life and the continued ability to learn. I told them love had everything to do with the matter and that the woman they sought had died, that I had seen her die in a burning caravan with my own eyes. I told them I was Ayesha and they must tell their prince I was another man's woman.

"I watched as they returned to the prince, hopeful that would be the end of it, but it was not. I gathered my hounds around me as the prince himself came with them in the small boat, stepping light and panther-like onto the sand, and walked slowly toward me. He said my name as it had been, looking with pity at me surrounded by dogs, and said I must remember who I was and return with him, that he would not leave me to live with these savages. I knelt then beside the aged and tired hound that had come with me to this place that was my home and hugged Angus's head to me. I looked quiet and proud at the prince who had almost been my husband but would

314

have never been *my man*. I told him, 'I know exactly who I am and it pleases me. I am Ayesha. I am Alive.'

"The prince had turned then in disgust from the woman who knelt before him and hugged dogs and I watched him go, breathing a sigh of relief. When Rune returned a few days later he was told of the scene that had occurred on his shore in his absence and he came to our room with the many gifts he had brought me with many questions in his eyes. He asked if I were truly happy, if I had wanted to return to my old life and simply not done so out of some fear. I told him clearly and long into the night that I wanted no more than what I had, that this was my life and it pleased me."

"Wow," Dristy said suddenly, slamming the journal closed and making Genie jump nearly out of her skin. "No wonder Jordan doesn't like dogs, I'd bet my booty it began right there!"

"Seems everything did," Genie said after a long thoughtful moment.

"I don't know," Dristy said thoughtfully. "That life explains so many things about the others, you know, the things she couldn't help but pursue through each life thereafter. But I have a hard time believing it all began with a mean twist of the Fates, simple chance..."

"I think it enough," Genie said. "Now can you bring her back?"

"There is something that bothers me still," Dristy said, thoughtful and ignoring Genie's prompting to end it yet again.

"What?" Genie sighed.

"The old crone," Dristy said, "feeling she'd owed her something and telling her she could pay her the next life." Dristy turned thoughtful eyes to Genie, "What if that were me again? What if I owed her from a life before that one and she repaid me in the one during the Crusades?"

"Just leave it," Genie said then. "We know where the notion of 'something more' began and it is enough, let's just wake her and start putting it together."

"I don't think so," Dristy said. "The crone spoke of owing her that much and of her tempting the Fates. Just give me ten more minutes. I want to do this right." Dristy said then, "Let's *really* figure this out."

Aizlyn's bearing changed dramatically before their eyes at Dristy's last words. Aizlyn sat up tall and straight, the blanket slid off her shoulders and made a useless puddle around her unnoticed as the two women watching were more consumed observing the disappearance of the red marks and welts that had been beneath it what seemed like no more than an hour before.

Aizlyn bowed her head at the neck, chin to chest, then returned to her regal stance before saying, "Let us figure what out?"

"I think I am Sarasvati again," Dristy said, leaning into Genie and whispering low. "This sucks, bad. I can feel my soul slipping as we speak. I shouldn't be playing god or goddess."

"So don't. Just see where she is and how she feels about life, assure yourself that was the beginning and then wake her," Genie said, growing antsy. "I would have thought it safe to assume she is a princess by her posture but I refuse to assume much more of anything with her this evening. You know what they say about…"

"Yah, yeah," Dristy said, "you, me, asses….I hate this, you know."

"It was you who wanted more. Just get it over with," Genie prompted. "*I* think we've found our chain and our wall for that matter. That was the first life where she doesn't seem to have had any deja vu. Be sure she was happy before that, so you can shut that damn no-such-thing-as-just-plain-old-fate part of your brain down. I am past hungry. Do it!"

"Are you happy?" Dristy asked, after another brief moment of beating herself up for playing goddess again.

"Of course," Aizlyn said with regal surety, "I am a princess." Then her face darkened with suspicion and she asked, "Should I not be?"

"I am not judging your feelings," Dristy replied, mentally kicking herself in the shin, "I merely wonder if you have ever longed for more?"

"Is there more?" Aizlyn sounded somewhat awestruck. "Is that what I am to figure out?"

Dristy wanted to cry suddenly as she recalled when she, playing Sarasvati, had mentioned to Aizlyn that she should feed the dog if she wanted to chase the love of dreamers, and then returned to find Aizlyn in tears over a poisoned dog. She had dismissed the thought that she had somehow planted the idea in Aizlyn's head in the first place as an impossibility. She had told herself it had been bound to happen and even thought, for just once in her life, that it had to be merely a coincidence that she had said to do it and then Aizlyn had. But Dristy didn't really believe in coincidence any more than Aizlyn did. Dristy recalled the old crone again, saying, 'I owe you that much.'

Dristy had to be sure as the terrible thought began to eat at her. She sent Aizlyn further back asking her again, "Are you happy?"

Aizlyn's reply came as swift and sure and proud as before, "Of course. I am a princess."

But when the inevitable "Should I not?" came from her open malleable heart and fell from lips eager to please her goddess, Dristy was truly visionary for the first time that whole day and answered, "You should be as you are if it please you."

Dristy began crying, slow heartbroken tears, as she sent Aizlyn even further back and again she heard, "Of course. I am a princess."

And again, "Of course. I am a princess."

Dristy started to sob.

Dristy's whole body shook with tears, washing clean her inner eye. She wasn't sure how or when or why, but she felt sure she was the first link in that terrible chain Aizlyn sought to break and be free of. She was positive it had begun with her, fourteen or so lifetimes ago, planting the idea there was more to life than being a princess in an impressionable young heart. Dristy cut a brokenhearted tearful look at Genie and saw Genie shared her pain, saw Genie knew what she knew in that very moment. Dristy herself had been Aizlyn's wall and she knew then beyond a shadow of a doubt this night had been planned by Genie as much for her benefit as for Aizlyn.

"You knew?" Dristy cried to her old friend.

"I thought," Genie admitted, "but I wasn't sure until I saw it, heard it, just now. I had even begun to hope I was wrong. When I saw that your friendship passed through many lives by the way she responded to you, even in this one, I actually started to think that was all it was that was between you. That you merely sought to guide her back to peace you knew she'd found in other lives because you had been her dearest friend in them. I hoped it was simply something you guys took turns doing, being the eyes for each other from life to life. I tried to stop you there, when I saw you meant to check the old crone. I told you to make it quick. But you just had to know, couldn't believe it a mere twist of fate."

"How?" Dristy sobbed. "How could it be?"

"You were the one so good at playing Sarasvati," Genie said then, "you tell me."

"I don't understand," Dristy said, wiping her eyes on her shoulder and nose on her sleeve trying to focus on Genie better.

"Neither do I, not completely," Genie replied honestly, "but I believed you lived your life to provide her this night, maybe because your sense of fairness indeed felt you owed her. You have educated yourself and trained for it ever since I have known you, and maybe it is what you, too, are meant to figure out in this time. In any case you have demanded much of yourself, karmically speaking, and Aizlyn and I have done our part in opening your eyes to the reason behind your need for such vision."

"I would have never caused anyone so much trouble," Dristy said then, glancing forlorn at Aizlyn who still sat staring blankly ahead, "especially not someone so naturally sweet."

"I know you would have never done so on purpose," Genie said carefully. "But from the day I met you, you had such grand ideas and vast vision of how the world was versus how it should be, why people did the things they did and how they could have done them better. You had all these thoughts spinning wildly in your head about so many things you felt should be set to right, and yet a part of your ideology was that each man had right to his own version of right. Do you see?"

"This is my lesson then," Dristy said sadly, rocking slowly back and forth. "I somehow knew my vision would be broadened this evening. I spoke so blithely of humanity's quest for fairness to her, and the constant journey toward being worthy of peace and yet *I* could not be fair enough to see each and every soul *is* worthy of peace merely by being willing to make the journey. I could not see it was *I* who have been truly *unfair*, even in this life, but especially back then. I said I was not judging her feelings even as I decide she was unenlightened because she did not *earn* her peace, and I think it a failing of merely being unaware there was more. *I* set her to a path to see and experience more because she did not feel as I felt, that there was indeed more to life to be seen. Yet I excused my saying she must do this learning so that she may have the peace that same path of the learning took from her?" Dristy started to cry again. "I am so going straight to hell."

"Well, then we all are, dearest," Genie said, nonchalant. "I've done my share of directing her lives," Genie laughed unabashed. "Now wake our girl and let's put the pieces in place."

"She's gonna hate me!" Dristy said, suddenly afraid to face Aizlyn in the here and now.

"No," Genie said smiling, "my Aizlyn is no good with grudges, thank God. Win on the other hand..."

"Oh, hell," Dristy said, worriedly remembering the tales of Win's particularly acute sense of undeniable joy at helping karma along.

"Don't worry," Genie said after a moment of enjoying Dristy's shiver, "Win has never been to my house."

The first thing that came out of Dristy's mouth after "peaches," now that the word was understood again by Aizlyn, was, "I'm so sorry." Then she began to spill desperate explanations that didn't make sense to her, let alone Aizlyn, about how it seemed impossible but she was Sarasvati and had *accidentally* set her to this path one fateful lifetime some fourteen lives before by encouraging her to seek something more of life.

Aizlyn stood and stretched, waking the dog in the process, and tried to make sense of Dristy's apologies as she headed up the stairs to let Angus out into the back yard to pee while she did the same. Dristy followed her thoughtlessly into the bathroom and Aizlyn found herself pissing to the jumbled tune of Dristy, still trying to make sense of how she could have been a god speaking from the future to her past-life selves and Genie nodding and chiming in with an occasional, thoughtful, "Hum, I suppose that could work."

Aizlyn flushed the toilet, washed her hands, washed her face, let Dristy stumble for a moment more as both of them wondered what she was thinking. Then she dried her face, put up a hand to silence them and said, "Is there anything to eat?"

Dristy broke into nervous giggles as Genie started to laugh outright and lead them all back to the kitchen. The peaceful interlude Aizlyn's unexpected response brought didn't last long though, as Dristy soon began to apologize again, needing desperately to hear from Aizlyn something that symbolized forgiveness.

"You were not Sarasvati, Dristy," Aizlyn said at last, realizing there was no way she was going to get to eat and process all the new things running through her head before having to share them with the world. "Not in past lives and certainly not when speaking from the future. You were merely a priestess in some, a friend and confidant in others, but always a wonderful part of most of my lives. You knew what to say and when to say it only because you said it then. *And* even then you only did and said what you thought best and I don't blame you at all, so quit fidgeting, will you, please." Aizlyn forced a smile for Dristy. "You have always been visionary and had wild ideas, but I have always been free to make my own choice as to what to do with what ideas you gave me. If not for your wondering aloud to me of things that might possibly exist just beyond both of us from the dark confines of that temple, we wouldn't be here right now."

"I know," Dristy cried, "I'm so sorry!"

'I'm not! Would you stop already?" Aizlyn begged. "I am glad you asked me if I had ever wanted more."

"You remember?" Dristy gasped, feeling a little weak in the knees, not just from the relief her soul suddenly felt at being so easily forgiven but also the awe that someone could recall so distinctly all of what had just been revealed in their regression.

"Parts," Aizlyn said evasively, "feelings and glimpses, questions and answers. I remember we have always been the closest of friends." She looked thoughtfully at Genie who was busy making sandwiches, adding, "And that Genie has always seemed a step or two ahead of us up the enlightenment ladder your wild ideas set our feet to. I remember her chasing butterflies."

Aizlyn laughed as she saw Genie's shoulders shake with good humor while bent over her counter. She added, "I remember trying everything on God's green earth to make Jordan other than he was and is, and it never making me happy, then trying everything again to avoid the need within me. I remember Papa and Grandmother and Angus, even Jadin. I remember Rune showing me there was more."

Genie smiled happily, not looking back at them, cutting the crust from the sandwiches and then slicing them in half. Dristy looked a tad longing, still studying Aizlyn's face.

"Have I helped at all?" Dristy asked then, hoping the memories had shed light for Aizlyn.

"Yes," Aizlyn smiled softly, "you always did. I think I know what I am meant to do. I knew but I didn't, ya know, and now it is clear."

"What?" Dristy begged. "Tell me!"

Aizlyn leaned against the counter thoughtfully for a moment then said, straight-faced, "Torture you for another three months with my twisted inner demons and convoluted mind games, then give up completely, sacrifice Angus to the gods of what if, and slice my wrists with a dull, rusty butter knife."

Dristy's eyes bulged and Genie spun, sandwich in hand, to face her, aghast and accusatory, "Bull shit!" they cried in unison.

"Yeah," Aizlyn said grinning, taking the sandwich from Genie's lax fingers and shoving it in her mouth.

"You know what I find intriguing?" Genie said after a brief thoughtful pause that followed their laughter and involved eating half her sandwich. "It seems your feelings for Jordan changed each life but only slightly. Beginning right after your first life with Rune we saw you try to accomplish that kind of fulfillment with him. We saw that your resentment and discontent stem from more than one small, empty place or all of them, over time, in each life that you were unable to. In one you love him but find resentment wanting more of his love. Then, frequently, you found you hate him if he won't let you have the dog, like you know the dog somehow leads to the love you wanted. Then in that one scary one that you quit breathing in…"

"I quit breathing?" Aizlyn cut in suddenly.

"Yeah, but only for a second," Genie said quickly, dismissing Aizlyn's look of frightened suspicion. "What's important is you are breathing now and we found out you died, at least once, full to the rim of simple, overall, discontent, having missed out on all of it, with regard to chasing the dream. Then we found another life, one where you were obviously born fey, avoiding all of those things involving Jordan completely, following your soul to the tee in chasing the dream, but obviously that life didn't please you either, you said it hardened you and you spoke of sacrifices. We know you came back, again and again, to repeat old mistakes, so we have to wonder if that route was to the tee after all. In the life you and Jordan were just friends because you couldn't dance, you seemed content knowing him, but we found nothing of the dog to have led you to the next step. You referred to Angus as the mongrel that spooked the horse that crippled you."

"Well, we could go back and see?" Dristy suggested. "We only stayed briefly in each, maybe that was a different dog and she found Angus later, shortly after we spoke to her?"

"No," Genie and Aizlyn said in unison, their eyes meeting briefly as if questioning each other's reasons for being so adamant. But neither posed the question and as Aizlyn grabbed a second sandwich, Genie just continued, "The important things were found out already, we found where the chain began- with her, by your suggestion or not, wanting more." Dristy flinched reflexively, and Genie continued, "We found a princess standing on the wall and wondering if there is more to life, and the chain sprung from right there. Now I am seeing that her happiness lies not just in following her desires-following the dog, presumably, eventually coming to a man named Rune- but also in coming to terms with Jordan as a friend, being okay with him not loving her more than his other wives, maybe just loving each other in another way, like in that first life we came to and found them as friends. Maybe she needs to find a way to be okay with all of these different aspects of herself, rather than just avoid some of them each life. Do you see?"

"Well, she seems to be coming into some of that on her own without this regression, from what you tell me," Dristy said thoughtfully. "So far she has condensed a lot of these lessons that may have come one per prior life into this one already. As I said, she came out of the womb already a Windell, which if other lives can indicate, put her in a position to meet Rune eventually. She has already been through many different feelings for Jordan, condensing many lives' feelings into one, and she's found the dog. So now we just have to find her something more, her cliff, her Rune, which the dog is, *presumably*, meant to lead her to somehow. Maybe then we'll have found a way to rip the chain free as she said."

"Guys," Aizlyn said, mildly annoyed her life's mission was being discussed as though she were not there, "I'm right here."

"Yes, we see that," Genie laughed, "and we are trying to figure out why. What Dristy says fits with some stuff your mom said in the letters too." Genie continued unabashed, and noting Aizlyn's surprised look, she added, "I got them and read them myself. You went through these weird stages with Jordan in your youth, first hating him, then grudgingly accepting him, then befriending him. Now it seems you have become his lover, left him behind, found the dog, become his lover again and then again and now you are slowly breaking away and trying to figure out how to make that okay with your soul. Maybe you are condensing all the lessons, of all your lives, into one, to bring all the small moments of peace with you from each life into one big peaceful happy ending?"

"My gosh," Dristy said, smiling wistfully, swaying a little as though that thought had struck a whole new chord, "wouldn't that be a trick?"

"I have Zen moments, I call them," Aizlyn said, walking to the door to let Angus in when he scratched it. "I have been coming to see that I do need to make peace with Jordan before I can be completely happy and tonight only made that more clear to me. We are intertwined too thoroughly, through far too many lives, and though I see now we cannot share the kind of love I cannot help but want now that I have seen it, our souls do need to be close. The love I want is not the kind he can give and I need to accept that once and for all and quit trying to find it where it doesn't exist."

She was thoughtful a moment and wrapped her arms around herself, shivering, not because opening the door had let in a chill, but because suddenly she heard her mother whisper in her ear again, confirming her thoughts.

"Our friendship cannot be sacrificed." Aizlyn said after a moment of reflection, "and I need to make peace with my Grandmother too or that will be yet another regret. But to do either of those things I will need to make all the different aspects of me come together."

Aizlyn looked at Genie pensively, then looked down at Angus, scratching his snout as it nudged her hand. "Then, we need to find Rune."

"Yeah," Dristy laughed, "no shit, good luck!"

"No really," Aizlyn said seriously.

"No really," Dristy said, just as serious. "I know you need to find him, but I came across his name in the baby book when I was at a loss as to how to deal with you being all catatonic and it means *hidden*."

"Catatonic?" Aizlyn asked.

"Yeah," Dristy replied, adding quickly, "but Genie figured it out, she just had you write it all down like it was just a bad dream and she was your mother telling you what to do with it to be free of it."

"Where?" Aizlyn asked.

"In your journal," Genie answered. "In the basement."

Aizlyn sat once more on the blanket in the middle of her friend's basement and paged through to the back of her journal. She found the entry. Her friends had told her she had quickly scrawled out the story, of a particularly scary life, after having been told it was only a dream, as though desperate to be free of it. They had said it was the only way she seemed able to relay it, it had scared the language from her. She knew why; this life's story began with the burning that had haunted her senses to this day, creeping up on her nose without warning, and blurring her vision with remembered smoke and panic. She remembered parts of it, but it was like remembering a dream, and she wanted to read it now to see what it might reveal.

Aizlyn read through it quickly, skimming really, since they were her words and thoughts and she almost knew them word for word already. The light in that dark corner of her mind was flickering now. When she was done, she simply closed the journal and stood up, walking to the window to light a cigarette. "I need to find Rune," she said again, "but right now I really need some sleep." Aizlyn looked out the open window into the chilling night. "Can we start this again tomorrow?"

Genie could tell Aizlyn had as much she wanted to process alone as she did and looked askance at Dristy with regard to the rain check. Dristy merely watched them both, thoughts of her own still spinning wildly.

"I'll be here," Dristy said and watched as Genie walked Aizlyn up the stairs. Dristy stayed behind picking up and putting away her things, the things that had helped her to reveal what she could, even to herself. Dristy refolded and put away her scarves and doused the flames in what was left of the candles. The process should have calmed her nerves but she still couldn't escape the nagging worry at the back of her mind, the thought that just wouldn't go away, the one she had been unwilling to share with Genie until she was sure.

Dristy bent to retrieve the card she had told Aizlyn to keep before they had begun from off the blanket and she nearly returned it to her deck without looking, afraid of what she would see. Dristy paused. She didn't believe in coincidence, she had thought to have Aizlyn do that for a reason. Dristy flipped it over, it was the death card. There was no denying when the spinning in her head stopped and she was suddenly sure of that nagging little fear.

Genie had not returned by the time she was done collecting her things, so Dristy simply left her a note and let herself out. She saw Genie's car was gone and assumed she'd decided to drive Aizlyn home. Dristy was glad of that, remembering the chill of the card she had read, as she got in her little nineties model sports car and headed for home.

Genie arrived back home a few minutes after Dristy left and went to the basement to fold and replace all the blankets in her trunk. She wandered around cleaning and putting away random things, hoping the answer would come to her. She put another shoe that had ended up on the floor back in the wall rack and told the little girl to sleep peaceful, then went back upstairs to her bedroom. Genie fell asleep with a memory tickling the very edges of her mind- where did she know that bouncer from?

Aizlyn crawled into bed with far too many memories, brought far too close, to even begin to pick one in particular and examine it at length. She was exhausted and so was Angus, he hadn't even bothered with the dinner she had offered. He'd simply followed her to bed. She fell asleep with her hand in his fur, gazing at a blank canvas in her mind, thinking about a particular shade of blue.

When Aizlyn awoke she was surprised to find she didn't recall having had a dream. She didn't even have the feeling she'd had one she couldn't remember. She'd thought for sure, after all she had seen and remembered, she'd have been plagued with a terrible jumble of them, but she hadn't been. She felt good and was happy to toss the covers back and set her feet to the floor. She threw the back door wide and tossed a little more food in Angus's still full bowl while her coffee brewed.

Aizlyn wandered into the dining room while the dog crunched his breakfast. She looked at the paints and pots and the empty canvases that took up the better portion of the table. Aizlyn glanced at the clock, it was still early, they wouldn't miss her for a minute still. She pulled up a chair, twisted her hair atop her head and stuck a paint brush through it to hold it there. She set a fresh canvas up and stared at it for a long time. Then she opened her pallet box where she stored the perfect mixes that she didn't want to dry out and stared at them for a while too. Finally she put a brush to thinner and began pulling the blue from the overcast sky of Genie's painting into the green of its grasses. She spread it in a wide swath over the center of the canvas and just stared. That was it! That was the color of peace.

The phone rang and she listened as the machine relayed Genie's demand that she get her ass up and get over there while she mixed her coffee in her thermal mug. Then she went and got Angus's leash again, rattling it noisily among his other things, calling him in from where he'd fallen asleep under a tree out back. Aizlyn glanced at Sarasvati again as she locked the door and took Angus and her for another walk. She really needed to put her shelf up and give Sarasvati her own safe place.

Aizlyn realized about halfway to her destination that she had forgotten her cigarettes, so she veered off toward the convenience store, taking the long route around the second block separating Genie's and her houses. She got herself a pack and a lighter and then cut through the alley between the store and the laundromat next to it, thinking to cut behind the three houses before Genie's and enter through her back yard.

Angus was still a few feet back, pissing his greeting to another tree Aizlyn had apparently found unworthy, as she'd walked ahead, gazing up and around instead, paying her awed tribute in her own way. The trees lining the alley hung low and close at their canopies, leaning hard over the back fences she traveled between. They made a deep comfortable shade, dotted with a wide variety of colors. She never expected such a creepy horror movie scene to unfold within such beauty.

Out from behind a tree, not five feet ahead, came a broken terrifying vision. The old woman lurched, one spindly leg fairly jumping forward as if with a mind and energy all its own. This, in turn, jerked her torso along for the ride and pulled her shoulders and head along a few horrible seconds after. Her elbows remained still, as though pinned to her ribs, and set to a tremble-worthy wiggling the limp hands that hung from the ends of her forearms. The other foot lifted, hovered, then landed, not four inches from where it had been, and her body followed through the scant space that bare foot had told it to travel with crooked terrible slowness. This apparition's thin body, covered only in an long white nightgown, looked as though any one of these movements should have shattered it. The old woman's hair, silver wisps, flew back from a mask of age-scarred-leather in a chill wind that came up suddenly to assist the nightmare in becoming more real. Her eyes, a creamy white blue that froze Aizlyn where she stood, looked deep into Aizlyn's own. Aizlyn was powerless, pinned by those sightless eyes as they drew ever horrifyingly closer.

The old woman's arm suddenly shot out, the elbow detaching from her ribs. She grabbed Aizlyn's arm in a viselike grip, her bony fingers pressed deep and far too strong into Aizlyn's bicep. That awesome, sudden pressure, and the fact of it coming from so feeble and frightening a creature, made Aizlyn scream. The old woman didn't flinch, hadn't seemed to hear it, she just drug Aizlyn down to her height and whispered, "I saw you die."

Aizlyn couldn't have screamed again had she tried, her knees went weak, her vision blurred, she slumped to the grassy floor of the access alley in a heap.

Next thing Aizlyn knew there was a young Indian woman leaning over her crying, she understood the girl's words though they were hasty, scared, and came out in a language she hadn't spoken since she was twelve. Aizlyn was suddenly back in India, in nineteen thirty-one, her body broken in a car crash caused by a mongrel racing across the road.

"Are you okay?" the young woman cried again. "Can you hear me?"

Aizlyn looked over, saw Jordan lying limp over the steering wheel, blood pouring from a wide gash over his wide, dull, unseeing eyes. She saw Angus, the mongrel that caused this wreck, legs and head sprawled at impossible angles and in too many directions at once to still be a living thing.

Aizlyn screamed again.

A middle-aged Indian man came out the back door of the Laundromat, bringing real-life color and words into the Technicolor scene playing out in Aizlyn's mind. He did not belong there, not in this life, and Aizlyn started to shake with dawning realization.

"What is going on?" the man demanded of the young woman leaning over Aizlyn.

"Great Gram has frightened her near to death, I think," the young woman replied hurriedly. "She slipped away from me while I was making her tea. She said something…"

Aizlyn sat up and looked around her then. Angus lay beside her, whole and well, looking askance at her with worried eyes. The old woman, who had just been labeled "Great Gram," was being led back into the rear door of the laundromat by the upset middle-aged man, who was cursing under his breath about incompetent daughters. The young woman was still crying.

Aizlyn said, "It's okay. I am fine. Your great grandmother just spooked me is all."

"I am sorry," the young woman said, wiping her eyes on her sweat shirt. "She forgets things these days. She wanders if I do not watch her very closely. She says strange things sometimes."

"Yes," Aizlyn admitted, pushing to her feet and grabbing up Angus's lead again, "yes, she does."

"What did she say that frightened you so much?" the young girl asked suddenly as Aizlyn began to walk away.

Aizlyn wasn't sure why the girl would want to know, or why she felt compelled to answer honestly, she just did. "She said she saw me die," Aizlyn answered, looking back only briefly.

"I am sorry," the girl called after her as she let herself in Genie's back gate. "She became a nurse back in India, after she seen a bad wreck, it haunted her I think. She has seen many people die. She forgets things these days. She says the strangest things."

Aizlyn could see why as she closed the gate, tucked her rational fears back into her pocket, and began to play with irrational solutions they called to mind. The old woman had lived long enough that she was seeing some souls return which she had watched leave. It could be confusing, Aizlyn supposed, with incredible calmness.

18

Sarasvati:

Goddess of the Arts, Learning and Knowledge

Aizlyn entered Genie's house and headed for the basement to be greeted by two somber, thoughtful faces. Dristy wasted no time. She handed Aizlyn the card from the night before and immediately told her she needed to come to terms with whatever it was she needed to, and be quick about it, because change was coming one way or another and she'd better make it her way because the alternatives might not be so nice.

"Well, good morning to you too, Sunshine," Aizlyn greeted Dristy, looking at the death card and shivering.

"I'm sorry," Dristy said, smiling bitterly, "Unless Genie has a better idea where Rune is *hidden*, in this lifetime, than I do, I don't know what else to tell you, except get your ass in gear, woman."

Aizlyn's looked at Genie. "Do you know?"

"I'm not positive," Genie replied honestly. "What's the hurry? You've got the rest of your life now you know what you're looking for. I think *that* is the change that was needed and it has already come, even if Dristy disagrees. I think you are there, just start implementing the changes you now must come to allow for the happy ending. Talk to your grandmother, make peace with Jordan. I'm still putting things together here about Rune."

Dristy looked long and hard at Aizlyn, remembering her terrible hunch the night before, that the card had made so solid for her. She knew she'd been correct. She knew Aizlyn knew it too. They were working with a limited time frame.

"When did you get Angus?" Dristy asked Aizlyn, drawing Genie's attention from her own musings.

"What's that got to do…," Genie began.

"*Over* three years ago," Aizlyn answered.

"Met any Viking-looking men lately?" Dristy asked then.

Aizlyn started laughing then, uncontrollable, stressed laughter. She sucked it in mid-laugh, an eerie thing to watch and hear, then said, perfectly calm, "I work in a strip club, honey, we live by a base and a war's on. I have met nearly every large male of European descent on this planet the last few months."

"Shit," Dristy stomped.

"What's going on?" Genie asked then, seeing that Dristy and Aizlyn seemed to have come to an understanding without her as their eyes locked and held.

"You and Rune, marrying for love, and being so damned and determined to have that or nothing," Dristy answered for Aizlyn. "All the lives, so quickly, one after another; didn't you think it odd? Aizlyn's on a limited time frame here. I noticed the pattern and now it makes sense. The dog comes into her life and three years later if she can manage to stay with him, Angus somehow brings her across a moment or means where she can meet Rune. Three months after that, Rune and she either get together, or something bad happens and they start again, trying something different."

"Whoa," Genie said, aghast, "what?"

"I am discovered by Angus in the burning remains of my caravan," Aizlyn began for Genie. "I manage to keep him with me and he keeps me safe. We find our way to you and you send us to Rune three years from when the Walker and he came across me. Three months from arriving on Rune's shore I take his offering of a sweet-smelling bar of soap he traveled across the ocean to get for me and am his, happily, from that day forward. Until one day the prince returns, set to destroy the savage people that have destroyed his betrothed's mind and I am made to watch as many I love die. Rune and I survive, but as we send many bodies out to the eternal ocean it is become a regret that Jordan and I had not made peace.

"Two lives thereafter I try to find that same kind of love with Jordan, to avoid the slaughter of so many for my own happiness," Aizlyn continued. "The first I think I only need to work at it and it will come on its own. The second I am drawn to the dog, seeming to recall it had not worked before but also sensing I cannot have both. I choose to try with Jordan again. I try different things those lives yet both times I fail. I never kept the dog with me and so I never met Rune.

"I am discovered by Angus after my caravan is attacked leaving a temple and I stay with his master in the Holy Land until we return to England," Aizlyn said then, almost in a monotone, as though keeping her emotions tightly reined so as not to have them run away with her. "Three years from Angus finding me I have come to stand on a cliff and watch as you and Rune approach in a ship. Three months from then you decide you love your Lord William and open the door for us to be together. Only, when Lord William returns to the Holy Land he is met by a vengeful prince, Jordan, and killed. These are the kind of endings I remember. I have within me a growing list of regrets. The lack of peace between Jordan and me which causes the deaths of those I love and that I never came to an understanding with Lady Windell haunts me.

"I think I came to try desperately to avoid those I love having to die for me to be able to find what more I now intuitively cannot help but seek. So I had married Jordan in the next life, trying to bypass such miss-steps, but I don't meet the dog. I don't travel, though I want to, and I seem to think it would have made things different. It doesn't." Aizlyn took a deep breath lighting a cigarette, shaking a little. "Next I try to avoid it another way, I am born fey, but the self-serving journey I set myself to changes who I am, who it is that Rune loved. When I meet Rune there is no great love between us, at least not enough to keep him by my side when I see his future and his death, and can only beg he trust me and remain. He does not. Three months from meeting him, I have not been able to change his course. I learn to be more careful what I sacrifice for love, because it may end up being the love I sought.

"So next I try being born among the poor," Aizlyn continued. "I set myself to a pilgrimage to the temple and even think to become like a nun. I find the dog but when I return I am made by my family to dance and watch the dog be denied me by my new husband. I resent him. The following life I try to lose that resentment, I seem to know it will come to no good. I try again to love him and in return earn the love I seek, but it fails. Next, I feed the dog and he poisons it. I try again to find forgiveness and not resent him. Then, I don't feed the dog so that it will at least live well, but I am incredibly disillusioned now. No matter what I try, it does not work.

"So I am born a man. I mean to chase my dream without fear of Jordan's later reprisals, we are friends, fellow princes, I have begun well. I mean to go by ship without the fear a woman must feel on those vessels when Angus is given to me, I travel with Lord Windell, to Britain," Aizlyn continued, far more calmly than Dristy thought should be possible. "Three years from that gift I am walking down a crowded street in London toward the smell of coffee and Angus knocks a woman into me. She is Miss Rune, of the house of Rune, she tells me, when I apologize and introduce myself and my rude dog. We fall in love over the next three months and I decide to make a proposal to her and her father but I am too late. You know the rest from the dream.

"I find and befriend a hungry dog, accidentally left at port when his master's ship leaves," Aizlyn said then, as Genie too lit a cigarette with shaking hands. "I can't help but feed the poor beast and it follows me home, where I continue to care for it in secret, fearing instinctively for it's life. Three years later I sneak out to take him some food and find him with an Englishman who thanks me for caring for his dog. We talk, he comes with the dog often during the three months he is to be there, I am falling for him but I am engaged now and it is highly improper. We are discovered. You know how that ended.

"I have once again been born among the poor as if to hide. I am walking down the street and a dog spooks a wealthy man's horse. It bolts, knocking me down and crushing my hip. I survive, but I am resentful of the dog now, I throw rocks at it when it wanders near my home, angry for its part in my crippling. The wealthy man feels responsible and befriends me, so we are friends now because I cannot dance, a gift from the dog I definitely recognize. One day Jordan takes me for a ride in his car so I can feel the wind in my hair." Aizlyn grew distant and thoughtful. "I am content in our friendship in those moments. It feels right, but then the mongrel breaks across the dirt road before the car, running toward a foreigner who stands on the other side, waiting for something or someone. Jordan and I hit this huge beast and as I lie dying, in the arms of a young woman who will in those moments decide to become a nurse, the foreigner comes to kneel beside me. He whispers something strange as I move toward the next life. He says, 'I am sorry, I tried to find both of you sooner.'

"I have came into this life trying to avoid anyone's death being the conduit by which I come to meet Rune by being born a Windell. But it seems in that I have already failed, because my mother died in India for me to be sent here to my grandfather, where I have yet to come to terms with my grandmother to be able to avoid that regret too. I found Angus on my own but that was before last New Year's, I remember kissing him on New Year's Eve and it is mid-March now. I am nearly out of time."

Aizlyn shivered, Dristy cringed, Genie started pacing furiously back and forth across the length of the basement. Absently she knelt and picked up another shoe and slid it back into its place. Then she turned and walked back to the open window where Aizlyn and Dristy were both lighting another cigarette. They all needed one.

"What about Gamble?" Genie asked suddenly.

"What about him?" Aizlyn said, still trying to think how she could narrow down her search. "I've already told you..."

"I love that name," Dristy said, not quite understanding the exchange between Genie and Aizlyn.

They ignored Dristy's comment, their eyes locking in debate. "I know him from somewhere," Genie said purposefully.

"Where?" Aizlyn demanded, suspicious.

"I don't remember," Genie admitted looking down finally.

"Well, I don't Gamble," Aizlyn said then, purposely playing with his name the way Genie had the first time she'd tried to bring Aizlyn's attention to him. "I am looking for Rune."

"That's fine," Dristy jumped in, finally realizing they were discussing someone they both knew by that name. "It don't mean 'to gamble.'" Dristy laughed when they both turned to her, eyebrows raised with questions.

"What?" Genie said finally.

"It doesn't mean 'to gamble,'" Dristy reiterated hopeful she was being helpful, "least not in the way we have come to think of it. It's from the old Norse, meaning full-grown wisdom. I think it began kinda like a safe bet, knowing the outcome before you wager, and lost its true meaning somewhere along the line."

Genie looked triumphantly at Aizlyn and grinned. "There, a safe bet for ya, go ahead, Win."

"Funny," Aizlyn snickered sarcastically, "but he has always been called Rune. I ain't messin around here, Genie. I have messed this up enough."

"We *are* talking about a guy you two know," Dristy asked finally, "right?"

"Yeah," Aizlyn answered, "a bouncer I work with."

"Well, how 'bout we quit quibbling over names," Dristy sighed as though they were naughty girls, "they do change after all. Yours has at least, hell, you got born a Windell this round. You could have forced him to take another family by taking his, ever thought of that? Wouldn't want to be born to fall in love with your own first cousin. And Rune and Gen were, at least in one life, Windell's great niece and nephew." She looked hard at Aizlyn, causing her to gasp at the realization, then turning to Genie, she said, "and concentrate on when you met him. See if that fits."

"I don't know, he started a few months ago," Aizlyn answered honestly. "I don't pay much attention really."

"More or less than three months," Dristy pushed.

"*Really*," Aizlyn stumbled, "I don't remember exactly."

"Genie," Dristy said then, sighing and trying her luck with her other friend, "where did you meet him?"

"The bar," Genie answered, "on my birthday."

"But you said you *knew* him?" Dristy prompted, adding hopefully, "From before then?"

"Yeah," Genie answered honestly, "but I can't remember where or when."

"Well, think," Dristy demanded, beginning to sway.

"Stop that!" Genie demanded, seeing what Dristy had started to do whether she had meant to or not.

"Stop what?" Dristy asked innocently.

"That!" Genie griped. "That hypnotic swaying shit. I'll figure it out, just give me a second."

Aizlyn's head was spinning again. What if she had forced Rune to be born into another family, making it impossible for her to find him? She hadn't missed how quickly Genie and her grandparents had bonded, how Genie had taken them as her own. What if she had forced Genie off course too? What if they had been meant to be brother and sister again and she had ruined that too? She was beginning to think up a whole new list of things she might have to add to her list of regrets to take with her into the next life.

Angus again came wandering down the stairs, only this time he came happily, at normal speed and with tail wagging. He walked up to Aizlyn and nudged her hand as if he wanted something. She was just asking herself how long it had been since he had been let out and reminding herself he had just had breakfast when Genie made her jump.

"That's it," Genie cried, "that damn new collar!"

"What?" Aizlyn and Dristy asked in unison.

"The day you came to get that new collar," Genie exclaimed, "I remember now. You came into the swap-meet all puffy-eyed saying Angus needed a new collar. I knew damn well you just needed to talk because you and Jordan had split again, just by lookin at ya. After I'd pried it outta ya without calling you out on it, making him the new collar, and you left, Gamble walked up..."

"And...," Dristy pried when Genie fell silent and thoughtful.

"He just asked about the woman with the dog," Genie said then. "Said he thought he knew her from somewhere." She looked at Aizlyn then, adding, "I know how you are so I just told him you were a bartender and if he went to bars, which I imagined he did since he seemed a young fun loving kinda guy, he'd probably seen you there."

Aizlyn's spinning head went into hyper-drive. "You told him which bar?" she demanded.

Suddenly Aizlyn was recalling the night she had found out he only worked the nights she did, that he took the same nights off that she did. Suddenly she was thinking he had seen her, started to obsess over her, got a job where she worked and begun to stalk her in earnest. Suddenly she was thinking she was crazy. Gamble wasn't a stalker. Was he?

"No," Genie said thoughtfully, "I don't think I did. No I didn't, I wouldn't have. I know how you like your damn privacy."

Aizlyn let out a sigh of relief, thank God the cows were just winking and dinking.

"That was how long ago?" Dristy asked then, calling them back to the reason for the conversation.

"Two months, three weeks, one day," Aizlyn laughed derisively at herself for knowing so well, adding, "and some random number of hours, I'll figure out later."

"So if Rune is this guy, Gamble," Dristy said cautiously, "we have this week."

"It's easier to see Gamble as a stalker than as Rune," Aizlyn said sarcastically, still sure she sought a man named Rune who would turn her belly to butterflies, not a twenty-one-year-old kid with perm-a-grin.

"Rune is a stalker," Dristy laughed, causing Aizlyn to pause. "I recall him hunting you down in as many lives as you did him."

Aizlyn was thinking hard now, the Win and Miss Windell portions of her brain pulling her every which way but easy. She realized both of her friends were still looking expectantly at her so she just took a deep breath and said, "I dunno, guys…"

"Well," Genie said then, "I don't wanna steer you wrong. I like the guy, I liked him instantly, but I know how important this is to you so, obviously…I'm just saying."

"Look," Dristy said, "just keep an open mind and an open eye these next few days, that's all you can do, that and pay close attention to all the signs."

Just then they heard Scruffy announcing Nathan was coming home from school and all such conversation ended. It wasn't that Genie didn't want him to know that there were quite a few views out there in the world, she just didn't want him learning about them right then, in this situation. Not in this scary way, where they were so closely related to his Aunty Aizlyn. Genie gave them both the mommy look that said "behave or die" and they all put out their cigarettes and were in the kitchen refilling their coffee when he made his way through the house to them.

Nathan was quizzed about homework and hunger as he hugged each of them in turn before laying over Angus's back and hugging him too. Aizlyn found herself seeing him again, the way she had the first time, as a young Viking lad trying to ride more than one uncooperative Wolfhound and coming into the longhouse with multiple scrapes and bruises for his efforts. She shook her head quickly, trying to clear it, and begged off staying for the after-school meal by saying she had a lot she needed to do. Dristy followed her to the basement where she gathered her things, then gave Aizlyn her phone number and told her to use it without hesitation if she could be any further help. Aizlyn said goodbye to both of her friends, then she walked home with Angus. She had her dream journal and box of letters in her arms, and a million new questions flying around in her head.

Aizlyn considered her feelings as she hung the small wall shelf and put Sarasvati in her place, then stared at her, trying to remember. She was confused by the way memories faded like dreams no matter how clear they had been during her regression. She could understand Genie's inability to say for sure whether she had known Gamble other than from the swap-meet, no matter they had been kin, because she'd just spent the previous day running through life after life where he was right there and still couldn't recall enough to be sure either. Genie hadn't even had the relative benefit of a recent regression to make such things more clear and Aizlyn, though she had for a few minutes thereafter seen a few things quite clearly, was still left now with just feelings and glimpses.

She shrugged her shoulders as she gazed at her statue. It wasn't that she worshiped this goddess anymore, that wasn't why she put it there, it was more that the figurine represented to Aizlyn not only all the arts but learning and the pursuit of knowledge. Aizlyn wasn't really hoping the little statue would enlighten her, she had merely hoped looking at it would remind her of something. She gave up after awhile and wandered back into the dining room to be greeted by the painting she had begun before she was even fully awake and had any coffee that morning. Now why had she thought that was the color of peace? Ahh, yes, the cliffs, and that magical area of water you could see from them.

Aizlyn walked around the painting, like a panther debating the taste of a wounded thing, for quite awhile. Then suddenly she lunged for the kill, planting her butt in her chair and whipping her hair up for a paint brush to hold out of the way. She pulled her pallets to her and began unveiling the scene, the edge of the cliff where it met the water, the many fallen rocks, piled low against it amid the boiling, frothy reunion. There was no sky, the waters just continued from there and up the canvas, all that the eye looking down from that cliff's edge could see.

339

Aizlyn was critical and picky; every hue had taken her far more time than she felt it should have. By the time she was done, it was well past midnight, she'd still not had a meal and it still wasn't perfect. The glittering calm of the circular patch of magic water hadn't shown her peace anymore than looking at Sarasvati had made the light in her mind stop flickering and just shine.

Aizlyn put on a load of laundry, emptied the ashtrays and fed the dog. She put her mother's letters away in the top of her closet and put her journal back in the nightstand drawer. Finally it was the normal everyday things that saw her somewhat more peaceful, if only in body, as she wandered from the shower, to the dryer, to bed.

Aizlyn woke to a knock on the door, sounding persistent and not for the first time. Angus sat up as she rolled out of bed and pulled on a large heavy robe, she patted her thigh and told him to come with her to see who it was. It was her Papa, come to make sure that the powerful Mustang he had given her had not harmed his granddaughter. Aizlyn smiled, told him she was fine and held the door wide for him to enter. He hesitated, and Aizlyn looked past him to his own old Ford pick-up and saw her grandmother staring blankly ahead from the passenger seat.

Aizlyn took a deep breath and said, "Oh, crap, Papa, just go tell her, Jordan and I aren't liven' in sin in here, we split up a few months ago. I'll get dressed and put on some coffee."

Aizlyn left the door hanging wide in invitation and walked back to her room to drag on her sweats and hoodie, then walked to the kitchen and put some life on to brew. When she walked back to the living room she found her grandparents on her porch in a heated debate. Her grandmother had apparently seen the statue. Miss Windell started pulling her hair out, Win started to boil, Aizlyn said, "Oh for goodness sakes, Grandma," Aizlyn said, shocking even herself into listening, "It's a simple figurine, that Papa didn't burn it was a wonderful choice and a good thing, because it's mine and not for you to judge or destroy. It's not an idol to me any more than the cross on the wall over your stove is to you. I don't worship it, never have, it just

340

reminds me to learn what I can from each day, like your cross reminds you to pray."

Aizlyn silenced her grandmother's retort by quickly adding, "God is my Savior as surely as He is yours, Grandma, and he is Divine. Divine enough to know the difference between crosses and figurines and idols to false gods. Divine enough to know when I read a horoscope I am taking nothing from Him by seeing what His stars might have to show me. We don't have to agree on how we approach our paths to closer communion with Him, we just have to not judge each other, learn to accept each other, and love each other despite the fact they are different. Now if you'd like to come in and have some coffee with me, I would love to have you, I'm sure it's almost finished brewing. I would love to just talk to you." Aizlyn turned then and headed back toward the kitchen, leaving the invitation open, adding, "I love *both* of you."

Aizlyn was not surprised when she heard the old Ford fire up and drive away. She squared her shoulders, let Angus out, and left the door open as she finished mixing her coffee. She jumped and squeaked when her grandmother showed up in the kitchen a few moments later and poured herself a cup. Her grandmother laughed at her and then turned to meet the dog who came in from the back yard to greet this new woman who'd come to visit his home. It turned into a beautiful afternoon, full of pleasant heated arguments like she and Genie so enjoyed, while her grandmother ran her fingers through Angus's coat as though drawing the same calming energy from him that Aizlyn always did.

Her grandmother grilled her and was pleased to find she had indeed learned and retained and held to her soul a great many things she had tried to teach Aizlyn. And Aizlyn was pleasantly surprised to find she was able to retort and put in her two cents without blowing up the whole afternoon. She found it nice to have her grandmother in her domain, for once and thought her grandmother looked oddly at peace with Angus's butt plopped on the couch beside her while they talked.

They discussed such things Aizlyn found dreadfully outdated as men not dressing as women and vise versa, the old irrational reasoning behind shorts being bad for swimming in and her jeans in high school having been hidden in her locker or provided by Jadin. Aizlyn was pleased to be able to point out that her shorts revealed far less of her body, a far worse thing, than a skirt that floated up around her waist while you swam and that there were more jeans companies out there for women than men now. This of course led to discussion of God's unchanging perfect state, with regard to the laws He'd set forth, and then back to Aizlyn's assertion He was Divine enough to see His creation did change and had been designed with a free will that made it do so quite often. Aizlyn wasn't about to push into the deeper waters of her deep love for skinny-dipping, she was going to take this slow and easy.

Aizlyn was just glancing at the clock and wondering what she was going to do with the fact she needed to get ready for work, and not wanting to deal with that part just yet, when she heard her grandfather pull up. She said a silent prayer of thanks to the Divine and smiled when her Papa came to stand before the screen door, with the truck still idling, and announce they'd best get home before the groceries spoiled in the bed of the truck. Aizlyn watched her grandparents pull away, a huge smile still plastered to her face. Then she walked back in her house and shared the smile with Angus and the little figurine. It was a great start, she thought, as she headed for the shower.

It wasn't until she was rinsing her hair that she remembered she'd wanted to ask her Papa about the dogs. Hadn't the Windell and Rune houses always had dogs? Papa had Shanks but never a dog, not that she could recall. She told herself she'd have to call him in the morning, as she wrapped up her hair and began putting on the Armor of Win. She loved that the Win part of her had come out to help today but was still quite adamant that Miss Windell and the blending part that was Aizlyn remain home. It never paid to take your true self and all those emotions to work, she was still quite sure of that.

Win still drove the Mustang to work though, she couldn't resist. Win found herself singing right along with the radio, "let your hair down girl, let it rain down on me..." and smiling as she pulled into work. She found herself looking ahead to the door for Gamble to push it open for her, and he did. Win smiled up at him as she passed, headed for her bar and whatever dreadful shot Gina had mixed up and waiting. Win took over the bar and lit a cigarette, watching Gamble take his seat by the door, then watching Jovan walk in.

Some styles Jovan wore were lost on Win, making little sense, a thing she blamed on spending so much of her life overseas, but this girl owned all of them. Tonight Jovan wore a strange combination of fatigues hung low on the hips and drawn up on the calves. She'd paired them with a soft pink short-sleeved sweater that showed off a belly ring and a pair of shiny, strappy pink heels. Her hair was bundled off to one side in a pink scrunchy under a camo hat. Win cringed inwardly, it wasn't for her, but damned if the girl didn't pull it off.

Jovan tossed her purse on the bar for Win to set under the counter with hers and then let out a huff of disgust. "Men are so stupid," she pouted. Can I owe you for a shot?"

Win made no comment as she chilled a large shot of whiskey and poured it into a short glass for the girl, awaiting the inevitable expounding that would follow after Jovan had swallowed it.

"I mentioned, just mentioned," Jovan exhaled heavily, airing her mouth to the burn of the liquor, as she exploded her feelings on the bar, "that I thought I could make more money as a dancer and Jason went nuts. He started ranting how he'd seen this coming, knew he shoulda never let me start working here."

Jovan's mouth puckered with her irritation, which came off quite cute as Win nodded for her to continue.

"*Let me! LET ME,* like he owns me or somthin'. Can you believe that? He's lucky I even talk to him about what I'm thinkin of doin. I could be like my momma and just not say a word, do what I please and you can like it or lump it, swallow it or leave the table." Jovan paused and made another adorable face that could have meant the shot just hit her and had tasted bad but Win knew it was not the shot she hadn't liked but rather the thought that had just crossed her mind when she added, thoughtfully, "Dad left her though…"

Jovan stared at her for a long thoughtful moment and Win became thoughtful as well. Win thought about the fact she didn't want the girl to become a dancer either. She had selfish reasons she could admit to: it was hard to find a good waitress, one who could keep her head in this environment, kept things clean, worked hard and was honest with the tip out. She was a gem and Win didn't want to lose her to the stage. But there were others she didn't want to consider. Win liked the girl and didn't want to see her swept away on the tides of all the other things that seemed to inevitably wash out even the most likeable girls. The stage was a true gateway drug if there ever was one and Win knew it, had seen it first-hand. Win knew drugs came in many forms too.

Win had watched more than one innocent take her first shy, sober steps on the stage with clouded visions of all the cash their biggest dreams could need, only to be fired a year later because they couldn't keep their heads up out of their own drug-induced drool between sets or they were doing things on the side that weren't exactly lawful. They'd fall for the "just once" that promised the night to speed by and the money to fly that became "just one more" and "just one more, I'll give you a free dance." They'd go for the "huge money at the hotel", "*just dance* for me and my friends we'll tip you good." Next thing you knew they were in the dressing room thrashing through their bags in a clear moment, screaming "Who stole my money?" because they couldn't recall where they'd spent or left it. Or worse, they were missing shifts for a private gig, and never heard from again.

There were a few who accomplished it, and they were truly Win's favorites, they took it like Win and worked it for the job it was, but that was just a few out of the many dozens Win had seen and Win didn't like Jovan's odds. Win knew Jovan was in school and had good big dreams, she wanted her to fulfill them, needed her to fulfill them like she had yet to but still told herself she would someday. Win needed that hope. But those were the reasons she didn't admit to because they were personal and shouldn't apply. Those were the thoughts that caused her to pull up short in her thinking and wonder if she was going to be required to comment to get Jovan going again so she could quit.

"He gets mad I spend so much on my clothes, you know," Jovan said at last, as if she needed to state more reasons why he deserved her holding onto the anger that seemed to be fleeing her quickly. "But I make more money when I have a new outfit. He doesn't get it. I earned it, you like it?"

Win told her she looked awesome, careful with her wording, no need letting her know it made little sense to her, just let her know she looked amazing. Again the silence grew as Win wondered if she shouldn't say something, interject some further bits that might encourage the girl along the right path, but she was finding it difficult to let the silence go.

"How come you never danced?" Jovan's question sent a shiver through Win. Not only was she being presented the perfect opportunity to open up and maybe help by shedding some light for the girl, but the words of the question itself seemed to echo into the eternity that had been stretching through her head lately with more meaning than she could fathom.

Win tried and failed to find words that would work. She realized she had shooed Miss Windell so well this evening she wouldn't even come when called upon. Finally all that worked its way off her tongue was, "I can't."

"You can't dance?" Jovan repeated incredulously. "I've seen your hips jump sexy a time or two when the music hits ya just right. You're full a shit."

"No, I mean," Win hated this feeling, explaining herself, opening up, but she tried, for some reason she felt she needed to, "I can't handle the stage, the lights, everybody looking at me." She was amazing herself with every word she heard stumble over her teeth. "Truth is," she added, liberated by the moment, "I get horrible stage fright."

"Serious?" Jovan looked stunned.

"Yeah," Win grinned and exhaled deeply, plunging on. "I can dance if no one is watching me directly, ya know? Like I can go out dancing with my girl, Genie, matter a fact I was supposed to Saturday night for her birthday, but no worries, I'll set it up for this Saturday. Point is, if I feel the pressure of someone watching my every move, I freeze up."

"Wow, why?" Jovan prodded, interested in this new side of Win she had never seen and leaving her own problems completely behind.

"I don't know," Win said, honest and thoughtful, taking Jovan into her confidence even deeper. "I always thought it started when I was twelve and my grandmother started telling me my dancing was of the devil. I started learning in India when I was a kid, I loved it, it was my first passion even before painting but it was *too* sexy, a stumbling block to men, ya know?"

Win cocked a crooked grin at Jovan, and Jovan laughed outright at that, a bursting giggle that settled into a twinkling happy sound. Then Jovan said, "My dad said that same crap when Momma let me wear daisy dukes. So what happened? You just quit?"

"I hid in the barn to practice. I thought that's how the stage fright developed, you know, always trying to hide it, looking over my shoulder. But recently I was told something that let me know it started back when I was nine and I froze up at a recital." Win paused and smiled, "Seems I've always been unwilling or unable to perform on demand, only when *I* want to."

"Sounds like the Win I know," Jovan smiled back and laughed again. "I knew you grew up in India. I knew you painted. But I never knew that Win had any problems." Then she pinched Win's upper arm lightly and added, "You are human."

"Yeah, well don't tell anyone," Win laughed. Then taking the opportunity so beautifully provided her, she added, "There's another reason, though. I mean I could have gotten past the stage fright with a few shots I'm sure, why not, everyone else does. If that wasn't enough we both know there's other stuff here to be had but...," she paused, making sure Jovan was truly going to hear what she meant to say, "I've seen waitresses head for the stage, the money seems easier, no clean-up after work, just sit around and have the guys buy you drinks and hand you money all night."

"But it's never like they think. It's much harder than that." Win's tone was soft with sadness for those she'd witness fail, as she glanced down the bar. "They find, eventually, that the guys have lost some measure of respect for them, then they lose some for themselves. It's a little different for those who start there, a little, but to end up there, well…. And the money isn't any different after the first week or so of shock factor; them seeing you there not here, wears off."

"You can't come back either," Win said looking back at Jovan, "and that's not coming from me, I'd let ya. But forever after all the big tips you used to get for just plain good service are promised for after you dance for them again or show them your tits just one more time. If it's about the money, don't be silly, girl. If it's about showing Jason he doesn't own you, be careful what you sacrifice…"

Win heard her mother's parting words, her own words, drop from her tongue and was shocked into silence. It was as though the words had moved unbidden from a whispered memory wearing hip-huggers to a mouth that she no longer owned. She didn't regret them though, the sharing had seemed right, not so scary as doing so by accident with a tall blond bouncer who smiled too much. Jovan stood stunned and quiet for a minute and Win did too. They both seemed to absorb the moment and take from it everything they could, and there was a lot to be had.

"You know, we have worked together for nearly six months and that is the most I think we have ever talked," Jovan said at last, laughing again but thoughtful still. "You're not really a hard-core bitch, you just dress that way."

"Yeah, well don't tell any one," Win said, smiling back and, returning to form, she pointed toward a booth in the corner where two guys had just taken a seat moments before.

Win studied her own actions this evening while Jovan got their drink orders and had decided not to worry about it by the time the waitress returned. Despite the fact she'd shown there were openings in her armor, she seriously doubted that Jovan would use them against her. She made the drinks and watched the waitress go earn her tip and simply told herself not to make a habit of it, not everyone could be trusted.

347

Win glanced at Gamble again, who was returning to his seat after having shown those customers to their booth and walking around the club to observe everyone there so far that evening. Win found herself wondering if it were possible he was Rune, then laughing at herself to shove the thought back. Win thought she'd know when Rune came into her life, because the butterflies would too. But when he brought his grin up to the bar, a few moments later, to ask for a glass of water, she found herself unable to resist just one question.

"Do you have a dog?" Win asked, surprising even herself again with the question, as she handed him his water.

Gamble stood there, his grin faltered and became thoughtful, just looking at her, and she began to wonder if he was going to answer. She realized she really didn't deserve for him to. She was the one who'd set up the rules, she was the one who'd told him she wasn't willing to discuss the more personal aspects of herself at work and wasn't going to go outside of work with him either so she could. She was just thinking, maybe that was what he was thinking, as he stared at her, not giving her an answer. Maybe *he* was *showing her* how something felt.

Ah, sweet karma, she was about to laugh.

"No," Gamble said finally, passing the glass back for her to refill.

Gamble continued to watch her, as if he expected the answer he had decided to give would lead her to ask another question, but it didn't. As she handed him his glass back, now full again, she sighed, it was enough, he could go now. His grin returned full-force when she nodded toward the door and the customers he needed to attend.

She then proceeded through the remainder of the night to greet each customer who came to her bar with a leading, and mildly dim-witted, sounding, "Hi, I'm Win, what can I get for you...," hoping for a name that was followed by butterflies.

19

Gamble: Full Grown Wisdom

Win drove home that night mildly annoyed, but at nothing in particular she could chase away with rationalizations. She hadn't really wanted to find Rune in a place like that anyway, now had she? But that didn't make it any better not to have found him. She didn't have a whole lot of time left, if Angus was any indication this life. She let herself in, taking her shoes off in the living room, and headed through the dining room to the kitchen to let Angus out. There she came face to face with the painting that hadn't come out just right either. She took a step back and looked through the arch again at Sarasvati, then she huffed and went to feed and relieve her favorite man.

When she returned to the dining room, coffee in hand, she saw it, suddenly. She knew what was wrong with the painting. She whipped her hair up, still wearing half of the Armor of Win and not even thinking of the paint she might get on it. She sat down to make it right.

Aizlyn pushed back from the painting not quite an hour later and smiled. Taking another few paces back, she stared at it. Barefoot in leather pants and strappy leather top she walked around it, and smiled more as it followed her. She had placed the small dark Viking vessel slipping dead

349

through the center of the circular patch of calm. It was become the iris in the eye of the mystical water that was peace, and that eye followed her where ever she walked in the dining room. She was pleased. It was perfect!

She woke early, again having suffered no confusing dreams. She rolled happily out of bed, she had plans before work. She took Angus with her and went to have the painting framed, it belonged in her bathroom by her shower and it needed sealed properly so it wouldn't be ruined by the constant moisture. Then she took Angus to the park where she ate a sandwich she'd picked up at a deli and wondered absently why no large Viking types with a dog like him came to talk to her.

Well, half the day had gone right so far. Aizlyn returned home and hung the painting while Angus watched, one eye on the large bathtub, hoping he wasn't about to be forced into it. Then she went to find her phone, and re-make the trade with Al that should have seen her off last Saturday. He agreed, but said he needed her to work for him again, though he knew he owed it to her, he still had a date he wanted to keep that weekend and would need at least one of the nights off. Aizlyn agreed despite the trade being unfair, since she had already worked one night for him. She still wanted to go out with Genie and meant to invite Dristy too, it would be worth it. She hoped! She had a feeling it was going to be her last best chance of finding Rune too.

Aizlyn then called and made reservations for a table for them at a nice garden patio bar where they could enjoy a good meal and conversation before heading out to get down to the serious fun of dancing till their lungs hurt. The last call she made before getting ready for work was to her grandfather. She desperately needed to know why he had never had dogs. It was a bothersome bit at the back of her mind, flashed upon by the flickering annoyance of a bad fluorescent bulb. Hadn't the Windells always had dogs, in every life? Hell, for that matter wasn't that how the Windell and Rune houses had been joined in the Crusades? It seemed to her she had to be missing something important.

Aizlyn called and got her grandmother, with whom she chatted pleasantly, about a new cookie recipe, of all things, until her Papa could be located and handed the handset out in the barn. She wasted no time but rather asked him right out the gate, "Papa, how come we never had dogs when I was growing up?"

Her grandfather's pause was so long she'd have thought the phone had died had she not still heard the faint buzz in the line. Finally he said, "My brother raised dogs, big old Wolfhounds like your Angus. He brought two back after taking a trip to Britain with his college rowing team before World War Two tore Europe apart. Those dogs were his most prized loves after your grandmother." Papa paused, sighed, and added, "That's what the letters were about, Aizlyn, my brother was the one your grandmother loved so much it nearly broke her. When the war broke out and he went to fight, he left the dogs with me. He never made it back and I sold them and their pups. I didn't want them around to hurt her with what memories they'd invoke. I was pleased to see her meeting Angus yesterday didn't seem to cause her any pain."

Aizlyn's head started spinning again. She was recalling Windell sitting on the edge of a bed made of piled furs before a fire she kept high, gazing thoughtfully at a chest that had belonged to his brother's wife and saying, "sometimes you win, sometimes you lose." She was recalling the Crusader who had spoken with love for the father of Rune and Genevieve, a man Rune had said had never married because he couldn't have the woman he loved. He had raised two very different-looking children, obviously given him by two different women, but never taken the love vow before Odin. The Windell and Rune houses were linked by more than just dogs then, they were probably sprung from two brothers who'd loved the same woman more than once.

"Did your brother have any children?" Aizlyn was frightened the answer would somehow make her related to Rune when she found him, if she found him, but she still needed to know.

"No," Papa replied, "just the dogs. What is this about, Aizlyn?"

351

Aizlyn's grandfather seemed to suddenly become aware there might be more to this conversation than a search for more knowledge spawned by a conversation with her grandmother yesterday about dogs and having read the letters he had seen to it that she gotten.

"Nothing, really, Papa," Aizlyn answered, unable to word the problems even had she wanted to right then. Then something else occurred to her and she asked, "Who bought the dogs? Do you remember a name?"

Her grandfather must have assumed his wife and Aizlyn had talked about Angus and the stock of his kind which her grandfather had sold before her mother was born, because the question caused him no further wondering.

"An older gentleman, called himself Rune, had a strange accent," her grandfather said, unaware how Aizlyn's heart jumped. "He had bought a large plot a land out this way and seemed to have a deep affinity for the huge hounds. He had one with him, as I recall, when he came about the ad and bought the lot of 'em from me."

"What happen to him?" Aizlyn said, nearly breathless.

"I imagine he's dead now honey, he had to be in his fifties when he bought my brother's dogs, but his stocks still out there, still bred by some distant relatives," Papa paused, thoughtful. "Ya know, come to think of it, that could be where your Angus came from. Their land is somewhere out this way, you found him driving home from here, didn't you?"

Aizlyn wanted to die. She remembered how it felt. She remembered dying, in the early thirties, with Rune coming to her side and saying, 'I am sorry, I tried to find the both of you sooner.' He had lived out that life with the dogs, alone, while she piddled in the in-between. He'd had to leave the dogs to distant relatives because she'd not returned, again not given him children...

"Papa," Aizlyn said, suddenly nauseous, "I gotta get ready for work. Thank you for telling me all this, it helps."

"I love you, Aizlyn," Papa said after another brief pause, "good luck at work tonight."

"Love you too, Papa," Aizlyn said quietly.

Getting ready for work that night was hard. All Aizlyn wanted to do was run over to Genie's, cry on her shoulder for a bit then borrow her internet and look for Wolfhound breeders in the area to somehow find out where a man named Rune was buried. She dragged on the Armor of Win, purposefully using it to hide from her own emotions, more so than hide those emotions from the intoxicated masses.

Aizlyn dried her hair, thinking about a long lonely life. If he had been near her own age, maybe a little older, when he'd come to her village in India and found his dog only for it to cause her wreck and end her life, then he'd have had to have been nearing eighty when she finally chose to come back. How horrible that he probably came to the end of his days while she was fighting to comprehend dreams meant to lead her to him. Win couldn't even force a smile when she put on her lipstick.

It truly was hump day and she barely made it over the hump when she pulled up to work and it came to her that how long she had thought she had left to find him was probably irrelevant now. Since Rune had probably died about the time she'd begun dancing lessons in India, she needn't worry that her time was almost up. She'd thrown everything out of whack, made Genie get a new family, made Angus come into the world without a Windell or a Rune to lead her to, made Rune leave alone, old, with nothing to show for it but some hounds he had to leave to others to care for. She had driven the SUV to work in a slump, and didn't even look up when Gamble opened the door to the club. She had just slipped silently by him, hoping the music would put her together right for the evening ahead.

She noted Gamble taking his place by the door with another thoughtful look replacing his grin and making her think, once again, that she shouldn't have taken her mood out on him. A pleasant greeting for a pleasant young man was not so much to force from yourself to make another's evening go easier. She was no longer surprised that the Miss Windell side was reprimanding her at work. When he came to the bar for a glass of water, grin conspicuously absent, having been replaced by a pensive thoughtful look she knew she'd put there, she didn't resist Miss Windell making reparations.

"Sorry I was rude earlier," Win said, handing him his water, "just had a bad day is all."

"Anything you want to talk about?" Gamble asked, grin returning slowly with the realization of opportunity. "I know a great place for coffee..."

"No," Win said, fighting a grin of her own, something about his was contagious if you let it be.

His grin was firmly replanted when he left.

Win didn't bother leading all the tall white boys with blond hair to tell her their names. Win didn't rightly care, she knew none of them was Rune. She passed the whole night in a slump, just this side of the hump. No matter how hard she tried to make herself push it away, something she was usually phenomenal at, she just couldn't be free of her deep sadness. It was worse than waking from a dream where you had a musket pressed to your head and meant to use it. Win just barely made it through, by looking forward to the relief of the evening being over so she could crawl into bed, get through the night, and go see Genie tomorrow before having to come right back here.

Win was doing no better when she drove to work the following evening. Her afternoon at Genie's had done nothing to lift her spirits permanently. Though it had been pleasant to tell her friend of their new Saturday plans, and watch her bounce around, calling Dristy and telling her too, her mood had fallen off quickly when they'd begun browsing the internet. They'd found the Rune estates, begun by a dog-breeding home builder, but they also found out he had died in the early eighties, and had been buried somewhere on the property. The picture of the founder showed her a large older man, standing alone but for a slew of hounds, before a long low structure he had built to house them all, and had broken her heart.

Win pulled into work worse off than the night before. Gamble met her with his contagious grin ready to help if she'd let it. Win smiled back, but the smile never made it to her eyes as she headed for the bar. She stopped Gina, thinking she would at least enjoy the shots tonight, and mixed them herself. Gina swallowed and sighed appreciatively before leaving. Win was smoking her starter cigarette, leaning on the cooler and considering what made a guy so brave and crazy that he just kept smiling no matter how many times you shut him down, when a huge man with blond hair came down from a darkened corner booth.

This large boy asked her for a refill in a manner that said he was disappointed to have had to come get it himself but not enough so to lodge a complaint. That's when Aizlyn realized Jovan was late. She didn't bother trying to get this large man's name, it couldn't be Rune, in her mind Rune was dead. She just made him the drink, apologized for not having seen him up there, all hidden in the dark, and wondered where Jovan was. It was when he turned to walk away, squaring his broad shoulders as though knocking loose the burden of having to come down to get it, that she began to wonder. What if Rune was back already? What if Rune hadn't dawdled in the in-between at all? There was something familiar about that large frame with the smallish butt and thickly muscled legs.

Her eyes must have narrowed with her musings because Gamble came up to the bar just then and asked her, "My little brother wasn't rude, was he?" Gamble looked back to the large man returning to his corner booth. "Sometimes he doesn't think how his actions might be perceived. I think sometimes he should have been a girl, the way he expects people to look after his feelings but doesn't think to look after theirs. Guess I shoulda asked him if he wanted another drink sooner."

Gamble saw the look Aizlyn was suddenly giving him and mistook it for him having put his foot in his mouth. He added quickly, "I don't mean all women are like that, just, you know, you gotta tread easy with girls. They see it for more than it is if you head toward the bar and don't ask 'em if they want one too..."

"That's your brother?" Win asked, cutting his explanations short. "What's his name?"

Again Aizlyn watched Gamble decide whether or not to answer her, knowing that if he chose not to it was what she deserved. She figured she'd just have to find a way to find out on her own if he didn't. Gamble didn't make her. He just grinned at her and said finally, "Dustin."

"And he's younger?" Win asked then.

"Yes," Gamble replied, grin broadening, "does this mean you have to answer one of my questions now?"

Her mind was whirling viciously, confused, and it was with that confusion written on her face that she turned to look at Gamble, when his question registered. He took her questioning look at him as a yes and said, "Its personal, I warn you." He laughed as her face turned even more confused, and then asked, "Is that your real hair color or do you have it highlighted?"

"What?" Win was lost now, her dark hair, near black but for the odd red browns, wasn't a thing done on purpose, who would do such a thing? She had been tempted to dye it more than once, ready to have a normal color.

"It seems like it should be all black, is all," Gamble said quickly, thinking maybe he'd insulted her. "Just wondered if the browns and reds were highlights or something."

"No," Win said absently, still trying to figure out something about the tall blond in the darkened corner booth and not focusing at all on the question or her answer. "I'm only half Indian. I think the odd shade is an accident of my mother's lighter mahogany."

Jovan came in just then, apologizing for her lateness and the conversation ended but not Win's musings. The witches that brewed what ifs in the cauldron of her Aizlyn-mind began working overtime. What if Rune had been forced to take a different name, as Dristy had told her to bear in mind was possible? What if he were back already and was this young Gamble or the even younger Dustin? How was she to know? Where were the butterflies?

She watched Gamble walk away, truly watched, for the first time. His broad shoulders were squared, and he too had thick muscled legs attached to a smallish butt and torso. Before, she had thought him 'born-to-run-a-foot-ball', now that build was forever set in her mind as Viking. What if neither were Rune, he was still sleeping in the in-between, and she was being delusional, seeing things that weren't there as she had seen Nathan, as he had been, when she'd seen him hugging Angus?

Win had come to no good answers when she was forced to put all of it away and be Win for real and work. She was not so amused to find she now resented having to be Win, to work, and was unable to be Aizlyn to think. She was not amused to find she had another question she wanted to ask Gamble, much later, as they sat at the bar and she counted the bar's money. She went over her approach a few different times, realizing it was unfair of her and might even seem incredibly rude to suddenly become all interested questions about Gamble's brother. Finally she saw no other means but to be direct.

"So what was your brother in here for tonight?" she asked without looking over at Gamble, as she wrote down the total for the tens and picked up half the twenties.

"His twenty-first birthday," Gamble answered after the briefest of pauses.

Win was putting some possibilities together quite well now when Gamble threw her off again.

"You always wear those anklets?" Gamble asked, taking another swig off his beer.

"Always," Win said, finishing her counting.

Gamble seemed satisfied with the answer and sat back. She realized he was trading answer for answer and that tickled her memory as something Rune might have done, trade. So it started to fall together in an odd way, if she'd thrown Rune and Genie off and they'd had to find different families then Dustin might be the younger brother Rune had expected to be a younger sister. They were *all* Pisces, and that seemed right, somehow. Gamble might be the name Rune had been saddled with by a mother who wasn't in tune enough to listen to his soul before it came, but it still didn't work perfectly. Win still felt he'd have a dog. Win still felt she'd be all butterflies if it were Rune sitting not three feet from her. Win wasn't risking being wrong either, not when they worked together and not with another young horse that could throw her so easily. Definitely not when the real Rune could walk back into her life in the next few days if he had wasted no time.

Win put the money away and allowed Gamble to lead her to the door and then out to her SUV. She went directly home, wanting nothing so much as a good long bath and some time and space to think. Win let herself in, removed her boots, patted the dog, then followed him into the kitchen to let him out and feed him. She let him back in, then locked the door while her bath ran and she put Win's clothes away. She put her hair up in a knot to keep it out of the bubbles and relaxed into the water. She was still trying to make it work in her head, still coming up on the wall that was Gamble not owning a dog, when suddenly she felt that same odd feeling of bathing in the open, floating in a large cool pool in the middle of a wide glade. She heard a man's deep happy laugh in her head and her eyes flew open to be greeted by a calming blue green eye.

There, right where she'd hung it, was something not Aizlyn, nor Miss Windell nor even Win could deny. That painting she had worked so hard to perfect, the scene of a Viking ship, acting the iris, passing through the calm magical center of a circular area of the ocean that spoke of inner strength and peace to her soul, was just as surely the color of Gamble's eyes. Aizlyn had compared his eyes to such a scene and wanted to paint them or their hue from the very night she had seen them so clearly under the bright exterior lights of the club. What about the butterflies and dogs then, she asked herself, as realization tried to seat itself.

Other thoughts kept knocking those two things aside though, as she remembered things he had wanted to know of her: what her sign was, whether this was her true hair color and not black, whether she had always had anklets. She recalled Gamble asking about whether she had nightmares and remembered him telling her of one in which he'd been stabbed. Aizlyn remembered how "let your hair down girl…" seemed to always be playing in her mother's car on her way to work and then, finally, Aizlyn remembered Rune telling her he dreamed of her hair falling all around him every night when he slept.

Suddenly she knew why Gamble was so brave and crazy, why he was so damned determined to leave the door open no matter how often she tried to close it. He'd been looking for her too, and maybe that inexplicable grin meant he'd been sure he'd found her long before she'd even realized she was looking for him. Maybe finding out why her hair wasn't full black and that she'd always worn anklets had only been bonus questions. Maybe the fact she was a Cancer truly had pleased him, as she'd thought his tone implied. Once again Aizlyn found herself in a hurry to get through the sleeping hours so she could get back to work and talk to him. She wanted to prove to the Win side of herself there would be a damn good reason he didn't have a dog. There was, after all, a good reason his name wasn't Rune, if all her other assumptions where right.

Aizlyn drove the Mustang to work, singing loudly and happily with the radio, and when her song came on just before she got there she turned the radio way up and pulled her hair down from its perpetual ponytail that kept it out of the bottles. Aizlyn was going to bartend tonight and prove Win wrong. It wasn't until she'd turned the car off, when the song was done, that she realized Gamble hadn't come to the door again and why. Only then did she remember he didn't work Fridays, because neither did she, and there was no point. He had a contractor's job, if Jovan was right, and was only there to stalk her.

Aizlyn was crushed then. If her timing was right, then she only had tonight, maybe tomorrow, if she was lucky. She had no idea how she was going to talk to him if he wasn't working tonight and she wasn't working tomorrow. She threw open the door of the club and Win took over, now she was emotionally upset, and sought to make it right. Win walked to the bar and made the shots at Gina's request and then sat on her cooler and stewed. Win began trying to convince herself that the absence of dogs and butterflies made Gamble the wrong guy, just to calm herself, while Aizlyn pouted about his beautiful blue green eyes and all the other things that she felt made him right.

Jovan came in and the night began and slowly Win won simply because she needed to, to do her job, and earn their money. There came a lull around midnight and Win lit a cigarette and stared at the smoke as it rose slowly in the still air, then suddenly it shifted as though someone had blown on it. She looked up to see Gamble standing before her register. She hadn't heard him but obviously he had been laughing. She told herself to focus as Aizlyn cried, "See, just like in the dreams!" in her head.

"Can I get you something?" Win tried to be calm.

"A beer, please," Gamble replied, "I'd like to start a tab if you don't mind."

He'd reached back behind him, pulling out his wallet, and Win stopped him with her best smile.

"You work here," she told him, "I don't need to hold your card."

He folded his wallet back up and put it in his back pocket, then headed for the end of the bar while she dug in the cooler for the brand she remembered was his. She rang up the bottle and pulled the receipt, to put in a cup to add up for him later, and noticed a card that had fallen from his wallet. She glanced at it, not wanting to pry but unable to miss the drawing of a Wolfhound's unmistakable head in the corner of the card or the word breeder that jumped out at her. She picked it up to return to him, and couldn't resist reading that the breeders were from Ireland, not local.

She was confused and thoughtful while she tried desperately to concentrate and twist open his beer with trembling fingers that had suddenly decided not to work properly. She walked to the end of the bar, still trying, and stood before where he now sat completely lost in thought. He reached out, took the beer from her hands as she stood pondering absently, and twisted it open easily with another priceless grin.

When his fingers brushed hers, taking the bottle, she found the butterflies. Suddenly Aizlyn was screaming about the odd comfort of a large male protector that only turned to butterflies when she'd realized she wanted him to be more. Win was trying desperately to calm herself and ask him about the card as she returned it to him.

"Thought you didn't have a dog," she said, hoping she sounded nonchalant.

"I don't," Gamble said, grinning hugely, and accepting the card back, "I bought a young male from these people a little better than three years ago to add fresh blood to my family's stock. He ran away though, and now you have a dog."

Win was going to die right there. These cows weren't merely winking and dinking, these cows were dead drunk on the witches' most potent what if brew yet.

"Angus was yours?" she demanded. "Why didn't you put an ad in the paper or report him missing? I looked, I checked." Win paused. "How'd you know *I* found him?"

She was unable to get her answer right away as Jovan came up to place an order and then apologized. Why would Jovan apologize, she wondered, what was Jovan thinking she had done? She caught a look from Firefly and realized that, whatever it was, that girl was thinking it too. She found herself swept up in a train of orders that started to flow again. She saw Gamble finishing off his beer out of the corner of her eye, just about the time she found a break in which she'd normally have lit a cigarette. She pointed at the beer cooler, wordlessly asking him if he wanted another.

Gamble nodded that he did and she retrieved it, ringing it up and dropping the receipt in his cup. Suddenly she was wandering why he was there. What if he hadn't come to see her, as she'd assumed? What if he was waiting on someone else? She brought his beer to him and was surprised when he knocked those thoughts aside by picking up their conversation where it had dropped off twenty or so minutes before.

"I saw you at the swap-meet buying a collar for him," Gamble grinned. "He's unmistakable. Besides, he seemed happy, I wasn't about to tear the two of you apart. He wouldn't have believed me anyway if I tried to tell him he was mine. I'd already bought another, anyhow, to add new blood to the line."

"But you said you don't own a dog?" Win replied, holding his eyes as best she could while the butterflies wreaked havoc in her abdomen.

Again she was called away before getting her answer, by an apologetic Jovan, and this time she had to ask her why she kept saying she was sorry. Jovan surprised her saying, "Well, it looks like you're finally sitting up and taking notice of him and I hate to interrupt."

"Finally?" Win asked.

"Yeah," Jovan giggled, thinking Win was playing coy, "You know he's had eyes for you since he came lookin' for a job he didn't need and askin' if we had a bartender who owned a Wolfhound."

"When was this?" Win asked breathlessly, happy to have it settled, he was indeed there to see her and not waiting for another woman to meet him.

"'Bout three months ago," Jovan laughed, "you know…"

Win was pulled away from a second conversation by a customer who wanted another pitcher. Then another customer and another, so that by the time she was done with them Gamble was ready for another beer and she took it to him, happy to get back to the answer he was still waiting to give.

"Nope, no dog for me yet," Gamble laughed, accepting the beer and again picking up their conversation. "Figure I'll pick a bitch from one of the litters one day, when I meet one that's picked me."

Win looked up just then to see a man standing by her register, fidgeting angrily. She recognized him immediately as the man she and Genie had helped karma handle Saturday evening. He motioned her over and Win walked calmly out from the bar, directly up to him, since it seemed he had no desire to be loud about his indignation. Win was aware Gamble and the other on duty bouncers were watching her closely and felt comfortable enough when she stood before the man without the bar between them.

"Can I help you?" Win asked, as if having no prior knowledge of him.

"Yeah," he gritted angrily, "you can refund my credit card."

"I'm sorry, sir, but I can't do that," Win said calmly. "You spent the money…"

Suddenly his arm shot out, gripping her bicep where it was still tender from the old crone's death grip. Win flinched more from the unexpectedness of the action than from pain and quickly held a finger out to her side to stay the wary bouncers, including Gamble.

"I know what you did," the man fairly spit in her ear.

Win looked hard into his eyes then down at his hand. She turned back to pin him with her eyes, showing him something recalled from another life, something evil that had lost her Rune once. She gritted back, low and menacing, "You haven't the faintest clue what I did. I know everything about you now, *everything,* more than just your credit card number and up-town address, more than your phone and My Space info. I have the most lovely picture of you to prove it, too." Win smiled then and it was a mean smile, as the man's hand dropped and he went pale. "I'd hate to see your picture all the rage on My Space, it's not flattering. I'd hate for the cops to become suddenly interested in your street. How 'bout you just walk away, never show your face 'round me or my girls, and hope I forget what it looks like? Hope I forget why I have all those things…"

The man stepped back like she had burst in to flames, "You'll pay for this," he said in a failed attempt to bolster his courage.

"You better hope not," Win smiled prettily, putting on a false sweet Southern drawl. "I just know the first flat tire I get, I'll probably not be able to help but remember you."

The man spun on his heels and stomped from the bar, grunting curses under his breath. Win turned to see Gamble grinning big and appreciatively at her. When she walked over to give him another beer, he asked what all had been said and laughed loud and long over the tale. What remained of the night went smoothly, as Win filled orders, then returned as she was able, to talk to Gamble. By last call, Win was nearly as sure as Aizlyn was that Gamble was indeed Rune. She walked to the end of the bar with his last beer and couldn't resist one last question for him.

"So were you here to meet someone tonight and got stood up?" Win asked just to be sure.

"Not sure," Gamble said then, not giving her time to ask for a better answer or even digest that one he added, "Now my turn. Firefly is misled, isn't she, everyone here is, you like it that way? You don't really have a fiancé, do..."

The phone rang just then and she was released from his eyes when they turned to the phone and she followed them and just stared at it as it rang again.

"You gonna answer that?" Gamble asked her.

Aizlyn was suddenly afraid and saw her hand tremble when it reached for the phone. She gave the caller her normal, professional greeting, only to stumble when she heard the voice.

"Jordan?" Aizlyn asked, beginning to shake on the inside now, as she turned away from Gamble's questioning glance and toward the cooler in shock. "Why are you calling here and so late?"

She listened, as her heart slowed to a dull aching thump, taking in all his witch's hour explanations, apologies and excuses. Suddenly the music faded and she found herself within a true Zen moment as Gamble came to stand beside her and point at his tab, indicating he was ready to leave. She began adding with one-half of her mind while the other half realized Jordan was more lost than she'd ever been. Jordan was trying, just as surely as she was, to come to terms with a deep abiding love he had, paired with the inability to make that enough. He too still sought the easy communion of two souls before either of them had thought to seek more.

Slowly, she turned into the phone and gently set him free. She told him it was okay that he was okay without her. She let him know that their friendship bound them far tighter than any marriage within neither of them would find peace, and that the friendship would never go away. She told him she understood his deep desire to see her happy, to be part of that happiness and how it kept him coming back but that he needn't keep trying. She let him know that he didn't need to sacrifice his happiness, returning to her again

364

and again, trying to change for her, simply to give her some measure of happiness which detracted from his own. She understood his inability to walk away thinking he was taking it from her but assured him his happiness was just as important as her own. She let him go, knowing he kept her undying love and she would always be his friend, even as she pointed to the total she had just come to for Gamble.

Win walked to the end of the bar and hung up the phone as Gamble held out his credit card to her, his ever-expressive eyes seemed sad and she looked down at it blankly, wondering why the sudden change. She suddenly remembered his question about Jordan and that he had just heard her on the phone saying his name. Then she remembered the total she had just given him, and why she was now holding his card. It was too much too fast as she bent over the machine, the lights came up and she swiped the card. Then something about it flashed in the light, and caught her eye.

Gamble Rune.

She stared at it, punching in the total, watching it print, watching him sign his name. Aizlyn looked up then and said the stupidest thing. "I know you," she said, breathless from suddenly chasing butterflies. She knew how stupid she had to sound the moment the words flew out of her mouth. Of course she knew him, they had worked together for months, they had just talked off and on pretty much all night. Aizlyn handed him his card and forced herself to look up.

Aizlyn remembered those eyes, and Win and Miss Windell would not deny it, they were become so blended by all the spinning, caught up in a maelstrom of butterflies and ocean-views, they totally forgot they might have once. It was only Aizlyn now as she watched Gamble's face fill with the most amazing grin, a grin that made her feel divine and not the least bit silly for her comment.

Gamble said, "Does this mean I can take you for coffee now?"

Aizlyn started laughing long and happy, then finally she replied, "You want to take me for coffee?"

"To begin with," Gamble laughed too.

Aizlyn drove Gamble back to the club to retrieve his truck sometime after dawn. She had finally taken pity on him when his answers came out more and more frequently as yawns and it had dawned on her the poor guy had probably worked all day and now she'd kept him out all night. She'd asked for the bill to be brought, even though he protested, and Aizlyn had to assure him it wouldn't be the last cup of coffee they shared. She watched his every movement as he stood, paid, and tipped the waitress at the truck stop without seeming to notice the admiring looks he drew. The waitress had watched them leave and given her a smile which Aizlyn remembered; pleased to see someone as happy as you wanted to be, something like envy, but kinder.

Aizlyn found herself inviting Gamble to get Jon to cover his shift the following night and join Genie and Dristy and herself at the Garden. Then she'd had a sudden epiphany and asked him to bring his brother, Dustin, along too. She'd sat in her mother's car with "let your hair down girl…" playing softly over the idle of the engine and watched Gamble get slowly into his truck, roll the window down and start it up. She'd called to him, asking if he was sure he was good to drive home. She was suddenly frightened that she may not have made her choice clear enough to the Fates, afraid they'd take her from him again. She threw her mother's Mustang into park and jumped out, ran up to his truck and threw the door open. Aizlyn toppled him onto the bench seat, he'd barely had time to face her as she landed nearly on top of him. She'd grabbed his head in both her hands and lowered hers, slowly letting her hair fall all around him, then kissed him slow and passionately.

When she raised her head his eyes were dark, inviting her to drown. Aizlyn smiled. "You sure you're awake enough to make it home? You're good to drive?"

"Oh," Gamble said, leaving the invitation open, "I'm good."

"I bet," Aizlyn said, licking her lips at the memory as she pushed his door closed again, "I'll see you tonight then, Rune."

"I'll be there, Ayesha,' He grinned, turning himself again to face the wheel.

Aizlyn flew through the front door of her little house in the middle of the dead end still, riding high on the swirling winds left behind by the butterflies. He'd called her Ayesha, he did remember too! She stopped dead in the center of the living room, where Angus lay in the middle of the floor, licking the paint off Sarasvati. She was in shock, he had never used his great height to steal food, let alone a figurine. She was dumbfounded, what was he thinking. Angus raised his head, taking note his human had finally returned home, and stood up leisurely, as though nothing was out of the ordinary. He walked back to the kitchen to wait for Aizlyn to let him out. She did.

Aizlyn went right back to the little statue and picked it up, looking at it every which way. If there was something tasty about it, why wait till it was on a shelf? Why not lick the little goddess when she'd sat so easily within reach for days on the coffee table? She flipped it over again and that's when she saw the note rolled up and stuffed up into its hollow center. So Sarasvati had something to show her after all. She pulled the note out and sat down.

"Aizlyn," it read in her mother's handwriting, "I don't believe in coincidences, and neither do you, not if I've done you right. If you've found this then it was time. I had a dream once, my dear one, right before you were born. I saw a woman child of India, all the trappings and jewels and bright silks of a goddess draped about an ageless girl. She was hollow, though, like this statue, but where it holds a musical instrument she held a shackle. She cradled it like an ailing child, with a care that seemed to age her but make her more beautiful in a broken way.

"She spoke, and I heard her in my heart, though her lips never moved. She said, 'I have seen clearly, all can be right, I simply must be allowed to dream. The chain must be broken. I should be strong enough to seek out what is hidden and love the river enough to let it flow.' Her eyes had flown open then as if startled that I could see her or just realizing I had heard. She had whispered my name in question then. 'Windell?' she'd asked. 'Yes,' I had replied. Then she had begun to cry and said suddenly, 'Will you help me?' 'Of course,' I had said, for what else could I do? This woman child began to fade then and I heard her final words echoing in my heart when I woke: 'Be careful what you sacrifice for love, for it may end up being the love you sought.'

"I found out I was pregnant with you that very day. I definitely could not think it anything less than meant. I named you Aizlyn, and tried all I knew to help you dream. I sought to teach you all I could to help you with whatever it seemed you wanted to find that was hidden, and accept all things and let them flow by understanding them. When you found this statue and wanted it so badly, your answer of, 'she will show me something,' reminded me again of the dream that came often to memory when watching you grow. I know this has all been meant, everything, to this very moment, and I pray I have helped. Aizlyn, whether Grandmother has you saying 'you reap what you sow' or you still call it karma, just remember to let it flow, seek what is hidden and always dream. The rest comes easy in the harvest.

"I love you Aizlyn, Always."

Aizlyn held the note to her chest and breathed deeply, the sweet depth of incredible peace of mind. She rolled the note back up and took Sarasvati to the dining room table to remind her to paint her. Then she fed the dog, locked the door, took a quick shower and went to bed.

That evening Aizlyn sat with Dristy waiting and was pleased beyond words to see Dristy, so obviously pleasantly surprised by her blind date when Gamble and Dustin arrived a few minutes later. Aizlyn was also pleased to see Bill had made it back to town in time to join them as he walked in with Genie close on their heels. They spent the early evening eating and drinking wine and enjoying the comfortable companionship of old friends. Then they spent the later part of the evening dancing like fools till they could hardly stand and Aizlyn didn't mind dancing that night, even with Gamble watching her so closely.

Aizlyn found herself reflecting as the night drew to a close and realized she'd almost gotten this one completely right. The only low note in the entire night was that someone had still had to die for her to make her way to this moment. Her mother hadn't been careful enough of the sacrifices she made. Her mother had done everything so right and deserved so much better.

368

Gamble had caught her mood sobering and asked her about it. She was honest and explained as they walked back to their vehicles. Gamble had just grinned, as ever, as he closed her car door, and told her it would be all right.

And it was when she said, "I am ready."

Part 3

The Future

20

Tressa: Harvester

Aizlyn placed Sarasvati on her shelf in the den, now she was truly done unpacking. It was late but the moon was high and bright as she walked to the window and gazed out at the stream than ran behind the long low structure she called home now. There was a place where the stream widened, hidden just back in the woods, in a small clearing that she sometimes called the washing vale but mostly just called heaven. She was pleased as she thought of where she'd been and how she'd come to this moment, she always was when she stopped to reflect.

Genie had come by that afternoon bearing a house warming gift of homemade brownies and her three year old daughter who was already showing signs of a terrible shoe fetish. Nathan had run off chasing the dogs, after a brief hug, with a brownie hanging half out his mouth and came in later with a scraped knee. Jordan had called, full of excitement over his newest business venture, while Genie sat patiently awaiting her return to their conversation and coffee.

Angus scratched the rear door demanding reentry, Aizlyn had long since realized something's never changed and that wasn't a bad thing. He was followed in by his mate and three puppies and she thought, other things did, all the time, and that wasn't bad either.

She turned off the lights, checked the coffee pot, took a quick shower then banked the fire before crawling into bed to snuggle the man who'd already been asleep for at least three hours. She saw the clock read three thirty three and heartily agreed as she closed her eyes to dream.

I saw a field of daisies waiving in a soft breeze and there came walking through them a woman child, a true Ozark beauty, in a flowing, white cotton gown. Her soft brown hair blew back from sun gold skin as she pressed her nose into the handfuls of those flowers she had gathered on her journey.

I heard her thoughts within my soul, she said, 'there is no path but what I make, I need to reap what I have sewn.'

This woman child took note of me suddenly and smiled pure love my way. She said, 'I would be Tressa, will you help me?', 'Yes,' I said, it was the only reply my heart could muster. Then I heard her voice, as it echoed into silence in my soul then, 'Sometimes you rein them in, sometimes you let them run.'

Aizlyn nuzzled into the dream and realized it was Gamble's arm when he asked her why she was smiling in her sleep. He always wanted to know what she had dreamed. Her eyes fluttered open and she fell into the calm, magic waters of his eyes. She smiled, and sighed deeply, "We're going to have a daughter."

www.ingramcontent.com/pod-product-compliance
Lightning Source LLC
Chambersburg PA
CBHW020838030726
47493CB00028B/308